Dedicated to
my fellow members at
The Vault
speculative fiction writing group
in Louisville, Kentucky,
in particular,
Geoffrey Mandragora,
William Levy,
and
Richard Roberts.
None of this would come out as coherent
without your helpful comments
and suggestions, gang!

February 14

It all started shortly after dawn on the most dangerous day of the year—Valentine's Day.

One minute I was engrossed in taking names and kicking ass—you know, deep into a video game—when the familiar black-and-caramel muzzle of my canine partner got between me and the screen.

And the arrow.

The first I became aware of the danger was when his teeth snapped down on it a foot away from reaching its target.

Me.

It was old-school design. The only bit you might call high-tech being the pink and red feather bits at the tail end. Beelz had it gripped between his teeth and had amped up his growl as he turned demon-red eyes to the being hovering near the ceiling.

A cupid wearing nothing but a red sash with a quiver of those dainty fletched arrows on his back.

"What the frick!" the curly blond-headed, bow-wielding tike snarled around the cigarette clamped between his front teeth. Based on the deep octaves of his voice, as well as his language and smoke, I made the deduction: this weren't no kid. I'm a P.I.; it's what I do.

Beelz spat the stick out and hustled around the desk to leap at the intruder. He might be a hellhound but as his preferred form is that of a dachshund, the leaps were getting him nowhere near his target.

And cupid was nocking up another bolt.

I took cover beneath the desk. "Who the hell wants me to fall in love with them?" I yelled at the little bundle of lethal joy. I certainly didn't want it to be any femme with Otherworlder DNA. A human, now… Except a human wouldn't have hired a *real* cupid. Mostly because few knew they actually existed.

"No one, slick. I was hired to take you out." Ash cascaded as the cigarette bobbed. Don't talk and smoke at the same time should be up there with chew with your trap shut. But, hey? He was an *assassin*?

"Pretty lousy camouflage. In that get up"—or lack of one—"you don't exactly blend into the surroundings, pal."

Beelz kept leaping and added a bark, obviously agreeing with me.

"What camouflage? I ain't wearin' no camouflage. Youse The Raven, right?"

No one had asked me that since November, but the answer lingered on my tongue. I'd said it enough times last fall. "Fictional character. Yeah, I've got the same name, but that's all."

"Not what I heard, buddy. Let's just get this over with. Crawl out and take the medicine I come ta give ya."

Hmm. Supply a target or evoke my décor-singeing modicum of magic. Decisions, decisions. But, since what prestidigits I could toss leaned more toward human flame-thrower, and I really didn't want to burn the house down, there had to be a third option.

"How much they paying you?"

"Whadda you care?" the cupid snarled.

"I'm willing to top the offer so you don't shoot me," I said.

Only the sound of Beelz's now half-hearted snarls filled the room as our visitor considered.

"What if I said it was a million?"

"I'd say you were lying through your teeth. Nobody hates me that much." Well, right now they didn't. At least… I couldn't remember ticking anyone—or anything—off recently enough that they'd want to whack me. I'd been busy writing a book so the only interaction I'd had lately was with the humans who supposedly found me endearing.

"Doubt you could match my price, Raven," chubby snarled.

"Farrell," I corrected. "The name's Bram Farrell. The Raven is not a real person. I think if you'd just take a gander at this room, you'll see that I probably can match—if not best—the amount you agreed to."

I'd inherited a cushy joint. No need to describe the place. Just saying *mansion* should fill in the blanks. All it'd taken was making sure my creator bit the big one.

"Oh," the fake toddler mumbled. Sounded like he was eyeballing the décor.

Beelz gave an exhausted sigh and stopped trying to get a piece of the hit-tike.

"I'll throw in extra for the name of your client," I offered from my burrow safely beneath the desk.

"No can do," Babyface said.

"Professional ethics?"

"Never met them. Just an envelope dropped in my quiver at the wedding chapel I frequent. Gave me the address, a picture of the target—you—and a hefty down payment."

"How hefty?"

"Fifty Gs."

"Fifty thousand dollars?"

"Nah. Fifty pieces of gold. The places I frequent don't trust paper, pal, just coin."

"Any particular kind?"

"Spanish, Roman, Etruscan—whatever ya got."

Great. All I had to do was denude every online offering of antique gold coins. Collectors would be gnashing their teeth as it disappeared from circulation. Since denomination didn't matter, I might be able to buy myself a reprieve for under a hundred thousand. Heck, I'd spent that much my first six days outside of a bookbinding back in October. I was, after all, still a fictional character—The Raven—even if currently packaged in something that was certainly puncturable by an arrow.

"You on a timeline?" I needed to know. There would be shipping involved.

"End of the month," chubby said.

In that case, expedited shipping.

"There somewhere to get in touch when I've got the horde gathered?"

"Little Chapel of Bliss in Vegas," the assassin said. "Ask for Ernie."

Ernie?

"So, youse wanna shake on the deal or what?"

"Going with *or what*. Cool with that?"

"Totally chilled," he said. Well, he should be. It was the middle of February in Detroit for Grendel's sake.

There was a sorta *poof* sound, but I was taking no chances. "He gone?" I asked Beelz.

He barked a *coast is clear*.

I crawled from my hiding spot and back into my upscale executive chair. The laptop had decided to take a rest. Hopefully, it hadn't exited the game in progress because it'd taken forever to get to that level of play.

But now I had something a bit more important to sort out. Someone was honing that hating feeling. Question was, who in the real world was it?

***

I'd done an awe-inspiring bit of bank balance reduction exercises by the time my Gal Friday showed up for work at nine. When the Dragon dictation software had discovered dragons in both fictional and real worlds weren't Raven-friendly, it had joined the protest movement. That meant that, if the next Raven Tales volume was to get spun, help of an officesorial bent was required—and required fast. Hiring a keyboard aficionado had, therefore, landed the number one spot on my New Year's Resolutions list. Spots two and three said *spin tale* and *survive what comes next.* There'd been no other resolutions. That last one pretty much covered things.

Rather than get anesthetized with interviews, I'd taken the quick solution and hired Naomie, the wannabe writer who'd been the only decent person I'd met at the lone scribblers' meeting I ever attended. Since I'd offered her more than triple the salary she'd made serving complicated coffees at extravagant prices, she'd started working for me immediately. As she did most of the work by transcribing my recorded ramblings—and kept her hand in the coffee game since I'd bought one of those super-duper set ups to keep my cup running overeth—she deserved every penny I threw at her. Figuratively, not literally, of course.

She worked under a misconception she hadn't a clue existed: she thought I was a real person.

I suppose I'm the first *homo fictionalus.* At least, I think I am. The early decades of my existence had been restricted to the printed page where I'd survived the numerous attempts by paranormal, supernatural, and legendary things to kill me and had done unto them first. Then my creator magicked me across the machine-stitched binding into the real world. Oddly enough, life on this side turned out to be much the same as it had been between the glossy covers. Including me being the last guy standing.

The first book of the new set of Raven Tales had left Detroit for the publisher's New York City corner office a week back, which meant Naomie and I were temporarily superfluous to the literary world and enjoying the state.

Life in a higher income bracket hadn't changed my secretary-cum-administrative assistant much. She'd stopped wearing silver skulls, much to my relief, but that was it. She continued to sport unnaturally deep black locks and the wardrobe of drape-y, form-concealing layers of black, but, considering my hair, clothes, car, and dog were the same light-sucking shade, strangers probably thought Raven Central lacked color spectrum creativity. The Amberson mansion from which we worked dazzled with it though, and the two-dozen crimson roses sitting dead center on her desk looked right at home rather than out of place.

If any human *had* hired Ernie for the arrow-of-love delivery—rather than the arrow-of-possibly-instant-death—I wouldn't have minded in the least if Naomie had been the one to hire him. The vase bursting with red-budded glory wasn't there because it was a nice thing to do for the girl who worked for me. More me feeling my way into how romantic interaction with a full human—as opposed to fictional or previous human or passing for human—sweetheart might work.

She squealed in a very ego-satisfying manner the moment she spotted them and rushed into my office to deliver a thank-you strangle. One I quite enjoyed as her arms were around my neck and her head was buried against my chest. As she pressed close, my torso was very aware that, under those layers of black, she was hiding the sort of willowy female chassis I daydreamed about. Her hair smelled like vanilla, so cookies came to mind—she possibly being one. Then she let loose and returned to her guard post in the wide foyer and, sadly, reality returned. Apparently, I needed to do more late-night Internet searching for ways to indicate my interest to a girl in this world. But she had left my office with a bright smile on her face. After six weeks together, I knew Nomes took the job of being the first line of defense against anybody who wants something from me seriously.

Or her video game was already wrapping its mystic lure around her. That was tough competition to beat out for her affections.

As it turned out, Naomie was going to have her work cut out for her that day. And we weren't even talking an assassin, here.

While coin dealers the world over busily packaged up pirate treasure for shipment to my door, I faced that all-consuming question of the self-employed writer the world over: restart my interrupted gaming vice or stream *Doctor Who* via Amazon. In other words, a non-gold coin needed to be tossed to choose the procrastination path my morning would follow. When the aroma of freshly-brewed designer coffee reached me, I put off the flip in favor of donuts and caffeine. I might not have trained Beelz to do tricks, but Naomie's indoctrination had included strong hints about daily baked goods delivery. I felt sure there were maple bars awaiting my attention. The way to my heart is through my sweet tooth. Cupid intervention is not required when pastries beckon.

With noshing in mind, I ignored the doorbell when it pealed. Sounded suspiciously like someone was using the button to support their weight. Naomie would see to it. We were expecting an invasion later in the day when Alexis Muldoon's plane arrived, but that was hours away. I doubted the caller was another assassin. It was too early for a second one to show up. More likely someone with less lethal aspirations. Naomie would make short shift of them with an overload of perkiness alone. She wouldn't want to have her own video game of the month decide to reset itself.

Because the path to the kitchen would take me through the foyer and, thus, make me visible to the visitor, I lingered in my office, waiting for her to deal with our intruder. It took a second irritatingly persistent toll before I heard Naomie's office chair roll away from her desk. Her boot heels echoed on the parquet. The front door was too well-mannered to creak on its hinges when she answered the knell.

"Yes?" She sounded nothing like her usually effervescent self. Naomie may dress like a Victorian widow, but she has a Pollyanna personality.

"Beck Ritter of 4th Estate to see Mr. Farrell," the visitor announced in the sort of whiskey-toned female voice that could make a report on hog futures sound decadent.

Intrigued, I leaned back in my chair and craned to catch a

glimpse of Naomie in ninja mode. There was a full-length mirror in the hall positioned just right for such entertainment possibilities.

As expected, my pet human was attempting to block the way into the house using her willowy form as a barricade. Not expected was the long, lean, short-legged length of my investigative hellhound partner. His dachshundric Clark Kent disguise cloaked his true, self-assigned duty as her backup. Probably did it because Naomie kept a supply of dog biscuits in her desk drawer and was generous in their dispersal. She didn't know about his secret identity.

"Mr. Farrell has no intention of selling the property," Naomie stonewalled.

Actually, I did, but that was neither here nor elsewhere in the current wibbly-wobbly space-time continuum.

The sultry-voiced woman stuck on the doorstep was muffled against the rigors of Detroit in February, but she was determined.

"I'm not a real estate agent; I'm a reporter."

It might be news to Nomes but not to me. I knew what 4th Estate was in political jargon. Or, more importantly, I'd read that 4th Estate Reporting Bureau, or FERB as detractors termed them, dreamed of crushing Reuters, The Associated Press and other news agencies out of existence. Beck Ritter's name was already synonymous with the fall of political and corporate giants.

What was she doing slumming it at my door?

Yeah, so it was the door of a mansion filled with expensive furnishings and sat on a hefty stretch of real estate, having its own mini forest and a half-mile long driveway. Sure, I'd done nothing to deserve it. Far as the world at large was concerned, I had simply sprung from a fortunate gene pool, not from an inkwell.

"You don't have an appointment with Mr. Farrell," Naomie said. "The person you need to contact is Delia Maddox of Maddox Public Relations. She handles all publicity dealing with The Raven Tales, the late Calista Amberson, and Mr. Farrell." Delia's address and office number tripped merrily from Naomie's lips.

Beck Ritter made no move to write it down. I noticed she'd edged her foot across the threshold far enough to make it impossible for the door to be slammed shut.

"A PR person?" Ritter sneered. "I'm sure she has created a lovely spin on who Bram Farrell really is. What was his name before he ingratiated himself into Calista Amberson's graces? I've already spoken to the only man who actually qualifies as her nephew, and his name isn't Bram Farrell."

Ouch.

I knew who she meant. I'd done my own research on Calie via the trusty Internet last fall. If the guy thought he had a chance of reversing her will in his favor, he didn't know how dangerous Team Raven could be. Other than Naomie, every woman in my cadre was a witch, members of Calie's former coven. While I was clueless on whether the legal eagle in the bunch was an upper echelon magic user, she was at the top in her judicial aerie. She'd crush the dude considering he was just the illegitimate son of Calista Amberson's sister-in-law and what I'd inherited was the fortune my creator had built *after* her Mr. Amberson's demise.

Still, it would be a pain dealing with inheritance litigation. I'd be forced to wear a suit. First, I'd have to buy a new one. The Dolce & Gabbana one I'd acquired around Thanksgiving had suffered irreparable damage in the aftermath of Black Friday.

Ritter's announcement left Naomie speechless, but my dachshundric buddy stepped up to bat in her place. His growl revving, Beelz bared his fangs.

Beck Ritter glanced down to where he stood between Naomie's booted feet and took in his red eyes. "What's wrong with the dog?" she demanded.

The usual answer was "gene pool defect" rather than "he's a demon", which would have ruined the alter-ego thing.

She went with something entirely different than the usual spiel. "Rare and very infectious disease," she said. "We've all been vaccinated against it, but if you're interested in a slow, disfiguring decline to an ultimately painful death, I'll see if Mr. Farrell has a moment to spare. He usually conducts interviews with Beelzie on his lap to calm the dog."

To help her sell the story, Beelz hacked in the direction of Ritter's door-stopping foot. Whether she believed any of the story—which I doubted—her reflexes to escape a coating of dog drool were excellent. Ritter jerked her foot back.

"Have a nice day," Naomie wished insincerely and slammed the door shut then locked it. She had to practically kneel on the floor to exchange a paw-to-fist bump with her backup, but the exchange seemed to satisfy both dog and secretary.

I rolled my chair back to the desk and reached for the phone. Delia's private number was on fast dial. "Trouble in Motor City, cuz," I told her.

All it took was delivering Beck Ritter's name to have my witchy pseudo-cousin swear quite creatively.

***

To some guys, having women figuratively drop from the sky onto their doorstep would rate a high-five. The news piranha was merely the first to show up. At least we were expecting Alexis Muldoon.

A little over three months back, just before my creator curled up her toes in Wicked Witch of the West fashion, Delia and I had instigated a Calista Amberson replacement search on the Web. At the time, I'd been the only one willing to let The Raven Tales stand on twenty volumes and not continue from a different pen. Delia had sideswiped me with the suggestion that I be the one to write further titles. "Just write up the adventure you managed to live through," she'd said. Naturally, that had skewed the replacement search all to hell.

Fortunately, Calie's agent and publisher decided my contest entry sounded most like The Raven as Calie had written him. They'd no idea I was *that guy*. However, as it might seem like thimble rigging to the other contestants to have me inherit the job of author as well as Calie's fortune, a second-place spot was awarded. Alexis Muldoon had taken it hands-down with her Raven prequel novella, a young adult tale of teenaged Bram Farrell's early years as a magic user and Otherworld crime disabuser. The editor saw further dollar signs in her future and—*shazam!*—the fledgling Teen Raven series was given the go to launch. As a result, Muldoon wanted to put me through a third degree on the type of things this fledgling Raven might have done based on my own youth.

Trouble is, I sorta lacked those early years. I'd flowed from Calie's pen on the cusp of twenty-nine years old and, over twenty years later, I was still hanging in at twenty-nine years old.

I had a plan, though. Whatever Muldoon wanted to know, I'd

make up a lie on the spot. I just hoped I remembered what I'd said later if she made reference to it.

Muldoon was staying at a hotel, but once her luggage was dropped off, Delia was swinging by the estate with her in tow. I would have preferred dinner at a restaurant, but that didn't have the personal touch my faux cousin thought would play best.

Or as she phrased it, "It's Valentine's Day, idiot. The best restaurants will be mob scenes." Thus, we would be having dinner at Raven Central, also known as the Amberson Estate.

Fortunately, there was one among the coven girls who seared beef to perfection, and she had jumped at the chance to handle kitchen duty. The house did have top-of-the-line everything and in grand sizes since Calie had enjoyed entertaining. Not cooking, though, just entertaining.

After the hasty departure of the last chef to rule the kitchen, none of the built-in toys got the attention they deserved. I tended to eat out. The spatula-and-tongs-wielding witch had been itching for a chance to use the snazzy super-sized, built-in grill set up in the patio area off the kitchen. The fact that it was February, temperatures rivaled a deep freeze, and it had been snowing, had not deterred her. She nearly swooned with joy when approached about doing the cooking, gushing something about the outside grill even having a smoker tray.

Since nothing but knives, bullets, and fire did me any harm, my diet leaned heavily on items consisting largely of sugar, bacon, bourbon, and former longhorn. Just the promise of mesquite-flavored porterhouse steaks made me weak. Mention of vegetables was made, but I tend to tune such talk out.

Delia gave me a heads-up when she and our contest winner were ten minutes out. As I'd switched to video solitaire in anticipation of being interrupted, no angst was incurred in shutting the game down.

As the day had progressed, more snow had fallen. The guy who trimmed the grass switched to plowing snow off the driveway in winter, leaving me just the area near the door to deal with. I'd done the morning burn on the entry steps before Naomie arrived, but it was now dark, and to be hospitable the porch was in serious need of a fresh scorching. Needed privacy to accomplish that, though.

The tricky thing about living in a world where the existence of magic is kept at a need-to-know level is keeping Naomie clueless about my hidden talents. Rather than tip her off, I suggested she make a fresh batch of coffee, then prepared to steal out front to pretend to use a shovel and salt on the porch. But before any of that could be accomplished, Naomie closed in on me, plucked a stray hair from my sweater, and did a light brush down the sleeve. Then, as if she had just realized how such sweet attention to my haberdasherial éclat might be seen, she backed off, her smile flickering a bit. A warm blush rose in her cheeks. I quite enjoyed the flushed tide rise and fall before she hustled off to the kitchen and coffee duties.

By the time the headlights of Delia's car made an appearance on the drive, the house was bathed in the scent of fresh-brewed designer coffee. I had no taste nuances to discern how this flavor of the month differed from the month before; that was Naomie's department. My hand was wrapped around a tumbler of Evan Williams 86 proof. Figured I'd need fortification.

Earlier, I'd piled wood in the fireplace in the front parlor. Well, it used to be the front parlor. It was a media room now. The 110-inch flat screen gave that away. Anyway, when Nomes bounded in from where she'd been keeping watch at the front window to head for the door, I took advantage of her absence to shoot a small ball of fire at the hearth for an instant campfire. Made the room look cozy. Some might say romantic, but there were enough table lamps lit to downsize that notion.

The sound of the outer door being opened was the signal that it was show time. Beelz jumped down off the sofa where he'd been curled up. By the time Muldoon entered the manse, I was in Raven pose, shoulder holding up the archway, arms crossed over my chest, weight on one leg, the other bent, the toe of my recently acquired Tony Lama's kicked tip-down on the carpet. Beelz was planted at my feet. Figured he wanted a front row seat.

With Naomi holding the door wide and Delia ushering Muldoon ahead of her, front seat wasn't a bad position.

Muldoon's website featured a picture that lacked any hint of personality. In it, her dark hair was scraped back and she wore a generic suit. That seemed so out of place in the Raven universe, I wondered if she really looked that... er... boring. Okay, make that *conservative.* I knew she was from Tucson and taught composition at a community college. To my mind, that equated to college credits up the Kalamazoo, which flows far to the west of Detroit so doesn't really count. However, that was pretty much the sum of what I did know about Muldoon.

There wasn't much of her in sight when she stepped over the portal. Detroit winters were a far cry from those in the Sonoran Desert. Muldoon had a scarf wrapped from nose to chin and the fur-trimmed hood of a parka pulled far enough down to leave only her eyes showing. Pretty blue eyes, at that. But I already had a built-in preference for Naomie's sparkling emerald ones—and not entirely because I gazed into them over shared pastries most mornings.

"Ah, warmth!" Muldoon sighed moving farther into the foyer. "I knew it was going to be cold in Michigan, but it's still a surprise."

She had a nice voice. Not sultry like the reporter who had visited earlier, but feminine, soft, and a touch breathless—probably from the unaccustomed deep-freeze air temp outside—that was Muldoon's.

Then she shook back the hood, unwound the scarf, and revealed a tousled batch of brown curls, a slightly cold-reddened nose, gently curving lips, and a slight dimple to the left of her smile. It hadn't made an appearance in the dull photograph on her website. Her hair had not been cropped and corkscrewing on the website pic either. In any case, Muldoon in the flesh didn't appear dull in the least, which was a relief. She was going to be creating a younger version of me in her stories and the word *dull* just would not suit any version of me.

Yes, my ego kicked in even if the character she wrote would not be me. At least, I didn't think he would be.

I pushed up from my position. "Here, let me take your coat."

"I'm not sure I'm ready to give it up yet," she said with a smile.

"Not to worry. We have a force field to keep drafts out of the house."

Muldoon laughed and allowed me to divest her of the coat. I dropped it over the chair by Naomie's desk. Spot-on assistant that she is, Nomes plucked it up and hung it in the closet. I hadn't even realized we had a coat closet.

"Thank you, Mr. Farrell," Muldoon murmured.

"Oh, please. We're all casual here at Raven Central. It's Bram."

"And I'm Lex." She offered her hand.

We shook. "Welcome to Casa Amberson," I said and introduced both Naomie and Beelz.

She made instant friends with the hound by kneeling and offering her hand.

He led with a paw.

Drinks were offered all around as everyone settled into seats. The fire crackled picturesquely. No one was surprised that the Arizona import took a chair near it. She even held her hands to it, soaking up heat before turning back to us locals.

Oddly enough, we were all lined up on the sofa. I'd settled into my usual spot, feet on the cushy leather upholstered coffee table, Beelz was next to me, his muzzle resting on crossed front paws, then came Delia, her wool-trousered legs curled beneath her, and Naomie had a hip perched on the far arm. I wondered whether Muldoon felt she was back in front of the classroom with all of us facing her. Writing young Raven Tales would be a part-time job for her until it took off—something we all expected the new series to do. Heck, I certainly hoped it would. As owner of the Raven franchise, as Delia now called it, I would be receiving a share of the royalties generated by Teen Raven. I had big plans for those funds, too.

"Well, do we chit-chat or get right to business?" Muldoon asked, the steaming mug Naomie had supplied her cupped between her hands.

That's when Beelz clicked his low warning growl on just before the doorbell chimed.

I turned to Delia. "More company?"

"Not that I was expecting. Sandra's already in the kitchen working on dinner."

"Yeah, I let her in when I made the coffee," Naomie added.

The bell ringer leaned on the button longer, though whether their goal was to instill a sense of urgency or to irritate us, well, they were doing a damn good job of combining the two.

I got to my feet and Beelz jumped down, preparing to do backup duty. "Be right back," I said, then paused and added, "Unless it's a Girl Scout taking cookie orders."

Yeah, like a Girl Scout was going to meander down a half-mile driveway, past woods with lots of tall, spooky-looking trees to reach a mansion in the middle of a field in the dark.

Naomie, not realizing I was being facetious, hastily told me what her favorite cookies were. Well, we probably *did* need a fresh supply of afternoon sweets to stay powered up for the video games.

The dinger donged a third time before I got to the door. Beelz's teeth were visible and perhaps a bit longer than regular dachshund dentures. His growl had passed WARNING and was revved for IMMINENT ATTACK. I hoped our unexpected guest wasn't another hit man because that would make a very poor impression on both Lex Muldoon and Naomie, who were clueless about our early morning visitor from Vegas.

"No going savage Great Dane, hmm?" I said. "Low profile for both of us around the norms. Got it?"

Beelzebub stayed alert rather than give me his usual nod of compliance.

I was not going to like what was waiting on the opposite side of the door, but there was no way around it. I had to open the damn thing and just hope it wasn't someone interested in making a financial killing by killing me.

Just to play it safe, I planted a sturdy shield wall between us and whomever was on the other side of the door.

A blast of arctic wind swept in—and so did a woman in a long red dress and a furry white coat. I let the shield fall the moment I recognized our caller. Oh, she was dangerous, but not in an assassin-ish way.

"I need your investigative skills to find my great-grandson, Raven," she said without preamble.

Considering the latest female to come visiting was a vampire, the day was just getting better and better, wasn't it?

***

Timing-wise, she couldn't have hit a worse one. Not that having a vampire drop by ever made it to my wish list. I could understand Beelz's attitude now. The last time he'd seen Miss Sweden 1934, he'd turned her into a chew toy.

She got better.

Now she needed me to dust off my P.I. kit? Well, I'd been kicking my heels for a few days and she was offering a case that would get me away from Muldoon's questions, make it easier to avoid Ritter's possibly damaging queries, and make my schedule diverse enough that if there were any other hit folks gunning for me, I would be harder to find.

"Not exactly available to chat this minute, Ingrid," I told her.

She sighed. "I've gone by a number of names over the years, but Ingrid has never been one of them."

"Still bad timing, Brigid."

"Wendy," she corrected. "Is it possible for you to meet me at The Red Dragon after midnight?"

Hopefully, Muldoon would be ready to head back to her hotel long before then.

"As long as I'm not what you're drinking," I said.

She ignored that quip and simply tugged the collar of the fur coat up to cover dangly diamond earrings and her own luscious neck. "I'll see you then," she murmured and turned back to where a cab waited in the driveway.

I stayed where I was as it maneuvered around Delia's cherry red Toyota Prius sedan and Naomie's previously used lime green Chevy Spark. I assumed Sandra, our cook for the evening, had parked around back.

Once the taillights had vanished and our most recent visitor was on her way back to town, I shut the door. "Weird, huh?" I mumbled.

The dog sitting on my foot yipped in agreement.

I hunkered down to give his coat a rough-up and delivered a scratch under his muzzle. "You won't be able to go into the dragon's club, you know. The city has that pet discrimination law that's tough to get around, but if you want to come along, there's a nasty alley to hang out in. I barbecued a couple vamps in it, but I can't guarantee that level of fun tonight. Still, you're welcome to join me."

He gave a double yip which I knew meant he was up to the challenge and looking forward to shaking down either rats or cats lingering near the dumpster behind The Red Dragon.

In the media room, I could hear Muldoon asking Naomie how she'd landed her job of Bram-wrangler.

My chirpy secretary was bubbling over with enthusiasm. "He even wrote me into the new book," she gushed. "I was so surprised. The boss does all kinds of nice things, though. He even had roses waiting for me on my desk today."

Sounded like she would award me a halo and polish it brightly if the way the day was going supplied enough thrills and chills to become another Raven Tale. After all, she was a major player in

Beelz's and my life now. She would appear in our next adventure. We'd grown accustomed to her perk.

And everything else about her, too. We were keeping her, even if it meant lying like crazy to keep our secret life hidden from her. For her own good, of course. We were killers, after all.

***

There had been some rearranging of the seating during my absence. Naomie had stolen my spot and was leaning forward eagerly as she answered Muldoon's questions. Lex was probably taking it all at face value. Nomes seemed to be painting me as her Galahad for rescuing her from food service. She didn't mention that I also paid her extravagantly for what amounted to very little work. Sure, we'd both put in long hours to get that Raven Tale manuscript done in record time, but until another needed to be written, I paid her to tinker with her own writing efforts (which, unfortunately, had more enthusiasm than content) and to indulge in her vampire romance novel addiction with the occasional gaming time. Oh, and to make coffee, of course. The fact that I'd wanted to rescue her within minutes of meeting her last fall had nothing to do with anything.

Yet.

I was still new to this world. I needed to take things slow where Nomes was concerned. At least, that was my current mantra, even if it was a rather long one. I needed to do that extra Internet research about romance, after all.

As they seemed to be getting along, I was willing to lend Naomie out and, thus, keep Lex out of my hair during her stay.

Hopefully, during Q&A sessions neither of them would tumble onto the fact that the fictional Bram and I were one and the same. Considering it looked like I'd be working for a non-human on a case again—or is that previously human? It is so difficult to be politically correct when it came to vampires, were-beings, zombies, and ghosts—it was probably best to keep Nomes busy elsewhere.

Beelz hopped back onto his own place on the sofa and rested his muzzle on Naomie's thigh, though he kept his eyes on Muldoon. Probably trying to decide if he needed to guard me from any incursions she might make. Knowing how quickly he took to the females in my life—and there were a lot of them—it wouldn't take long for Lex to win him over.

Oddly enough, she hadn't asked what was wrong with his eyes. She couldn't know he was a hellhound. Heck, even Naomie bought the gene pool disparity story and she'd recently typed an entire manuscript where he was identified as a hellhound. But then, it was just a story to her, right?

I took Nomes' previous position on the sofa arm. "Not a Girl Scout so no cookies were ordered."

"Who was it then?" Naomie wanted to know. "It's kinda late."

"Not for missionaries, apparently. The visitor wanted to know if I'd been saved. I told her yes and that I was happy with my congregation, then closed the door." The closest thing I had to a congregation were the passel of witches I'd inherited. Delia was their titular leader now though they didn't meet on the estate grounds any longer. I merely used their professional services in this world.

Delia gave me a look. Other than Beelz and I, she was the only one capable of recognizing *essence de vampire* in the air. "A job," I said softly. She'd know what that meant. Fodder for another story.

Muldoon shifted her attention to me. "I don't know what your schedule is like, Bram, but will you have a few hours tomorrow to answer questions and possibly toss about some ideas for the junior series?"

"Morning, afternoon or evening?" I asked.

"Whichever is most convenient."

It would mean sharing my breakfast pastries, but doing the Q&A in the morning would free me up to begin investigating after lunch and not need to worry about delaying follow-through on a lead if I got one. It seemed a bit off kilter for our Nordic vampire to still have human relatives, but it wasn't impossible. I had no idea what her life had been like before joining the ranks of the blood-suckers.

"Naomie gets in around nine. Would that work?"

"Absolutely. I'll just need directions on how to get here. Since Delia picked me up at the airport, I haven't rented a car yet," Muldoon said.

"No problem." I took my wallet out and set a business card free. "We have Burt for situations like this."

Burt was nearly the first magic-free human I'd met after crossing from fictionland. Calie'd had his cab on retainer, which meant I hadn't needed to know my way around. He knew his way around. Continuing with the contract suited us all very well. Particularly for me since Burt knew hundreds of places to eat in Detroit. It was his purpose in life to introduce my stomach to every single one, too. I not only had Burt's number on speed dial, I knew it by heart. I didn't need his card.

"Just give him a call and he'll swing by with his cab. I'll give him a heads-up, so he knows you'll be in touch."

"Great. Thank you," she said and reached for the card—

Which is when the house exploded.

***

Okay, it wasn't the entire house, just the back patio, but that blew out quite a few windows rather successfully.

"Sandra!" Delia gasped.

"I'll find her," I said and vanished.

Make that *appeared* to vanish. Black smoke was rolling through the place, so it probably seemed like I did a djinn-like *poof* to them.

When I called her name, it was coughing rather than an answer I heard. Our cook for the evening was on the floor and bleeding, but it looked like cuts from flying glass rather than anything else.

"Easy," I told her. "As long as you aren't bleeding out, dealing with the flames out back should probably take precedence."

"What?" she shouted. Obviously, the explosion had put things on mute for her. I hoped it was temporary.

"Delia! Call 9-1-1," I yelled. "Paramedics and fire department." Then I grabbed the fire extinguisher from under the sink and headed out to blast any flames.

By the time emergency services arrived, the only flickers were those attempting to keep everyone toasty in the media room fireplace. February had invited itself into the house via the R.I.P. windows across the back and in the kitchen wing. I strongly doubted obtaining enough plywood to prevent its entry would be possible that night. By the time the professionals finished with things, every home improvement mega store would have sealed their entrances for the day.

"The propane tank in the grill setup exploded," the firefighter in charge of giving bad news told us.

"But I had it checked two days ago," Sandra insisted through the oxygen mask she'd been given. "Everything was in good order."

"We'll have an investigator out to look at things tomorrow morning," he said. "If for no other reason than to assure your insurance company that it was an accident."

I took my own oxygen mask off to thank him.

He recommended I put it back on. "You probably inhaled far too much smoke though that was fast thinking with the extinguisher. Don't forget to get it replaced."

"Adding it to my shopping list right under a shit-load of plywood," I promised. There was a good chance that finding an insurance company willing to cover me for anything would soon be difficult. They'd had to pay out a bundle to replace my Mustang when it had gone to Valhalla the day after I'd driven it off the lot back in October. Having my off-site office (as in, not on the estate) bombed before anyone but the bombers could stop by for a visit hadn't gone well either.

Once the paramedics left with Sandra to ensure they'd found all the glass punctures she'd incurred, I tucked Naomie into her car and told her the office would be closed for a couple days while repairs were made. Then I escorted Delia and Muldoon to the Prius. I also cancelled the morning meeting since the mansion wasn't exactly warm any longer and asked my trusty PR witch if there was someone on our go-to list to call for repairs.

Naturally, there was a coven member with the connection we needed. She promised to pass word along and offered her guest room for my own getaway. As she didn't know I never slept and, thus, didn't need a bed, I told her thanks, but I'd already made arrangements. She didn't need to know those arrangements were holding down a booth at the Denny's in Sterling Heights which was open all night. I'd head there after leaving The Red Dragon. Fortunately, there was still time to make the meeting with the vamp at midnight.

It was only as the fire department packed up the last of their equipment that I realized another city employee had come to visit.

"Car survive this time, Farrell?" Detective Chad Durkin asked as he pushed away from where he leaned against his own vehicle.

He'd sort of given me an assignment early in November, one that I hadn't made any more headway on than he had, but I knew that wasn't what he was here about. He had me on his radar. If my name popped up in connection with anything, he was going to turn up.

"Yup, lucked out this time. The garage survived unscathed." It was probably a lot warmer than the house was, but not enough for a guy and his hound to live in.

"Think this was an accident?" he asked, gesturing at the blackened barbecue area, then shoved his hand back into his coat pocket before it could freeze off. Since I felt like body parts were attempting to go arctic on me, I didn't blame him.

I sighed. "Wish I could say yes, Durkin, but…" There was no reason to finish the sentence. He'd get the gist.

"Regular human or otherwise?"

Yep, he knows about the Otherworlders. He is the only non-magical human employed by the city who does know and keeps quiet about it. Heck, no one wants to get the modern version of a Section 8.

"No idea," I admitted and wondered whether I should tell him about the visit from Ernie earlier in the day. "Maybe the fire marshal will find something to tell me which way to lean in finding the answer."

Beelz trundled from wherever he'd been resting and sniffed at the DPD dick's pant leg.

"You have a dog?" Durkin sounded stunned. Not surprising since Beelz had kept out of his sight last fall. "There isn't one in the books."

"Not the older ones, but he's in the new one," I said.

That's when Beelz raised his head and Durkin got a gander at his eyes.

"Ah," the cop said. "A hellhound. Didn't think they resembled dachshunds."

"He doesn't always. What brought you to my door, Durkin? Other than the malfunction on the grill."

"Just making sure I haven't lost the only guy who can find the ghoul for me," he said.

The ghoul in question being one Solomon Prisk. Durkin had tied his name to a host of missing person's cases but had not been able to find Prisk.

So far, I hadn't either, but I hadn't looked very hard 'cause it was winter. In other words, too damn cold to entice me out during optimum ghoul-hunting hours. Which were long after the sun had called it a day. I *had* attended another Friday night poker game with an odder-than-usual batch of Otherworlders these past months in the off chance of finding a ghoul in attendance. Apparently, ghouls didn't play poker. None had shown, in any case.

"You've got talents the rest of my department lacks," Durkin reminded me.

Considering his department included a vampire working vice at night and a werewolf on SWAT, I would've thought he'd had things covered without drawing me in as an unofficial consultant.

"Got time for a coffee some place warm?" I asked. When he agreed, I did a magic douse on the lights and fireplace, and lobbed shields over all the destroyed windows and doors. I hoped like hell they'd keep February and further miscreants at bay until physical repairs were in place.

Beelz hopped into the recently replaced Ravenmobile and we were ready to go.

Durkin lead the way to a pizza place. As a substitute for the steak dinner, it came in a close second.

February 15th

Valentine's Day came to its official close with no further disasters. An entire new day clicked into place. Meeting a vampiress in the dead of night would no doubt kick off a fresh batch of calamities. Maybe I'd get paid for enduring them, though.

When midnight struck, my stomach had been appeased, Durkin was back to his regular work, and Beelz had inhaled the meatball sandwich I'd ordered as take out for him. There were still cooing couples abroad, but they were mostly on their way back to cozier surroundings when I pulled into a parking spot outside The Red Dragon.

On the way to the door, I passed a few stationary cars with motors purring, but the steamed-up windows proved St. Valentine's magic had done its job. Necks were definitely being nibbled on but not, in most cases, by one of the undead. Whether Beelz took note of the rocking vehicles or not as we ambled by, his tail turned chipper metronome when we reached the mouth of the alley I'd promised him. He vanished inside before I hit the club's main entrance.

Oddly enough, The Red Dragon is owned and run by a red dragon. I've seen him in both sinuous lizard form and the mock-human glamour he stuffs himself into. He's unpleasant in both manifestations. I'd made his acquaintance at Thanksgiving when he'd been hot to acquire a heavenly brass horn and I'd been determined he wouldn't. Well, determined that *no* being got hold of it as the damn thing was scary on an apocalyptic level. The only moniker I'd heard used to reference the dragon was The Collector. I pictured his horde looking a bit like a storeroom for the brass sections of Ellington, Basie, Goodman, Miller, Chicago, Blood, Sweat and Tears, and a couple thousand marching bands. He has a thing for jazz music and his club features a live band every night. Their repertoire is strictly big band swing tunes, although there are only four guys on stage. Oddly enough, only one of them plays a horn—a saxophone.

They were still on stage when I slipped in the door a few minutes after midnight. So was the former Miss Sweden 1934, aka Wendy.

Or, as the sign out front had announced, "The sultry vocals of Detroit's own Wendy Whilsen." As I'd taken her for the vamp in charge of call girls and extremely friendly escorts including gigolos at our first stare down, singing at the dragon's club seemed rather like a demotion.

I doubted she was a native of Detroit despite the sign. More like a coffin-berthed immigrant from one of the North Sea nations, though she could have already logged in eight or more decades on this side of the Pond. She had squashed any hint of a foreign accent from her voice, though.

A few couples were still holding down tables or out on the dinky dance floor swaying to the music. The vampiress was the only femme who gave off fatale vibes. Ones that had nothing to do with her being a bloodsucker. No, she was sex personified.

Her fur coat had hidden her dress when she'd stopped by the mansion. Now that it was on full display, I wasn't surprised to find there was more skin than fabric on the top half of the outfit. The floor-dusting skirt made up for its absence in a shimmer of clinging red silk.

Her smoky voice turned Cole Porter's "Night and Day" into the song of a siren. Each breathily delivered note infused the very air in the club with vampire pheromones.

As the bulk of the Valentine's Day crowd had scarpered out into the cold, I commandeered a table in the back of the room and ordered my bourbon of choice. As the temperatures were doing the limbo, seeing how low they could go, I asked for a double. Anti-freeze for humans. Or pseudo-humans, as it were.

Wendy gave me a mid-croon nod, acknowledging that she'd spotted me. Considering I was far from sartorially elegant, layered against the cold in inky black shirt, crew neck sweater, jeans, and had tossed a similarly toned pea coat on the chair next to me, I blended into the shadows easily.

The dragon's wait staff was all female, and the last time I'd visited, they'd been outfitted as Playboy Bunnies. Tonight, their outfits were Valentine red, leaned toward oriental with a Mandarin collar, had long sleeves, and glittered like an explosion at a sequin factory. The crimson costume ended at thigh level with black fishnet stockings taking over. A pretty little blonde had just delivered my order when the dragon himself loomed tableside.

"Farrell," he growled.

"Collector," I snarled back.

"Whaddaya doing here?"

"What any guy's doing for Valentine's festival. Hoping to get debauched." When he just glared at me, I tipped my chin toward the undead songstress. "Late date with Wendy."

He pulled out a chair and sat down. I suppose when you own the club, you don't have to wait for an invite to join a customer. "Sure you don't qualify as her dinner?"

"I have been assured by Palermo himself that what my veins contain has more in common with what's in a magenta printer cartridge than a blood donor bag." Palermo is the centuries'-old head of the Detroit vamp syndicate though I still think of him as Old Renaissance.

"She don't get off 'til we close," the dragon hissed—which isn't easy when few of the words used supply those nicely hissable *S*s.

"I'm not allowed to be a music lover in the interim?"

"Let's say you have a strange way of showing it, Raven. You've only been in my joint twice and both times were Thanksgiving weekend."

How could I forget? He'd had a mutant moron begin tenderizing me in the alley before the vampires tested their luck with me. It hadn't been good luck for either them or me, but at least I'd limped away.

"I've been busy. Now, I'm not," I said. "You might have heard that I lost my last girlfriend? If you heard how, I'm sure you'll agree I needed time to recover from the disappointment."

It had definitely put me off Otherworlders as romantic partners. Could that be why Naomie had landed on my daydream menu, because she *wasn't* an Otherworlder? Hmm… worth considering or not?

But now was not the time to put much thought into it, though. I had a vampiric looker interested in having me dip into my PI bag of tricks again.

"Oh, yeah. I heard about the succubus. You treat Wendy the same way and I'll personally make that magenta in your veins boil."

"Duly noted." Though that just meant I'd have to beat him to the punch if things did turn pyrotechnic of their own accord.

Wendy's song ended with light applause. The sax man took the mic and announced they were taking a break and would be back in fifteen. Rather than follow the men to whatever barely breached original packaging The Collector kept them in off stage, the blonde vamp in the red gown stepped off the platform and headed in my direction. She had as plastic a smile planted on her kisser as the wait girls did.

I pushed my chair back, getting politely to my feet. The dragon stood as well, offering her his already warmed seat. Wendy slid into it, the upper parts of her torso making the skimpy silk covering those regions do interesting things. I know because I come from a land where the males take full advantage of all opportunities to take in the scenery.

Miss Sweden 1934's deserved panoramic postcards as well as photo ops.

The dragon maneuvered Wendy's chair closer to the table. Living dangerously—considering he was still lurking—I regained my seat.

"If Farrell gives you any trouble, my dear, I'll be glad to see if he tastes like chicken or blue spruce," he offered.

My guess would be a rather bland, wood pulp pudding. Only art books get the upgrade.

The smile she gave him was as false as the one she'd given me across the room. "I'll be fine," she assured him.

Yeah, but would I? She wanted me to find her great-grandson. If I didn't… well, she might develop a taste for ink.

Wendy and I both waited until The Collector wouldn't hear our topic of conversation.

"Need to wet your whistle with alcohol or do we get right down to business?" I asked.

She leaned forward slightly and snagged my tumbler of EW. "I'll just share yours, Raven," she purred.

I was gent enough not to get possessive about my poison. "Just so you know, I don't work cheap," I said.

She peered at me over the rim of the confiscated glass. "Word is that you didn't charge the succubi for the investigative work you did last autumn."

"Ah, but that case was to clear myself of the murder charges, cupcake. Finding your missing relative is something else entirely. I don't work nine to five on a case but stay on it until it's solved. There are several things that determine my price. Like, is the missing person a norm or a night person like yourself?"

"Eric's not been turned, if that's what you're asking. He doesn't know what I am or who I am, and I've kept my distance from the family so that my lifestyle doesn't intersect with theirs." Wendy sipped my bourbon, then set it back in front of me. "However, you and I both know that doesn't absolve beings in the Otherworld community from involvement in his disappearance."

I nodded. My fingers drifted over the condensation on my newly-returned glass. "Since there is an off-chance magic is involved, the rate per hour is going to be executive level. There's also a deposit paid up front and non-refundable." You know, in case I don't live through things.

She didn't even blink at the concept that I was going to bilk her if magic was being used—whether it was by me or others. When you are the only P.I. in the neighborhood capable of fielding spells, the sky is the limit. Wish I could have charged what I had in mind back home. Unfortunately, hocus-pocus powered investigators are so common in fictionland, services can be had for the price of a fast food combo meal. If there is a coupon deal to use, the case keeps the books in the black.

The only thing I was surprised about was where in that slinky gown she'd managed to tuck the folded bills she slid across the table to me. Under the cover of my cupped hand, I flipped the corners up, counting. Purely for tax purposes, of course.

"Consider that a deposit toward those billable hours, Raven," Wendy murmured. "How soon can you start?"

As my covert tally had come to $3,000, that was a very easy answer. "The moment you give me the details."

***

His name was Eric Winthur. Wendy had never met him, but she'd attended every evening sporting event he'd participated in from high school to college. She'd done the same for his father, her grandson, after learning that the daughter she'd left on the doorstep of a Stockholm orphanage had grown up and immigrated to—of all places—Detroit when her engineer husband had left Volvo for a job at General Motors. Mentally doing the math, I realized that I'd been nearly on the mark by linking her to 1934, though I'd done that based on the cascade of blonde waves spilling forward in Veronica Lake/Jessica Rabbit fashion.

Yeah, it's weird that I know actresses from a by-gone era considering my age on paper, but my creator had logged in a lot of years before inventing me. And I do mean *a lot*. The vestiges of Calie's knowledge surface at odd times, too, meaning, I really killed at those trivia games. Of course, I'd met Jessica Rabbit in fictionland. She was in a book before she made it to Disney movie fame.

According to Wendy, Eric was working on a Master of Science at the university's Dearborn campus, his field of specialization one of local interest: vehicle electronics and controls. He lived off campus, but Wendy wasn't sure where since he'd recently broken up with his girlfriend/roommate and been kicked out. He held down a full-time job as a mechanic at an independent auto repair where he did second shift fiddling with vehicle electronic systems (no surprise), brake pads, and late-night towing services for Triple A and similar concerns. It was on one of the latter jobs that he'd vanished.

As had the stranded motorist who'd made the call.

Fortunately, Wendy had a clandestinely-shot photograph of her great-grandson taken in a sports bar. She'd already emailed it to me since, even if her outfit for the evening had had pockets, carrying a cell in one would have ruined the whole look. When I hit enough icons to bring it up, the tiny screen on my phone was filled with the wide grin of a bearded Viking. He had her Nordic coloring, the shoulders of a competition-level swimmer, and the height of a resident of Asgard. Yeah, he was a regular chick magnet. Made me wonder about his personality since, if he hadn't been kidnapped, he would have spent the just-passed Valentine's Day crying in his beer or trawling for a hook-up.

Wendy was chock-full of names to pass along. I hastily thumbed to my official investigator's tech notebook and keyed them in. Former girlfriend, college mentor, best friend, parents, employer. All starting points. All regular humans. If there were non-humans involved, I'd have to trip over them myself.

When the band members drifted back on stage, she asked if I had any further questions. I was sure they'd surface but needed to do a bit of pondering first. It wasn't like dropping by to talk to any of the names on my list was possible at this hour. Now, if they'd been Otherworlders that would not have been a handicap. For the most part, non-humans prowled the night.

However, so could I.

She sashayed back to the mic. I tucked her hefty deposit into a front jeans pocket, dropped a twenty onto the table, downed the remaining antifreeze in my glass, then grabbed my coat. I was turning the collar up around my ears, preparing for re-entry into the arctic chill, when the TARDIS arrived. It was either that or the ring tone on my phone. I went with the most likely scenario and re-snagged the cell.

"Raven," Ruth Lund's gravely tones snapped. "You still looking for that ghoul?"

"Solomon Prisk? You know where he is?"

"I know where his cousin is," she said. "He's sitting in a booth here at The Bridge and he's got two humans with him. Girls who should know better than to hang with a guy like him, but as they're all dolled up, I doubt they've got a drop of common sense between 'em. Get your tail feathers over here fast, Bram, 'cause these damsels are in one heck of a need of rescuing."

***

When Beelz trundled from the alleyway in answer to a short, sharp whistle, he looked like a mutt that had just been to intimidation heaven. Not that hellhounds were allowed within whizzing distance of those gilded gates, but there was a definite swagger to his step. Which, I had to admit, was quite an accomplishment for a hound with a low-riding chassis.

"Ruthie needs us," I told him. "You up to further rumbling if necessary?"

The *yip* said it all. His adventures in the alley qualified as a warm-up for the major event. If, of course, convincing a couple of human Cinderellas that midnight had come and gone and they were one hell of a way from the castle gates turned into the main event of the evening.

It did have a way to go to beat out the explosion at the manse, after all.

Since the latest Ravenmobile's odometer had yet to crest a

hundred—the Mustang was that new—I tossed a shield over it to irritate the heck out of thieves or vandals once we found a place to park. The neighborhood wherein The Bridge nestled was in one of the more battered-but-not-yet-condemned areas of the city. I'd spent a lot of my first week in town within bare blocks of the bar and had collected enough bruises to know the area was a very dark part of the proverbial woods.

Fortunately for us, Ruth's brother Ralph Lund had no problem allowing hellhounds in his place. Beelz led the way in when I yanked the door open and was blasted with cranked-up heavy metal music and a cloud of smoke that mixed the scents of tobacco, hashish, and marijuana into eye-watering soup. Two steps in and the aroma of sweating Otherworlders of various gene pools nearly beat out the toxic smudge.

Ruth materialized from the crowd immediately. Part troll and part dwarf, and just shy of waist-high, she probably wove her way through the crowd's legs like they were trees in a forest.

"You took your time," she snarled at me.

Made me wonder how she'd sound if she didn't like me, which she did. "I was at The Red Dragon. We practically flew here."

Her look said, "Whatever". "We're a bit crowded tonight," she said. Like I hadn't noticed. "Maybe you should carry Beelzebub, so he doesn't get stepped on."

I looked down at him. "You want that?" He was particular about being treated like a package. Fine with it if a female was going to be cuddling him but evaluated things on a danger scale of his own design otherwise.

In answer, he morphed into a Great Dane, apparently uncaring if shedding his disguise would stun any non-humans. Only Ruth's eyes grew large when he did.

"Oh, that'll work, too," she allowed. "The ghoul's got the norms trapped in the fifth booth back. Do what you like with him, but only after he's paid his bar tab, huh?"

I snapped my heels together and gave her an equally snappy salute.

Ruth looked at the big box-sized Beelz. "How do you stand being around him all the time?"

The hound shrugged but he gave me his best grin.

To reach the fifth booth back, I pushed past a couple of Ruth's troll cousins, slipped between a dark elf and the Valkyrie he was chatting up, dodged a guy who looked like an accountant but smelled like a werewolf, and kept my distance from the lone succubus in the crowd. When she caught sight of me, she made a hasty exit. Excellent thinking on her part.

Solomon Prisk's cousin's human glamour was a throwback to Pacino as Serpico, but he'd added a gold tooth. It glinted even in the dim lighting of the bar. He had one of the human girls trapped through the simple expediency of sitting on the outer end of the banquette seat. She didn't look like she minded.

Where Naomie's idea of fashion is shapeless black layers like those Winona Ryder wore in *Beetlejuice*, this girl had gone for the Goth tramp look. Lots of skin in view and lots of tattoos, too. She'd worn a spiked dog collar as jewelry. Her hair color came from the same bottle as my secretary's, but it looked like she'd hacked it with hedge trimmers then created spikes with Elmer's glue. In honor of Valentine's Day, she'd dressed things up with lipstick and nail polish that leaned more toward raspberry than cherry.

There were several empty glasses on the table, their rims smeared with raspberry lip gloss. They certainly explained why her giggle had a pitch that could shatter crystal. Fortunately, the barware at the Lunds' narrow little tavern was generations shy of anything that delicate.

It wasn't until I was standing at the booth that I caught a glance at the girl wedged as far back in the opposite seat as she could get. Her lipstick was definitely candy-apple in color and unsmudged, unlike her friend's. Her eyes were heavily kohled and were unnaturally wide. Her gaze darted from the couple across from her to the strange assortment of other patrons. An untouched mug of troll beer sat before her and she had the lower edge of her bottom lip firmly gripped between her teeth.

"Naomie!" I gasped.

Beelz had lagged behind me in the crowd, apparently lingering to help himself to something's unattended meal, plates being much easier to reach in Great Dane mode. At my exclamation, I caught his instant drop back to dachshund form from the corner of my eye.

"Boss!" Naomie gasped back at me. But I saw her shoulders relax. Her teeth freed her bottom lip. Yep, Sir Bram had come to rescue her. Everything was—or soon would be—fine in her world once more.

"What the hell are you doing here? Do you have any idea how dangerous this place is?" I demanded. Okay, maybe I snarled it. The Bridge catered to folks who snarled. It was catching.

The ghoul pushed to his feet and found that, even standing, I had the height advantage. I saw the balk, but he decided to brazen it out.

"Clear off, slick. This party's doing fine without you part of it."

His shirt was unbuttoned to display a hairy chest and a gold amulet on a thick chain. I grabbed a handful of both fabric and chain, dragged him up on his toes, and leaned into his upturned glare. "Pal, the Seventies called and left a message. They want the wardrobe back."

"You don't scare me," he growled.

"You know who I am?" I countered.

"Yeah. The guy in the books. The Raven."

True, but Naomie and her friend didn't know that. "Fictional character, bucko," I said and added a nasty grin. "But if I *were* The Raven, what do you think I'd do to a slime ball like you?"

He tried to shrug me off and found he lacked the traction to do so. "I ain't doing nothin' wrong, Farrell. Leave me be."

I glanced over at Naomie. "Time to go."

She scooted across the bench so quickly I wondered whether Ruth had begun waxing the seats. Her friend, however, stayed where she was.

I leveled a glare at her. "You, too, sugar."

She took a deep breath, folded her arms across her awesomely displayed rack, and turned mulish. "No," she said. "I'm enjoying myself."

"You won't for long. This piece of shit"—I shook the dangling ghoul until his teeth rattled a bit—"has already slipped you happy drugs. He likes to make stupid little girls disappear. He'll sell you to anyone with cash in hand and let them do whatever they want to you. If they happen to kill you, he'll just charge them extra and arrange to have your body disposed of."

"You're just trying to scare me," she insisted adamantly.

"Apparently doing a lousy job of it, too," I said and turned my attention back to the ghoul, letting him drop back to his feet. He staggered a bit but caught himself on the table. "You've got a relative

I've been asked to locate. Solomon Prisk. You think he'll like hearing that you and I had a nice cozy chat?"

"We ain't having no cozy anything, Farrell," he said.

I smiled in a way that was far from friendly. "You know that, and I know that, but do you think Sol will believe it if I tell select people how helpful you've been in giving me information about him?" Not that I'd be grilling him about Prisk quite yet. I'd hunt him down for that treat in the very near future, though.

The ghoul's expression alone said his cousin wouldn't take his word as line-and-verse in the bible of the streets. His bravado packed up and left.

"Fine. Take 'em both with you," he snarled, then pushed through the crowd toward the bar. Not a one of the self-absorbed customers had paid any attention to our contretemps, and they ignored his shoves as well. Life went on for the regulars at The Bridge Bar and Grill.

In his absence, Ruth surfaced and glared at both Naomie and her friend. "You're both barred from this establishment," she announced. "We don't like troublemakers."

Naomie's friend gaped at her. "Troublemakers! He's the troublemaker here!" She pointed at me.

"He's the woodsman like Chris Hemsworth in those movies," Ruth corrected. "I called him to save your scrawny neck. Now get the hell out."

Naomie was already on her feet and buttoning a long trench coat that looked like it had seen duty in World War II. She spotted Beelz at her feet before she finished. "Oh, you brought back up!" she cried and swept him up in her arms, getting super emotional. Tears of relief leaked from her eyes.

Beelz took care of washing them from her face. Didn't seem to mind that, with them making her eyeliner run, they wouldn't be exactly tasty.

The much-less-warmly-dressed girl continued to glare at both Ruth and me as she shrugged into a dark anorak that left bare legs and toeless knee-high boots on display. Since I was pretty sure she'd been the one to drag Naomie to The Bridge, I wished the head cold from Hell on her.

Ruth pushed a way through the crowd for us. She'd found another use for a carving fork, jabbing customers who didn't move fast enough to suit her. Naomie, with Beelz in her arms, was right on her heels. I had to manhandle the resistant girl ahead of me. Once we were on the street, she yanked her arm from my care.

"Who drove?" I snapped.

"Tiffany," Naomie said and pointed to a much-abused antique Chevy El Camino. In the dark it was difficult to tell what color it was. Other than rust, that is, and that had nothing to do with paint.

"Get in your vehicle," I ordered Miss Recalcitrant. "Naomie, the Mustang's that way. Beelz will escort you. We'll follow your friend to her place, then I'll drop you at yours." I had the remote in my hand but used it just to make the lights blink on. Had to decommission the force field before she reached it, after all.

Our secretary set Beelz on his feet and hung her head. "Yes, sir," she whispered, totally whipped by her disastrous evening out.

I waited until Tiffany had settled in her car, buckled her seat belt, and turned the engine over. It coughed rather than hummed. She tried to ram into me, but I'm quick on my feet.

Robbed of the satisfaction of running me over, she took off down the street at a clip that had passed the posted speed limit before she reached the cross street, then barreled through the stop sign there without slowing down.

Naomie was cozy in the shotgun spot and clutching Beelz in her arms once more. "She's going to try to lose you," she mumbled, still whipped by her disastrous adventure.

"She'll try," I said and tossed her a grin as I buckled in. The car was already purring. "What do you say we make sure she goes home then head to Denny's for a huge breakfast?"

"Breakfast?" she echoed in surprise.

"Well, that and an interrogation, sugar. I doubt it was your idea to visit that specific bar tonight." I pulled away from the curb after the retreating glow of the El Camino's rear lights.

Naomie buried her face against Beelz's coat. "I'm sorry, boss, but it really was my idea," she confessed.

***

It's impossible to claim I was speechless, because… well, by now you probably know that is next to impossible. "You what?"

"Well, Tiffany was saying that she wanted someplace really different to visit rather than the places she usually goes for fun. I sorta said it was too bad places like you wrote about in *Raven's Moon* didn't really exist because they were just the sort of place that would appeal to her."

Ahead of us, Tiffany squealed tires as she took a right too fast. The Ravenmobile did the turn at the same speed but with less histrionics. We began closing on her. "Places like The Bridge, hmm?"

"Honest, boss, I didn't know there was such a place, but, for fun, we got on the computer and fed in the name and Detroit. I was surprised when a website came up immediately," Nomes confessed. "After that, there was no stopping her."

Yeah, Tiffany had looked like that sort of person to me, too. A selfish idiot, not a lick of common sense in her head much less the rest of her. You'd think she was trying to be me.

I was a bit stunned to learn The Bridge had a website, too. Obviously, Ruthie was the one covering things across the promotional board because I couldn't see her brother Ralph caring that much.

"Why didn't you call me for help once you saw the joint, Nomes?" I demanded.

"Why would I call you, boss? Even if I thought about doing so, you had the house fire to deal with. I wasn't about to call my dad or brother. They'd have lectured me. Maybe get in a fight with someone in the bar. One they were sure to lose by the looks of those people."

Tiffany tried to shake her tail—us—by swinging her El Camino into an alley. I knew this neighborhood and she clearly didn't. I pulled over to the side of the road and waited for her to realize it was a dead end and back out.

"At least Ruthie was smart enough to call me," I said.

Naomie's eyes widened in surprise. "That mean little lady's name is Ruth? Boss, you called one of the characters who runs The Bridge in the book Ruth."

"Yeah," I agreed.

"You can't use real people's names in fiction. You shouldn't use the names of real places either unless they've given you permission. Well, unless they're like franchises 'cause those are everywhere."

Well, yeah, I knew that, but did it really apply to people who weren't human? Personally, I didn't think it should.

"Wait. They knew who you were at The Bridge. And Ruth had your phone number!" my secretary gasped. "They even let Beelzie in the place and that's a health department violation."

This interrogation was not headed in the right direction. Somehow, she'd turned things around so I was the one running the gauntlet. "Does Tiffany even know where she lives?" I asked as the beat-up Chevy inched out of the alley then turned back the way we'd come.

"Maybe not," Naomie admitted, "but she's got GPS on her phone."

"If she thinks to use it," I mumbled, doing a U-turn. Not an easy thing to accomplish on the narrow street.

"How many times have you been to The Bridge, boss?"

The tone was innocent, but I suspected her intent. I looked at Beelz. He got the message and distracted her with a thorough face-washing.

It didn't derail her, though. "Boss?" she said.

"Never been there at night, just in the afternoon when searching out interesting locations to use," I said. Which was a lie. Oh, not that I'd only been there during daylight but that I'd been doing research for the book. I'd been pulled within the confines by Otherworlders claiming they had a job for me to do. I stayed in touch because I liked Ruth Lund and she was a good link to the Otherworld underground community in Detroit. Ruthie ran a hell of an efficient yard sale, too.

"It is a great location, and, I gotta say, you described it to a T in *Moon*. And, boss?"

"Yeah?"

"You were totally awesome when you yanked that creep off his feet with one hand. Very Ravenish."

I sighed theatrically. "There goes the secret identity thing."

"Yep," she agreed. "Totally blown if you really had one."

Mentally, I mopped my brow in relief. Despite the lineup of odd and scary characters patronizing The Bridge, she hadn't tumbled onto the fact that the only humans in the place had been her and Tiffany.

And I wasn't that sure about Tiffany. I mean, she was strange…

But, apparently, she'd remembered to ask the GPS lady for assistance in getting home. No further attempts were made to lose us. When she turned into the parking lot of a shabby two-story block of apartments, I pulled in behind her. Neither Naomie nor I got out of the Mustang, but we watched in silence as Tiffany headed inside. She only staggered a bit. Considering how many glasses on the table had been smeared with her lipstick, I was amazed she wasn't crawling. When Naomie told me a light had just gone on in her friend's place, I got back onto the road, headed for a late night breakfast.

"I want to make sure about something," I told my secretary. "You are not to go looking for any vampire headquarters at One Detroit Center."

"As if there really were an office of them there," she said.

"I know what you read," I warned her, "and we're going to keep all vampires in the pages of those romance books or in the Raven Tales. No playing *Buffy* after office hours."

"Boss, in the vampire romances, the heroine never stakes the hero."

"Then I'm instigating another rule, Nomes. No blood-sharing with anyone you run into who claims to be a vampire."

"Okay," she agreed, but there was a laugh in her voice.

She didn't think I was serious. That was good and that was bad. Though the days were getting longer, the sun had usually beat it before Naomie left for the day and there was at least one real vampire who might stop by during that hour or so on her way to work at The Red Dragon.

"Your lectures are nothing like those either my dad or my brother would give me," Naomie confessed.

Not in the least surprised on that. "Okay, let's turn to business for a bit. You know when that reporter showed up this morning and you thought she was in real estate?"

Naomie made a hum of agreement. Beelz decided her face needed washing again and went to it. He loved her because she never wiped dog spit off until he left the room. I made a bet with myself that when we hit the restaurant, she'd head for the restroom first. She might scream when she saw that her eye makeup was smeared across her face. Tears had started the destruction, but hellhound drool had provided the *pièce de résistance* to the disaster.

"Well, it isn't common knowledge, but I'm thinking of selling the estate," I said.

"Really? Why? It's gorgeous."

"It's far too big for a guy and his dog. Besides, I'm thinking of building a place next to the St. Romaric cemetery."

"There's really a St. Romaric's?" she gasped, then narrowed her eyes. "Boss, is every place you used in *Moon* a real place?"

"Taking the Fifth on that. This stuff about the estate is top secret, Nomes. Not even Delia knows about it yet, so no spilling the beans," I warned.

"Who *does* know you're going to sell the estate?" she asked.

"Only you, sweetheart. Only you."

I cruised up to a cross street where the light had just turned red, so it was more than a glance I gave her. Her eyes were wide again, and she'd put a gloved hand up to her mouth—which was gaped open. Yep, I'd stunned the heck out of her with that.

"Oh, boss!" she breathed. "I'm honored with the secret. I'll keep it even under torture."

"Don't lose any digits over it, toots. Just keep it on the low-down. In fact, you can spout what you said this morning if anyone asks about it in the coming weeks."

"Got it. You aren't interested in selling anything but books."

"Perfect." The light changed and, moments later, we pulled into the Denny's lot.

***

I'd already ordered coffee for me, hot chocolate for her, and a lumberjack slam for myself by the time she finished in the restroom. The evening's adventure had apparently given her an appetite because she asked for a slam for herself.

"Have you got a notebook with you?" I asked.

"Boss, I'm a writer. I'm never without a pen and paper," she insisted.

"Get it out. While the office may be closed while repairs are made on the house, I have some things you can research for me. Find out what you can about…" I gave her the names Wendy had supplied.

"Real people again? You can't keep using—"

I held my hand up to stop her. "This isn't for a book. This week, you're working for B. Farrell Investigations."

"We're gumshoes?"

"Not exactly," I tempered, "but, just in case, order some detective movies to use as instructional manuals. We don't have time to read."

***

It was 5 a.m. when I dropped Naomie at her apartment. Building-wise, it wasn't that much different from the one Tiffany called home, but the neighborhood was a step or two up. Beelz and I walked her to the door rather than sit in the car. When a neighbor cracked their door to see who was making noise at that hour, Naomie wished her a good morning and smiled widely. From the glare the woman gave me, I'm guessing she thought Nomes had spent the night in Valentine debaucheries with yours truly. Wouldn't have put it past my trusty secretary to have made extra noise to give the snoop that idea on purpose.

If only it had been true.

While Naomie hadn't worked at Raven Central long, those six weeks had been jam-packed as I'd dictated and she'd pounded the keyboard, turning my first days in the real world into what passed for a fictional Raven adventure. Beelz and I both liked having her around. I hoped that served as a good enough reason for me to entertain fantasies about a cozier relationship with our pet human. Whether or not it was, those dreams danced like sugarplums quite often in my head. I was playing this hand so close to my vest, I hoped I recognized a royal flush when—if—she dealt it.

The real world was so damn complicated. Still, wasn't wishing myself back to fictionland, though. I liked it here.

"Sleep in," I told her. "When you surface, do the research and give me a call when you've got something. In the meantime, I'll deal with the house repair dudes and endure Lex's questions."

"Got it," Nomes assured me.

I looked down at Beelz in his favorite position—sitting on my foot. "We waitin' 'til the door's locked?"

He nodded.

I faced Naomie. "You heard him. We want to hear locks slamming in place."

She saluted, then got down on all fours to kiss the hellhound's snout.

He gave her a dog kiss on the lips.

"That was from both of us," I said, envying him a bit. "Now… locks?"

Which was when she stunned the heck out of me. She went up on tiptoe and brushed a light kiss on my cheek. "Thanks for rescuing me, boss," she murmured as she backed into the apartment, shut the door, then, in quick order, clicks at both doorknob and deadbolt sounded as she shoved them into place.

I looked down at Beelz and murmured, "Wow."

He gave me a canine grin, then headed for the stairs.

Personally, I would have been happy to just stay where I was and bask in that moment.

Yup, total sap.

Beelz had to clear his throat to get me moving.

But moving toward what?

***

It was still too early for anyone to show up at the mansion, be they fire marshal, insurance inspector, or work team. I'd need to beat them all to the estate so the magical shields were down. Nothing humans liked worse than walking into an invisible wall. It was a pain to find someone to wipe the memory of what caused the concussion away, too.

Considering I'd finished that giant breakfast not long before, donuts had lost their appeal, though coffee hadn't. Inside the pages of a book, I drank overly-sweet Turkish sludge claiming to be coffee. In the outside world, I'd grown accustomed to the designer coffee mixes so I headed for one of the local Nirvana spots. As it appeared that Naomie didn't intend to sanction my use of real places in future Raven Tales, I would only be allowed to say I went to Starbucks. I *didn't* go there, but I *did* soon have a large latte in hand.

Beelz was sacked out, having burrowed his way beneath the mountain of blankets I'd tossed onto the backseat, so I popped the trunk open and retrieved the backup laptop I kept there next to a bag with more than one change of clothes. The first thing I'd learned last fall was that my wardrobe didn't hold up as well out here as it did inside a book, so I carried spares.

With Naomie taking care of the Internet-related search for Wendy's list of names, I was at sixes and sevens, though it felt more like twelves or fourteens. But I had to wait until after sunrise, and activities with humans could commence once they stumbled grumpily out to snarl at the breaking dawn. In mid-February, that meant things would begin to lighten up around 7:20 a.m.

An hour and a half to kill. I plugged into the coffee house's system and logged on.

E-mail messages from the various gold suppliers told me that my expedited purchases were all in the shippers' hands. Chances were deliveries would begin arriving on the sixteenth. I made a note of which services were being used so I could have the packages rerouted since there would be no one home at the mansion for a while. Where should the packages of gold be rerouted to, though?

Only Beelz, Ernie, and I knew about the cupid's unsuccessful attempt to poke arrows in me. Did I want Delia to know? No, I didn't. Did I want Naomie to know? Hell, no. I could have things rerouted to The Bridge, but that was an even worse idea. There were things patronizing that joint capable of smelling out gold. The safest place would be at the police department, care of Detective Durkin, but I had a feeling he wouldn't cotton to that, plus, with my luck, things would arrive when he wasn't at his desk buried in paperwork.

It is definitely a handicap to have a limited number of people to count on.

Where did a fella stash close to a hundred grand in antique gold coins? I needed a vault, security guards. I needed… Damn. I needed a bank.

It took a few minutes to find Zeta's number on my cell. It wasn't near the top of my list like Neva's was. (The phone had assigned the insurance witch the top spot under "Contacts" due to my frequent claim calls.) Zeta was an assistant bank manager and handled the various accounts for Team Raven.

The phone rang long enough to read a 400-page book. Well, maybe not quite that long. When the chime ended, it was replaced by an extremely groggy female voice. "'Lo?"

"Darling, kindhearted, lovely, Zeta. Sorry I broke your beauty sleep."

"Bram?" she croaked. I heard fumbling and a curse. "Do you know what time it is?"

"A little after 5:30."

She groaned.

It was muffled. I wondered if she'd pulled a pillow over her face. I knew she was back when there was a very audible sigh.

"I wonder if a curse would work on you," she said.

"Too late. Already cursed. I'm in this world, aren't I?"

"What do you need?" She sounded world weary.

I have that effect on the coven girls. "You might have heard we had a bit of a contretemps at the estate last night."

"A what?"

Okay, she hadn't heard. "Don't worry. Sandra seems to be all right but for cuts from flying glass after the grill exploded on her."

"WHAT?"

She was definitely awake now.

I assured her that I would be checking on my injured chef-for-a-night, though I didn't know if she was home or the hospital had kept her trapped. I then moved on to the business at hand. "With the house not in habitable condition, I've got a bit of a conundrum. I have some items being shipped in and the value of them requires a safe delivery spot. How big is my safe deposit box?"

"What's being shipped?" she countered. Sounded a bit suspicious, like she expected illegal goods.

"Antique coins," I said. "I'm starting a collection but found so many of interest that a hundred of the things are headed my way. Most have an expected delivery date of the sixteenth. Can I reroute them to your branch and into your care?"

A deep sigh was my answer. "Yes, Bram. Do you want me to open the packages or just keep them for you?"

Told her she could decide based on the size that arrived. "Thanks, Zeta. I owe you one."

"Considering it's still the middle of the night, you owe me big, Bram," she said, though it sounded a bit like a threat. Then the line went dead. Flowers were not going to suffice as a payoff.

Fortunately, while the early morning shift at every delivery company I called was slow to answer—and unhappy with my request—they accepted the change of drop-off address. A little after six, I got a call from the home repair company Delia's contact had put on alert and promised to meet them at 7:30. I'd barely finished with the call when the cell rang again.

"You off anything last night?" Detective Durkin asked.

"You mean as in tick off? Probably," I admitted.

"As in kill," he said.

"Was tempted but only tempted," I assured. "Why do you ask?"

"I'm standing here in the alley across from a place called The Bridge, Farrell, and there's a stiff with your signature written all over him," the detective said. A very strange place for him to be considering it wasn't located in his precinct.

As no autographs had been asked for or given, I had one question. "What is he?"

"I'm guessing, 'cause I'm no expert on this stuff, but I'd say a ghoul."

"ID?"

"None."

I knew the glamour would have vanished once the thing was dead. Full body disguises immediately return to the used enshroudment shop in the nearest Otherworld dimension, leaving the true carcass behind. Clothes and accessories were rarely part of a glamour, though, and easy to acquire. All it took was illegal entry into a clothing store at night. Wearing duds seemed to be the thing that ensured humans that a beast or being was just like them. Might've been a bit creepy as a borderline human, but still accepted as one of the guys.

"Is he dressed like a cross between Serpico and Mr. T? Gold chain and amulet around his neck?"

"Yep."

"And the signature you mentioned?"

"He's been toasted," Durkin said.

Yeah, that did sound like me. But I hadn't done it. I wouldn't have done it. At least, not until he'd told me how to find Solomon Prisk.

"I was in The Bridge last night. One of the owners, Ruth Lund, called me to come rescue a couple of human girls the ghoul had trapped in one of the booths. There was a slight difference of opinion, but he was headed toward the bar and alive the last I saw him," I said.

"You got an alibi for later?" He had to ask. He was in cop mode.

"Was socializing with a girl until around five this morning. He been dead longer than an hour?"

"Socializing with a girl? Is that what it's called now?"

"When the girl is one of the humans rescued from the ghoul and she happens to be my secretary, yeah, that's what it's called. We did it at Denny's in a booth in the back in the corner under bright lights, Durkin. How long has the ghoul been dead?" I snarled. I had some attitude left over from earlier.

"Longer than an hour," he admitted. "He's not smoking at any rate, though in these temperatures, maybe he wouldn't for long. You know his name?"

"We didn't develop a close enough rapport to exchange monikers, though he knew who I was. Who found him?"

"Anonymous call. The 9-1-1 operators know they need to buzz me if something sounds like it's been taken from one of your books. We term 'em *freak-outs* because the person reporting a possible Otherworld situation is either scared shitless and incoherent or beside themselves with glee and incoherent."

"I sense a theme," I said. "I hope you're not calling me to get rid of him."

"Nope. A couple of guys proudly displaying bite marks on their necks ambled up and told me they'd take care of it."

"Vampire minions. I suspect they use the alley as a club house."

"In this weather?"

"If they're served as hors d'oeuvres before the main course, they're probably hyped up on vamp spit and don't even feel it. The body still there or have they taken it away already? If it's available, maybe I should take a gander."

"It's still here just not in the alley. One of them went across to the bar, swung up onto the fire escape and pulled himself up to the third floor where he banged on the window. Couple minutes later, a really short little lady in pink bunny slippers, nightgown, and robe with curlers in her hair swung the main door open and waved the guys carrying the ghoul inside," Durkin said. "She wiggled her fingers at me and grinned before she closed the place back up."

"That's Ruth. She's very popular. Probably took one look at you and decided you were the man for her. She's little but she's feisty."

"She's ugly."

"Goes with the gene pool," I said and explained about her split parentry.

"So what did your dust up with the ghoul entail? Anything that could have resulted in his sudden demise?"

"I did tell him I was looking for Sol. Could be he made a call after I got the girls out of there. Could be whoever he made the call to wasn't happy about being disturbed."

Durkin grunted in agreement. "You think your name got added to a hit list?"

"My name is already on a hit list," I said and told him about Ernie's visit.

I would tell you his comments on the subject, but this is beginning to look like it might turn into the next book. Naomie would look the words up as she turns my dictation into pixels on a screen and attempt to use them. She's currently as jaded as she needs to be.

I just prayed that our adventure that night hadn't landed Naomie's name next to mine on anything's list of folks to put six feet under

***

Since I had some time to kill, I swung by The Bridge. Durkin was gone and so, as mentioned, were the ghoul leftovers from the alley across the way. One of the Lunds' cousins ambled out of the bar while I was there and asked if I wanted to see it. I figured the deceased was either in the cellar or the freezer in the kitchen—but did I really want to have a private viewing?

Now, if I were back in fictionland, I would have said "yes" faster than a sneeze, but this was a totally different Detroit from the one back home. There, I would have recognized a burn pattern and been able to identify the neck of the woods the perp came from just by the scent of what had been singed out of the air. There, I knew people.

This side, I knew bupkis and bupkis don't get a guy anywhere.

I passed on the makeshift wake, at least temporarily, as I had better things to do. 'Sides, either Ralph or Ruth would offer me a drink to send the ghoul off, possibly in their furnace. There was a good chance it was one that harbored hungry flames. The sort that hadn't been upgraded since Prohibition ended. That was a sight I was willing to forego, plus it was too early in the day to imbibe even an Irish coffee. Hell, the sun wasn't even up yet. I told Ruthie's kin I'd be back later and to keep the ghoul handy for my next visit.

I was about to slip back into the cozy, electronically-warmed driver's seat when something pounded on the hood of the car.

Beelz popped up from his cocoon in the backseat, ears perked, stance alert.

I shook my head at him, basically telling him to head back into his blanket fort.

He looked to the vandal, to me, and decided to take my advice and re-burrowed into his warm nest.

The car accoster was big and he was ugly. He had an Internet divinity degree and a couple fresh bite marks on his neck.

"You dent it, you bought it, Hammer," I growled, throwing in a glare for good order. Yeah, like I'd insult the car by letting him buy it. Considering he had more in common with the sartorial elegance of a homeless person, the only thing he'd be able to cough up to even repair the Ford would be dubious or disgusting in nature.

"Whaddaya think yer doin' leaving victims in my territory, Farrell?" he snarled.

Why is it that when an Otherworlder gets deaded, everyone immediately thinks I did it? I'm sure there are other things that have good reason to hate the recently-corpsed, too.

"You mean the alley? I'd no idea you'd marked it, though considering what it smelled like when last I enjoyed the ambience, I should have guessed hind legs had been lifted."

"Ha, ha. Ain't you the clever one," he growled.

Actually, yeah, I was. This was not a battle of wits—because he was severely lacking in that department—but one of insults. If only I knew the point system used.

"Well, killin' that ghoul in my alley didn't do nothin' to improve that *ambience*."

Even Martha Stewart couldn't come up with a way to do that. "Know you'll be disappointed to learn this, Hammer, but Farrell Exterior Improvements was not called to do a remodel. Ten to one, it's someone else who doesn't like your face or that of one of your crew."

He glared at me, then rounded the front bumper so he could get in my face. "We don't got enemies," he said. "We got customers who enjoy seein' us."

Enjoy was probably a poor choice of word on his part. *Customer*, too, for that matter. *Victim* suited what the people were, like a bespoke suit from Savile Row.

I opened my car door. “A case of Febreze followed by a campfire’s worth of pine scented candles will do wonders for the place, Hammer. Now, move out of my way.”

In answer, he shoved the door hard and then gave me a similar shove. Considering I’d parked in front of The Bridge, I stumbled into the mushy gook that coated the middle of the road. Nearly slipped.

That encouraged Hammer. His left hand grabbed my coat lapel to drag me closer to his knotted right fist. I hoped he had enough padding in his glove to soften the blow he was telegraphing. Magic wasn’t going to do diddly for me. He was too close in for any flashy stuff. I needed space, a bit of distance, to play my trump cards. I might light up vampires in close quarters, but Hammer wasn’t among the undead yet. He just worked for them.

Of course, the last time we’d tangled, magic hadn’t followed me across from the page yet. He probably didn’t know it had seeped back into my play manual. He wouldn’t be expecting magic and I could do tricky small stuff that didn’t involve fire.

As his fist sailed toward my face, I pulled a mental rug from beneath his feet. Hadn’t realized I was standing on the same metaphorical rug. We both went from opponents with firm stances to feet flying. I landed on my back in the slush with Hammer sprawled across me. The power behind the intended punch failed. He slapped me hard across the face as a substitute.

My hands clutching his lapels, I rolled in the direction his flat hand sent me, reversing our order. The triumph was short-lived.

One of his boys materialized next to us, dragged me up and off the preacher, then delivered a roundhouse of his own.

I stumbled back, tripped on the opposite curb, then met a third hooligan as he stepped from the alley. My right eye connected with his fist, then my face kissed the far-from-disinfectant-washed brick, and I was back in the filthy gray-tinged snow. Whoever had made a Good Samaritan effort on the walkway had dumped the surfeit snow at the alley entrance. Only the trail beat by those viewing the roast ghoul or escorting his crispy remains from within, cut into the mass.

I did not attempt to make an angel in the frozen muck, though I did make a dent.

Managing to regain my feet, I faced the unholy minion trinity. “What the hell? Hammer, I’ve got better manners than to drop a vic in your…" I glanced around, "…well, place of business. I didn't kill the ghoul. I only threatened him last night. Heck, some time has to go by between a warning given and a warning acted upon. Law of the jungle." Not that jungles leaned toward wind chills using zero degrees Fahrenheit for a Maypole.

"Then consider this *your* warning, Raven," Hammer barked and dusted his knuckles across my jaw. It was nothing like tidying up with a bouquet of fluffy feathers. More like shirring off a bit of marble that doesn't look like David.

Michelangelo's statue, not Beckham.

In any case, I went prone again.

The moment Hammer and his crew stepped over me to see to household duties in their tainted alley, I thought an avalanche of fresh snow into being and let it drop four stories to bury them. Sadly, it was only temporary. But long enough for me to drag myself up and plant my soggy yet freezing self behind the wheel and make tracks out of the neighborhood.

***

I stopped at a McDonald's to use the men's room to change—and examine the latest battle damage. I was going to have a shiner. The jaw complained but still worked. Handy that I kept a fresh set of clothes in the trunk. I'd sorta danced to this tune before. The lesson had been learned. Not many others, but that one, yeah. Totally ingrained now. Perhaps a first aid kit should be added to the trove, though. I left the store sipping on a latte. Hey, you use the facilities, you thank them with some custom and I was thirsty.

I beat the repair guys to the house with barely fifteen minutes to spare. While I waited, I popped the various shields out of existence and pinged the trunk of the Ford open. Then I started gathering items. My main laptop, Naomie's PC and printer, spare ink, and a ream of paper were already tucked in the cavern where the spare tire lives when a salt-washed, dark blue pickup pulled in behind me.

"Whoa. That's a heck of a mess," a man said as he dropped from the cab. "What happened?"

"The barbecue gods took exception to our attempt to grill out last night," I said, introduced myself merely as Farrell and shook his hand.

"What were you cooking?"

"Porterhouse. Sadly, the slabs are somewhere in there, though probably frozen and inedible now."

He winced over such mindless destruction and, hands shoved into the pockets of a work-weary, well-padded, blindingly-yellow ski jacket, rocked back on his heels. "Insurance adjuster look it over yet?"

"Expected but when one will arrive, I've no idea. How long before I can move back in?"

He blew vapor clouds for a bit, musing on an answer. "Depends on the weather. Won't be able to start today in any case. Replacement windows will need to be ordered. I'll get wood up across the missing glass and any mangled doors, though. Probably can measure to figure what's needed but until your claims guy comes…" He left the sentence unfinished.

When the insurance lackey showed, he'd probably tell me the same thing only insert *fire marshal* as an excuse. I probably didn't need to hang around for any of this.

"Do what you can," I said as I fished out one of the B. Farrell Investigations cards and handed it over. "Call me before you leave the place. I'm gonna grab some clothes."

"Gotcha," he said and headed for his truck.

I was a bit relieved that he didn't get in and drive off but retrieved a clipboard, pen, and zippy tape measure.

I glanced at my watch. Still too early to call Lex at her hotel to deal with her questions, but as she was probably used to getting up for early class sessions at Pima Community College back in Tucson, there was a good chance she'd be awake somewhere around eight. If I just drove over and called her from the front desk, another item on today's To-Do list could be scratched.

The fire damage was limited to the back patio and kitchen, though smoke had billowed through the rest of the joint. Since I'd sealed it tight before leaving just before midnight, the taint of propane miasma remained. Considering the main floor drapes were custom made to fit windows close to fifteen feet tall, many of the rugs were rare antiques, and I really liked the cushy furniture, I added an army of professional smoke removal types to my tally of calls yet to make. This being-a-homeowner was damn time consuming. Once things were in motion, Naomie could attack with a carton or two of air freshener aerosols to take care of any lingering unpleasant smells. Hopefully, it wouldn't be as uphill a battle as Hammer and his boys needed to overcome.

Before I headed back inside, I checked on Beelz.

When I opened the car door, he poked his nose out from his blanket fort. "You need anything while we're here?" I asked.

He shook the blanket off a bit more, gave it some thought, then mumbled something at me.

After nearly four months in his company, he'd trained me well to know what he said. "Donuts? You're already hungry after the double order of sausage patties I got you barely two hours ago?"

He did the yip code for "yes" and burrowed back out of sight.

Mutts, I mused as I shut the car door. And I'd heard cats were dictators. They had nothing on a hound from Hell.

Once inside the house again, I took the steps to the upper level two at a time. There was no telling how long until move-back-in day would come around so I decided I'd just snag everything I owned and toss it on top of the computer stuff in the trunk. Once, that would have meant a single trip, but I'd shopped a bit since then. Besides my basic everyday Target wardrobe, there was a tuxedo with *accoutrements*, a suit that no longer looked like I'd forked over $3,000 for it, dress shirts, a tie to go with the lone suit, dress shoes, the dated boots, and the Diesel Weiter jacket I'd arrived from fictionland wearing, black athletic shoes, and assorted socks and boxers. I was already wearing my favorite sweater, pea coat, and the black Tony Lamas I'd taken a fancy to. I was mentally juggling the benefits of using a sheet over the poufy steel gray comforter to wrap it all into one giant hobo's bundle when I reached the door to my room.

A door I never closed these days but that was now shut and sporting a piece of paper dangling from a nail hammered dead center.

Sorry I missed you, someone, or something, had printed in block letters on it. *Kill you next time.*

***

If you've read *Raven's Moon* you won't be at all surprised to learn that I backed away slowly and made my way back downstairs.

A guy only needed to have one room explode on him in a lifetime, right? I'd had my limit.

Back out in the cold, I fumbled the cell phone from my pocket, found Durkin's number and hit DIAL. Considering it hadn't been that long since he'd called me about the ghoul's demise, he was having a heck of a long day. I was about to make it longer.

"I'd like to order a bomb squad guy delivered to my place." I said when he answered. "It seems Ernie isn't the only mercenary hired to see me planted."

"Geez, Farrell. Somehow, I thought you managed to make friends rather than enemies," he grumbled. "You sure there's a bomb?"

"No, but there's a 50-50 chance there might be. Could be a crossbow primed to loose a bolt at the first person through the door instead. Could be a bucket of acid balanced above said door to baptize me. Could be a black hole primed to suck me in."

"Better chance on the first two," he said. "I'll call it in and head your way myself."

"Thanks, Durkin. You're all right. I don't care that the vamp and werewolf cops whisper different. I've got your back," I said.

"Farrell. Shove it up your—"

I hit the END CALL button.

It is bad customer-to-contractor manners to allow the latter to be blown to smithereens, so I suggested the repair guy might want to head to Home Depot because someone was about to arrive to look the place over. I didn't tell him they might have sirens wailing when they did. He headed out. I got back in my Ravenmobile, told Beelz what was up, then moved the car, hopefully, out of blast range should one occur.

I nearly backed into an SUV that came barreling down the drive toward me. The driver swung the wheel, sending the vehicle into a slide that parked the hulkish thing sideways on the snow-coated pavement, blocking my escape. The door flew open, and the reporter with the phone sex voice jumped out.

This day was just getting better and better and it wasn't even 8:00 a.m. yet.

"Hold it right there, Farrell!" She stormed toward me. "Beck Ritter of 4th Estate. I thought you might try to slip away before regular business hours when I couldn't get passed that strange girl yesterday."

Naomie was strange? Okay, the way she dressed was, but a guy couldn't ask for a more enthusiastic employee. She got excited and went super perk about everything at Raven Central. Of course, she could just be psyched about doing little work for an extravagant wage. I sorta hoped Nomes was hyper-thrilled because she got to hang out with me all day, too, though.

Ritter was a problem but dealing with her was the lesser of two evils when one of the evils was a possible quick trip to the remainders table at the morgue.

I let the car window cruise down and stuck my head out. "You might want to move your car, Ritter. The police are on their way and won't take kindly to you blocking the drive."

That stopped her in mid-stride. Then she looked beyond me to the house. "What happened?"

It was comforting that she sounded stunned. "Propane tank on the grill blew its gasket."

"There was a fire," she said.

"Excellent observation," I countered. "Your reputation as a reporter is well deserved. Now move your damn car."

"So you can get away again?"

"So it won't get damaged if the house blows up."

"Wait."

I pictured wheels turning beneath her knit cap as she tried to catch up. Well, it *was* morning. From the reaction I'd gotten from Zeta already, it appeared the human brain was slow to kick in right off the bat every day.

"You said the police were coming. Is there a gas leak or—?"

"Listen," I cut in. "There is a Denny's…" I gave her the address and promised to meet her there as soon as the police were satisfied that everything was fine.

"You'll tell me about what's going on then?"

"Only if I'm allowed to. One never knows with the police," I claimed because I was damn well *not* going to tell her anything about being the Number One pick on the assassin's Top Forty jobs list. Blaming the police was nearly a reflex action. I'd done it frequently in the first twenty Raven Tales volumes. No reason I couldn't begin doing it in the current set. Might as well toss it into real life, too.

"They'll be here soon," I warned. "Move your damn vehicle."

"Denny's. If you don't show, I'll hunt you down," she warned.

Hell, she'd hunt me down again even after I did show, though I wouldn't be in a hurry to get there. She did get back in the monster car and leave.

Five minutes later, a police van arrived.

It looked like the sort of RV to use on a Raven camping trip. It was large enough to hold living essentials, but the bright yellow letters on the black finish ruined any stealth qualities. If the estate sat closer to the road, the only thing the neighbors would have read on the side were the ones that said, "Bomb Squad."

Considering I knew more non-humans than humans in Detroit, I was still stunned to recognize the broad-shouldered guy who stepped down from the passenger's side. Of course, he wasn't totally human these days. He was a werewolf. That wasn't noted in his employment record.

"I thought you were SWAT," I said.

"Hiya, Farrell. I am part of the SWAT team, but I worked with explosives in the military and the squad was shorthanded. Some bug going around."

Whether that bug was a cold, the flu, double pneumonia, or Tsetse fly, it sure the hell wasn't going to get near him.

The man with him came around the front of the van. "You the guy who called it in?" he asked. "What have we got?"

"Maybe nothing. However…" I told him how my office had headed to Valhalla back in October. "I thought when the grill exploded last night that it was an accident, but considering there's a note nailed to my bedroom door that wasn't there when I left last night, I'm taking no chances."

"Man, you really must have ticked someone off. Could it be whoever gave you that shiner? It looks fairly new," the stranger said.

I rubbed my aching jaw. It didn't throb as much as my eye. "Sorta related to a girl who needed rescuing late last night." Which, in a roundabout way, it had. If Naomie and her chum hadn't needed saving from the ghoul's clutches, no one would have even considered me as a suspect in the thing's murder. At least, I don't think they would have. Hammer had just been at the end of the accusation line that morning.

"What do you do for a living, sir?" the bomb squad regular

asked. He used his police voice, the one that makes you feel like a suspicious character even if you weren't one.

Even I would consider me a suspicious character, though.

The werewolf gave him a wolfish grin. "He's a writer."

Rather than trip merrily up the stairs as I had, they opened the van. The werewolf nixed a coin toss to see which of them would go in, insisting that he was the more expendable member, the one who didn't have a family. The regular bomb squad guy didn't push it, just helped him suit up. When the gear was on, the werewolf looked more like a NASA dude about to take a stroll outside the space capsule than a cop.

"Is your cell phone off, sir?" the human cop asked. "If not, please turn it off. If you got a call, the signal might set the explosive off if it's rigged that way."

I switched off. The werewolf in protective gear lurched off toward the house. It wasn't the warmest seat, but perching on the hood of the Mustang with my feet on the bumper was front row viewing. I noticed that Beelz had left his blankets behind and had his snout resting on the dashboard between his paws, demon-red eyes fixed on the mansion.

The werewolf didn't have to open the front door. I'd left it open when I'd galloped down the stairs and out of the joint. As he disappeared from our sight, Durkin strolled up. Apparently, he'd left his car on the street and done a hike rather than get within damaging distance.

"You might want to move behind your car, Mr. Farrell," the bomb disposal cop said.

"Might want to get the dog out of it, too," Durkin suggested.

Considering I didn't live within his precinct's borders, he did turn up a lot. Wondered whether his captain knew about the detective's extracurricular hobby. The one that involved keeping an eye on doings in the Otherworlder community. From afar, of course.

I noticed Durkin hadn't come any closer than the back of the Ford and was eyeing the police van, as if evaluating whether it offered better protection if something did go wrong.

In fact, once Beelz was sprung, all three of us headed behind the van.

If this were a movie or TV series, we'd have known how the

werewolf was progressing. As it wasn't, time ticked by at a crawl. I hunkered down, Beelz on alert between my feet.

After what seemed like a week, the werewolf stomped his way back to us. He had the note in his hand, and the shield over his face pushed up. "Nothing there," he announced, "but considering the cheerful wording of the message, I don't blame you for not taking a chance."

He handed the sheet of paper to the other bomb squad guy. Probably to prove I hadn't called in a prank call.

Durkin looked over the cop's shoulder. "That's nowhere close to Farrell's handwriting, so I'd say the threat is real." Which was true. This note was legible, whereas my handwriting resembled claw marks left by an infernal being. "It look like that of anyone you know, Farrell?"

"Nope. Would be handy if it did." I'd know who to go after.

Durkin and I had a deal. If the perp on any case I handled was human, the creep was turned over to him. If it was nowhere near the human genome, it was mine to do with as I saw fit. Human vigilantes, he hated. Borderline human doing vigilante chores among the Otherworlders, he sanctioned. Sad that Detroit wasn't Gotham, though. It would be cool to have a Raven signal in the night sky, like Bruce Wayne's bat one. Of course, that would really cut into my social life. If I had one.

The werewolf was divested of the protective gear, the paperwork was signed off on, and gloved hands were offered all around. "I didn't catch your name last time we met," I told the wolf after he'd squeezed my fingers into unconsciousness.

"Dawes," he said. "Dave Dawes."

"Dawes. So actually, your name is David David." Dawes is an old nickname for someone christened David.

He grinned. "Quirky, huh?"

"Quirky doesn't begin to cover it," I told him. "No sign of anything dangerous?"

"Not even a mouse was stirring," he said.

"Dave, any mouse hanging around would have been a popsicle considering how cold it got last night." It would also be a surprise inhabitant. Having a hellhound as a resident seemed to discourage all kinds of vermin. Not demon vermin, but bugs and rodents lacking demon ancestors. "Thanks for checking things out, gents."

"Just doing the job," the werewolf grunted. "See you around. Maybe Durkin will decide to host another poker night."

"Like hell," Durkin snarled. "I think Farrell cheats. He did walk away with the lion's share of the matchsticks last time."

"So he did," Dawes agreed then swung up into the cab of the van. Before he closed the door, I heard the other cop say, "What's with the dog's eyes?"

"Allergies, I heard. Being around Farrell makes him sick," Dawes said then laughed. He waved as they headed back down the drive.

Durkin didn't move. Hands in his pockets, his head tucked down between the wings of his upturned coat collar, he stared at the mansion. "Why'd you go upstairs?"

"Clothes," I said. "Now I'm thinking I'll just buy new ones. Just in case."

"Don't blame you. I'd do the same. You up for coffee or breakfast? I'm calling it a night. Hell, the sun's finally up."

I sighed. "If only you'd made an appointment earlier. Currently, my social schedule runneth over. The writer who'll be spinning some young Raven books is in town and expecting me to answer questions about my non-existent childhood. She called it fodder for her stories."

Durkin chuckled. "Considering you're made up, inventing a childhood should be easy for you, Raven."

"It's remembering what I make up that might be the problem."

"Not for a guy who can take on and beat things not of this world," he said.

I snorted at such *naïveté*. "If only it were as easy as you make it sound. Unfortunately, she's not the only one. Beck Ritter is expecting me to show for breakfast. I think she's planning to have grilled Raven with her sunny-side-ups."

"The news piranha?" Durkin dropped a hand onto my shoulder. "It's been nice knowing you, Farrell. Won't be anything left of you but singed feathers when *she* calls for the check."

"That's what I'm afraid of. Appreciate you making my false alarm a priority, detective."

"Better safe than dead," he said. "And I don't want you dead, Farrell. I've got too many uses for you."

I offered him a ride out to the street, which he accepted, then we parted ways, him heading home, me bee-lining it back to Denny's. I wondered if there had been a shift change since I'd left a couple hours ago or whether the same waitress would take my second breakfast order of the day.

It wasn't a familiar wait person who greeted me when I came in out of the cold, though. It was Alexis Muldoon.

She was seated next to Beck Ritter.

***

"Bram! Over here!" Lex called, slipping from the booth they'd snagged. She waved her arm as a direction finder.

I took a deep breath and maneuvered my way through the tables.

"What happened to your face?" she demanded when I reached them. She tilted her head to get a better view of my purpling-up injuries.

"A dude who thought I did something I hadn't. Case of mistaken identity. In the wrong place at the wrong time."

"Was he arrested?" she asked, slipping back onto the banquette seat and scooting over to make room for me next to her.

I shook my head, stalling as I dreamed up a reason why the phantom guy wouldn't have been jailed. I sure hadn't called anyone to report Hammer's alterations to my appearance.

"No reason to involve the police. The woman with him was quite prepared to use him as a rake over hot coals for ruining their Valentine date."

"A far more appropriate sentencing than an arrest?" Ritter suggested.

"A far worse one," I agreed.

It looked like both the gals had tossed their coats onto the unoccupied spot next to Ritter so I tossed mine there, too, then dropped down next to Lex.

Ritter looked tempted to pursue the matter, then switched topics. "Did the police find anything at your home?"

"If the cops did find something, they didn't tell me about it," I admitted. Stick with the truth when possible, right? The chance that what I'd tell either of them would qualify as honesty in any guise was slim. Far closer to the "oh, look, a bunny!" maneuver. With luck, if I salted my misdirection stew with grains of veracity, it might be tasty enough to satisfy them both.

Well, at least Muldoon. Ritter would be the trickier customer.

There were coffee mugs before both of them but no plates. “Have you already eaten?” I asked.

“We were waiting for you.” Lex offered me the menu.

I had the thing memorized. I’d be getting a slam, of course, just a different one than I’d had when Naomi and I had sat two booths over not long ago.

“I was expecting Ms. Ritter so appease my curiosity, Lex. How do you happen to be here? It isn’t exactly next door to your hotel.” Because Delia wanted to impress the heck out of Muldoon, she’d booked a place that would stun Lex with architecture, views, and services. We’d plunked her in the center of Detroit at 1 Park Avenue, The David Whitney Building. Hell, the name *and* the address had class. Depending on whether my PR witch had swung it or not, the view from Lex’s room was likely that of the Detroit River and Canada on the other side. Denny’s was a gigantic step down to the level where mere mortals lived.

“She called and invited me to meet her here,” Muldoon said, then added, “It was very handy to have the business card you gave me yesterday. Your friend the cab driver was very nice and arrived within minutes of my call.” Well, he would. When a fare was in the wind, Burt drove like he was in tryouts for NASCAR.

I turned a steely gaze on Ritter, but as I had a hell of a hill of things to hide, it was disguised as a mildly curious one instead. “How did you know Lex was going to be in town or where she’d be staying?”

Ritter pointed to herself. “Investigative reporter, Mr. Farrell. Ms. Muldoon’s name went on my radar the day the results of the Amberson replacement contest were announced. As did yours.”

Damn, I’d dug my own grave in telling Delia to launch the search last fall.

“In fact,” Ritter said, “I’m a bit surprised that, as a supposed relative of Ms. Amberson, that you were allowed to participate in the contest.”

“If you need a copy of the rules, Delia Maddox can supply one. You’ll find that there is no clause in it that would exclude me.”

“Was that to ensure that the contest could be fixed so you won?” she pressed.

"Nope." There really was no exclusion statement, but that was because Delia had written the rules before I'd turned up on the scene. Calie hadn't wanted anything to do with the contest, but once she was gone, only what the publisher said counted. Delia thought I should do the books. To appease her, I wrote a short story entry, figuring there was no way in Hell it would merit notice, but it would get her to stop harping at me. "Raven's Rest", as it was titled in the hope I'd actually get a rest, set up the twist to make Calista's Raven cross from page to reality. Which was how I'd gotten here. The rest was just a mishmash of detecting, magic, danger, and destruction back home in the land of flights of fancy. Since there was often downtime between books, I'd simply related a case I'd been on when Calie hadn't been typing.

All the writers participating in the competition had been given a number so their name, if well known, wouldn't influence the judges. When presented with the entries, the editorial team considered the top five entries, then the publisher who'd worked on Calista Amberson's Raven books had awarded me the contract.

Apparently, crossing your fingers in the hope that you *won't* win doesn't work well.

As Lex had taken a chance with a teenaged Raven entry, she'd caught their attention, too.

So I really *had* won fair and square. Upon discovering my name really *was* Bram Farrell, the marketing department found religion. Or perhaps that's *founded* a religion. Deification by corporation. The emails they clogged my system with certainly appeared to lean in that direction.

Lex sat forward in her seat. "If you'd read Bram's entry, you'd know he nailed the story elements and narrative style Calista Amberson had in place. I have to admit, because I was curious about the entry that beat mine out, I asked to read it. Honestly, I was surprised when it was sent in an email the same day, and stunned over how perfect it was for the Raven universe when I read it."

"I can get you an advanced copy of that, too, Ms. Ritter," I inserted. "They're using it as a promotional teaser before the new book comes out."

"By email today, Mr. Farrell?"

"Maybe not that fast. The publisher isn't as willing to share it quite yet, but I'll pass along your request." As I said it, I snagged my phone and called Delia. "Beck Ritter of 4th Estate would like to read 'Rest' to prove that I supplied decent copy in my contest entry. Do we need approval from NYC to get her one?"

"Told you we needed that story when you tried to wiggle out of writing something," my faux cousin said. "I'll call and get the okay, but there shouldn't be any trouble. Hell, if she writes about this, it's free publicity. Where does she want it sent?"

"Hold on. I'll let her tell you." I passed the phone across the table to Ritter so she could fill the request herself.

While she supplied an address, the waitress arrived. Turned out, at least some members of the wait staff hadn't changed since I'd been in earlier. "Well, you're a popular man with the ladies," the same waitress from six hours ago commented, glancing briefly at Lex and Ritter.

"It's one of the first things I learned how to be in my Gigolo 101 class," I said with a smile.

"And yet you bring them here," she said.

"They ordered the economy threesome package. A meal out among the common folk, sitting on the sofa for a couple hours of channel-surfing on the tube while drinking beer, a quickie, and Bob's your uncle. I've got a business card if you're interested," I offered.

She smiled. "Sounds a lot like life with my husband, except without a girlfriend included. But now I know why you always order a huge breakfast. Which set up will it be this time?"

Lex pointed at me as Ritter slid my phone back across the table. "See, he even babbles like The Raven does in the books. Is it any wonder he won the spot?"

Ritter didn't answer. I wondered how bad that was going to be for yours truly.

I let the girls order first then gave mine. Mine included as much food as theirs did together and then some. Naturally, there was a side order of sausage to go for Beelz, though considering that I had stopped to get him those donuts, he might not be ready to inhale the links quite yet. Depended on how long I got trapped at the table.

Ritter vetoed killing the time with chit chat before the food arrived. She went into reporter mode. "Lex was telling me why she's here in Detroit, about the sort of questions she wants answers to about your life, Mr. Farrell."

While Muldoon had obviously urged Ritter to use her first name,

I wasn't going to be that easy-going. This was strictly business. She already suspected it was going to be funny business, and not of the "ha ha!" kind.

"That's what she told me, too," I allowed.

"What sort of things are on your list, Lex?" Ritter asked.

"I want to know what Bram's life was like at the age I've chosen for the teenaged Raven," Muldoon said. "Like where he lived, what sports he might have been in, what school life was like, who his friends were. Things like that."

I leaned back and stretched my arm out along the back of our bench seat. "You could come up with whatever you want. It isn't like I'm the Raven in the flesh."

First lie told but one that held water very well.

"I'd still like to hear about it and only then decide whether to do a different take on the Raven universe. Since I got the editor's call late in December, I've reread the twenty books Calista Amberson wrote, looking for any hints but her Bram Farrell's past is never alluded to. It's like he simply appeared fully grown."

Which I had.

"If having him grow up in Detroit turns out to be the best option, then I'll need to discover more about the city while I'm here. So where did you grow up?"

Calie had actually supplied some of these lies last fall. She'd handed me my fake biography on nicely printed pages, and in a file folder, no less. "Nope, I didn't grow up in Detroit. My dad had itchy feet and enough money to cater to them. Whenever we settled some place, he hired a tutor and I had a run of intensive schooling, and then we'd go back on the road toting a load of textbooks to read. So my schooling wasn't exactly kosher."

Lex mused on that silently. Ritter jumped into the void.

"What were the names of these tutors?"

"Ritter. Do you remember the name of every teacher you had in school? Heck, you would have spent nine or ten months with each of them. I spent a month or so—three, tops—with them so their names were erased from my memory banks the moment we moved on."

She looked disgruntled but tried for a comeback. "What is your father's name?"

"Whatever Lex decides to make it. He won't mind. He was

christened Ambrose, which means he never uses it. Just goes by Farrell."

"Mother?"

I turned to Lex. "Your Raven need a mother in the scenario?"

"I haven't decided. Keeping the cast of human characters to a minimum is necessary, I think, but if she's not one of them, why isn't she there?" Muldoon asked.

"Abducted by fairies," I said then turned to Ritter. "That's what I'm going to claim, too. Not everyone needs to have their privacy stolen just for a story."

Ritter glared at me. "Or for an exposé?"

"Especially in that regard."

Lex's forefinger was stroking her nearly empty coffee mug. "Hmm. Calista wasn't from Detroit, was she?"

Ah, here I could go with the truth, and choose between that of the real Calista or the one who stole her identity, fortune, and disastrously wed Skip Amberson before turning to writing about *moi*. "Nope. East Coast socialite, but you can get all that from the Wikipedia entry about her or at The Raven Tales website."

"Did your father ever include Detroit in his roaming?"

"Nope. Albania to Zimbabwe and the harder it is to get to, the better he likes it."

Lex sighed.

Ritter might have been grinding her teeth. "Then how, exactly, are you related to Calista Amberson?" she demanded.

Methinks the investigative reporter was losing her cool.

I shrugged and went with something that wasn't on that handy fake bio. "I only met her occasionally when her travels intersected with ours. Since she was introduced to me as Aunt Calie, I just figured she was some sort of relative. Could have been a cousin or just one of those friends that is considered family. As she didn't have children of her own, I was as close to family as she wanted."

"But Calista did have a nephew through marriage. Her husband's sister's son."

"She did?" Lex sounded surprised.

"I was under the impression Calie cut relations with them, particularly after Skip ran through both his and her fortune and then died, leaving her with his debts," I said. Another truth, by the way.

Not that Calie had ever been interested in anything but Skip Amberson's social connections and wealth. "She certainly never felt they deserved anything from her when she rebuilt her life here in Detroit. The things she left me were those she attained on her own as a widow." Whoa. Another truth. I was on a roll.

Ritter hadn't gotten her reputation as a shark by giving up early, though. "I attended the memorial service for Calista Amberson, Mr. Farrell. You were there, along with quite a variety of her female friends and media hungry A-List types. Even local fans of her work came to give their condolences, but not your parents. Why not?"

"Why should they show?" It might have sounded like I growled the words, but I figured some emotion needed to be displayed to sell the scenario. "We weren't doing roll call or dispensing demerits for no-shows. Besides, Dad is somewhere unreachable by modern technology or a runner dashing off into some jungle with the post." Which is another truth because if Calie's muse back in fictionland cared to fill the father bill, he was unreachable. He and I did look an awful lot alike.

"And your mother?"

"She's not of this world any longer." Which was not a lie. I'd been conceived in Calie's imagination, and she was dead. Hopefully hung on a slow roasting spit in one of Samael's playrooms in Hell. If she was frequently basted with coronal mass ejections from various suns as well, I'd congratulate Sam on his ingenuity in creating the prefect final reward. If ever a soul deserved an eternal flame-licking, she did.

If you think I'm being overly vicious, well, just remember what I was configured to do as the Raven. That's deliver just deserts to evil-doers. Hadn't done the deed myself, but had made it impossible for Calie to complete the final step of her plan and that made her easy pickin's for The Devil.

To show I was finished answering Ritter's questions—even if it was a temporary reprieve—I turned to Lex. "Personally, I suggest you stick with Detroit for a setting. You can jot down things Calie wrote because most of The Raven's Detroit is not specified by street names or anything else, and she made things up to suit what she wanted. You can do the same. If you want a tour of the city, just call Burt. He loves this town, but he loves day-long fares even better.

Since the retainer Calie had him on is still in effect, you won't even be the one fielding that exorbitant fare. If you have a scenario in mind, swear him to secrecy and seal the deal with a steak dinner. He'll find a good spot or two you could use."

"That sounds like a good idea," Muldoon said. "I'll give him a call when I get back to the hotel and set things up. Can I impose on you to give me a ride back to the Whitney?"

"Not a problem," I assured her. As the food arrived at that point, it felt like the waitress cavalry had sashayed in to rescue me from further questions.

***

By the time the three of us parted company, Lex was geared up to write an origin story for how sixteen-year-old Bram Farrell became The Raven, her first item of business being to rope Burt into that tour of possibly good locations. She'd doodled on a scrap of paper, doing the math to figure out what year she might use. I told her sticking a date in screwed things up. Part of the formula Calie had put in place was that the years might go by for a reader, but, inside a book, The Raven was always the same age. He (me) rarely took more than a week, and sometimes less, to solve things and punish the perp. The trick was, once one Otherworlder type was killed, that type couldn't be used again. How boring to only kill vampires, right? Where was the challenge in that?

Ritter was taking notes the way I usually do. She clicked on a recording doohickey that could be plugged into her computer later. Lex and I made her put her hands in view and swear not to give any story or writing points away. She might have crossed her legs, but not her fingers, which would have made the promise null and void. Or at least that's what I've heard.

She did mention that I was being very helpful in getting Lex up and running without telling her what I thought should be in the stories. Just before Ritter clicked her device off, she pinned me with an "I am reporter, let me see you squirm" gaze. "You seem to know Calista Amberson's Raven volumes extremely well."

"Like I lived 'em," I said, standing up. I dropped a large tip on the table and grabbed the bill. Since we'd talked Raven books, I was pretty sure I'd snagged my first write-off for the year.

Lex decided she didn't need a ride back to the hotel after all. She needed Burt to show her the sights immediately. As Raven Corp still owed her a dinner, I asked if she'd be up to eating again around seven. If so, I'd pick her up. "Nothing formal, just casual wear," I added. Delia always wanted to know if she could dress up when we met to talk company business, an idea I avoided as though it involved a plague of water-buffalo-sized toads.

No, I've never seen any toads that size, but that doesn't mean they don't exist.

"Ritter, it's been terrifying. Are you happy with what you pried out of me?" I asked, shrugging back into my coat and buttoning up.

"No comment," she countered. "I may call you for a follow-up interview."

Now I was *really* terrified, but pulled one of the B. Farrell Investigation cards from my coat pocket. "As there obviously will be no one at Casa Amberson for a while, here's my cell number."

She studied it. "You're an investigator as well?"

"Investigations for writers. I gather research. Or rather, I had planned to do that before landing the writing gig. I'm not, nor have I ever been"—at least not in this version of Detroit—"licensed as a private investigator. Nor licensed to kill either. I'm very boring in real life."

"I have my doubts on that, Mr. Farrell. Tell me one thing. Why has the address on the card been inked out?" she asked.

"Oh, that?" I shrugged. "The office sorta blew up." Since that left both ladies temporarily speechless, I *amscrayed.*

***

I headed for Target, my preferred joint for clothing replacements, but before heading inside, I called Delia to find out how Sandra was doing. Turned out, the doctors had admitted her to the hospital the night before. A precaution, Delia said, since she'd been tossed across the kitchen as well as served as a target for glass shards. Her hearing had cut out on her for a bit there, I knew, and she might have a concussion. They were playing it safe. I asked which hospital and for Sandra's room number.

Beelz indicated he was fine in his cozy nest in the backseat. He'd finished his latest breakfast of the day quick enough to catch the attention of the folks at Guinness. Not the brewery, the record-keeping ones. When I asked if popcorn was needed, he let me know it was extremely necessary to his wellbeing, then disappeared beneath the mound of blankets again.

Half an hour later, restocked with a week's worth of the same items I wear every day plus two large boxes of chocolates (discounted now that Valentine's Day was past), and a large container of buttered popcorn, I headed for the florist. I'd bought all floral tributes from the same one since arriving in town and snapped up yet another bunch of posies in a vase. Buying spree behind me, I headed to the hospital.

Sandra had enough pieces of tape on her face to look like she'd been in a hell of a battle. Her arms and hands were wrapped in gauze. "You'll never win first prize at the costume contest with only half a mummy outfit, sweetheart," I said.

"Then it's back to the pink princess dress after all," she announced with an overly dramatic sigh. Wondered whether they'd given her some dandy pain killers. Her cheerful dial was definitely switched to high.

"The tiara wouldn't suit anything else. Bet you rock the princess look." Actually, since she was a rather portly dishwater-blonde pushing forty that was an out-and-out lie. To keep her roly-poly, I handed her the box of mixed chocolates. Not a one had nuts in or on it. I don't like nuts messin' with my chocolate and planned to help her make a dent in the treats. The second box was tucked in my trunk so Beelz couldn't help himself while I was otherwise engaged.

"This is for you," I said, handing her the candy. "And depending on what type of patient you are, these"—I set the vase of flowers onto the table next to the pitcher of water and lone plastic cup. This lack of beverage ware is, I believe, the way hospitals discourage visitors from lingering—"are for either you or the nursing staff."

"Oh, Bram," she murmured in a chiding tone, "I've been a model patient to ensure that none of them does try to steal any of the flowers." There were three other vases of them lined up on the wide window ledge, probably all from her coven sisters.

I maneuvered the lone chair, a moderately cushy affair with padded arms, around so she wouldn't have to twist to see me. "Hearing back to normal?"

"Yes."

"Head giving you any problems?"

"Nope."

I leaned closer. "Okay, now tell me what happened. Every detail."

"It was probably my fault. I've never used that model of grill before," she said.

"Sugar, look who you're talking to. The guy with far too many *things* that don't like that he's no longer confined inside a book."

She took a deep breath. Hesitated.

I reclaimed the box of candy and unwrapped it. "You obviously need to be fed rewards for giving me information," I said. "Dark or light, cream, nougat or caramel?"

"Dark cream."

I popped one in her mouth. "Mind if I imbibe?"

"Help yourself," she suggested, though her mouth was full.

A light caramel disappeared so fast it was as if I'd learned consumption speed from Beelz. "Last night, you said something about having checked the propane tank a few days ago." I said, interrogation mode flipped on.

"I have a much smaller grill at home that uses one, so I do know what I'm doing in checking the connection," she said. "Although mine is from a different manufacturer, there was nothing wrong with the one at the mansion and the tank was full. I don't understand why it exploded. It hadn't been on long. I'd just put the steaks on the grill and gone back into the kitchen to check on the vegetables steaming on the stove when BOOM!" Her hands illustrated the word, fingers thrust out quickly from her palms.

Time to see whether the fire inspector had visited the scene yet. I found the card Durkin had given me with the number to call. While I waited to be connected with the proper person, Sandra enjoyed another couple chocolates. I snagged another to keep my strength up.

"Mr. Farrell," a man's voice greeted. "Detective Durkin told me you'd be calling."

"He probably passed me your number so I wouldn't pester him," I said.

The fire investigator chuckled. "That does sound like Durkin," he agreed. "I'm still working on my report, but I found a few pieces that had nothing to do with making dinner."

"Don't tell me. They belonged to a timer."

"Good guess."

"Could it have been activated when Sandra opened the grill hood?"

"I didn't find anything attached to the pieces of the hood, but it would be the best way to ensure injuries, if not a fatality, when someone was present. You weren't the one at the grill then?"

"No, someone who knows how to cook was. Fortunately, she'd just returned to the kitchen when things headed to Hades." Which is not a place, but a guy who lends the sort of alliteration to things I find hard to resist.

But I digress. The fire investigator was still talking, after all. "A lucky move on her part then," he said. "Do you happen to have an enemy who might have done this, Mr. Farrell?"

There was no way I was going to mention Ernie's attack yesterday morning, but I was wondering whether the gravelly-voiced cupid had cornered the market on killing me.

"Not that I know of," I said. "If I think of someone, you can be sure I'll let both you and Durkin know."

But only if the miscreant was human.

"Any other questions?" he asked.

Yeah, I had a lot of questions but none that I could toss at him. "Think that's all I was curious about right now." Thanking him for taking the time to make the hackles on my neck rise, I ended the call.

Sandra was considering the selection of bonbons, but she seemed a bit jumpy. Probably from what she'd overheard from my end of the conversation rather than a sugar high.

"I owe you a big one, Sandy. You got caught in the crossfire of something I didn't even know was targeting me. Name the favor or the price," I told her.

"You know quite well that I offered to do the cooking because we're all fond of you," she said. The *we* meaning the coven. She was a witch, after all. "But I wouldn't turn down an upgrade on the grill set up in my backyard, though a smaller one would do."

Didn't have to think about it. "Done," I said and stole another chocolate, one of the vanilla creams this time. I needed energy. There wouldn't be any popcorn left by the time I reached my car, just a hellhound with a buttery-flavored licker. "Anything else you need while I'm here?"

Sandra shook her head then put a hand to her temple. Some brain matter was still a bit scrambled or she had one hell of a headache and was covering up the fact. "The doctor says he'll probably release me later this afternoon. I'm fine, Bram. What about your injuries?"

"Received in an entirely different incident, sugar. Nothing to worry about. Since you're on recovery road, I'm outta here. Got some investigating to do. Take care, darlin'," I urged and, leaning over, kissed her brow.

***

Next stop was The Bridge to view the ghoul's toasted remains. As much as I would have liked to ditch the viewing, putting it off from earlier was the best I could manage. I'd worked up my courage since then and was as ready as I'd ever be to face what remained of Serpico.

This time when I got out of the car, Beelz slipped through the narrow opening between the front bucket seats and jumped down to the street. I'd barely got the door to the bar opened before he scooted between my feet, darting into the warmer environs, heading directly to the fireplace. He curled up, nose to tail, on the hearth rug and uttered what sounded like a giant sigh of contentment.

I hadn't even realized there was a fireplace before. Not that I made a habit of hanging out at The Bridge. It was not just dim; it was usually damn dark in the joint. The front windows were miniscule and covered with electric beer logo signs and security bars. The door was of a metal that might have had manmade bullet repellent qualities or had been heavily warded to resist a rain of something much hungrier than buckshot. There were scars that indicated someone had been unhappy with the tavern's service in the past.

In this neighborhood, I wasn't surprised. But I was downright flabbergasted at the fireplace, though. I could have sworn it hadn't been there last night or on my previous visits, but a time-worn batten board wall with rusted license plates decorating it had been. Now, there was a roaring fire licking at rock that looked like it had been mortared in place around the fourteenth century. The thing was tall, it was wide, and would have looked right at home in a troll's hovel in the old country, but was as out of place as a *Blade Runner* replicant waitress would be at The Bridge, though either'd be nice and cozy to get close to.

Ruth looked over her shoulder as I leaned back against the outer door to close it. She had a stepstool out and had mounted it to wipe down one of the booth tables. "Ah, I thought you'd be along. Want to see the stiff?"

"The roasted ghoul? Yup. Did you always have that fireplace?" I demanded, pointing at the thing.

Ruth grinned. "Always been there." Because there was a twinkle in her eye I tumbled to the ruse.

"But it's usually glamoured to look like a regular wall."

"Ah, can't put anything over on you, Raven," she said.

"Like hell, you can't. Where's the unmourned deceased?"

She scrambled off her perch, stuffing a rag into her apron pocket as her feet hit the floor. "Follow me. Hammer wanted to dump him in the river, but that's pollution so I discouraged him."

It was hard to picture tiny Ruth's method of deterring Hammer. Other than blackmail, though in this case she could call her half-giant brother to back up any threats she cared to make.

I didn't mention that, considering the size of the miraculously-appearing fireplace, the Lunds were shooting plenty of pollutants into the atmosphere themselves. Still, I had a wood-burning hearth at Casa Amberson and did light it often. There's something soothing about the crackle of a fire.

But then, I have a preference for the crackle of roasting Otherworlder, too. Flame is about the only thing to ensure some of them stay dead, and even with the limited magical repertoire I'm packing, it's comforting to have that element in spades.

It wasn't far to the corpse. They'd tucked him in a toy-house of a shed in a dinky service yard behind the building. Might have been an airshaft between closely built structures once. There was a heavy-duty lock on the door. While a fresh layer of snow had fallen earlier, the accumulation had been tramped down by a horde of foot traffic. Probably that of the dudes involved in relocating the body.

I huddled in my coat, collar turned up, gloved hands shoved into pockets, chin tucked down as far as possible. Ruth went out in shirt sleeves and apron. As she twisted a key in the lock, she glanced back at me.

"You need a scarf," she said.

"No, don't think so," I countered. "Things can grab scarves and throttle the bejesus out of you. Between you and me, Ruthie, bejesus is a real pain to step in or clean up."

The lock clicked open. "With you, the lack of it would probably make you ten pounds lighter," she said.

Or dead. Either was possible.

"I suggest you take a deep breath, Bram. The aroma of confined roast ghoul isn't something you forget, as much as you might try," she warned.

The scents in the narrow yard weren't of fresh anything, not even the arctic-like air gripping the city. But Ruthie was right. The moment she swung the door open, breathing was impossible. A cesspool might have seemed minty by comparison.

Could have used a gas mask. I made do with my gloved hand over mouth and nose. Had to duck really low. The shed was built to accommodate the miniscule Ruth, not her hulking brother.

The ghoul hadn't received careful or thoughtful placement in the shed. He'd been dropped face-down. I used my foot to nudge him over and wished I hadn't. The gold amulet was fused to his skin. Ghouls come in a variety of toadish shades and textures, none attractive, but blackened and cracking wasn't one of them. Oddly enough, the human clothing he'd been wearing was still intact. He'd burned from the inside out.

"You think it was that spontaneous combustion thing that happens to humans sometimes?" Ruth asked.

"Don't think they've proved anyone does that, sugar. 'Sides, this is a ghoul, not a human."

"According to the documentary on TV, it's very real. People just burn to ashes within five or six minutes, but don't set anything around them on fire," she said.

"A documentary on television, huh? Not something validated by a medical degree class on the Internet?" Neither sounded like a source a proper investigator set any truth behind. And I was a proper investigator with a history of solving multiple crimes. Sure, I'd done them in enough volumes to weight down a long bookshelf, but the cases I'd solved at the end of October had been here in the physical world, not on the notional plane I called "home".

"Think I've seen enough," I said, backing out of the building. Nearly brained myself on the low lintel.

"You want we should keep him?" Ruth asked as she relocked the door.

"Wouldn't wish that on my worst enemy, honey, so no. Does the community have a witch doctor or alchemist who does autopsies like a coroner?" Not that we'd had someone like that back in the land of whimsy, but then, we had regular doctors, like the various alternative Watson clones—guys who knew there were things that did more than just go bump in the night. Was worth asking, though. This world shouldn't, if you went by popular theory, even have an Otherworlder community.

"We had a zombie who'd been a doctor, but since it turned out he was using the deaders for grocery shopping, the vamp mafia cemented a deal with him. Used real cement so he didn't last long," Ruth said.

"So no, huh? It would be handy to know what killed him. You think our vic there had kin in the city other than Prisk?"

"No idea, but I put the word out on *The Virginia*."

I looked at her blankly, totally lost.

"Raven," she huffed, "we don't use a grapevine to pass word along, we use a poisonous one, to go with the type of stories relayed. Back in the day, there was even a printed copy for a while, then the thing that cranked the press was found pressed in it. We all figured he ran a rumor a reader didn't care for. Anyway, the print copy had a logo and a name, *The Virginia Creeper*. We've shortened it since then and put it online. 'Course you've gotta know the magic word to access it."

I wondered if the magic word was *please* and whether I could make use of *The Virginia* myself, but didn't ask. Another time when my schedule wasn't as jam-packed, I'd give Ruth the third degree on it.

"Could you tell me if any of the Prisk family members drop off that vine?"

"Particularly one named Solomon?"

"As I hear it, he has quite a business going disposing of unwanted bodies," I said.

"Probably creating a few of them as well," Ruth suggested. "Sure. I've got your number. When something asks why I count you among my favorite people, I tell 'em I've got the hots for you."

"And they believe you?" Actually, I was a bit appalled at the idea.

"Sure, they do, Bram. You're sorta hunky."

When my jaw dropped, she cackled with delight. "Gotcha. Like sprinkling salt on them fine tail feathers. 'Sides, you ain't my type. You're too straight."

I'd met one of Ruthie's beaux in the past. He was in no way straight but bent as a mangled paperclip. What brains he might once have had had been beaten out in the ring leaving him stupid, cruel, and deviously sly. Damn right I wasn't her type. I was smart, plus those other two things.

It was long past time I left, but I had one last question.

"If you drop a hint on *The Virginia* about having a body to get rid of, think it would hook Prisk into getting in touch?"

"I'll post it and see if he bites," she said.

"You think he'll be reluctant or vengeful considering our deader supposedly was a relative?"

"It's business, Raven. Doubt he'd care."

"Then, on that note, I'm outta here, cupcake. Keep me in the loop."

As had become the norm that day, the moment I collected Beelz from his short snooze before the roaring fire, my phone did its TARDIS landing impression. This time it was Naomie.

***

I was feeling a bit guilty that Wendy's case had been put on hold nearly since she'd handed it to me, but you wouldn't have known that by the way I answered the cell.

"What the hell are you doing up already?" I demanded of my secretary. "You can't have gotten enough beauty sleep and had sufficient time to do that research for me already."

"Could and did, boss. How much sleep did you get?" Nomes countered.

None, but that was normal. "Enough," I said to cover.

"You want me to read off what I found or you wanna swing by to pick up the print-outs?"

I glanced at my watch, a classic 1701 Pontchartrain from the

Detroit Watch Company, black dial, silver case and hands, Swiss movement. Delia had surprised me with it at Christmas. I surprised her back on Boxing Day with something dead and furry that had sleeves. I hadn't thought Delia had a squeal in her until she saw the coat. Anyway, it was edging on four and that dinner with Lex was at seven. Three hours to accomplish a bit more.

"I'll swing by and pick you up," I told her. "There's someone I'd like you to meet and then we'll head to the Whitney and reclaim Lex for dinner. Think she'd go for what's available at the snack bar at the bowling alley?"

"You're taking her bowling?" Nomes gasped.

"Taking you both bowling. If they'd let Beelz in the joint and he could nose a ball down the lane, we'd have teams," I said. "As it is, it's every contender for themselves."

"That's a real downshift from the steaks we didn't get last night," she pointed out.

"True, but as Lex is writing about a teen Raven, her protagonist is going to be more inclined toward burgers, tacos, and pizza rolls, right? We'll call it setting her stage."

Devoted secretary that she is, Naomie totally agreed with me. I told her my ETA, then called Clarissa Ponce and asked if she was up for a brief bit of entertaining. After telling me she knew I'd be calling her—she's a seer—Rissy said yes.

"I'm bringing my secretary along. Just a warning, but she thinks I'm normal."

Rissy snorted. "You mean she doesn't know magic exists."

"And I want to keep her that way, so no calling me Raven. Deal?"

"I knew there had to be a reason you were bringing me that box of chocolates in the trunk of your car."

Seers! I think she does these things to get my goat. If I had a goat, I'd turn it over to her.

Neither Beelz nor I had ever been inside Naomie's place. Actually, until earlier that day when we dropped her there, I hadn't even known where it was. From the way the mutt was grinning, I knew he was anxious to see her. He galumphed his way up the stairs and, impatient for me to keep up with him, dashed down the hall, then scratched at the door to let her know we'd arrived. He was already in her arms and engaged in cleaning her face by the time I ambled up.

"Ah, I missed you, too, Beelzie," Naomie cooed, unconcerned over how thorough the tongue-lapping was. Then she turned that bright smile my way. "What did the two of you do today? Find a motel to sack out in?"

"Actually," I said as she backed up enough for me to enter the apartment. "I ran hither and yon while the Big B either snoozed in the backseat or ate a variety of things considered all wrong for the canine diet."

Since her arms were full of contented dachshund, I closed the door and locked it. "You'll be glad to know that the fire inspector has been and done his look-see, and that window and door replacements are being ordered. I haven't been by since the repair guy was there this morning, but there should be a plywood force field protecting the kitchen and keeping uninvited visitors out." Or at least make them work up a sweat to get inside. "Which reminds me, I've got both our computers in the trunk. Mind if we turn your place into an auxiliary office until it's possible to move back in?"

"Sure," she answered, that Pollyanna lean in her personality making the invasion sound like a treat. She grinned. "I'll have a really short commute."

"Heck, every day can be extreme casual day, Nomes. Bathrobe and slippers the rule," I said. Of course, I then wondered what the bathrobe would be covering. Since it was winter, I doubted the diaphanous sleepwear of my daydreams would be it.

"So you didn't get to sleep until after arrangements at the house were made?"

I sighed. "Actually, while I was waiting for the city's guy to arrive"—though it had been bomb squad rather than fire inspector—"that reporter showed up again. Couldn't come up with a good enough reason to duck her, so let her do the interview. Told her to head to the Denny's you and I'd just left. When I got there, Lex was in the booth with her. Ritter called her. Ergo, I had another breakfast and talked teen Raven for a while."

"Then you found a motel room," Naomie said.

"Then I went shopping, visited Sandra in the hospital, and… well, here we are. Mind if I borrow your shower before we head out again?"

"You don't have to ask, boss. Have at it."

Beelz indicated he'd like to find a spot to curl up, so she dropped him onto the sofa.

It was a nice sofa. Bright red and a nubby fabric. The type of rolled arms that are great to use as a footrest when stretched out to ponder things. Otherwise, the place was small, but then, nearly anything would look small after the mammoth proportions of Casa Amberson. Nome's TV was of the 24" variety, her coffee table was two down-sized parson's tables that were battered enough to shout, "Found curb side and cleaned up!" There was a beanbag chair with a fuzzy dark blue blanket to hide what appeared to be a hideous bubblegum pink cover, and generic white toss pillows on both sofa and disguised chair. Next to the beanbag pod, she'd built a make-do side table entirely of Raven Tales hardcovers. A miniscule lamp and a paperback paranormal romance with a red tasseled bookmarker in it jostled for space atop them.

"Very patriotic color choices," I said giving the place the once-over. The only thing it looked like she'd spent any money on was the sofa. I was guessing it was of recent acquisition. Like, since her income had taken that giant boost when she'd entered Ravenland. Considering her entire wardrobe consisted of shapeless black layers, I was rather surprised that she'd branched out into brighter colors when decorating. But then, this was being noted by the guy who wore black everything nearly every day himself.

"The place is a work in progress," Naomie admitted.

"There a table we can use for the computers or should a stop to snag card tables be made when we head out?"

For an answer, she led me behind a half-wall. It separated a dinky eat-in kitchen from the living room. The table here was regulation dining size and had mismatched chairs at either end. The table was shoved up against that token wall. If the chairs had been anywhere else, it would have been impossible to stand in front of the stove and open the door. Or the refrigerator, for that matter. They were cozied up next to each other with a sink on the opposite side of the stove.

"Will this do?"

"If we put the printer on the floor beneath the table, yeah. I can live with that," I assured her. "I'll bring 'em in."

As it was the largest piece, I brought the printer and its supplies in first, though I had one of my Target luggage bags on top of it.

Shower and clean clothes and I'd be a new man. Might even manage to get rid of the trace scent of cooked ghoul that clung to me. That would be a definite improvement.

Naomie was nowhere in sight when I bumped the door open. "Nomes?"

"In here," she called.

I eased the equipment to the table and followed the sound of her voice. She was in the bedroom standing before a beat-up-elsewhere-before-snagged dresser. A smaller version of the same coffee maker we'd had in the mansion's kitchen held center stage on it. Supplies rested in a plastic tray to one side, mugs on an identical tray on the other.

She grinned at me when I poked my head through the open doorway. "Figured you might need some coffee to stay awake, boss. It would be very embarrassing if you passed out while lining up your throw and slid down the alley in place of the bowling ball."

The intoxicating aroma was already wafting through the room. I closed my eyes and took a deep breath. "You keep this up and I may just have to marry you," I threatened, then headed out to get the remaining computers, the promise of steaming Nirvana a damn enticing carrot to make the trip a quick one.

***

Newly refreshed by the shower, in clean clothes with coffee mug in hand, I dropped into the cushy, welcoming embrace of the sofa. I'd received permission to drop my feet onto one of the scarred mini tables so, with Beelz's muzzle resting on my thigh, I was one contented fellow. Naomie silently handed me the research she'd printed off earlier on her home computer set-up and left me alone while she rustled around the kitchen, rearranging it for mini office duty.

It turned out that my vampiress's great grandson was quite the genius in his engineering field. Nomes had found newspaper articles about his wins at science fairs in elementary school, junior high, and high school, but also local medals at swim meets during his high school and undergraduate years. The printouts included abstracts of papers published in journals I'd never heard of, but also in *Popular Mechanics*. She had compiled a list of social media from Facebook,

Twitter, Instagram, and LinkedIn, plus she'd sent me emails with links to a couple of old YouTube videos he'd done. In them, Winthur showed how to do a fairly elementary—to his mind, at least—adjustment to correct what appeared to be a common problem with some automobile electronic systems.

His former girlfriend's Facebook account supplied cozy selfies of the two of them. Lots of them. A few were even of Eric at the auto repair shop in his company-sanctioned, grease-stained uniform. In another, he was grinning at the camera while leaning against the hood of a tow truck. He'd been driving one of those, maybe even the same one, when he'd disappeared. It seemed Kismet that the license plate was clear to read in the shot Naomie had printed off, although, since she'd pasted more than a single photo on a page, I had to squint at it a bit. While squinting, I unearthed my cell again and called Durkin.

He sounded grumpy when he snarled his name. Apparently, he hadn't gotten much sleep after parting company with me earlier in the day.

"How stands my allotment of favors?" I asked.

"About three quarts low," he said.

"Since when did favors start being measured by viscosity?"

Durkin sighed. "Viscosity, Farrell? You been living in a thesaurus?"

"Sorta," I admitted.

"Whaddaya need?" He sounded world-weary, but then, that was his default switch.

"A license plate run. It's probably been run already during the official investigation, but I need to know if the truck was found, and, if so, where it was found." I rattled off the number, then had to give it slower so he could write it down.

"You go look at our dead ghoul?" he asked.

"Yes."

"And?"

"Wasn't quite what I expected," I said.

"In what way?"

"Can't say."

"Can't say because it's something you haven't come up against before or can't say because there's a human who is clueless about what you are who might overhear?"

"Both," I said.

"Must be a strain," he mused.

"What is?"

"You keeping to such short responses. Hell, some of 'em were a single word."

Yeah, that wasn't like me at all. How did people stick to such brevity?

"Talked to your guy at the fire department," I announced, throwing caution into a meat grinder by lining up eight words in a row.

"Yeah, me, too. Somebody doesn't like you very much, Raven."

"Hard to imagine, isn't it, Durkin? I'm so warm and naturally cuddly."

"That describes your mutt, pal, and that's saying something since he's… not exactly AKC material," Durkin said.

The pause said it all. He, too, had acquired a possible eavesdropper who wasn't in the magic loop. "Go easy on the murder and mayhem on your beat tonight," I said.

"My beat frequently encompasses the entire city, my friend. Hard to avoid murder and mayhem within the parameters. Where will you be in case I get a call that sounds like you're in the middle of disruptive circumstances again?"

"Disruptive circumstances?" I snorted at the very idea. There was no *being in the middle* of anything for me. I was either the target or targeting an attacker. "Should be a quiet night. Taking a couple ladies to the bowling alley." However, I added the closest street crossings near the lanes. Let's face it; I hoped there'd be no need for him to be called to the scene, but the way the past thirty-four hours had gone, there was no telling.

***

Within half an hour, Naomie and I were on our way. Beelz stayed behind in the apartment. He'd already claimed the beanbag chair as his.

There were no cars in the driveway when I pulled up at the curb before Clarissa Ponce's home. That meant her nephew, his wife, nor either of his teenagers were at home. Either those who worked were stuck in drive-time traffic or headed to pick up one of the kids from whatever kids did after school. I sure had no idea. There was a good chance I'd learn a lot about what teens did once Lex wrote the first Young Raven Tales book.

Rissy was waiting for us on the ground floor. I noticed there was a coat tossed over the newel post at the bottom of the stairs. It looked rather like it might fit her tiny form. An umbrella rack sported a veritable bouquet of canes in various colors with a variety of carved handles not far from it. Rissy wasn't using a cane though.

"Bram!" she greeted me, a wide smile deepening the wrinkles on her face. "Oh, and who's this? Competition for me for your affections?"

Clarissa was eighty-seven going on twenty-five. I'd met her when an archangel supplied me with her address in November. Since the archangel was one with an address inside the Pearly Gates, that gave her high marks as a person. Even if she did plan to live to be over a hundred and twenty-three just to irk her relatives.

I introduced Naomi, who gushed about how excited she was to meet someone who was a fortune-teller.

Rissy didn't disabuse her for using a term that conjured up sideshow gypsies but turned to me instead. "Be a dear, Bram, and run upstairs for my tarot cards," she requested and told me where to find them. "But put that box of chocolates you're hiding behind your back in the middle dresser drawer under the sweater with a reindeer with a bright red nose on it. I know none of the family or visiting care-giving staff will find it there. I'm just not into sharing my riches with just anyone," she told Naomi in an aside. "Particularly not the creamy, chocolate-covered type."

I did as bid, managing to avoid banging my shins into the electric chair contraptions on either the lower staircase or the one that lead to Rissy's third floor loft-like garret. Naomie admitted to similar territorial behavior regarding chocolate so I heard both ladies laughing as they moved down the hall and into the kitchen.

When I rejoined them, Naomie was on tea duty while answering questions about herself. Oddly enough, it suddenly dawned on me that I knew very little about my secretary. I'd liked her at first glance back in October and had felt sorry for her when the others in the writer's group had panned her efforts. She'd been so open and clumsy as she'd offered what she believed was helpful feedback in return that it had hurt when they'd shown no appreciation.

Something about that encounter had stayed with me, though, and made me think of her occasionally. I'd never wanted to immediately rescue someone who wasn't being threatened by an Otherworlder before, but that was the way I leaned right from the start where Naomie was concerned.

At the tail end of December, I'd walked into the bookstore, found the group gathered and tearing into her latest effort. I slipped her a fresh latte and a note. *Have contract to write a book. Want a job as my secretary?* it read.

She'd stopped paying attention to what the pompous academic was ripping into her about and turned to me, eyes wide and mouth agape.

"I'll take that for yes," I'd said, grinning. "Ready to come away with me?"

She'd stood up so fast, the papers on her lap had spilled across the bookstore's gray carpeting.

Currently Nomes was telling Rissy that she had a brother who was a whiz at killing computer viruses but stopped when I pulled out a chair next to the elderly woman.

"Yes, Naomie, he'll have a cup. Three sugars," the seer said. She made it sound like she'd read the way I liked it in the stars rather than that she knew my preference from previous visits. Since meeting her in November, I'd made a habit of stopping by every couple weeks.

"Now, what is it you wanted to ask me about, dear?" Rissy rested her hand on mine.

"Foresaw the candy but not my purpose, huh?" I asked.

"A girl has to have her priorities."

"You told me you couldn't see things that involved you, Riss."

"The esoteric allowed me to see the candy in your hand and my number on your cell, Bram. There are ways around nearly everything, which you know quite well."

It was that deviousness that I like most about her. "Minx," I murmured and was awarded with a happy smile. "Okay, I've got a missing person. Around twenty-four, twenty-five. What will help you most? Picture or further details, though I'll warn you, we haven't got much. Nomes found what there is on the Web, but that's not going to narrow in on him or who decided to make him disappear."

Rissy gave it some thought. "Picture, I think. Probably the less I know, the clearer my path will be. I'll need to hold your hand though, Bram. That will give direction to the search."

I retrieved the printout of the selfie Eric Winthur's girlfriend had taken before their breakup. It was the best natural shot from the batch. "Never a problem holding your hand, gorgeous," I said, passing her the photograph.

The seer grinned across at Naomie on the other side of the table. "If I was younger, I'd steal him," she said, then turned her attention to Eric Winthur. "Nice looking young man. Viking heritage clear to see. I'd have hit on him sixty years ago, maybe even forty or fifty years ago."

"You have a one-track mind," I told her.

"Just not dead yet, honey," she said and batted impish, though faded, eyes at me. "Okay. Let's get started. When the tea is ready, just slide the mug over, Naomie."

My secretary repeated the formula Rissy considered the perfect cuppa, which included a precise count on the drops of lemon juice to add, then the old woman entwined her fingers with mine and closed her eyes.

We waited. The tea kettle whistled Nomes back into action. Steaming mugs were carefully placed within reach. I ignored mine but noticed that Rissy found the mug and took a sip without breaking her concentration or opening her eyes.

"Oh!" she said suddenly. "Interesting client."

"Uh uh," I agreed.

"He doesn't know."

"Nope."

"She fears this has something to do with her."

"Yup."

Rissy chewed on her bottom lip. Not the corner as Nomes does but dead center. "I can't say that it doesn't but can't say that it does."

I sighed.

She was quiet for quite a while. I wondered whether she'd dozed off. Across the table, Naomie stared at the seer, totally fascinated.

"A friend. Male? Female? It isn't clear. Could be both. Connected to a place of entertainment. I see laughter, drinks raised as though in a toast."

I waited. When she didn't add anything else, I had to ask. "Alive?"

She paused, squinted as though that would make the vision in her mind clearer. "Yes but injured. Confused."

I lifted our joined hands and kissed the heavily veined-back of hers. "That's enough, darlin'. Don't want to exhaust you."

Rissy released my hand and took a deep breath, her face alight with pleasure. "Oh, that was fun. I haven't done something like this in so long. Fortunately, I'm not in the least bit tired either. It was exhilarating! Good thing, too, since we're going bowling."

"You're coming with us? Oh, that's great!" Naomie gushed. "And it was awesome watching you work, Mrs. Ponce."

Rissy made a sound, clearly dismissing the comment as rubbish. "Nonsense, dear, and the name is Rissy to friends. Ms. Ponce to the hordes. I never married, just flitted from lover to lover. So much more fun that way."

Naomie's eyes were wide again and glittering like Brazilian emeralds after a master cutter has polished them to life. My eyes might be green, too, but they have more in common with the olives dropped in martinis, only without pimentos added.

"Curse of the seer, Nomes," I said. "She saw none of them were the right guy for her."

"It's one scary gift, honey," Rissy told her. "Wouldn't wish it on anyone but wouldn't want to give it up either. Come on, drink up. Isn't there another member of our team that needs to be picked up yet?"

Before we left, Rissy took an already-written note from her pocket and pinned it to the refrigerator with a flower-shaped magnet. It not only said she was out with me, it gave the name of the alley, the address, and told her nephew's family not to wait up for her.

***

"Bowling?" Lex repeated as she settled into the front passenger's seat in the Mustang. Naomie had chosen to be in the backseat with Rissy. They'd brought the tarot cards along and made do with the space between them for a layout table.

"I spent considerable time pondering how best to help you on your quest for sites populated by teenagers," I said. Actually, I hadn't. I'd never been bowling and figured that, unlike any of the witches from the coven or Durkin, Lex couldn't make the excuse of a previous commitment to duck out on me. Burt would have been happy to show me the ropes—did they have ropes in the sport?—but, as he belonged to a regular team and had regaled me regarding the number of trophies in the case at his home, it would be too embarrassing to have him grind me into the dust. If any of the lanes had dust on them, that was. Probably didn't.

Lex donned a thoughtful look. "It does have some merit," she admitted.

"Plus, the food available is prime pickin's for *your* Raven. Fortunately, we're of an age to indulge in something more than a soft drink."

"Like your Raven's Evan Williams?"

"More like Bud Lite," I admitted. A shame no local craft beers were likely to be on the menu, but this was wholesome family entertainment, right? "Rissy? You old enough to drink or have a false ID on you?"

"Packin' a false one," the octogenarian announced. "Even has a decent picture on it."

"Just checking," I said. "I'd hate to be arrested for leading you astray."

"You really aced that Gigolo 101 class, didn't you?" Lex commented. "All the girls love you."

"'Cept Beck Ritter," I pointed out.

"You've simply got too mysterious a past. That set her journalistic hackles on alert," she said. "The more you cooperate, the faster those hackles will lie down for a rest."

"Yeah? Sounds like you know what you're talking about. Living down a past bad experience yourself?"

"Yes," she admitted. "It's called three years working on a journalism degree before realizing I lacked the verve needed to become a Beck Ritter."

"So instead of taking on recalcitrant government officials, A-List celebrities, and lowly but mysterious writers, you decided to kick some Otherworlder butt in Ravenland," I mused.

"Don't forget, I've got a few years of being the terror of college freshmen with my deadly red pencil in composition classes," Lex reminded me. "I've killed more run-on sentences, sliced off more dangling participles, blasted more incoherent thesis statements, and demanded more rewrites at the point of a threatened sharp drop in GPA than you could beat with a stick."

I glanced over at her. "Good to know you aren't the violent type."

She laughed. "You play The Raven so effortlessly, I'm jealous. Hell, you've even got the snipe down pat. I hope I can do the same."

"It's a science," I allowed.

We arrived at our destination, and I pulled into an open handicapped spot so Rissy wouldn't have much of a walk to the door. I left her in the care of the girls while I found a spot that wouldn't get the car towed or ticketed. They were debating the menu offerings of things not recommended by dietitians when I caught up. There were no tables to eat at, but cup-holders on the seats by the lanes the counter guy told me as he handed over four plastic mugs of domestic beer. Lex and Rissy had gone off to find an open lane. Naomie was soon burdened by a large tray with three orders of chicken fingers, a taco, a chili dog with cheese, a double burger with cheese and bacon, and a large order of fries. Everything but the chicken fingers was mine. It had been hours since I'd downed that second breakfast. When we rejoined the rest of our party, Lex immediately returned to the counter for a tall stack of napkins. I had no idea why she thought we needed that many. Maybe she was going to take notes on them?

The girls all dug into their miniscule meals but sent me off to acquire bowling shoes, three ten-pound balls, and whatever weight I took a fancy to. Being the guy with a harem in tow was time-consuming. When I finally was allowed a moment to deal with the chili dog, they waited until my mouth was full to tell me teams had been decided upon. My partner was Rissy. She batted her eyelashes at me when I said, "You're kidding."

They weren't.

Naomie was the first one finished with her food so she stepped up to the scoreboard. She filled in names in quick order. Seemed she'd done this before, which was good to know. Now, all we needed was more Raven Corp employees willing to take ball in hand, and we'd have a team to challenge Burt and his buddies. It was going to be a long wait 'til that happened.

Rather than flip a coin to see which team went first, Nomes and Lex allowed Rissy the honor of the first roll. I was on to the taco as she carefully scooted up to the line and released the ball. It didn't look like it had the *oomph* to make it to the pins. I gave it a push with a thought and added a slight correction to the trajectory, keeping it from the gutter. The ball had enough momentum to scare four pins into fainting dead away.

Nomes and Lex cheered. When Rissy turned back, I doubted I've ever seen a bigger smile on anyone's face before. "Thanks," she whispered as she reclaimed her seat next to me.

"We're going to kill these bitches, but not by too flashy a score." I whispered back.

"Damn right," my doddering partner agreed. Her face was still glowing with pleasure. Team Risam (as Lex decided to call us) took the first game by three pins. The only cheating done was to improve Rissy's aim. It turns out that when a guy has made a career of taking out miscreants with wind thrusts, fireballs, and assorted other magical folderol, knocking down a bunch of pins at the end of an alley is child's play.

It was when I returned to the counter for another round of beers that I spotted possible trouble brewing in this corner of the Motor City. A familiar face caught my eye. Our gazes met and his dropped quickly. A moment later, he pushed off the wall he'd been leaning against, made some excuse to the guys with him, and followed the arrow that pointed toward the men's room. Five seconds later, my phone went into massage mode. A text was already working its way across the screen when I palmed it.

might need backup. you in? styles

So, Durkin's vice vampire's name was Styles. I was learning all kinds of things today!

in, I answered. **when?**

i call you come

I shoved the phone back into my pocket, handed the counter guy a twenty for the beer refills, stunning him by waving off the change, then took the mugs back to my ladies. "Saw a buddy I need to talk to for a minute. You gals okay with a short respite?"

They each assured me they were, though Rissy caught the sleeve on my sweater and pulled me down. "Careful. Short one has a knife, crew cut has brass knuckles," she whispered.

"Third guy?"

"The vamp will take him. He's hampered by the norms. No lightning moves."

"Good thing my hocus is the silent kind of pocus," I murmured, patted her hand, then ambled back toward the front door.

Styles timed his reentry to coincide with mine. We were even with his so-called friends when he bumped my shoulder. He glanced at me, his eyes narrowed. "You!" he growled and grabbed a handful of my sweater to drag me off to the side. "Where's my money?"

I glared back at him. "Don't owe you nothin', pally," I snarled under my breath.

"Trouble, Angelus?" the guy with the crew cut rumbled.

"Not yet," Styles… well, I suppose he growled again. I was running out of good thesaurus suggestions.

The vice vamp gave my shoulder a shove, knocking me back toward his friends. I twisted to let myself fall forward into the short one. Wished Rissy had told me where he was hiding his knife, but at least I was forewarned. Making it look like I was trying to catch my balance, I sorta accidentally rammed my fist into his gut.

"Sorry," I said, acting the total innocent and, backing up, stepped on the hulking third guy's foot, then appeared to lose my balance and grabbed crew cut's shoulder to catch it, giving him my own version of the Vulcan Death Grip in the process. When he sagged, I used the bent-over knife guy's shoulder to steady myself and death gripped him, too. Oh, not to worry. The hand in the right spot was prestidigitation. With the physical contact, it was possible to knock them unconscious with a thought. I'd done it a few times inside a book. Was nice to know the knack had followed me across finally.

"Whoa, dude! You sick?" I said, dragging crew cut to his feet and draping his arm over my shoulder.

"Hey!" The guy Rissy told me belonged to the vampire's mercies coughed as he realized things weren't quite what they appeared.

Styles had his own version of the death grip. I didn't see him move but doubt anyone else did either. His maneuver stiffened his opponent. The vamp tucked the guy in the corner against the wall, making it appear he was just standing there. Before anyone could notice Styles had gotten out of my face, he was back glaring into it.

"Listen, Shumsky," Styles said.

I looked up. "Shumsky? Who's that? My name is Timberlake."

Styles did a good impression of looking stunned. He looked closer at me. "Damn. You aren't Shumsky. Sorry, buddy. My mistake."

"Dude, your friends don't look well. Maybe they need some air?" I suggested.

"Told 'em those burritos from that food truck were trouble," he muttered loud enough for even the temporarily frozen staff behind the food counter to hear. "Would you mind helping me get them outside?"

"Not at all," I agreed, polite to a fault. While I dragged the comatose crew cut out the door, Styles made an effortless delivery of the tall stiff and the short knife guy. He'd barely dumped them at the side of the building when he called his catch in.

"Appreciate the assistance, Farrell," he said when his cell was back in a deep coat pocket.

"Angelus?" I demanded. "You're stealing names from *Buffy the Vampire Slayer*?"

"Angel wasn't using his formal name, so why not?" he countered.

"He does occasionally where I come from," I countered back.

"Where'd you pull Timberlake from?"

I resisted doing an eye roll. Naomie did them and I didn't want to steal her shtick. "Dude, one of good ol' Justin's songs was on the sound system. Details. You gotta use what the gods put at hand. By the way, I had a close encounter with Dawes earlier today. Claims he's a David. So what are you?"

"Hal."

"Not Vlad, huh?"

"Lousy name for undercover." Which it was. Someone would think he was Russian. Vampire wouldn't even come in a close second.

"Just curious, but what are you arresting them for?" I queried.

He pulled knife guy's jacket open and tugged on an inner pocket, opening it wide enough for me to see the neatly packaged little drug treats, then flipped the jacket back into place. "Best get back to the ladies you left languishing," Styles suggested.

"Yeah. If I'm not there to fight them off, the oldest one will start enticing guys back to her place," I said.

A minute later, I was downing my beer and watching Rissy take another shot at knocking some pins down. The first roll was a gutter ball, but that was because the manager from the snack bar distracted me with a fresh beer. "No charge," he said quietly. "Thanks for getting them out of here." Seems Styles and I had fooled only the drug pushers with our performance.

I gave him a nod and a wink, then turned back to deal with Rissy's unhappy face.

***

By eleven, the Ravenmobile was down to two occupants: Naomie and me. Lex was back in her hotel planning on another day of fun with Burt chauffeuring her around. Rissy was back in her attic digs, a spot she had chosen over something on the main floor much to her nephew's chagrin.

"You hungry?" I asked.

"You are?"

You'd think that in six weeks of rubbing shoulders with me that she'd have noticed I burned a lot of energy. Even if all I was doing was killing zombie hordes on the laptop.

"Beelz will expect a treat when we get back. He may have chowed down on the furniture."

"Then I hope it wasn't the sofa or the beanbag chair. Everything else looked chewed on when I bought it," Naomie said. "There's an all-night market a couple blocks from my apartment. They'll have dog food."

I glanced at her. "Are we talking about the same dog? The Long B thinks he's a person. He's not good with pizza, but meatballs are an entirely different thing."

She sighed. "No pizza places open this late in my neighborhood. Does that mean we need to go back to Denny's for takeout?"

"Nah," I said. "We punt." Not far up the way there was a convenience store with a 24-hour sign blinking out front. It was blinking because it was one seriously old sign. Filaments were probably using walkers and wheelchairs to do their job inside the tubes.

"Stay in the car with the doors locked," I said. "Won't be but a couple minutes."

When I pushed the door open, I found the place had been updated maybe once since the sign had gone up. The tile was worn but not by as many feet as one might expect. Paths clearly showed that the way to the beer cooler was popular. Another customer was standing before it, contemplating the available selection.

I found my way to the grill where foot-long hot dogs were lolling on slow-turning rollers. Since Beelz usually nosed buns away, I grabbed a narrow-waxed bag and shoved as many of the wieners in that would fit. That decimated the hot comestibles available. I moved on to breakfast delicacies and added two bags of those little donuts with the talcum powder coating. Yeah, the hound was used to larger donuts, but I could toss these at him for entertainment's sake. Added a bag of chips, another of pretzels, a couple candy bars, then dumped them all onto the counter before following the beer cooler trail for something to wash it all down. Damn, I missed my Evan Williams. Quality bourbon and domestic beer are so far apart in alcoholic content, they don't even qualify as kissing cousins. Or long-lost ones either. My shopping done, I was set for the night. Where I'd *spend* that night was still a mystery.

I'm a P.I, I solve mysteries. I'd figure it out.

The guy behind the counter rang everything up without comment. I handed over the legal tender.

Nearly the moment my wallet was in sight, the guy who'd been giving the beer a stare-down slipped up behind me. "Just lay it on the counter, buddy," he said and shoved something into my ribs.

"It will feel warmer in my pocket," I said.

"Oh, funny guy, huh?" He didn't sound in the least bit amused.

He obviously wasn't too smart either. The idiot was standing where I could see what he was holding in one of the concave security mirrors. It was a long-necked condiment bottle. He was also facing the camera affixed to the ceiling above the door.

"You aren't going to pull the trigger on that hot sauce, are you?" I asked. "It'll make a hell of a stain to get out of my coat. I might need to send you the cleaning bill. You got a card?"

The guy behind the counter wasn't checking the mirrors and obviously didn't believe me about the hot sauce. His face was pale, and he'd developed a twitch at the corner of his eye. "Just give him the money, mister."

"If I do that, he'll just want yours, too."

He looked at the guy carrying the hot sauce. "Be glad to give it to him," he said.

"He'll just come back for more. Do what you want, but I'm

keeping mine. I'm fond of that wallet and the dead presidents keeping warm within it."

The bottle pressed harder against my ribs. "I'll drill ya," the idiot said. "I swear, I'll—"

Which is when I turned and took him down with my elbow. Might have broken his nose. He was definitely holding it and whimpering as he curled into the fetal position at my feet. I bent over and snagged the hot sauce weapon. "Call the cops," I said to the clerk. "Tell them he tried to kill a paying customer with a condiment. I think that's worth ten to fifteen in the slammer."

"I'm sorry, so sorry," the incompetent felon whined. The way he was dressed shouted *homeless,* but he didn't smell of life on the streets. Or the least bit human. "I just ain't—"

Which of course is when my phone evoked *Doctor Who.* Naomi, of course. "Sorry, gotta take this," I averred. *Averred.* Lovely sounding word. Just had to use it. "Nomes? There something you'd like me to pick up?"

"Did you just take that guy out, boss?"

I *pshawed.* "He started it."

"I called the police," she said.

"Good girl. You want ice cream?"

"I, ah…" Couldn't make up her mind.

"Something with chocolate, then. I'll be out as soon as the law arrives. Stay where you are with the doors locked. Don't even think about getting out of the car," I ordered and tucked the phone back into my pocket.

"Let's hear what you're going to tell the cops when they arrive," I said, hunkering down next to the amateur footpad. "Choose the answer that best suits your situation. A) Haven't eaten in three days. B) Wife or daughter or son is sick, and you need cash to pay a doctor. C) Saw the opportunity and couldn't resist. D) All of the above."

"Huh?" he said.

"Insanity plea. That just might stick. That was certainly the stupidest thing you could have done tonight."

"Man, I was desperate."

For the sake of the human behind the counter, I played along with his homeless act. "You could have asked if I had something to spare for a meal or a place to stay. It's damn cold out there, buddy."

He was dripping blood on the not-all-that-clean floor. Well, couldn't blame the guy at the register. People had been tramping snow in all day. Keeping the floor dry was a full-time job in this weather. "Add a box of tissues to my tab," I suggested. "If you don't mind getting them off the shelf as well, that would be great."

No way was I going to leave the amateur felon's side. He'd scramble out the door on all fours to escape. I had a far better use for him than letting the cops have him, though.

"You planning on filing charges for attempted robbery when the police arrive?" I asked the counter guy when he handed me the tissues. I ripped the box open, pulled a few out, and handed them to the dude on the floor—a glamoured ghoul. "He didn't actually ask you to empty the register. You volunteered to do so."

That seemed to take the clerk aback. "Guess I won't," he admitted, "though my boss is going to be ticked that I didn't."

"So don't tell him," I suggested.

"You filing charges?" he asked.

"Still have my wallet and all the things that live inside it," I said, "so whether I do or not depends on our friend here. He did threaten to shoot me with hot sauce."

The thing on the floor stared at me over a bouquet of fluffy white, diaphanously thin paper. The tissues were liberally doused in something that resembled blood. Even smelled a bit like it. Not human blood, though.

"What do you mean, it depends on me?"

"I have a job you might be able to do, though I'll warn you, it could be… well, we'll say uncomfortable." Which was a nice way of saying dangerous. Very dangerous.

"You ever hear of a guy named Solomon Prisk?"

From the way he paled, I knew he had.

I'd slipped my wallet back into my pocket, but now I pulled it out again and casually folded two Benjamins and a couple of Sam Grants in half. Held them out to him between two fingers. "I need to get a message to him," I said. "You agree to seek him out and deliver it, and I'll call us square. This…" I lifted the bills. Like the thing's eyes hadn't been glued to them since I made sure it saw the picture on each. "…is payment in advance for your services. Give him this card."

The ghoul didn't take the money. It took the card. Looked at it.

Swallowed hard. "I'm a dead man," it whispered. A very good possibility, in fact.

Outside, a police car rolled into the lot, the lights on the roof auditioning for a side job at a dance club. I rotated my body to keep the officers from seeing the cash. "Time to decide."

It took the downed thing barely a second to make it disappear from my hand and into a pocket. My business card went with it.

As the first officer came through the door, I was helping the ghoul up. "False alarm," I said. "He got too close to me at the counter and, hey, it's late. I overreacted and cracked him one."

They looked at the blood on the tissues. "That right?" they asked the thing.

"Yeah, my fault totally," it insisted.

"Anyone interested in pressing charges?"

We all declined. I shook the glamoured ghoul's hand. "Hey, you still want that hot sauce?" I asked. "If so, I'll put it on my tab."

"No, I think I'll just head home and put ice on my face. Sorry I startled you." Thanking the cops for coming, it slipped past them and out into the night.

The guy behind the counter looked from the lingering cops to my bagged purchases. Asked if there was anything else I needed.

Because I'm into memorable dramatics, I smacked my brow with the heel of my hand. "Damn. Nearly forgot the ice cream. Thanks for the reminder."

The cops were still in the store when I strolled out with the supplies. Naomie leaned over in the seat and unlatched the driver's side door. I passed her the bundles.

"The police wrote down your license plate number," she said.

"Not surprised."

"So what happened?"

I grinned at her. "I believe I hired a snitch."

February 16th

In our absence, Beelz had requisitioned the use of Naomie's bed. It had been neatly made when we left. It now looked like a canine orgy might have been in progress. That or he'd built a pillow-and-blanket cave. Nomes wasn't in the least concerned. She rough-housed with him a bit while I lined the hotdogs up on a mound of napkins and gave them a quick nuke in the microwave. It, like the coffee machine, was housed in the bedroom atop a tall, narrow, distressed cabinet. Lacking appropriate mutt tableware, I found an aluminum foil pie pan in the cabinet above the stove, tipped the warm-once-more hotdogs in it, and set it on the floor in the kitchen. My domesticity continued with putting the ice cream in the freezer and gathering up the rest of my comestibles.

"Well, see you around nine or do you need to sleep in a bit to catch more Zs?" I asked.

"I thought you hadn't gotten around to finding a motel earlier," Naomie countered.

I was honest enough to agree I hadn't. "I'll just flit here and there. If necessary, there's Beelz's pile of blankets in the backseat. I'll be fine."

"Boss," she said.

"Nomes?"

"Let me show you something." She headed back into the main room. She did the arm thing that the babes on the afternoon game shows do to show off a prize to be won. The kind that cries out for a *Ta-Da!* "This is a sofa."

"With that level of observational skills, you could be a detective," I told her.

"Sofas can be slept on, boss."

"I'm sure Beelz will let you share the bed he's claimed."

"Slept on by *you*, boss."

"Nomes—"

She folded her arms over her chest and turned one damn scary gaze on me. She wasn't going to flinch on this.

"I'm really not tired," I said.

"You go to Denny's again to hang out for hours alone and they'll start charging you booth rent."

They probably would.

"Really, Nomes. I'm fine."

She crossed to the door, checked the locks I'd already thrown, then slipped a security chain into place as well.

"I'm not tired," I repeated.

"I believe you, boss. Half an hour ago, you were playing Raven again. Adrenaline, as I understand it, takes a while to dissipate."

Dissipate? Who was she, using words like that? Going all mature and concerned on me.

"No adrenaline was involved. It was a quick take-down and I released that former jailbird into the wilds."

"What makes you think he was a former jailbird?"

"He wasn't in jail right then. Believe me, sugar, I know miscreants." Particularly of the non-human variety. The ghoul had a high GPA in that regard.

"You," she said, leveling a deadly forefinger at me. "Sofa." It received a designated point as well.

I sighed. "I'm a nocturnal creature. I tend to watch movies all night. If I gave into the temptation to flick the set on…"

She headed back into the kitchen. "You want the ice cream or popcorn? Popcorn probably goes better with the beer."

Beelz trundled out of the bedroom. Came to a halt and cocked his head.

"Looks like I'm staying," I said.

From the other side of the half-wall, Naomie was gathering snacks. I heard the tab on one of the beer cans snap, then another. "Have you seen *Galaxy Quest*?" she asked. "I think you'll like it, boss. Until you told me we were going bowling, it was on my watch list for the night."

Five minutes later, we both had our feet on separate battered fifteen-inch-tall tables, a large red plastic bowl of popcorn between us and cans of beer within reach. She missed the end of the movie, falling asleep, her head sliding from where it rested against the back of the sofa to land on my shoulder. I put my arm around her, and once Tim Allen had bested the evil alien, I carried her into the bedroom, tucked her beneath the covers, then went in search of another movie to watch.

***

Two more movies and a sunrise later, Beelz found his way out of the bedroom just as I finished washing half a dozen diminutive donuts down with some orange juice I'd found in the refrigerator. I gave him a full dozen in the shiny pie pan, refilled the soup bowl Naomie had converted to a water dish, and whispered that his job was to guard Nomes. Promised I'd come get him if it looked like backup of the Great Dane vein was required. He morphed to it when the chips were not only down but had been pounded into subatomic particles. I'd only seen him do it three times, once to turn Wendy into a chew toy, once to kill a demon, and then at The Bridge the other night to keep from getting stepped on.

I left Naomie a note on the keyboard of her office computer, suggesting she give Burt a call and do a ride-along with Lex as she searched for inspiration. Added that she should take Beelz with her.

My day was allotted to tracking down what had become of Eric Winthur. Hopefully, there would be no further dodging of hit folks to be done.

***

The first port of call was to the university's Dearborn campus to hang around outside a classroom. Earlier, I'd pieced together a schedule for Eric's girlfriend, Jamie Rand, from comments in her Facebook and Twitter accounts. Instagram had supplied a picture of her with a group that included one of her instructors. Trawling the school catalog, I pinned him as her anthropology prof. She'd mentioned a test in the 10 a.m. class in a post, so I simply strolled into the Anthro office, told the secretary I was supposed to meet the PhD outside his classroom but had left the room number at home. Could she supply it? She supplied it.

This wasn't the first time I'd wheedled information from a college department secretary. Maybe Lex was right about me. Maybe I should be *teaching* a Gigolo 101 class.

It wasn't the professor I was waiting for, though. It was Ms. Rand.

Students began straggling from the classroom as they finished the test. Jamie was one of the last to emerge. She wasn't hard to miss. A guy with Eric's looks would have snagged a peach and she was indeed that. Burnished, long, brown locks, brilliant blue eyes, long lashes, smooth dusky skin. The rest of her was bundled in layers, preparatory for reentry into the arctic air.

"Jamie Rand?"

She was startled but smiled tentatively at me. "Yes?"

"Do you have a moment to speak to me about Eric Winthur? I've been asked to look into his disappearance," I said. Already had a card in hand. Passed it to her.

Jamie glanced at it. Knew the moment she narrowed in on that *Investigations* because her eyes widened slightly. "Yes, of course, Mr. Farrell."

"Appreciate it. Is there someplace where we can get a cup of coffee?"

She suggested the student union and led the way. We both hit the coffee bar, but I paid for the lattes.

"I'm sure the police have been over this with you already, but they aren't into sharing their records with people outside of their department, so forgive me if you feel like you're stuck in a *Groundhog Day* loop. But, since you've had time to think about things, if there is something new you've remembered since talking to the cops, please include it," I begged and assured her I'd share it with the proper authorities—Durkin, to be more precise, whether the case was on his docket or not. Him, I trusted.

"That's all right, Mr. Farrell. Where would you like me to start?" she asked.

"How long have you known Eric Winthur?" That seemed like a good place to kick things off, sorta take her back to happier times, maybe even supply a hint of what led to his disappearance. In any case, she relaxed as memories were revisited.

"We met here on campus when I was a freshman and he was a

senior," she said. "Bumped into each other in the hall and then seemed to keep bumping into each other. Finally, he asked if I'd like to grab lunch with him."

At a guess, I figured he'd found reasons to be within bumping distance after that first encounter. I sure the heck would have.

"We found we had common interests and what began as a friendship just grew into something more. Last year, we decided to move in together. Things were fine, but then he started getting calls at strange times. Eric wouldn't tell me what they were about, but he always left immediately. Even if he got one of the calls in class. One of the other grad students in his department stopped me and told me to tell Eric he'd missed an awesome presentation by a guy from Chevrolet. That was how I found out he was skipping classes."

"Is that unusual for him?"

"Very unusual. The guy lives and breathes electronic components."

"Sounds like a one-sided conversation, Ms. Rand."

She laughed lightly. "Yeah. I'm sure my eyes glaze over the same way his do when I get psyched about the possibility of being chosen to be part of a dig. He is very supportive of my career, as I am of his. We have plenty of other things in common without needing our future jobs synching."

"These strange phone calls and his refusal to explain them. Were they the reason for your breakup?"

This time she sighed. "Not really. It was because he *was* skipping classes and might not graduate on schedule because he'd missed so much. We were going to graduate together, me with my BA and he with his MS and then talk marriage. But rather than submerge himself in his final thesis project, he'd gotten totally wrapped up in a genealogical search."

Uh oh. That didn't sound good considering who my client was. And *what* she was.

"Eric's grandmother was the one who started the search for ancestors. She'd been born in Stockholm, I believe, but her mother left her at an orphanage late one night and never returned. She is determined to learn who her mother was and see if she has other blood relatives."

Wendy hadn't told me what year she'd left her daughter on that doorstep, but that daughter was now probably close to Rissy Ponce's age or a couple years older. It sounded like Mrs. Winthur belonged to the same generation.

Jamie wasn't done with her story yet, though. "Because his grandma doesn't get around well and peering at faded scans of documents sent via email is difficult, Eric took over the search. Basically, all they had was a black-and-white glamour shot from the early Thirties of a woman, and a couple names. Whether the woman in the photograph went by either of those names, they still hadn't determined.

"But Eric thought the woman looked familiar. He didn't know why, but he'd stare at that picture for hours, just zoned out," Jamie said.

I sipped my coffee thoughtfully. "Did Eric or his grandmother have a theory or an idea they were pursuing regarding the photo?"

Jamie nodded. "His grandmother is sure the woman is her mother, and if you look at photos of Grandma Winthur in the late Fifties and early Sixties, there is a strong resemblance. Anyway, Grandma's theory is that her mother left her behind to try her hand in the movies in America. Greta Garbo and Ingrid Bergman were actresses she loves to talk about, saying that since they made it in Hollywood, there was a good chance that other girls from the Nordic countries had tried to catch a director's eye as well, her mother possibly being one of them."

This was skating very close to Wendy Whilsen's story, though it had been a vampire don, not a movie mogul, whose eye she'd caught.

"What did the police think about Eric's family history search being tied to his disappearance?" I asked.

Jamie wrinkled her nose. "They brushed it off as unimportant. I even showed them the portrait and all the detective did was agree that the woman was a *looker*."

I could find out very quickly if the cop who'd interviewed Jamie had been Durkin, but it didn't sound like him to brush off any lead, no matter how insignificant it might seem. Right now, I wanted to see if the mysterious photo was indeed Wendy Whilsen, because if it was…

"Could I get a copy of that portrait, Ms. Rand?

"Of course, Mr. Farrell. I have a scanned copy on my computer as well. I like Eric's grandmother and have kept in touch despite breaking up with him. With Eric missing, I've helped her send queries out to other genealogy enthusiasts. Sometimes the glam shot needs to be attached to the email. If you'd like, I can send you a copy as soon as I get home. Eric had copies of it made at a photo kiosk as well, so I've got physical copies to share if you need one of those, too."

I told her to hold onto the extras, as an electronic copy worked for me at this point, then passed her another business card, pausing only long enough to scribble an email address on it. As I rarely get a chance to distribute any, I have tons of the cards. Well, maybe not *that* many.

"Do you think the search for this ancestor or the woman in the photo could be tied to Eric's disappearance then?" Jamie's voice quavered slightly. She hadn't stopped caring about him even if the romance had hit the rocks. Probably had only done so temporarily.

All I needed to do was find him and their ways would stop being parted. Imagine that. The Raven, repairer of romance and broken hearts.

Nah, I'd lose readers with a schmuck-y motto like that. Destroyer of demons, etc., was a much better catchphrase.

"I think the fact that the police didn't follow up on it and he still hasn't been found make it a very viable new trail to follow, Ms. Rand," I confessed. "You wouldn't happen to have any of Eric's other research laying around?"

Jamie nodded. "Oodles of it. He may have physically moved out, but he hadn't come around to pick up most of his things before he disappeared. There are three file boxes of scanned and photocopied stuff, though I'll bet a lot are duplicates. Filing paper documents is not one of his strong suits."

"Would you mind if I borrowed them to go through?" As a creature of paper myself, there was always the chance that something in the boxes would speak to me.

She sipped a bit of her latte, stalling for think-time, then dug in her backpack and unearthed her cell. Within moments, she'd found the number she wanted and connected with the other person.

"Grandma? This is Jamie. I need to ask your permission to do something. There is a private investigator looking into Eric's disappearance and he'd like to look at all the research Eric had about the woman in the photo. He thinks there might be something in the boxes that will help locate Eric. What do you think we should do?"

I liked that she was still close with the missing man's family. She wouldn't have said *we*, including herself in their fold, otherwise.

My mind had bolted out of the gate without waiting for the starter's pistol though. If the photo really was of Wendy and someone within the vampire community discovered there were humans searching for information about her, I could see Palermo giving an order to put a halt to it.

Rissy had said she saw Eric injured, but *only* injured. She hadn't specified what the injury entailed. I hoped it wasn't two fang marks and an unauthorized withdrawal from his blood bank.

"Yes, ma'am," Jamie said, then ended the call. "Mr. Farrell? Grandma says, 'go for it.'"

***

Rather than have Jamie ill-at-ease with a strange man (and they don't come much stranger than me) in her home, I gave her Naomie's number and caged hers for my perky secretary. Nomes was thrilled to be included in the investigation when I touched base with her. I suggested she and Burt snag the document goodies after dropping Lex back at her hotel later that afternoon. That worked well with Jamie's schedule so, while Eric's girlfriend headed to her next class, I went on to my next interview. It was with the kid's boss at the auto repair joint.

The moment I pulled the Ravenmobile up to the garage door, an appreciative group of men in canvas coveralls stopped working on other vehicles and drifted out into the cold to drool on my hood. It was that kind of machine. Burt, Beelz and I had all drooled upon seeing the twin of the current model last fall. Burt had gotten blurry-eyed when miscreants had set it on fire as an incentive for me to drop a case. Not that that had worked, of course. When the insurance check had finally arrived, I'd stopped dictating *Raven's Moon* and rushed off to order an exact replacement: solid black Mustang Shelby GT 500 with all the perks except silver stripe detailing and spoiler. The stripe would have killed the stealth thing and the spoiler just gave things with claws something to grab onto.

"What sorta problem you got?" one of the men asked, his eyes never leaving the car. As the name embroidered on the left side of his uniform said *Nolan* and I was looking for a Nolan Frye, I closed the car door and said, "Same one you've got. I'm looking for Eric Winthur."

"Don't tell me the kid screwed something up with the electronics. Hell, he's the best man I've got for those things."

"Nah. The car's still under warranty for everything." I passed him one of my cards.

He looked at it. "A private dick?"

"There are those who leave off the *private*," I said.

All three of them laughed.

"Do you have a few minutes to spare to answer a few questions, Mr. Frye?"

"There a possibility I could take this baby for a spin if I do?" Frye wheedled.

"Depends on the answers."

"Many of them?"

"Probably enough to make it wise for the dazzling repartee to be exchanged out of the cold," I said. Maybe it was a strong hint. Despite my many layers, and having just exited a toasty warm Ford cocoon, Father Winter was attempting a fast freeze on my toes, nose, and various exposed parts. Needed to put one of those ear covering knit hats on my shopping list. Maybe fur-lined boots rather than the Tony Lamas. I'd miss the extra height the heels supplied, but most people would think six-two in stockinged feet was sufficient for most men's needs.

Frye waved his boys back to work and led the way toward a small office. The walls were lined with shelves of boxed replacement parts, parts catalogs, automotive magazines, and dealer detail sheets. The desk was wide, metal, battered, and barely left room for Frye's padded desk chair and the two unpadded folding chairs before it. I pulled one away from the wall as much as possible to avoid giving myself an inadvertent concussion on the edge of a metal shelf bracket. The scents of motor oil, grease, rubber, and substances I couldn't name drifted in from the bays. Country western music hits mixed with advertisements for local firms and national products blared from the multiple speakers. "Could you give the door a shove,

Mr. Farrell? It's one thing to have the radio blasting when I'm processing invoices, another when a conversation needs to be had."

I leaned forward and gave it the required shove. On the back of the door, below the glass pane that looked out into the shop, was an old-fashioned pin-up calendar featuring a twenty-something woman in very skimpy lingerie. To keep warm, the model had added a bright red feather boa that framed the rest of her nicely. Doubted the door ever got closed if a female customer needed to go over paperwork for a repair. Some would have fits, others would shrug. Maybe roll their eyes.

I wondered how Naomie would take to the idea of getting one for our office when we moved back into the mansion. I'd sell it as *inspirational.* She'd probably go for it if I bought a Boris Vallejo/Julie Bell fantasy illustration one. Mentally, I put it on the growing shopping list.

"So, what do you need to know?" Frye asked.

"Had Winthur been missing work, getting calls that had him asking to duck out early?"

"Neither. Until he went on that late-night emergency call, he was the kind of kid a man hopes will stay on, although I knew that wasn't going to happen. He's nearly finished with his college work and was lining up interviews at the Big Three."

That's Ford, Chrysler, and General Motors, to you non-Detroitites.

"Heck, if he had been getting calls and asking off, I would have figured it was one of them calling him to come in to talk job placement," Frye said.

Time to take another track. "I understand he recently broke up with his girlfriend. Did he seem despondent, lackluster, absent-minded over that?" Since I knew what Jamie Rand looked like, it was how I might feel. They had been considering the *M* word, after all.

Frye leaned back in his chair. "Quiet. Not joking around as much with the other guys as he had previously. But women tend to come and go when a man least expects it. At least, they have in my experience."

Considering he was forty pounds overweight, had a pronounced, natural tonsure, and the mark of his profession discoloring the skin around his nails, he wasn't exactly an award-winning specimen. The women who *were* curious enough to take a chance probably took to the hills when they found the sexist calendar.

Pretending I hadn't already talked to Jamie, I tossed another idea at him. "Did he mention another woman had caught his eye, then? Or that his girlfriend had found a replacement for him?"

Frye shook his head. "Don't know about her, but Jamie was the only girl he ever talked about, and he could go on about her for hours. She's a looker, and the few times she stopped by here, I could swear she had no plans to replace him. Hell, when she looked at him, you'd have thought he'd stepped off that mountain where the gods live in those old Greek and Roman tales. Worshipped the ground the kid walked on, or near enough to. Then he came in looking like death warmed over a couple weeks back and said they'd broken up. But time heals all. He's a good-looking kid. I figured he'd be talking about a new girl before long."

I nodded sagely, then went off on a different tangent.

"He into any particular sports? Fantasy team stuff? Betting on his favorites?" If anybody would know this, I figured it would be the guys with whom he worked.

"Small change stuff," Frye said. "We'd all throw something in the pot for bets on the Lions and the Pistons. Wins are split even-steven."

I hadn't suspected gambling but wasn't the sort of investigator who left stones unturned. Maybe overlooked until I tripped on them at times, but occasionally it took more detail before an information stone even looked like a stone.

"He ever talk about the genealogy stuff he was doing for his grandmother?"

"You mean the search for The Babe? You seen that picture he had from the Thirties? Talk about a looker. From what I remember him saying, they weren't sure who she was but thought she was a relative. There was something about her that reminded me a bit of Winthur, but only now and then. Couldn't tell you if it was cheekbones, a similarity around the eyes or what, just that it was there. Why, you think looking up family members who woulda croaked long ago is dangerous? Hell, the gal in that picture would be over a hundred now. Not much of a chance she'd still be around."

I agreed with him, but I had one last question. Well, maybe two.

"Winthur took a call for emergency road service just before he vanished. Are the calls recorded to authenticate billing to Triple A and various insurance companies with similar benefit services?"

"That's a good idea, but no one's requested anything of that sort when we present invoices. They want a copy of the log. Time the call came in, what the problem is, where the vehicle is, and which company membership card is being used. It's a form thing. Used to be all paper with three copies, one going to the customer who made the call. Today, it's all electronic. Winthur set up the form but no further information was ever added. The service ID card that was given over the phone was missing one number. One in the middle of a long string the company said. As no service was supplied; they felt it was a waste of time to contact any of the customers it might have been, and the cop who interviewed me didn't think it was worth pursuing either. He said that if he'd been the one calling for help, if no one had shown within half hour of their expected arrival time, he would have called elsewhere, and he'd figured that's what this motorist had done."

Yeah, it definitely hadn't been Durkin's case. He wouldn't brush something like that off. Heck, one number missing? A computer could run the list with a stipulation of gathering all Detroit area card holders, or even all Michigan and Northern Ohio ones. It might take a couple days, but Eric Winthur had been missing for much longer than a couple days.

I had one hole yet to fill. "Has the tow truck Winthur was driving turned up?"

"Yeah. Cops found it in River Rouge. Door was locked but the driver side window was smashed. The toolboxes had been pried open and cleaned out. The gas tank had been siphoned and the tires and hubcaps stolen. So had the license plates. Cops used the serial number to track it back to us," Frye said. "When I saw it, I was surprised things under the hood hadn't been cannibalized or the upholstery ripped apart, but it was a relief that replacement and repairs would be easy to do to get it back up and running."

"I suppose you've cleaned it up by now, but would you mind if I took a look?" I asked, not that I knew what I was looking for. Inspiration, perhaps.

"Won't mind at all, Mr. Farrell, but considering the cops put it in their compound as evidence on the case, I may never see that vehicle again," Frye answered. "You have any further questions?"

I admitted I was fresh out but asked if he could send me a copy of the service order Winthur had set up. When he said he would, I scribbled an e-mail address on another card, handed it to him, then shook his hand. Because he'd told me a lot of stuff that probably didn't mean a hill of cocoa beans, yet might have something crawl free, I let him sit behind the wheel of the Ravenmobile and gave him a tour of the perks I'd upgraded to.

It took a while to evict him from the car, but I'd barely gotten back on the road when I called Durkin.

As usual, he snapped his name in answering. "What now?" he demanded.

Caller ID is a bitch. He always knew it was me when I called. Gave him time to dial up a snarl before he growled his name. Like I didn't know who I was calling.

"You been on duty long enough to fancy lunch? I'm buying," I said.

"And I am obviously expected to supply answers to whatever itch you're currently scratching in exchange," he countered. "Yeah, I could eat. Just stuck at the desk shuffling paper. Where you want to meet me?"

I nearly said Denny's but going there with a guy would no doubt ruin my reputation now. Sure, Burt had been the one to introduce me to that particular location, but that was long before my post-Valentine's Day visits with the girls.

"You name it," I said. "Chances are the lovely GPS computer gal will guide me there."

"Easy to fall for those types. You do know it's a computer?"

"One with a voice that started life with a real girl."

"Who was possibly missing the looks to go with it," he said. He'd probably become a pessimist after raiding a sex phone call center for some reason.

"Don't ambush my dreams, Durkin. Name the joint."

He named one and was already holding down a booth when I found it. My computerized dream girl either hadn't wanted me to go there or she'd taken up with one of those possible assassins that were after me. She had me turn the wrong way twice. Once, her misdirection had wanted me to turn into a dead end—perfect ambush territory if I'd ever seen it. Fortunately, there had been a sign telling me it wasn't a through street. It only took one mention that your name was on a hit list to make a guy a bit jumpy. Of course, she could simply have been as new to the neighborhood as I was.

Durkin's choice of eatery was a dank bar not far from the 4th precinct that shouted *cop hangout* to me. But hey, it was a safe place to relax because nearly everyone in the joint had your back. The 4th was Durkin's *official* stomping grounds, but as the only one-hundred-percent-human cop in town who knew there were things that could do worse than just go bump in the night, the entire Detroit area was his extended beat. Considering there was more than enough to keep him busy in his own neck of these woods, he'd given me unofficial cachet to police the Otherworlder residents when necessary. He just wanted to be in the loop. Particularly when humans might be involved.

"I already ordered for you," he said.

I slid into the bench seat across from him. "What delicacy am I anticipating?"

"Burger, double beef, two kinds of cheese, bacon, token salad stuff on top, and Jack Daniel's Master Blend barbecue sauce dripping down the sides."

"I had no idea Heaven looked like this joint."

"Southside of Heaven," Durkin corrected. "Figured you'd want fries with it and as I can't have a civilian leaving here with booze on their breath—"

"And ruin your reputation as an upstanding officer of law and order," I interrupted.

"—you're having a cola. I didn't specify a brand."

"Doubt I'd know one from another," I admitted. It wasn't something that slid over my palate often. "And you're having?"

"A friggin' salad. Got a medical coming up and they aren't going to like what the scale says."

That's when the food arrived. His friggin' salad had chili poured over the top and a bowl of chips alongside it, so I didn't feel the least sorry for him.

"You in the loop on the Eric Winthur case?" I asked, coating my fries with a thick layer of tomato blood.

"Name seems familiar but not making a connection."

"Missing person. He might have landed on that list of yours. By the way, I'm hoping to finally pin down something a bit more concrete on Solomon Prisk for you. That vic the other night might be related to him and I put word out on *The Virginia* in connection with the episode."

"The what?"

"*The Virginia.* Just found out about it myself. The… er… you-know's version of a grapevine. Haven't heard anything yet, but the whisper only went out yesterday afternoon."

"You figure out what… uh…"

"Served as the evil chef?" Exchanging information without referring to details was not the easiest task I'd ever juggled, but then, Durkin was searching for ways around it, too. I gave him the old negatory head shake as I bit into the burger. Five stars for Southside eatables, whether it was Heaven or Detroit. Let's face it, you gotta love this town to consider a chunk of it akin to Heaven quite yet. Too much of Hell still to get rolled out of the Motor City.

"This Winthur have a connection to your particular neck of the woods?" Durkin asked, picking up the bottle of dressing a guy from the bar snagged for him. He pounded thick splats of creamy ranch onto his salad, inserting calories to it by the bushel.

"Yes and no. He doesn't—at least I don't think he does—know that he has an ancestral link to it. You know, similar to yours."

"He has a lotta great-grandmothers who turned banshee like mine did?" he asked quietly. Well, that was why he knew about the Otherworlders.

"Vamp," I said around another bite.

"Passed or current?"

"Latter."

Durkin stabbed a forkful of iceberg, dunked it in the ranch, then scooped up a bit of chili. "There you go again," he said before filling his mouth.

I alternated to a couple ketchup-drenched fries. "Go where again?"

"Single word answers."

"Damn, I hate when that happens. It's going to ruin my reputation as a rambler."

"Yep," he said around a second forkful.

We were both quiet for a bit, concentrating on the food. Then he said, "So?"

"So. The detective on Winthur's case was lucky to pass the test to get to your honored heights," I said. "According to the people I talked to, 1) he dissed treating the place where Winthur's vehicle was found—a company tow truck, if you're curious—as a crime scene and 2) although the kid has been fixated on a genealogical search to the point where he's skipping classes his final semester at the U, and has broken up with the cutie with whom he'd been talking wedding bells, this cop considered those things not worth pursuing."

Durkin was grinning when I finished. "There's the Raven we all love to tune out. Are you going for a Guinness record for run on sentences?"

"My lad, even I fall short of their standards," I told him. "So am I right? Is this dick a real dick or what?"

He savored more enhanced rabbit food. "One can only hope his name *is* Dick as well to top that off. But you're right. He's an idiot."

"Thank you," I said.

"Considering it's obviously not in my precinct, what do you expect me to do?" he asked.

"Durkin, Durkin, Durkin. You call and ask the imbecile assigned to the case what he can give you because you have been compiling a tally of unsolved missing person cases in the hope that some details will jump out and do the chicken dance to catch your attention and, thus, lead you to the perp." I sighed. "It isn't bad enough I have to maneuver my way through the shadows, now I have to do the thinking as well?"

"Yeah, it's the pits, ain't it, Farrell?" He was grinning.

"You know I'm right."

"Your ego's already cresting Matterhorn proportions so I'm not plopping a cherry on top for added height, pal. I'll touch base with them," he promised, then went off on a different tangent. "Whaddaya think the chances are for the Wolverines winning the game on Saturday?"

Again, an aside for non-Detroiters: Wolverines attend the University of Michigan. Not the animals, though sometimes it's hard to tell with college students. Or so I've heard.

"No idea. I'm constantly amazed that they manage to keep the balls inflated, much less lob them off those foot-long claws," I said.

"Hugh Jackman spends a couple pre-season weeks with them to teach the basics," Durkin answered with barely a pause. Yeah, he's getting far too used to me.

***

After lunch I swung by the mansion to see how things were going.

And found *nothing* was going. The blown-out windows and ruined doors were merely gaps hidden by wide swaths of plywood. I used my key to enter the main building and found that particleboard made it impossible to visit the disaster site from the inside as well as the outside. It was warmer in the main part of the house with the gaps filled, though. Almost livable.

Almost. It stilled smelled of smoke.

The only problem with camping at Naomie's was that it prevented me from roaming off for a touch of night hunting. I don't need to leave the city to do it either. Until the mansion was back to normal, my style was majorly crimped.

Granted, I hadn't left the house much since my last case at the tail end of November, but now that I had a new case, it made me itchy to stay put. Could have something to do with "staying put" sounding a lot like "sitting duck" for a professional killer.

I decided to tour the place and tally up what was on the list of things the contractor would be repairing. One of the back rooms on the lower floor had lost part of a window, another had spider-web-like cracks. Both were boarded over.

I headed up to the room directly above and found more spider webbing had been covered over. The other rooms were intact, just the taint of the fire that had followed the explosion remaining. I headed to the basement and checked on things down there. Another boarded-over window, this one missing, but it hadn't been on the side of the house where Calie's enormous wine collection was stored. Well, maybe it only appeared enormous to a fellow who preferred bourbon. There were at least ten cases, though. I needed more friends to gift the damn stuff to.

Having checked the premises, I headed for my office. Of course, it lacked a computer currently, but my cell was willing to connect to the server. At least the Web was still in reach. I found a company that took care of smoke-damaged drapes, upholstery, and carpets and gave them a call. They promised to have someone out the next day to give an estimate. I told them to skip the estimate and could they begin working tomorrow?

Sensing a chance to stiff me well and proper, the gal who managed appointments said, “We’ll have a team out around nine then, Mr. Farrell. Will that suit your schedule?”

It most definitely would as I wouldn’t be the one on-site. Naomie would be.

Which got me thinking about the advisability of her being here alone with the steam cleaners.

“Didn’t I just talk to you?” Durkin demanded in answer to my ring.

“It’s your lucky day. You get to deal with me more than once,” I said. “Listen, has Dawes got pack buddies who do security?”

“I can ask. Why?”

“My secretary will be at the mansion alone tomorrow while strangers go at the carpets and stuff to get rid of the smoke smell. Considering someone has it in for me, I’d rather have someone looking out for her.”

“You have a secretary? When did that happen?”

“January. I have damn books to write now, you know,” I growled.

“She one of yours or one of mine?” he asked.

“Dude, I’m one of a kind. There is no one who qualifies as one of mine. But, no, she’s clueless about my secret life. She’s one of yours.”

He was silent long enough for me to wonder whether he was still on the line. “You’re fond of her so she’s a weak link. Someone who could be used to get to you.”

“Bingo,” I said. “I’m leavin’ Beelz with her, but he’s limited in what he can do since he’s gotta keep his Clark Kent disguise on around her.”

“Odd,” Durkin mused. “The hound wasn’t wearing glasses when I saw him.”

I sighed. “You need to test that standup act on one of those TV talent shows. See if they can find whether you’ve got a lick of any.”

He laughed. “I’ll talk to Dawes. You want he should give you a buzz?”

"Best way to sync schedules that I know of," I said then ended the call. The damn thing let the TARDIS land immediately. It was Ruth Lund.

"*The Virginia* supplied someone I think you'd best meet," she said.

"Another ghoul?"

"Nope. Someone who can probably tell us what killed the one in my shed."

"You've still got him?" I'd thought they would make him vanish during the night.

"It's not easy finding someone who raises demon boars, Raven."

"I'd no idea that demons were bores because their parents reared them that way," I quipped.

"Oh, you're a barrel of squid monkeys," she snarled. "Pigs, idiot. Pigs with tusks. They'll eat anything and leave no evidence. You can't just bury an Otherworlder on the sly. There's always the chance some contractor will decide to dig the site up and then the archaeologists, biologists, and the Project Blue Book guys from Wright-Patterson will be crawling all over the place."

"Project Blue Book closed in 1970, Ruthie." Don't ask me how I know. There's a lot of stuff I know but don't know how I know it. Blame Calista Amberson for inadvertently pouring gibberish into my imaginary head before turning me into her pet golem in this world.

Ruth made a sound that, for a human, would constitute a guffaw but had entirely different overtones when a troll/dwarf made it. I believe she doubted the veracity of my statement.

"And here I thought cremation would be the answer," I murmured. "Silly me."

"The ghoul was already part charcoal," she said, although I was under the impression that only wood could be converted to charcoal status. But what did I know? I cooked my victims' husks. I didn't deal with making their remains vanish.

"So, who is this someone you think can solve our cause of death conundrum?" I asked.

"Come on over and find out," she invited. "He's scheduled in for a look-see at quarter to four. Be there or—"

"Be square?" I queried.

"Or miss the fun," she countered.

***

Within the past thirty-eight hours, I'd been to The Bridge late night when it was packed with the true scum of the earth and early in the day when it was deserted. Now, midway through the afternoon, there were a few customers, but when I arrived, nearly all of them were gathered around a booth in the back near the still-in-sight and roaring fire in the beyond-antique fireplace. The closer I got, the weirder it got. There were a couple male things at the bar, but a gaggle of females hovered over the man holding court in the booth.

Ruth spotted me and shoved the twittering femmes out of the way to make room for me. They had to shift again when the man got to his feet and offered his hand. I shook it. Automatic response. Don't know what I was thinking.

"The Raven in person," he mused. "It's an honor I thought impossible to be awarded."

"The Raven?" I countered. "Sure, my name's Bram Farrell but…"

"He's the Raven," Ruth assured.

I heaved a sigh. "Secret identities don't last long at The Bridge."

"Ruthie's Rules," Ruth said. "I call 'em as I see 'em."

The stranger gave her a slow smile. He'd taken the Gigolo 101 class, too, apparently. "Fortunate for me, then, that I don't have a secret identity. Now, a secret profession is an entirely different thing."

Ruth hooked a thumb at him. "He's a necromancer."

"New to town," the stranger said. "I'm Nate Townshed."

He was about my height, pale, blond and coiffed as Chris Hemsworth on a long-haired Thor day but with downsized pecs. I guessed him at around my perceived age. As a necromancer, he might be older than he looked. Like me, he wore black, but his was a business suit complete with vest, silver watch chain, and storm-colored dress shirt sporting silver cufflinks. The Van Wijk knotted black silk tie was icing.

The women around us included a princess of Faerie, a Valkyrie, a dark elf, and a selkie. Oh, and Ruthie, of course. Not a one of them seemed able to take their eyes off him.

"Nate Townshed, hmm?" I mused. "Somehow that doesn't sound like a necromantic name."

"Yeah, I know." He sounded apologetic about it. "But Benedict Cumberbatch was already taken."

The ladies twittered.

Ruth got us all back on track. "The boys have business to discuss, so either you tarts order something or hit the streets. Those johns aren't going to come in here looking for candy, you know."

She still had to shoo then off with a flap of her apron. Which was quite a trick considering she barely came up to their waists.

Now down to three, and two of us towering over her, Ruth rubbed her hands together in anticipation. "All right, gents, let's head out back."

I was still bundled up. Townshed reached back into the booth for a snazzy overcoat. Being a necromancer paid well, I suppose. But then, not everyone was content with a Target-heavy wardrobe like I am. Ruth sensibly donned a cape she might have lifted from Red Riding Hood's closet. It was lined with wolf fur, in any case.

I indicated Townshed should go through the door ahead of me, allowing me to size him up. "You're human," I murmured, a bit surprised.

"And you're not," he countered. "Well, maybe a touch here and there. Golem?"

I hated to be termed that even if I met most of the requirements. "Fictional," I countered.

"I told Nate about our problem, Bram" Ruth said.

"Which problem would that be, sugar? There tend to be a myriad of the things."

"About getting rid of the roast and sorting out how he happened to be roasted, of course. Nate's got a demon sow with a litter of shoats that will take care of the disposal problem, but he knows a lot—"

"A bit," Townshed corrected.

"—about curses that kill in rather nasty ways."

"You probably know far more than I do, Farrell," the necromancer said.

Wasn't about to admit I knew diddly about such things. I didn't kill via curse. I tossed variations on elemental sources.

"This one has me stumped," I returned. 'Cause, well, it did. I was totally clueless on what had cooked the ghoul. "Ruthie's rooting for the instantaneous combustion thing that occasionally does in the odd human here and there. She's the expert. Saw a show about it on cable. I'm not buying that. And not just because our vic isn't human."

"Interesting," he mused.

Ruth had the lock on the shed door open, but not the door itself. She dipped her hands into her apron pockets and freed two flashlights. She handed one to each of us. "Time to take a deep breath, gents. It's the last breathable moment you'll have for a while."

"You forget, Ms. Lund, that I work with the dead and not necessarily the recently dead," Townshed said.

"Take a *deep* breath now," I recommended. "Trust me. This is one nasty-smelling stiff."

I followed my own advice before Ruth pulled the door open. Unfortunately for the necromancer, he hadn't taken our advice and inhaled sharply in surprise when the scent hit him.

"Told ya," I said, though the comment was muffled by the gloved hand I had pressed over my nose and mouth.

By the glow of the flashlights, if anything, our deader was even less appealing than the day before. He'd been freshly-dead then. Now he was seasoned. You'd have thought that, considering the overnight temperatures, he'd have frozen solid. Instead, he looked fresh from the oven.

If an oven had been involved.

"The Devil!" Townshed gasped.

I didn't think he was calling for Samael, but you never know.

"I'm not surprised you couldn't identify what killed him."

"Other than the roasting," I said.

"It's a rare curse—"

Though it certainly had left the victim nowhere near a *rare* searing.

"—so few have seen one of its victims before. Frankly, from what I've read, there isn't this much left of one of the victims very often. You say it probably happened out-of-doors? If so, the air temperature might have prevented total consumption." Townshed was clearly thinking out loud. Or lecturing. I hoped there wouldn't be a pop quiz.

"What's this curse do exactly?" I asked.

"And what's it called?" Ruth added.

Townshed hunkered down next to the corpse, something I'd avoided doing. It still lay twisted, the result of the shove I'd given it with my foot the day before.

"The street name is Heart Burn," he said. "More properly, *Consumpta est Cor Meum*, or The Heart Consumed."

"That's a new one to me," Ruth admitted. "Is it ancient?"

Townshed tipped his hand back and forth. "It depends on what you use as the standard for ancient. Alchemic, yes, so it could date back before current era. There were some nasty sorcerers making deals with demons as far back as the Hittite empire, but I'm more inclined toward the Renaissance or Age of Reason. Say fifteenth through eighteenth centuries."

Odd that I knew someone I suspected as having been around since then, isn't it? Palermo, to be specific—the vamp I figured had turned a certain knockout from the 1930s into the slinky Wendy Whilsen who sang breathy swing standards at The Red Dragon.

"How's it work?" I inquired.

Townshed planted a hand on his thigh and pushed to his feet. "It's a touch-activated curse. A double touch. It's not fussy over what a victim is, either. Testaments claim even demons and angels aren't immune to it; they just need to be in a physical form for it to invoke. It works whether planted directly to the skin or through clothing. Brushing against the target in a crowd or delivered via fisticuffs or a caress are the most common ways to confer it to the intended victim."

Now that was just…

"Eww," Ruth said. "You'd never see that one coming."

I totally agreed with her. On both points.

"That's merely the delivery method," Townshed continued. "The curse doesn't activate until the receiver either rubs or scratches the point where contact was made. As I understand it, there is a fluttering sensation. The victim may ignore it at first, but the repeated movement will promote an unconscious response to sooth the irritation. And that touch by the victim themselves activates it.

"If the contact point was over the heart, death will arrive swiftly. If delivered on a vein, the curse moves to the heart and then flares to life. A body's normal functions pump it throughout the victim, then the heart totally ignites. Depending on when the victim rubbed the contact point, hours could pass before the curse activates. Once it does, the victim is in agony from anywhere from two minutes to five. This gentleman," he indicated the roasted ghoul at his feet, "might actually have endured the pain longer if he was out-of-doors when it activated."

"Geez," I whispered.

"This is all hearsay, of course," Townshed qualified. "I'm merely giving you a summary of an entry in an obscure text from my library. Not many have ever seen one of the victims, and frankly, only an alchemist at the top of their profession can create this curse. They can't hand it off to an associate or hired assassin to deliver. It has to come from their hand, and wizards of that class rarely lower themselves to the level of paid killer."

Just what Detroit needed, a rogue alchemist hiring out as an assassin.

Great Grendal's balls! I hoped like hell they weren't one of the assassins determined to come after me.

"I'll be back within half an hour with the hearse to claim him, Ms. Lund," Townshed said.

Ruthie gave a heartfelt sigh. "I'll be glad to be rid of him."

"You have a card, Townshed? I think it would be wise to add you to the old Rolodex," I said.

"Absolutely!" He plucked one from his coat pocket and passed it over. "While my farm is as far from civilization as it was possible to be, I am in the city most days following my regular profession."

"You have a job beyond necromancy?" I blurted in surprise.

Ruth chuckled. "Yeah. A real kick in the pants job. He's a mortician."

That's when I turned my flashlight on the card. "Fontaine's Funeral Home?"

Townshed grinned. "You've heard of us then? It's all those billboards they've got, isn't it?"

"I like the ones on the sides of buses," Ruth piped up. "They're tasteful."

I tucked his card into my back pocket. "Hell, Townshed. I've not only heard of Fontaine's, I nearly had to use the services."

"For a dispatched Otherworlder?" he asked politely, though I thought there was a glint of interest in his blue eyes.

"Hell, no," I snarled. "For myself."

***

Jamie Rand had given me the name of the sports bar where Eric frequently met his buddies. As there was a game being televised that night, she said they'd probably all be on hand.

I had their names, of course. Wendy had supplied them. Also had a photograph from among those Naomie had printed off from the various social media sites. Now it was time to discover what they could contribute to my font of information regarding the missing man. It was too early yet to find any of them ensconced there, though, so I headed into Dearborn and my favorite place to shop. Even snagged a spiffy red shopping cart when I walked in the door.

I headed toward housewares first. Beelz needed a bowl that would fit in Naomie's food nuker. I bought two, one a backup in the event the one that went into the microwave was too hot to use when it came out of the microwave. Next stop was the grocery section. Two cans of Dinty Moore would see him through the evening. A box of twelve glazed donuts would see all of us through the morning, even if there were no sprinkles, chocolate, maple or cinnamon topping. No tasty filling. He and I were camping at her place, after all. One had to rough it.

From there, it was the pet department for an honest-to-goodness dog dish for water, a swing through the men's department for that hat to keep my ears from getting frostbite, then on to footwear for boots with furry stuff inside. Seems they thought winter was over. In any case, they had zip. I bought heavier socks instead. Added a pair of sunglasses, too. Sun glare off fresh snow is a bitch.

With Beelz and I taken care of, I turned to the next batch of items on my list. Needed to turn Nomes into something Eric's friends would want at their table while I pelleted them with questions. I tracked down a salesgirl in the women's department, told her what was required, then set her free. I took a break in the snack area with a bag of popcorn and a soft drink to wash it down.

When the salesgirl found me, she bubbled about the choices she'd made and why they were good ones. All I had to do was look at them to know they were. I shook her hand to show my appreciation. She might have been surprised to find a twenty had stuck to her palm when I let go.

I had enough bags to load into the car to give the impression I'd been shopping for the long-past holidays, but I was one content fellow when I slipped behind the wheel and gave Nomes a call to see if she was still out and about or back at her place.

"We just got here." She sounded a bit breathless, like she'd run up the stairs. I had a feeling that, when not burdened with something to carry, that was her favorite mode of locomotion. She certainly took the stairs at the mansion at a dash. "Burt's bringing the boxes in. Are we going to sort through them tonight? Should I order pizza delivery?"

"Nope. We're headed out for more investigating tonight. I'm in Dearborn so, depending on traffic, I'll be back shortly. See you then."

Less than thirty minutes later, I slid the Mustang next to her Spark.

Her place looked out over the parking lot. Burt's taxi was gone but I could see two faces in the window above me when I popped the trunk and climbed out of the Ravenmobile. One canine, one human, both with welcoming grins on their faces.

The door was already open when I hit the top of the stairs. Beelz rushed forth to leap about my feet. Naomie looked tempted to do the same but restrained herself, hovering in the doorway instead.

Beelz barked a couple questions at me.

"Yes, I brought you food, both for dinner and breakfast. You can have the pretzels I didn't touch last night in between," I told him.

He gave me a nod of satisfaction and trotted ahead down the hall and around Nomes. Probably headed for the beanbag chair he'd claimed. I might have to buy him one of his own when we were able to move back home.

"You always seem to know what he says, and he understands what you say," she said in wonderment.

"Hell, he understands what you say, too. He's a friggin' genius in the canine world," I said.

"No, it's different with you," she insisted. "He's simply got me trained to think he understands me, but it's probably body language he uses to make me do what he wants me to do."

"I've just been around him longer," I asserted, though that wasn't the case in the least. He'd understood every insult I hurled at him my first day on this side of the binding. At the time, I'd thought it rather embarrassing for a guy my size to be seen being walked by a hot dog, even if we did have the same taste when it came to the color of our coats.

It was only then that she seemed to notice the confluence of bags I was toting. "Did you get cold last night, boss? I'm sorry that there was just that one thin blanket to lend you, but—"

"You mean these things?" I let the bags slip from my grip to nestle on the sofa. A couple rebels spilled to the floor. "Not a bit of bedding in the lot."

It took a few seconds, but I rifled through the heaviest ones first and emptied them into her hands. "Dog tableware, food for dog, food for breakfast."

"Oh, that makes sense," she said.

She wasn't going to think the rest of it made sense. I waited until she deposited the things in her arms in the kitchen. As there was no counter and computer gear now filled the table, the stove was doing double-duty as a place to dump things.

"Now," I said, "let me tell you what's on tap for the evening."

With the remaining bags still taking up most of the couch, and me taking up a large part of the remaining space, Nomes perched on the cushy padded arm. She'd kicked her damp boots off near the door so her feet were covered in black knit socks and rested on the sofa cushions barely six inches from where I sat. The long, shapeless layers she draped herself in daily cascaded around her as she leaned forward, elbows on knees, chin in her hands. Those pretty green eyes sparkled with excitement.

I left Wendy out of my story, but I filled in a bit about Eric. She'd already met Jamie. I let her think Eric's grandmother had hired me, though it had been his vampiric great-grandmother, of course. Told her what I'd learned both from Jamie and Eric's boss. Then I did a mock drum roll on my thigh. "And now we come to the part where you become a different person to help me gather even more information. Hopefully, lots more."

Her eyes widened. "I'm going undercover?"

"Sorta," I said. "I need you to be a distraction."

"Me?"

I heard exclamation points get added. Where are those interrobangs when you need them?

"Of course, you," I said. "I'm not a distraction to guys." Maybe a threat, but not a distraction. "You, on the other hand, have all the necessary accoutrements. I simply bought some accessories to make you stand out."

I handed her all but one of the bags. "And, before you ask, no, I did not choose these personally. A very helpful salesgirl around your age, height, and build did so. I told her you wanted to make a splash, but in a tasteful way."

Did not tell her lingerie had been included and, well, I'm a guy—I *had* given that the once-over. I totally approved of my helper's choice. But then, I'd kinda implied the entire get-up was a make-up gift for my girlfriend whom I'd disappointed on Valentine's Day. Claimed a flight delay due to weather had trapped me in Denver. Heck, I'd been on a roll with that story. The salesgirl had bought it, and even told me that she wished her boyfriend was as generous. Yeah, I ruined things for her guy but good.

"Since I need to use the microwave in the bedroom to serve up Beelz's stew, maybe you should use the bathroom to change," I suggested. "When you're done, I'll grab a shower and we can be on our way."

"Okay," Naomie murmured, sounding hesitant. Just wait until she got a look at what was in the bags.

Nomes disappeared with the purchases. Before I could fill Beelz in on my day, there was a partial shriek heard from the bathroom.

"She just found the underwear," I told him.

Though it was difficult since I had to avoid words like *ghoul, necromancer,* and *death curse* in the telling, I laid out how the case was going as he downed the Dinty and indicated more was needed. As I nuked the second helping, I asked him if he'd mind watching over our girl the next day, though warned him there might be a werewolf there as his backup. "You'll be the only true canine on the premises. Don't know who it will be, but we can hope he takes direction well from you."

Beelz rumbled a comment.

"Yeah, I know. A far inferior being, but you take the muscle where you can find it, right?"

He sighed. I recognized it as reluctant agreement.

The bathroom door was still firmly shut and Beelz had

thoroughly cleaned the bowl free of any hint of stew when my phone rang.

"I understand you need a watchdog for your secretary tomorrow," Dawes said.

"Actually, I have a watchdog. A vicious dachshund."

The werewolf snorted.

I moved as far away as I could get from Naomie's current changing room so she wouldn't overhear the conversation. "She's a straight so Beelz can't exactly follow his natural inclination if there's trouble," I said.

"So I don't turn either."

"I get you, not another howler? Whoa, but yes, no matter what the provocation you don't turn."

"You think there will be provocation?" he asked.

"Hoping things will be quiet, but why take the chance?"

"Makes sense to me. What's she like?"

What was Naomie like? Hmm. "Once upon a time she thought wearing jewelry that consisted of silver skulls made her goth, but actually, she hasn't the least idea of what being goth entails beyond having an all-black wardrobe and black hair. I've a suspicion her locks aren't naturally black. Beelz and I humor her."

"Guessing here, but she doesn't know you're doing that?"

"Not so far. She's as innocent as the night is long at winter solstice. Enthusiastic. Bubbly, even. Perky. Totally devoted. Loves the damn dog and he loves her back. If he could morph into a two-legged form, they'd run off together."

Dawes chuckled. "Sounds like you envy the mutt."

Yeah, maybe a bit. He got to cozy up to her. Despite that innocent kiss she had given me on the cheek, I was still weighing scenarios to be able to do the same. According to the trusty Internet, moving into or lingering within each other's personal space indicated some sort of magnetic pull had been engaged. We'd been doing that ever since her first day behind the desk at the mansion. Of course, I'd been clueless about it being an indication of attraction at the time. I just liked to inhale her scent—a sweet combination of vanilla and lavender that was nearly as heady as freshly-baked cinnamon rolls. Other websites warned that there was a certain protocol involved in this world as couples danced around each other. Residents of the real world were sticklers on these sorts of things the so-called experts insisted. In fictionland, we just jumped each other. No waiting period necessary.

"Beelz has the much easier life," I insisted to Dawes. "He doesn't have to write books."

"I should meet her ahead of time," the wolf said. "Let's face it, a stranger my size might be scarier than a pixy with a lethal hat pin, though the pixy would kill her in a flash."

"A hat pin? How old are you? Not a female around wears the type of hats that require pins to hold them in place."

"You, my friend, obviously don't hang out with Steampunkers."

He was right. I had my hands full with Otherworlders. I knew Steampunk existed—hey, I'd watched *League of Extraordinary Gentlemen, Wild, Wild West, Legend,* and *Penny Dreadful*, though that last one is more Gaslamp fantasy—but I hadn't been curious enough to extend my knowledge.

"And you do?" I sounded stunned to even be asking.

"Damn right, my friend. As long as I'm wearing tweed, a weskit, have a pocket watch to check and a bowler set at a cocky angle, I can even go partially wolf and pose as a science experiment gone wrong. Now, beyond those far-from-fancy goth colors, what else can you tell me about her? She tall, thin, stout, short, pushing forty, have a boyfriend who might take exception to me hanging around?"

I considered a moment. "When she's got her two-inch heeled boots on, the top of her head is even with my chin. Soaking wet, she might nudge the scales to 110. Bites her nails. Chews her lip, sinking her teeth into the corner when concentrating."

"Eyes?" he growled.

"Two of them."

"Farrell."

"Green. Dazzling shade of emerald. Long, mascara brushed lashes."

"Skin?"

"Covers every bit of her, though I'm only guessing."

Dawes growled.

"Pale. There's a chance she freckles in the summer. I haven't been this side of the binding for a summer yet, though, so that's a mystery to solve months from now."

"Lips?"

"I believe they were mentioned."

"Yeah, but you were fixated on the way she chews on them," he insisted.

Fixated? Me?

"The shape, Farrell. Are they thin, full, bottom one plumper than the top?"

It was my turn to growl.

"Do you look at them and just want to taste them?"

"Secretary, Dawes. Sacrosanct. Drawin' the line. Hands off." Well, temporarily, at least.

"Okay, okay. *Pax,* fiction boy. If you had only one word to describe her, what would it be?"

One word. That was not my forte despite the flings I'd taken with single words lately. *Girl next door* was more than one word, though it was Naomie to a T. *Cute* didn't seem enough right. *Funny*, yeah, that could work but that was personality, not looks. Naomie was…

Beelz looked up, his muzzle turned toward the bathroom door. It opened hesitantly, then she stepped forth.

I nearly forgot I was in the middle of a conversation.

"One word, Dawes?" I said as I stared at Naomie. "Gorgeous."

***

"Whoa," Dawes breathed, and he couldn't even see her. "You need to introduce us tonight, Farrell. Where can we meet?"

I was on automatic. Gave him the name and address of the sports bar we'd be trawling for info. He gave me an ETA, but I had no idea what he said.

"This is so not me, boss," Naomie said as I ended the call. She stood in the doorway, the lights over the sink still glowing behind her, outlining her.

As I'd surmised, she really was a girl under all those concealing, draped layers she usually wore. The Target staffer had found a niche between fashion shoot and funereal widow, which was what I always thought Nomes had aimed for as her style statement. Now, a pair of spike-heeled boots reached above her knees, black tights covered her thighs, and a full but damn flirty black wool mini skirt was topped off by a dark charcoal-toned, loose sweater with sleeves long enough to nearly cover her hands. It had a tendency to slip off one ivory shoulder, placing a single bright red silky strap in view. When she hitched the shoulder up, the sweater dipped forward to display lots of blushing female flesh and a glimpse of the red lace and ribbons that constituted the rest of that slinky bit of fantasy wear. Well, *my* fantasies regarding her, at least. Nomes had done her eyes up, but not as drastically as they'd been on post-Valentine's night. Her straight black hair looked freshly brushed and plumped.

Every element I'd conjectured about Nomes during the hours of both day and night hadn't been delusions fueled by Evan Williams, but accurate as… well, damned if they hadn't materialized in living color. Okay, pseudo-color. Everything but the lingerie was still an off cast of black. Of course, I could not let her know she took my breath away.

Yet.

Further indications that she might feel the same about me were needed, the Internet had warned. So, counseled by that auspiciously glutted source of information—both accurate and as phony as a moon made of green cheese—who was I to say it nay? All my previous romantic conquests had been Otherworlder or fictional, or both. If nothing else, my movie consumption these past months hinted that the human female probably wasn't as ready to hear a starter pistol's report as I currently was.

"So not you, Nomes? That's the whole concept of going undercover as a distraction," I said to cover the direction my thoughts were galloping.

"I just don't see myself as the type of girl to distract anyone."

"Trust me, sugar. I'm a guy. You're distracting in that get up." Well, my libido was straining at the reins, in any case.

As Beelz's style was not cramped by human society's rules, he trotted over, circled her, came to a stop at her toes, reared up, and attempted to hump her leg.

To hide my case of canine envy, I pointed at him. "That's high praise, toots. Trust us—tonight, you're hot."

She disengaged from the amorous pooch. "Still not sure I can do this, boss."

"You won't be alone. I'll be right there, running through the entire repertoire of territorial poses guys do to denote possession of a girl." 'Cause as far as I was concerned, she was claimed property. *Mine*. "They'll stare at you, flirt with you, joke around to win a laugh from you, but the message being given is that you're going home with the guy you walked in with," I assured her. "Think you can act like you expect me to behave that way?"

How to describe the look on her face? Hmm. Stunned probably covered it, but then she perked up, obviously struck with a thought that had nothing to do with the remodel to her wardrobe. She didn't answer my question but instead announced, "I nearly forgot. I got you something today, too, boss."

I was pleased to note she didn't wobble on those lethal heels. Her usual long stride looked… well, awesome now that there was a long length of leg on display. Yeah, the gams were covered in cotton and plastic mock leather, but every streamlined inch was being hugged by that fabric. The skirt sashayed with each step.

I was in guy heaven just watching her move.

She found her purse. Bent over it.

Be still my heart.

"Here," she said after a quick rifle through it, then held her hand up. "I had a key made for you. This way you don't have to wait for me to get back, and you can lock the door when you leave."

Great Dagwanoenyent, blow me over. No female had ever given me a key to her place before. Not back home in fictionland. Not here in the real world. Not even Calie. She'd just expected me to be able to get back into the mansion without one.

"Nomes," I said.

"Common sense for you to have one, boss. Burt agreed with me. We stopped and had one cut after we dropped Lex off, but before we went to Jamie's." She waited for me to take it from her outstretched hand.

Felt like one of the labors of Hercules to do so.

So I didn't do so.

"Probably better grab that shower so we can be on our way," I said, tearing my eyes off her. Well, off the delightfully playful sweater that had slipped again. Best to remove myself from the scene. Take a cold shower rather than a warm one. In February.

“Sure.” Naomie dropped onto the couch and put her booted feet onto the short table in front of it.

Beelz jumped onto the sofa next to her, nudged her hand in a demand for attention, then put his head on her thigh, the lucky mutt. They were the picture of contentment.

I grabbed one of the Target suitcases acquired the day before and headed for the shower, change of clothes in hand. Before I closed the door, I noticed that the red strap peeking from Nomes’ new sweater was the same shade of scarlet as her lately-acquired sofa.

***

I’d describe the joint we expected to find Eric Winthur’s friends at, however, just saying *sports bar* should be a description in and of itself, just as *mansion* was for the Amberson place. The noise level was deafening, particularly when a player festooned in Michigan’s colors put the ball through a bit of recycled fisherman’s macramé. I think it’s called sinking a putt, but I could be wrong. Just in case, I planned to avoid responding to any and all sports-sounding questions, comments, or requests for my opinion.

My game of choice was called *Play It Safe.*

While I had a couple selfie downloads to identify Eric’s pals with, Jamie had given me a further heads-up on how to find them. “They’re doing an economy cosplay,” she explained. “Men seriously lacking a sports gene pretending they know what’s going on. One of them was working the campus bookstore a couple years back and got them all discounted team shirts to wear. Once or twice during the football and basketball seasons, they pull the shirts on and hit the sports bar. Eric’s the closest any of them come to being a jock and he’s only interested in swimming, nothing else.”

She’d been right; it was easy to spot the guys. They were the only ones with unfaded UM sweatshirts on. A simple observation around the room would have shown them the error of their costumer ways.

They were holding down a round table just off the long bar and beneath a large flat screen affixed to the ceiling mount. The TV was a slightly smaller one than I owned. The guys had either turned chairs to face the screen or were straddling them for the same view. Wasn’t a femme among them. Either it was guys' night out or none of them had stumbled across a girl who cared to engage in sports fan cosplay.

I had my arm draped over Naomie's shoulders, holding her tight to my side, as we ambled up to their table. I pinned one of the fellas with a look as his gaze left the screen and settled on Naomie. He nearly choked on a half-swallowed swig of beer. I'd bought her a better coat to go with the rest of her ensemble. Yeah, black but it nearly brushed the floor, was heavy wool, and sported a fake, fox-fur rolled collar. It had been buttoned up, keeping her camouflaged until we were through the door, then, though she had shivered doing so, she'd opened it to put the glories of her new duds to work.

"Vic Tanaka?" I asked.

Eric Winthur's best friend looked up. "Uh, what? I mean, uh, yeah?" he sputtered. It took an effort, but he forced himself to glance at me for a hundredth of a microsecond before returning his peepers to the more agreeable occupation of worshipping Nomes.

I offered my hand. "Name's Farrell. Mind if we join you? We're looking for Eric Winthur."

Something was in progress on the screen. As though required, his eyes flicked to it just as the rest of the men at the table stopped watching the game and admired my secretary instead. One of them jumped to his feet and offered her his chair. Nomes smiled shyly, thanked him, and swiveled into it. I had no idea she could do that sort of move.

"Winthur's not with us tonight," Tanaka said. "No idea where he is."

On the big screen, a player bounced a ball from one hand to another. Other players lined up on either side in honor guard formation, or a 3-D mirror representation of *The Last Supper*, only without the table. Or the long togas and shawls. An official in a black-and-white striped shirt gave a signal and the ball went airborne. An unseen crowd went bonkers and an irritating horn sounded. Everyone in the place turned their attention away from the various flat screens, continuing previously abandoned conversations. Even the folks in the well-worn team shirts.

"Any of you guys know where Winthur's got himself to?" Tanaka asked. He was faking the casual air. The white knuckled grip he had on the beer mug tattled on him.

I passed him one of my cards.

"Oh," he murmured and passed the card along to the guy on his right, who passed it along to his right, etc., until it returned to Tanaka's hand.

"I have a few questions, if you guys can give me a couple minutes of your time." To ensure that they would, I helped Nomes off with her coat. Rather than let her hang on to it—'cause she'd grip it tightly to her front if I did—I tucked it under my arm.

"Sure," one of the others said. "It's half time."

Is that like Happy Hour? From the way the wait staff was hastening away from tables to the bar or kitchen and then back to take further orders, it felt that way.

Seemed this table had a standing order for the night. A waitress slipped into the nearly non-existence space between two of the seated guys to place a fresh pitcher of beer onto the table. "Two more mugs?" she asked, glancing at Nomes and me.

I shook my head. Told her we were expecting a friend and would order when he joined us. She took off toward another batch of patrons.

Tanaka gestured toward the card on the table before him. "You think you'll have a better chance of finding him than the cops have?"

"Wouldn't have taken the case if I didn't think so."

One of the other men was attempting to chat Naomie up. Her voice was hesitant when she answered his sad attempt. Making it seem like a natural move, I dropped my hand onto her shoulder. The one the sweater had slipped off. Didn't give the rest of them even a glance.

"I'm trying to piece together Winthur's movements in the days leading up to his disappearance. Did any of you notice something out of the ordinary in the way he was acting?"

"Other than being in the dumps over Jamie giving him marching papers?" the man across from Tanaka asked.

"I've already talked to Ms. Rand. She mentioned phone calls at odd hours, missed classes. Anything you can add to that? Perhaps something you overheard him say? A name, an address?"

They exchanged looks, shrugged. "Nope. We got nuthin'," Tanaka admitted.

"'Cept the picture of that hot babe from the Thirties," another of them said. "If he wasn't fantasizing about her, I sure was. Figured she'd have one of those whiskey voices."

Didn't have to guess at it myself. If the picture was indeed of Miss Sweden 1934, I knew she did.

"Hey," the guy next to Tanaka said. "Didn't Eric say he had this weird feeling like someone was watching him?"

"Yeah," agreed the only guy wearing a dress shirt. Hell, he even had a pocket protector in the chest pocket and a tie pulled loose at the collar. His attempt to blend in was a classic dark blue ball cap with a yellow serif font *M* on the front. "He even asked me to hang back as he was leaving class to see if anyone followed him to his car one night. I didn't see anything suspicious, but then, everyone was fleeing the campus at that hour."

Naomie had been quietly talking to the guy next to her. He was attempting to flirt. I think she was attempting to flirt back. Neither had the least idea what they were doing. But it seemed she'd also been paying attention to what the other men were saying. She glanced up at me. "You mentioned a tow truck, but did anyone look for clues that might be in his car?"

Out of the mouths of babes. And a hot babe, at that.

"What kind of car does Winthur drive?" I asked the table at large.

"Decade-old Honda CR-V. Blue one," one of the guys said.

"Light blue," another corrected.

"Was he crashing with any of you guys? The car parked near your place?"

Tanaka shrugged. "Considering he disappeared while driving the company truck, I'd think it was parked near the garage where he works."

Not a single person I'd talked to had mentioned Winthur's vehicle. The case had seemed to revolve around the trashed tow truck. But if Eric thought someone was following him, maybe there were hints in his car about places he'd visited just before he vanished.

I leaned down and whispered, "Be right back," into Naomie's ear.

She gave me a deer-in-the-headlights look so I squeezed her shoulder for assurance. These guys were harmless. "Just let them drool from afar," I whispered, then headed out into the cold to call Durkin.

"I'm off duty," he said rather than bark his name.

I ignored that ridiculous statement. "Eric Winthur's car. Did anybody on his case happen to look for it?"

"Not a clue," Durkin admitted.

"Bet there are clues just asking to be found in it. I'm betting that if it was parked on the street near where he works, it got towed as an abandoned car."

"Damn, you're a pest," he said. "Since it isn't my case, I'll call in a favor from someone in Records and find out. It'll be tomorrow, though."

"Tomorrow works," I said and disconnected. I doubted I'd be allowed a chance to look over the car, but maybe getting a nudge to set an evidence team on it would move the official investigation along. I'd have to leave it in DPD hands.

That's when Dawes loped up. "You out here looking for me?"

"Nope. Irritating Durkin."

"Always a fun game," the wolf agreed. "Your girlfriend inside?"

"My *secretary* is inside and currently surrounded by slavering geeks."

"Want I should scare 'em?" he offered.

"Nah. If Nomes looked like she was interested in one of them, the dude would faint dead away. They're pretending they like sports."

"Like you know what any of that's about," he countered. "I'll snag a booth. You reclaim your girl."

I could run with that game plan. I pulled the door open and let him head in first.

***

Dawes had an unexpected superpower. In a bar crowded with rabid—or faking rabid—sports fans in the middle of a game, he found an empty booth within sixty seconds and had settled in.

I had Naomie's elbow in hand to guide her through the joint, but she nearly missed a step when she saw where we were headed.

"*That's* your friend?"

"That's your bodyguard for tomorrow."

She stopped moving entirely and turned toward me, putting her back to the wolf. "What do I need a bodyguard for, boss? I've got Beelz."

"Nomes," I said. "The security system is currently disconnected at the mansion and the place is isolated and far from the road. Add to that the fire inspector's belief that the grill explosion wasn't an accident. I'm having you oversee a staff of unknown steam cleaners, and there's a chance some of the workmen doing repairs on the house will be there as well. All strangers. All folks we can't run a security check on before they arrive because we don't know who will be there. Perfect opportunity for someone to walk in and walk out with you in hand. None of them would know if you were escorted away without your permission."

"You mean like kidnapped? Why would anyone want to do that to me? I'm nobody."

"They wouldn't know that if you're a lone woman on a fancy estate, sugar. They might decide you're an heiress."

"Boss…" she said, clearly not buying that scenario.

"Humor me, cupcake. I'm taking no chances where your safety is involved. Beelz wouldn't be enough of a deterrent to a determined man. I'm not saying I think you'll be in danger, I'm just not taking chances. Hey, if something happened to you, Beelz would go for my jugular. The mutt loves ya."

She glanced toward the booth Dawes had staked out. Two waitresses nearly collided in the aisle while gazing at him. He smirked and said something I couldn't hear.

"You trust him?"

"To keep you safe? Absolutely. To not hit on you? Not a chance in hell he won't."

"Hit on me?"

She still hadn't gotten over how much a change in wardrobe had erased her ability to disappear.

"When I talked to him earlier, he thought you'd be more comfortable if you met him before tomorrow morning," I said.

"I suppose," she murmured, but it was enough to get her moving again.

Dawes got to his feet politely as we reached the table. Although he had a long-sleeved tee-shirt on beneath a brown leather jacket, there was no disputing bench press muscles rippled beneath the surface. Wear-worn jeans molded to his thighs. The only way this cop could go undercover was as a bouncer. Eyes turned toward him from every table. And why not? With his squared jaw scruffy with unshaved shadow, his hair a barely tamed pelt of brown, and his eyes the amber of a gray timber wolf, he had *trophy* written all over him.

"Farrell," he said, offering his hand.

We shook. "Naomie, Dave. Dave, Naomie." Introductions short and… well, short.

He flashed her a grin that was all teeth. Wolfish ones, but human wolf. He looked amused as his gaze bounced between us.

"Pleased to meet you, miss. Hope this table meets with your approval," he murmured.

Nomes was jittery yet. She quickly slid along the bench seat across from where he'd been seated and jerked me to her side with a swift tug on my coat.

"Appreciate you giving up your day off tomorrow to do the favor," I said.

"Always glad to help a friend out, Farrell."

Nomes took a deep breath. As I'd draped her coat back around her shoulders, the effect wasn't as spectacular as it might have been. Wendy would have let the coat slip away and leaned forward to award a view of further cleavage. But Wendy was a blood-sucking predator. Naomie was prey.

"Boss, you shouldn't have asked him to work for you on his day off," she admonished in a skittish mouse voice.

"Dave's happy to do so, aren't you, Dave?" I pinned him with a look.

"Ecstatic," the wolf declared.

"I'm sure your wife or girlfriend wouldn't appreciate this assignment," Naomie said.

"No wife. No sweetheart. No problem, ma'am."

She blinked in surprise over being called *ma'am*.

"He's a cop, Nomes. Eats nails for breakfast, lifts perps instead of weights in the gym, but polite as a politician heading into election season."

Her eyes widened slightly at that. "Really?"

"Nails for breakfast? No. Bran muffins fresh from the oven are my choice," Dawes said.

"We do donuts every morning, don't we, boss?" she countered, turning toward me briefly. She flashed a coy smile my way as our shoulders brushed in the narrow space.

"Except for mornings when we go crazy and have Pershing rolls," I agreed.

"With icing dripping down the sides," she added.

It sounded damn decadent. The last time we'd had them there'd been a touch of glaze stuck at the corner of her mouth. Beelz had licked it free. I considered beating the dog to the job in the future.

"Are you a patrolman, then?" Nomes queried, apparently in interrogation mode.

"SWAT," Dawes admitted.

She frowned slightly and turned back to me. "You were on a case where the SWAT team had to be called? When?"

"Never," I declared. "We met at a poker game."

"Your boss cheats at cards," Dawes said.

"Do not." My magic had still been on holiday the night of the card game. Cheating had been impossible.

I was saved from further slurs regarding my character by the arrival of a waitress with menus tucked beneath her arm, a pitcher of beer in one hand, and three empty mugs clasped in the other. She put the drink set-ups in the middle of the table. "Sorry you had to wait, guys." Menus were distributed. "Should I give you a couple minutes to decide what to have? If you want a recommendation, our kitchen does barbecue ribs that will melt in your mouth."

Naomie handed the menu back. "Sounds good to me."

Did to Dave and me, too. Sides were discussed and chosen in quick order. The waitress had just scurried off when the sound of gunshots erupted out on the street. Everyone in the bar turned toward the windows, some rising to peer over heads to see better. A few smart ones ducked, some crouching, others hitting the floor. Winthur's friends were fighting for room beneath their table.

Dawes was on his feet immediately, badge in hand. I was just rising when he pushed me back down in the booth. His phone was already to his ear, calling the situation in. "Stay here," he growled and headed outside.

That so went against the grain but considering Nomes had a death grip on my arm, I stayed.

"Terrorists?" she whispered.

I doubted it but couldn't discount the possibility. However, considering my life had seen its share of things of a *demolative* nature… well, terrorists seemed a bit anticlimactic when compared with assassins armed with the Heart Burn curse.

Dawes stepped back inside swiftly and ordered everyone to stay put. He held his badge up where diners and staff could see it. "Nothing to worry about. Kids setting off firecrackers," he told the crowd. But he caught my eye and jerked his head to indicate I should follow him.

"Stay here," I ordered Naomie, though I had to pry her death grip from my arm. "I'll be back shortly. Dave probably just needs temporary backup for something."

That wasn't what he had in mind at all. He gestured with his chin to where a gaggle of kids were in full flight away from the scene. Occasionally, one looked back over his shoulder, a sadistic grin of delight stretching his mouth. They were laughing and hooting in triumph as they fled.

"Irritating but fairly harmless fun," he said. "Though I could still arrest them for disturbing the peace or nearly instigating a panic. It's a weird thing to do in this weather though, isn't it?"

I agreed.

"Feels more like a distraction to me. Could do with a second opinion." His gaze scanned the entire street, flitted over upper windows where drapes were drawn. As a second set of eyes, I concentrated on what the shadows might conceal. With the sun down and the buildings—mostly homes—built close together and featuring denuded but overgrown bushes in the yards, there were hundreds of places where a patient thing could be waiting.

If one was out there, I didn't get the feeling it was pointing anything lethal-from-a-distance at me. Otherworlders didn't feel the need to manufacture anything other than their traditional weapons—knives, swords, axes, cudgels. Things for close-in, hand-to-hand fighting. Either a long bow or a crossbow were too bulky and difficult to hide, so I doubted arrows or bolts were pointed our way. A professional assassin, on the other hand, would take to a rifle like a hellcat to crème de menthe. Still, while Ernie was an Otherworlder assassin, that didn't mean all the contenders in the Kill-the-Raven sweepstakes were non-humans, did it?

"A shield?" Dawes asked in disbelief when he sensed I'd popped one in place.

"Taking no chances," I said. He was probably jealous that I had talents he lacked. Not that he would have liked the restricted movements a shield created.

We waited a minute or two longer. "I'm getting nothin'," he admitted. "You?"

He meant the heebie-jeebies, the sense that someone was staring at him.

"The only non-humans I'm sensing are you and me, and the humans scattered about are reading as harmless ones." I dropped the shield. "We might as well go back in and eat."

"Might as," he agreed, but he didn't turn to do so. "Durkin says you're on a missing person's case. The table of geeks involved in it?"

"The missing guy is one of them, but they didn't tell me anything new." They hadn't. Naomie had been the one to bring Eric's car up as a possible clearing house for clues. "Weirdly enough, it seems everything is coming back to a genealogical search for the guy's great-grandmother. Even his buddies mentioned the glamour shot of the 1930s' babe he had. In fact, a copy of it was supposed to be headed for my web address. Let me snag the laptop from my trunk and see if it's come in yet."

I'd been backing up as I suggested it, headed toward the car, but the werewolf stopped me.

"Are you driving that decked-out black Mustang I saw you in yesterday morning?" he asked.

"Nothing else."

"Then if we don't hustle, you're probably going to need a ride home, Raven," he warned, and strode away from the bar toward the Ford.

The lot next to the place had been crowded. I'd parked part-way down the block on the opposite side of the street. Now, despite the invisible shield I'd tossed over the Ravenmobile, a gangly guy had managed to bypass it and shove a Slim Jim into the window well of the driver's door to open the lock.

Dawes and I closed in on him. "Hey, whaddaya think you're doing, slick? That's my car!" I yelled.

He gave me a brief look of triumph, yanked the door open, then dropped into the seat.

Which is when this Mustang, too, went to that giant car lot in the sky.

***

The explosion threw Dawes and me off our feet. His shoulder hit a historic fence of iron pickets. My head just missed it, trying to dent the side of a once-shiny trash can instead. A rain of car parts caught us, the smaller bits nearly acting like bullets. The wolf grunted as something struck him, but shook it off. For him, a graze would heal within a couple hours. Me, on the other hand…

Car alarms were howling in the tavern's parking lot. I heard them distantly, but saw people spilling out the bar's door. They were really convinced terrorists were at hand now.

It didn't help that the guy who'd flashed his badge earlier was on the ground.

I pushed to my knees. "I am never going to be able to get car insurance again in my entire life."

Dawes sat up and put a tentative hand to his shoulder. Flinched. "You could be right. How long did you have this one?"

"Thirty days today." At least it was longer than the thirty hours I'd had my first car. "Better call Durkin."

"Already did that. He's on his way."

That's when Naomie arrived.

She skidded to a halt in the slush, practically falling over me. "Boss! Are you all right? Dave?"

"Fine," the werewolf and I said nearly in unison.

"Go back inside, miss," he told her. "Farrell, you're going to have to help me keep any possible witnesses from escaping."

Naomie didn't budge. When she tried to help me up, I had to wave her off. "Nomes. Please. Inside," I murmured.

Only then did she notice the car. What was left of it, anyway.

Her hand went to her lips in shock. Her eyes were huge when they turned to me, her teeth clamped on that corner of her bottom lip once more.

"Yeah," I said. "Does having a bodyguard make sense to you now?"

The nod she gave was nearly microscopic.

"Now get out of the cold," I urged. "You might call Burt and put him on alert. Tell him we'll call when the police release us from the scene."

Her head bobbed. She took two steps backward, her eyes on me rather than the destruction, then she turned and pushed her way through the spectators and back into the bar.

The screaming wail of a couple of squad cars was already in the air. In the meantime, Dawes and I had our hands full preventing escapees. No one wanted to stick around. I certainly didn't blame them. Making a dash for home sounded wonderful. Trouble was, I didn't have a home to head toward, much less a vehicle to get me there.

Paramedics arrived in sync with the patrol cars. Dawes told them he was fine and shrugged off being looked over. Because I was already sporting injuries from Hammer's tender mercies, they wouldn't let me slip the leash. At least the latest knot on my head was declared minor and I was released to get into further trouble elsewhere. Rather than head immediately inside, I drifted to where Durkin stood watch over the flames dancing on the Ford's upholstery. A fire truck had joined the party. They banked the campfire.

"I really am going have to start carrying marshmallows with me," he commented. "This sort of scene is becoming a habit with you."

"You find enough of the guy who'd stood in for me?"

Durkin shook his head. "Haven't tried to look for the pieces, Besides, I don't do search-and-rescue for parts. We've a team for that."

"Lucky them," I said.

"Dawes said there was a bit of ruckus shortly before."

"Obviously when the bomb was planted, the kids were holding our attention."

"We're on the same page, then."

"Weird thing, though," I murmured.

Durkin barely moved, but he did shift to give me a look. "*Your* kinda weird?"

"I had more than the security measures Ford supplied on the car in place. After the grill episode, I began tossing a shield over the Mustang. Sealed not only to the pavement but sealing the undercarriage from excursions from below."

"Homicidal moles?"

"Or their near relatives. The guy with the Slim Jim shouldn't have been able to access the window well. My shields might be invisible, but they'll keep humans at bay as much as they will Otherworlders."

"You think our carjacking victim was a user?" Durkin asked.

"If he was, he wouldn't have needed a tool to trip the lock."

"Plus, he wouldn't have been stupid enough to get into the car if he'd known about the explosive," the detective added.

"Yep, but it gets more complicated than that. I'm a one-of-a-kind type of user. My shields aren't like those taught at Hogwarts. No one should be able to take my shield down."

Durkin digested that quietly for a bit, then snarled, "We're fucked."

"Are we ever," I agreed, and headed back inside the sports bar to rejoin Naomie.

***

I expected to find my secretary holding down the table, maybe making inroads into the ribs we'd ordered, but, instead, she was entertaining the troops.

Eric Winthur's buddies had found ways to wedge themselves into the booth. She was smashed up against the wall with two of them having taken over my place next to her. Three more were wedged into Dawes' side of the table, and two others were straddling chairs at the end. Beer mugs in various stages of being emptied littered the table.

Even stranger was that she had shrugged out of her coat and was so engrossed in listening to them, she hadn't realized the sweater had slipped down her shoulder, fueling nerdish dreams. A notepad and pen had materialized from her purse and she was jotting notes as they chattered at her. They were all so intent, I had to clear my throat loudly to get noticed.

Nomes looked up and nearly blinded me with a dazzling smile. "Boss! Is it time to give Burt a call?"

"Past time," I said.

Her cell was on the table before her. She didn't bother picking it up, but pressed the fast dial for the cabbie, then leaned forward to tell him to swing by. The men across from her went glassy-eyed as the sweater shifted. Nomes was clueless. "He'll be here in five," she announced brightly.

Three large carryout boxes rested in the center of the table; a reckoning slip pinned to the top by three separately-wrapped mints. The round kind with red swirls. I pocketed the candy and tossed payment plus a hefty tip down. One of the guys passed me the Styrofoam-corralled meals. She might call me *boss*, but he knew a lackey when he saw one.

Naomie delivered smiles all around and thanked the guys for talking to her and for their contact information should she have further questions.

I think she'd hijacked the Winthur case while I was nearly being blown up.

As Eric's friends hastily moved, she scooted across the bench seat. "Hope you don't mind that I asked to take everything home. Should we invite Dave to come with us or just hand him his meal?"

Dawes was busy interviewing a couple of diners. I stopped one of the wait staff and asked if she could slip the to-go container to him. As a fiver accompanied the request, she saw no problem getting it to him.

One of Naomie's worshippers helped her on with her coat. "So we can all leave now?" another asked.

"No, *we* get to leave. You have to wait until one of the cops has talked to you," I said, then dug a knife into each of their hearts by adding, "Shall we head home, sugar?" To put a cherry on top, I offered her my hand.

Nomes' fingers entwined with mine, her eyes glittering from beneath the shelter of long lashes. "Yes, please," she murmured.

Damn. She sounded like she'd been taking voice lessons from Wendy. Those two words dripped with temptation.

She hadn't a clue that they did. "Wait until you hear what the boys told me," she said as we slipped passed the cop at the door.

And the moment was gone.

***

"You know that picture the boys called The Babe?" Nomes demanded from the backseat of the cab. I'd let her share it with the boxes of delayed dinner and took my usual shotgun position next to Burt when he'd arrived.

"Yeah?"

"Well," she gushed. "Eric thought it looked really familiar. Not like he was comparing it to pictures of his grandmother, but that he'd seen the photograph somewhere else."

I hadn't seen The Babe picture yet, but since Wendy wouldn't have changed her appearance since being turned, though she might have altered the way she did her hair, I knew exactly where Eric Winthur might have seen a nearly identical photograph. There was one on the placard outside the front door of The Red Dragon.

"Gary wasn't sure, but he thought Eric had found where he'd seen it and had gone to talk to someone about the woman in the picture," Nomes said. "The other boys agreed with him. Apparently, they were ticked off he hadn't invited them along, but Naki thinks Eric didn't want anyone with him. Not even Jamie."

Naki? Mr. Tanaka had definitely been putting the moves on her. "Which one was Gary?" I asked.

"The guy with the tie. He's finishing one last class before graduating and already has a job with Chrysler though he's still Stewart's roommate."

I didn't even want to know which one was Stewart. It sounded like when she'd pulled on her figurative deerstalker, she'd been the one chatting the fellas up.

Then she changed the topic. "What do you think caused your car to blow up?"

A really nifty batch of C-4 wired to a pressure-sensitive detonator most likely, but that wasn't what I was going to tell her.

"Just guessing, but those kids with the firecrackers? When they tossed them in the street, some must have rolled under the car. Either the fuse was a slower one or it fizzled a bit. Whatever, it must have settled directly beneath the gas tank. When the firecracker went, the Mustang soon followed."

Burt threw me a suspicious look, but kept his trap shut. All I needed was for Naomie to buy the scenario.

"Does that mean you'll need Burt to chauffeur you around tomorrow?" she asked.

"Ms. Muldoon asked me to play tour guide again tomorrow, but if you need—"

I cut him off. "Nah. I told Lex you were the best guy for the job she needs done and that's finding locations for her stories. If Nomes doesn't mind, I'll borrow her car." There would be no stealth mode available in the lime green economy model, but I didn't want to pull the 1969 MGB Roadster from the garage in this weather. I'd already talked to a classic automobile dealer to include it, the 1909 Silver Ghost, and the 1935 Town Cabriolet my creator had owned but not used, in an upcoming auction. Another note for my To-Do list—call the guy to find out when pick-up of the vehicles would be. I'd do it first thing tomorrow after leaving Nomes in Dawes' hands.

"Sure, boss. Makes sense to me," she said. Her perk-o-meter was back online. "You can drop me off out at the house, and if the cleaners get done earlier than expected, Dave can probably drive me home." She was quite cheerful about the idea. With another female, I would have suspected she had flirtation with Dave in mind. With Nomes, I was pretty sure she was going to attempt to pry information out of him.

"If things run late, well, you've got your own key now to get in," she added.

"You're welcome for that," Burt said.

"Oh, so it was your idea, was it?" The query was accompanied by a fearsome Farrell frown.

"He didn't want to take it," Naomie supplied.

Burt glanced over at me, a lone eyebrow quirked. "Didn't want to take a key to a pretty girl's apartment?"

"Key to *my secretary's* apartment. Entirely different thing."

"Yeah, I can see it is." He sounded as amused as hell. "I like the new outfit, Naomie. Did he tell you you look great in it?"

"The boss said the idea was to look distracting."

"Did he now? Well, you nailed it."

"Let's turn this conversation to far more delicate matters," I suggested.

"Which are?" he asked.

"What to feed the dog. Take-out had not been the plan for us and if he doesn't have his own highly improper canine dietary requirements catered to, I'm likely to go hungry," I said.

Naomie suggested chili.

I was just glad Beelz preferred to sleep with her.

***

My key was baptized when Burt dropped us off. Naomie's hands were full with our dinners and the bag with Beelz's treat. She wouldn't give them up, forcing me to test drive my present.

It was still early. At least to me. Midnight had not yet been breached. Since I was currently burdened with the collar of domesticity that kept my roaming feet from roaming off to beat the mean streets, I settled for changing out of snow-dampened jeans and into another new pair.

"Why don't we watch some of those old detective shows you asked me to order, boss?" Nomes called from the bedroom. She was letting the various dinners take turns in the microwave. While he waited for his, Beelz was at his ease in the beanbag chair. "I downloaded some to your video collection at Amazon," she said.

If I couldn't play detective, at least I could watch others play detective. While programming my account data into her system, I noticed a couple barely-burnt candles on a shelf above the television. Why not, I thought. Cozy night in front of the tube with a bit of ambiance.

The twin flames leapt to attention. Beelz jerked his head up in surprise and on alert. I glanced back. Naomie was standing just outside the bedroom door, a plate in her hands, but her eyes on the candles.

Considering I was ten feet away when they flamed up, there was no way in hell they should have been burning brightly. Barely a second passed before I'd dampened them, returning the wicks to their slumber.

"Did you see that?" Naomie asked. She sounded stunned. Disbelieving and yet…

"See what?" I concentrated on walking the remote through the offerings.

"The candles."

"Candles?" I glanced up, saw her staring at them. "Hey, why don't we light them? Cold night, mini fireplace. You have matches?

Nomes shook her head as if to dislodge something. "I could have sworn they lit themselves then went out."

"Sounds like you've had too long of an exciting a day," I said.

"That must be it. If not, then it's magic, boss."

I laughed. "Magic, Nomes? That's just in books. There's no such thing as magic. It's not real."

She sighed. "Well, move your feet. With barbecue ribs, we are not eating off our laps on my new sofa." And with that, she slid a plate onto the make-do coffee table and handed me a fork.

February 17th

Naturally we had to watch *The Maltese Falcon*, but it'd been followed by *The Thin Man*, then the *Warehouse 13* episode in the final season, the one where Pete and Myka get sucked into a hard-boiled detective novel. It was sorta the reverse of what had happened to me, though all those black-and-white shows made me nostalgic for my own previous black-and-white existence back home in the land of anything goes. Only characters from comic books and graphic novels ever got colorized, though we never even noticed they were different than us text-bound characters.

Naomie, of course, didn't make it much beyond the opening scenes of *The Thin Man*. As I remained on the floor after our feast, slouched back against the couch with my legs stretched out, Nomes had the entire sofa to herself. She'd taken the sexy boots off, and as that had left those long legs highlighted by the black tights, I'd simply enjoyed the view.

Actually, I'd been a bit surprised she hadn't immediately changed upon walking in the door, getting comfy by returning to her usual gamine widow weeds. Could it be that she'd liked the attention she'd received that evening? If she went shopping and acquired an entirely new wardrobe of distracting outfits, I'd take it as a clue that I'd created a monster.

One that was easy on the eyes.

"If you're tired, why don't you go to bed?" I asked upon returning to the living room after liberating the last beer from the refrigerator. On the flat screen, William Powell and Myra Loy were into their Nick and Nora Charles byplay.

"No, I'm watching the show," Nomes murmured. Since her back was to the screen, her face buried against the back cushions of the couch, and a toss pillow beneath her head, she was fibbing.

I put my beer on the mini table I'd shifted earlier and headed into her bedroom for the quilted, monochromatic-colored comforter that looked handmade, along with a proper bed pillow. She was so out of it when I got back, even my lifting her head to switch out the pillows didn't wake her. While she snoozed in a cozy cocoon of padded cotton, Beelz and I shared the bag of pretzels. I wondered whether the mansion would be ready for us to move back in tomorrow night. I really missed sharing my evening with Evan Williams.

On the tube, Nick Charles maneuvered around his eager-to-investigate wife, and my mind maneuvered back to the various cases on my own detecting plate.

Top of the list was who the hell had taken the hit out on me and why?

Well, maybe that had slipped to the second spot because I really needed to know how something, or someone, had managed to dismantle my shield. As I'd told Durkin, that shouldn't be possible. I was a dimensional being unto myself. The hocus I pocused didn't depend on the rules for Earth-based users or the legendary types. The shield should have been both demon- and angel-proof, too. I would have prayed like heck to ensure that a god hadn't made me vulnerable, but there was no telling which god might be jerking me around by nixing my security measures.

But without the shield to protect me, I might as well have a target painted on my back—and front—as a visual aid for any hit type with me in their sights.

When the three shows were over, I checked on Naomie. Still down for the count on the sofa. The pretzels were long gone. Beelz had curled up in the beanbag chair for some shut-eye, but I still needed to entertain myself for hours before either of them stirred. Which is when my eyes fell on the boxes of Winthur family genealogical data and remembered Jamie had promised to forward a scan of The Babe picture to me.

Rather than turn on the overhead lights in the kitchen-cum-Raven Corp annex office, I liberated the small lamp on the table of Raven Tale hardcovers and set it up to provide light by which to see the laptop's keyboard.

The attachment file took its time opening. Nomes was making

do with a much slower web link than the mansion had. I'd have to upgrade that for her, too. It was the least I could do considering I was raiding her cupboards for anything resembling food. FYI—dry Frosted Flakes really lack verve when you're stuck washing them down with Mountain Dew. I suffered through the ordeal until the box was empty and there were two empty cans in the sink. Not that it took that long for the photograph to load.

It was Wendy Whilsen all right. Circa 1930s but I was curious about the location of the studio that had taken it. Fortunately, back in the day, studios stamped their name and, if you were lucky, the city and state or country in a bottom corner of the photograph rather than hide it on the back. It looked like something was on the right-hand side but enlarging the screen didn't help. It broke down into unreadable pixel blurs. Another item for my To Do list: call Jamie and ask if—

Wait. If she'd handed over all the research materials to Nomes and Burt, the original might be in the boxes.

I sent a quick *Thank You* to Jamie for sending the copy and lending out the boxes of stuff, then shut the computer off. I had old-fashioned research to do and it was not going to fit on the kitchen table even if I removed all our computer stuff. The living room floor, though? Perfect.

Pulling the first box over, I sat cross-legged with my back to the now-sleeping flat screen and started sorting.

It was easy to make headway because anything that had no relation to Wendy was superfluous to the investigation. The first box was mostly data about the family Wendy's daughter had married into. About the family who had adopted her. There were no glam pix of my vampiric client. On to the next box!

Traces of the golden vein for which I searched surfaced there:

- A copy of a baptismal certificate for Alfrida Nean dated March 27, 1933.
- A slightly smeared fax of adoption papers for Alfrida Nean, aged approximately three months, giving the adopting parents as Ansgar and Siglinda Rundstrom.
- What appeared to be a wedding bands announcement for Alfrida Rundstrom and Lucuz Winthur cut from a newspaper.

As it was written in something I wasn't Svengalish enough to read, I was guessing on that. Looked like the date might be 1954. Eric's grandmother had obviously brought it with her when they'd immigrated.

The rest of the papers were either black-and-white or faded Polaroid color snapshots of family groupings that were nearly indistinguishable from each other except for new, shorter members being added and others getting taller. The faces were stamped with the same good looks Alfrida and Lucuz brought to the gene pool.

And, yep, Alfrida did indeed look like a cloned Wendy Whilsen.

On to the third box, though I was losing hope. I'd started with the one with a large #1 on it and it had held data on the wrong branch of the family. The #2 box had those few tidbits but was basically grounded in the Fifties and Sixties with a few contributions by the Seventies. I feared that box #3 would be even more recent family photos.

And it was. Lots of newspaper clippings following Eric's father and then Eric himself through their schoolboy sports phases. A few honor roll citations for Eric, and his college acceptance letter giving him a generous swim team scholarship.

And then, at the very bottom, there was a pristine folder. No notation on the tab about what it held, but nothing else in any of the boxes had merited a file folder.

Being the suspicious sort, its place at the bottom seemed rather telling. Eric had hidden it there, I suspected. All the untamed papers had been camouflage.

Rather than open it immediately, I raided the refrigerator again, resigned to eating something that was supposed to be good for me. Nomes had carrot sticks and dark red Michigan apples. She slept through the noise I made eating both.

I had a carrot stick gripped between my teeth when I returned to the only place left to sit on the floor. With papers and photographs fanned out around me, I opened the file folder.

Wendy Whilsen's ageless beauty looked back at me from the original copy of what everyone I'd talked to thus far called The Babe pic. The name of the photography shop was clear to read, as was a very encouraging "Detroit, Michigan". No out-of-town searching necessary.

But the folder held even better clues. A torn ad from a real newspaper—one that was printed *on* paper!—for The Red Dragon Jazz Club. A very small picture of Wendy three-fourths of the way down announced her sultry stylings of classic swing tunes were a feature Wednesday through Sunday from ten to closing. The dragon was making sure no one would expect her on stage until after the sun went down, no matter what month of the year it was.

Eric had followed the ad to the website noted at the bottom and printed pages of it that had appeared pertinent to him. But the last goody in the file was a napkin from The Red Dragon with an address scratched on it in pencil. Generic, run-of-the-mill, graphite.

Who carried pencils these days? It seemed a nostalgic sort of thing for someone to use at the club. From my own few visits, I knew the wait staff used handheld computer screens to take food orders so they wouldn't have had a pencil to lend out. At the bar, no one wrote anything down; they just supplied the required poison and took your money.

So why an anachronistic wooden pencil? And I was guessing it was a wooden one, not part of a steel-toned desk set or of molded plastic. But if it was carried by someone who was holding down a seat at a bar where a vampiress took the stage five nights a week, there might be a reason to have a sharpened *wooden* pencil.

As conundrums went, this was one I was willing to take a stab at postulating. The answer was: someone who planned to use it as an easily-carried stake and knew they had the power to drive such a fragile bit of wood through an unsuspecting vampire's non-beating heart.

As enviable as the muscles Eric had developed through his medal winning swim career were, a human wasn't going to be able to do that. Well, not unless they were John Wick, and, as far as I know, other than appearances on the silver screen, his address was still near where mine used to be—in fictionland. Humans couldn't move fast enough, nor telegraph the intent and be neutralized either via a broken neck or snack-down on ye olde jugular before the lethally-honed point even touched their vamp target.

But there were some Otherworlders who could do the deed.

Particularly another vampire.

The napkin was evidence that Eric had visited The Red Dragon.

He'd probably gone to hear her sing, hoping to be able to talk to her during a break or as she left the club. The pencil-wielding something-or-other had sat with him. The kid had probably spilled the reason he was at the club. Had been convinced he'd made a friend in the stranger and been hungry for further information, particularly if he never got a chance to speak to Wendy. If she'd known he was in the audience, I think she would have mentioned it, but one never knows with blood-suckers. I needed to talk to her again.

On the other hand, if she had taken a night off that had happened to coincide with Eric's visit and he'd been disappointed, his new-found friend might have offered to act as a liaison for him.

I not only needed to talk to Wendy, I needed to ask the dragon and the barman some questions. I already knew the bartender mentally cataloged the faces and clothing of his customers. He'd rattled off particulars nearly detailed enough to give a shoe size back in November when I'd asked about a cable repairman who'd been a bit too conveniently on hand. The booze slinger said it was good for business to remember not only what a customer was drinking but what the customer looked like in the event he moved from the bar to a table.

My morning planned, I had to wait for Naomie to stir. I was stealing her wheels for the day and dropping her at the temporarily hobbled Raven Central mansion, so I couldn't take off until she was ready to leave. There was a bonus to her having conked out on the sofa, though. It was open season on the coffee maker in the bedroom.

It only took me fifteen minutes and an airing of demon, fae, and Klingon swear words muttered under my breath, to get the friggin' machine working.

***

Nomes was in the shower when I called Zeta to check on the incoming pirate treasure. She told me to come by the bank to count packages to make sure all shipments had arrived. If I believed the various tracking number assertions in my e-mail, they had. Told her I'd be by after dropping Naomie off. Then I called the guy from the classic auto auction place.

"Glad you called," he said. "I've been trying to get hold of you for two days."

I explained we'd had a problem at the house and that no one was currently in residence. When I had stopped by, it never occurred to me to check voice mail. Naomie always took care of that. She was far more efficient when it came to daily duties beyond donut consumption during office hours.

For a guy who thought he was awesomely free of ties, I'd become damn dependent on people since crossing into this world. Special people, considering they catered to me: Burt, Ruth Lund, Delia, Zeta, and the other members of the coven. Durkin. Naomie. Rissy. Hell, I'd even roped wolfboy-Dawes into the circle now.

"You have an ETA on when the vehicles will be picked up?" I asked car auction guy.

"Yeah. This afternoon between one and two, if that suits your schedule. Otherwise, it'll have to wait until the next auction."

Told him that worked for me, and the keys plus all required documentation for the authentication and provenance would be waiting on the front seat of each. When I said my secretary would be there to sign the legal paperwork his crew would have, I ran into a slight brick wall. I hadn't a clue what Naomie's surname was when he asked for it.

You'd think I would. There had been paperwork involved in hiring her. She received a paycheck that would need that important tidbit added. But I'm one catered-to dude. Nomes had signed on board the Raven train via the coven's resident legal eagle and was paid through the CPA witch's office.

I told him to hold on while I found out. Embarrassing, yes. I'm man enough to admit to a glitch when it trips me up, though.

Nomes had a landline phone, just like we had at the mansion. I used hers to call Helena, the CPA. It was easier to reach her than it was the attorney, plus I wouldn't inadvertently lose the guy on my cell. "I need to know Naomie's full name so it's on record when she signs for something this afternoon," I said when she answered her phone.

I've got every coven member's direct line. Had to cozen it from the resistant ones. Damn, it was good I'd aced that mythical gigolo class.

"For a former P.I., you're rather clueless," Helena said.

Former ???

"Her name isn't Naomie at all. It's Niela Enright."

What???

"While I've got you on the line, we need to make an appointment to do your tax return, Bram."

??????

"You might not have had any income as either a P.I. or a writer last year, but you did inherit a rather large estate from Calista. There will be taxes."

Which is like saying, "There will be an apocalypse later today. Film at six, if we're still here."

"I'll have to get back to you on that," I told her. "Keeping pretty busy with the repairs to the house so I can move back in."

"Understandable. Don't let it go too long, though. Tax season is my version of Black Friday. Things are jumping," she said.

I thanked her and got back to the guy on my cell. He made note of Naomie's true name and promised to keep me abreast of auction details.

That's when Nomes left the bathroom, freshly groomed and teetering on the line between Victorian widow and the hot chick from last night. She'd gone with jeans, the knee topping boots, and a variety of draped, form concealing items from her past wardrobe. "Whaddaya think, boss?" she asked.

"About what?" That she passed muster? That Dawes would be torn between keeping his eyes on her and his eyes where they were supposed to be—on everyone else?

"Do you think I've got enough layers on to stay warm at the house? I turned the thermostat down to sixty before we left the other night. No use heating the great outdoors with all the broken windows and stuff, right?"

Damn. Who was this creature? My perky secretary had previously hidden veins of common sense. She was thrifty!

"You'll find out when you get there," I said, "but chances are the main house is now sealed off enough to put the heat back to normal."

"Right." She gave a decisive nod and pulled on her new coat. "I'm ready when you are."

We hit the road.

***

Dawes and the construction crew were already on hand when I pulled the lime-green Spark up to the door. His left eyebrow rose, as did the left side of his mouth. So nice that I could amuse him so early in the day.

"Quite a comedown for you after the Mustang," he commented as I climbed out of the economy sardine can. Even with the driver's seat pushed back as far as the track allowed, it had felt like my knees were up around my ears. That simply meant another thing went on my list of things to upgrade for Nomes. A company car. Heck, I'd be at the dealership doing another replacement on my car anyway. I'd call it multi-tasking. Thrift in hours over thrift when it came to my pocket.

I explained to the wolf that a dealership-sized truck-and-trailer combo would be swinging by to raid the garage. When I mentioned what was hidden away inside said garage, Dawes stuck his paw out, demanding the key. He needed drool time before the vehicles vanished. He hadn't forgotten why he was there, though. When Naomie headed to the front door, her key to the place in hand, he stopped her, took the key, ran a check over the door for new intruder marks, then went inside and searched the entire joint before letting her enter.

She made the thermostat her first order of business. I headed around the corner of the building to see what the workmen were up to and get a possible move-back-in date. The contractor I'd talked to before was helping another of his men dismantle something around where a door had once proudly stood. He turned the entire job over to the other man and picked his way through patio rubble to my side. He explained what they were doing and pointed to where other teams of men were engaged in other chores. The only thing I understood was, "We'll have this area sealed off enough to keep winter at bay before we leave today. If you don't mind the smell of smoke, you can be back sleeping in your own bed tonight."

I just wanted to be back before my TV with a bourbon in hand. I was sure sleep was overrated.

The arrival of the two vans and teams dealing with cleanup in the mansion proper further warmed my heart. But as the temperature was still well below freezing, that was the only part of me feeling warmed. I left Nomes in charge of every man in sight and began my round of stops for the day.

The first item: find a security-level briefcase. Not exactly something I could pick up at Target, though I'm sure they would have made an effort. Took more than a single stop, but I found one that not even Houdini could have gotten out of. Mostly because it was too small for him to get into, but that's beside the point. By then, it was long past lunch, but I headed to Zeta's bank branch to view the gold horde. She was a bit scandalized that I planned to keep the coins from rattling in the briefcase by wrapping them in a kitchen towel set from Dollar General then binding it in rubber bands. We got rid of all the shipping materials, but I had her keep the achromatic-sided treasure chest in the safe. Had things to clear up before I could book a flight to Vegas to visit Ernie.

A Rueben at a Subway shop along my route filled the inner man and gave me troll breath, but as I was headed to The Red Dragon, I'd be able to cover it up with a slosh or so of bourbon. Now *that* made my mouth water.

As hoped, the bartender I'd siphoned information from in the past was on duty. He didn't bother to ask what I was drinking, just turned to pick the Evan Williams bottle from the soldiers lined up before the back-bar mirror. He slid a tumbler before me. "I'm guessing you're here for more than a drink, Mr. Farrell," he said.

"I'm that transparent, huh?"

He smiled. "Shamuses usually want more than something from a bottle."

Sounded like investigators stopped by regularly. "I've got a missing person I hope you might be able to help me narrow in on." I unearthed the printout of Eric Winthur. "This ring any bells?"

"Hmm. Paper. You're old-school," he commented, but he was looking at the picture. "You know you can keep photographs on your cell, don't ya?"

"That only works if you remember to charge it overnight. Paper, you don't have to recharge," I said and savored the EW. *Buddy,* I greeted as it slid over my tongue, *I've missed you, pal.* Which merited a second sip.

"This your missing guy?"

"Could be," I cadged.

"Yeah, I remember him. He came in to hear our songstress, but Mr. Palermo needed her that night, so she wasn't here."

"He was alone?"

"Came in alone. Didn't leave alone." Cryptic of him.

I took the hint and casually slid a fifty beneath the edge of the cocktail napkin. A twin of the one in my pocket with that penciled address on it.

As though polishing a condensation ring from the bar top, he made the greenback disappear.

"Left with one of our regulars. Used to be here during daylight, but, recently, he's only been in after dark. Never caught his name, but Ms. Whilsen probably knows it. She left with him a time or two then dropped him. He still hung around, but as he'd been a regular for a long time, I didn't think anything of it. I did overhear my employer asking her if he should bar the guy from the premises or arrange to have a restraining order to deter him. She said no, that, if necessary, he'd be taken care of. By which, I figured she'd mention the dude to Mr. Palermo and the problem would disappear."

It definitely would have, but Wendy had probably thought she could rid herself of the guy's attentions by having him for dinner. And I do mean, *for* dinner. Yeah, vampires had other uses for stalkers, which is what it sounded like this admirer had become. It was a long time until sundown and as I didn't know how to contact her other than through Palermo's auspices or via a drop by the club during her narrow band of working hours, I'd have to wait. Had a feeling she did not want Palermo to know about her human family's existence.

"What's this regular look like? You know, in case I run into him in an alley?" I asked.

He reeled off a grocery list: about five-eleven, medium brown hair tied back with something that looked like a leather boot lace, otherwise he dressed like he worked in an office that went for business casual in polo shirt, sport coat, dark blue jeans sans tears or wear marks, dark Nikes, and iron-rimmed glasses with tinted lenses that made it difficult to swear to the color of his eyes beyond dark.

I didn't need the haberdasherial info so I downsized it to casual, white-collar business. It was the physical characteristic that wouldn't change if he went for a different set of clothes. Not everyone kept their selection to as narrow a focus as I did, after all.

"Had a few pockmarks on his face, one near the bottom corner of his mouth, left side, and was clean shaven. Hands of an office worker, shoulders of someone stuck at a desk, average build but a bit stooped."

"Bad posture, huh?" I murmured.

"Not a bad-looking man but a bit too friendly, like it was a forced thing."

"Shoe size?" I asked facetiously.

"Standard clown."

I smiled at the quip, then realized he wasn't joking. "You mean broad like a duck's?"

"Like you could use 'em as paddles to row contraband across the river to Windsor."

"Extra wide thirteen or fourteens?"

"Around that, though I'm guessing," he admitted.

"If necessary, would you be willing to sit down with a police artist to compile a portrait of him?" If it turned out my latest suspect was human, Durkin's team could get involved as part of the missing persons canasta group.

But if he wasn't…

"Possible on my day off if neither my boss nor Mr. Palermo mind," the bartender cautioned.

Yeah, a human walked a thin line when his employer was a dragon—which he seemed to know. And one who had a close relationship with a vampire don.

"Thanks." I passed him one of my cards. "If this guy shows up again, could you give me a call?"

"If no one is against me doing so," he answered. "But considering he's been haunting Ms. Whilsen's heels, I don't think there will be a problem. Should he walk in the door, you'll get a call. If not from me, then from whatever bartender is on duty."

"Works for me," I said, but before going back out into the cold, I asked for a refill on my antifreeze.

And I called Ruth Lund.

***

"Can you take a peek out your front door and see if Hammer is in his office across the way?" I asked.

“You want me to do what?” she snarled.

“I’m not all that thrilled with the idea myself, Ruthie, but I need some questions answered and Hammer is likely the only one handy at this time of day I can ask.”

She sighed deeply. “Just a sec.”

Since she was on her cell, I heard the clump of her footsteps as she headed toward the street. Considering her diminutive size, her step was as heavy-sounding as a lass with the full DNA requirement for troll status. The door creaked in true haunted house fashion.

“Hammer!” she yelled. “Someone wants to talk to you.”

The phone didn’t pick up his answer—probably yelled from the alley on the other side of the street.

“Raven, that’s who!” Ruth shouted.

Silence.

“No, I don’t know what about,” she growled. “Come ask him.”

After another pause…

“He says he’s in conference and can’t be disturbed,” she relayed to me.

“Tell him I’ll be at The Bridge in fifteen and buying drinks,” I said.

“How many drinks?” she asked.

“As many as it takes, cupcake. I’ll even spring for lunch.”

She shouted the message, then said, “He wants to know if that goes for all of his boys.”

I sighed. “Yeah, all of them. How many are there? I might have to stop at an ATM.”

Fortunately for my wallet, counting Hammer, I’d be buying only five meals and uncountable drinks. When they stumbled out of The Bridge, they probably wouldn’t even feel the cold any longer.

“In fifteen then,” Ruth said. “I’ll go ahead and get their orders in the meantime. You need anything from the menu?”

God, no.

“Just ate. See you shortly. Save a booth just for Hammer and me, huh?”

“You got it, sweet cheeks,” she said and rang off.

I hit the ATM. Hard.

***

Hammer's food arrived as I walked in the door. He didn't bother to greet me, but Ruth did. Her howdy consisted of, "What are you drinking, bub?"

Not anything that came from a tap in this place. "You got any cans or bottles of trademark brand cola?"

"What do you think this place is, Raven? Chucky Cheese?"

"Something that goes well with bourbon and isn't troll-brewed, then."

"You don't like what we brew here, Farrell?" she growled.

"Found I'm allergic to it, Ruthie. Not putting your creative efforts down." Yes, I was.

She sighed deeply. "I'll see what I can find."

As she went in search, I worried about what she'd unearth. Though not for long. His mouth might be full, but Hammer was ready to talk anyway.

"Whaddaya want, Farrell?"

Business, it was. I leaned forward, forearms on the tabletop, elbows akimbo—which makes it sound like they were doing a rather festive dance, but they weren't. "Considering Palermo keeps you languishing on the want-to-be-turned lists, I'm guessing you keep abreast of who's getting turned and possibly by whom."

"And?"

"I think I'm looking for someone who was recently turned, probably since the beginning of the year." I trotted out the bartender's description of the man who'd formed a temporary friendship with Eric Winthur.

"Oh, him," Hammer mumbled around another huge bite of burger.

"He got a name?"

"Ya mean do I got a name ta give ya," he corrected, though he didn't offer it up. I wondered whether the late Ulysses S. Grant would be able to yank it out of him or whether Ben Franklin would be a better choice to wheedle it from him.

Hammer paused in his mastication efforts to guzzle something from an honest-to-goodness pewter tankard. "He's no friend of mine, so yeah, I'll give ya his name," he said, breathing troll-brewed... well, it was impossible to describe it in further detail without resorting to extremely uncomplimentary words. I'll leave things at: it was bad in an extremely toxic way.

"Harvey Wallbanger."

"You're kidding," I said.

"No, I need a Harvey Wallbanger as the price for the name, Raven."

It was far less expensive than I'd been prepared to pay. I whistled to the bartender—not Ralph, Ruthie's brother, but one of the troll cousins—and pointed at Hammer.

Pissant that he is, he waited until he'd downed half the drink before giving me what I wanted.

"The prick's a CPA. Has an office at the Center."

He meant One Detroit Center. Palermo had an office on a top floor there as well, though only made his own appearances at it in the still of the night. If lunch was brought in, there was no one around to hear the screams. I wondered if, when working late one night, Wendy's stalker had bumped into her in the elevator as she left for her Red Dragon gig and been struck by Cupid's arrow.

"Name?" I reminded.

"I'm gettin' ta it," he promised but indulged his thirst buds first.

During the pause, Ruth returned with an extremely dusty can of Diet Coke. The moment I saw the word *diet* I knew I wasn't going to like it. To delay having to drink it, I asked for a glass with ice in it. Clear ice, not a grit-impregnated icicle broken off an exterior window ledge or—worse—the mini shed where the toasted ghoul had been stashed.

She mumbled something that sounded like "Picky, picky, picky," as she headed back toward the kitchen again.

Across from me, Hammer belched. His breath had not been improved by the he-man cocktail. "Frost. Quinton Frost."

"You got a beef with Frost?" I queried.

"If it weren't against the rules of my game, I'd shove a stake up his pinched-cheeked ass and then go for his heart," the head vamp snack said.

"What did he do to give you such a loving feeling, Hammer? Refuse to back you up at an IRS audit?"

"He jumped the line, that's what."

"I'd no idea there was a line to the process. That *is* what you're referring to, right? He got the magic bite after being a contender for only a brief time?"

"Good guess, Farrell. He didn't even apply to Mr. Palermo for acceptance into the family. He short-cutted the leap. Found his way to a food lair, singled out a buyable fanged tramp, and took her home with him to do the deed. As I hear it, he had everything prepared. Windows sealed against light getting in, draft flaps along all gaps in the door, and enough locks on it to give Fort Knox a hard on."

I leaned back in the booth. "I was under the impression that Palermo frowns on kills he hasn't sanctioned."

"Does. Particularly kills where a turn happens. He thinks the vamp population needs to be maintained at a low number so they don't stand out."

"Is he hunting Frost?"

Hammer shrugged. "He wouldn't tell me if he was, though. I met the dude when he was looking for vamp hangouts. He made it sound like he was only interested in the vamp girl experience to see if it was anything like in all those novels. You hang around with vamp girls in those books of yours, Raven?"

I had. Psychos, every one of them. Wendy, at least, covered her killer instinct well. "Did Palermo obliterate the vamp girl Frost seduced into turning him?"

"Would if he could find her, but she vanished."

Vanishing vampires were becoming a theme in my life. There had been another one doing unsanctioned turns that I'd been hunting just days after entering this world.

"You think Frost is working nights at his office these days?"

"If he was, he ain't no more. Mr. Palermo would have paid him a visit."

It would obviously have been the last visit anyone had with the newly-fanged accountant.

"Which means, if Palermo hasn't found him, Frost is still out there, and instead of hunting vampires to engage with, he's hunting humans to nosh on."

Ruth returned with a cloudy glass, but crystal-clear ice cubes rattled in it. She smacked it onto the table. "That's gonna cost ya, Farrell," she snarled.

"How much?"

"An unspecified favor in the future."

"Deal," I said and spit in the palm of my hand to seal it. She did the same. We shook.

There were a lot of really disgusting things a P.I. combing this neck of the woods was forced to do in the course of an investigation. I hoped the favor Ruth would demand wouldn't up the ante on the disgusting scale. The handshake thing was bad enough.

When she left, I dug the napkin from The Red Dragon out and asked Hammer if he knew what was at the address written on it.

"Nothing good, that's what," he said. "That's one of the worst neighborhoods in the city."

Like this one wasn't?

"Interested in accompanying me to it?"

"Why in the world would I want to do that?"

I tucked the napkin back into my jeans pocket. "Because, if I'm guessing right, this is where we'll find Quinton Frost."

Those were magic words to Hammer. "When do we go?"

"Tonight. Think you can be there around eleven?"

Hammer nodded. "I'll even bring my boys for backup. Only thing that can bring a vampire down is another vampire. Or a horde of determined men."

Or a cheerleader type like *Buffy*. But since we were fresh out of cheerleaders, Hammer's boys would have to do.

***

My next stop was at a car rental lot. I asked what they had in black. They had a four-door Dodge Charger R/T sedan. When asked how long I would need it, I said until the insurance company paid out for my totaled Mustang. They didn't ask how the Mustang had gotten totaled, just had me sign on the dotted line and ran my credit card. Considering it was a debit card and there were a lot of zeros attached to it, it was no surprise that they even had a couple guys to follow me back to the Amberson mansion so I could return Naomie's car to her and then be on my way.

Progress had reached a point where Beelz and I would be able to move back in around 5 p.m. The cleaners had started on the upstairs and were now nearing the finish line on the main floor. Furniture was in the act of being moved back into the dining room, media room, and office. A separate team was doing a few last touch-ups on the upholstery.

Nomes told me someone had been out to take the custom-made drapes and antique area carpets away for processing at their plant and would have them all back in place before noon tomorrow. She had stripped all the beds and raided the towels hanging in the various baths and tucked away in cupboards and had been doing laundry all day to get rid of the taint. She'd tossed my clothes in for a run through the cycle, too.

"Not the tux or the suit or your leather jacket. I'll take those with me and drop them at the dry cleaners on my way in tomorrow. If you've got time to stop by to load the computers into the trunk of my car, I'll bring them back tomorrow, too. I know you and Beelz will be glad to be back home, boss," she said, though it sounded like she'd miss having us under foot.

Nomes had her secretary hat on and rolled right into details about the three antique cars. I now knew when they'd left the premises and when the auction would be. She presented me with the paperwork she'd been given. I opened the middle drawer on my desk and shoved it in.

Dawes admired my temporary car as the rental guys trawled back down the drive and out the gates. Out of her hearing, I asked if he'd stick around until she was ready to leave and, without her noticing him, trail her home just in case something had picked up my scent and made note of her car. Money exchanged hands via a handshake. I was getting very good at making these underhand passes of greenbacks.

Since I had things to retrieve at her place, I roamed the house looking for her. She was in the laundry room, a place conveniently located on the floor where most of the laundry was created—upstairs with the bedrooms. It was sandwiched between two bathrooms.

She had earbuds in and was singing along to a song I wasn't familiar with but doing so under her breath. My little mouse had no intention of letting anyone hear her song stylings. They were nothing like Wendy's, though Naomie's near-whisper was tantalizing. Tantalizing in an entirely different way than Wendy's. Nomes' were sweet, innocent, and meant for her ears only. I wondered whether she cut loose and sang at full lung capacity while in her car with the windows rolled up.

I propped my shoulder against the door jamb—the Raven

stance—and shoved my fingers into the rear pockets of my jeans. Beelz had followed me and settled in at my feet, both of us content to just watch her remove towels from the dryer and fold them against her torso. From the height of the pile—all snowy white ones—seemed I'd inherited a locker room's worth of 'em.

Nomes suddenly realized she was no longer alone, glanced over her shoulder, and flinched. A startled squeak acted as the final note of the song. "Boss! Do you need me to do something?"

"Yes," I said. "Stop working. The cleaners are on their way out and the workmen have gone. Time to head home. I have just one question."

She placed the towel in her hands onto the folding table and gave Beelz and me a wide, happy smile. The one she never gave anyone else. She had lousy taste when it came to companions. She preferred to hang out with a demon and a guy who owed his existence to a string of two million words. More, if you counted foreign translations.

"One question?" Her head tilted to the side. That impossibly black hair swung coquettishly. "I'm girded for it. Shoot."

"What do you want for dinner? To go or eat in an honest-to-goodness restaurant?"

Beelz stayed at his ease on the floor, but his head swiveled from me to her, waiting for an answer.

"That's two questions, or maybe three, boss."

The dog looked up at me.

"And the answer is?" I prompted.

The hound was in tennis match mode. His attention went to her once more.

She worried that bottom lip in thought. Damn, when had I become aware of her doing that? It was obviously a habit of long standing. She did it unconsciously. It was Dawes' fault. He'd asked for a description and somehow that tell had worked its way into said description. And my mind.

"Italian?" she suggested in a voice so full of indecision it made me want to grab her. Kiss her.

Beelz cocked his head, eyes on me, waiting for the next volley.

Back away, Farrell, I cautioned myself. "Pizza to go or sit-down regular meal?"

Beelz watched the verbal ball fly across the net again.

"Sit-down?" A tentative query through and through.

Since there would be no one to interview or run interference as Eric Winthur's friends and Dawes had done the evening before, the connotation would be that we were on a date.

Beelz's demon-red eyes rested on me, waiting for my return.

"Olive Garden or do you have a favorite elsewhere?" I asked, throwing the direction we took back into her hands.

"Olive Garden," Nomes decided with barely a thought. "Smaller, local places are date-night stops. That's not us."

"Not us," I repeated, though I wasn't sure whether I agreed or was a tad disappointed. "I've got one stop to make before picking you up. Shouldn't be much more than thirty minutes behind you if you head out the door right now."

Smile back in place, she saluted. "I'll finish putting these away tomorrow." It sounded like a promise.

"I'm not totally incompetent when it comes to putting towels away, and I'll have all night to get around to it." I pushed off the door jamb. Beelz got to his feet. "You. Out of here."

"Yes, sir!" Her happy smile was back.

***

My stop was at a supermarket. I owed Nomes a cupboard-refilling since I'd raided hers to even barer bones than it had been before. Beelz checked out the rental, giving it a thorough investigative sniff. He sneezed a couple times. Could have been the lingering scents of previous drivers irritating him, but I took it for discontentment. We'd both have to make do with the Charger for a while. I picked up something for him to eat and some comestibles for the night ahead.

When I got to Nomes' apartment it was a bit later than I'd expected, but the real surprise was that Burt's cab and Dawes' truck were both parked in the lot. Beelz was at my heels as I went into the building entrance, but he beat me to Naomie's place. Her door was wide open. I wondered whether there had been trouble.

Beelz barked a greeting. Or maybe he was demanding obeisance. As a demon, he did rank higher on the power scale than a werewolf, and probably me as well, though I was more diversified in what I could do on the nonhuman scale. Of course, the three wholly humans in the room were basically pets to his mind. We were all his servants, catering to his whims and needs.

Considering he'd hung out with Dawes all day and Burt was his regular ride to the groomer's, the only person in the room he had just a glancing acquaintance with was Alexis Muldoon.

In the tiny apartment there was barely room to walk. Naomie hopped up from where she'd been curled into the beanbag chair. Burt and Lex had the sofa staked out, and Dawes had confiscated one of the chairs from the kitchen and sat straddling it, arms crossed and resting on the back. He got up and closed the door behind me.

"Don't tell me this is an intervention I've walked into. What are you going to attempt to convince me I shouldn't do?" I asked.

"Eat donuts," Dawes said. "One of these days, they'll kill you."

Naomie's eyes fell on the bags. "I thought we were going out to eat."

"You and I are," I said. "Don't know what the rest of these clowns are doing."

"Clowns?" Dawes growled.

"Call 'em like I see 'em, pal. I thought you were just going to follow Nomes home."

"Was. She spotted me."

"Back to covert surveillance school for you, officer."

He ignored the jibe. "What's in the bags if you're moving out tonight, Farrell?"

I handed him one of them. He searched it for… well, hell if I know.

"Frosted Flakes, Mountain Dew, precut carrot sticks, popcorn, and Hershey's kisses?" he listed for everyone's benefit.

"Replacing everything I raided for late night snacks. Except for the chocolate." I grabbed the package, ripped it open, peeled back a red foil wrapper—the Valentine-themed packets had been 50% off—then tossed the treat to Beelz. He leapt into the air with the grace and twist of a rainbow trout trying to shake the hook from its mouth, snagged the candy, and had swallowed it before he hit the carpet again. Understanding the look he gave me, I unpeeled another and tossed it low and to the side. He fielded it nicely. "See? Entertainment feature for when there's nothing to watch on cable."

"You do know chocolate is bad for dogs," Lex said.

"Tell him that," I suggested, hunkering down. My demon partner and I did the paw-to-fist-bump thing Naomie had refined. "So what are all you people doing here?"

"I live here," Nomes said, her voice hovering on a giggle, if I'm not mistaken.

"Ms. Muldoon asked me to bring her by. I'm merely waiting in a warm place until my fare is ready to head out," Burt declared.

"Uh huh."

"I was not briefed on Mr. Zelinski's position in the operation," Dawes said.

I nearly asked who the heck Mr. Zelinski was, then realized it was probably Burt. I was so bad about getting surnames from the people on my payroll.

Dawes was still talking. "...so, as Ms. Enright's security detail for the day, I questioned his purposes in trailing us into the parking lot."

"He jerked Burt from the cab and patted him down." Lex sounded affronted at the action.

I glanced at Naomie. Her eyes were dancing some uninhibited tropical fandango of delight at the memory. If I asked her, the odds of her saying, "It was awesome," came in at even money.

"I didn't mind," Burt said. "He was doing his job."

Dawes took the bag of groceries around the corner and deposited them onto the table. A table that, when I followed him with my other two bags, I saw was missing the Raven Central computer set-ups.

Dave noticed the start I gave. "Took 'em down and stored 'em in her trunk while we were waiting for you."

I sighed, though whether it was over the way things kept getting out of my control or relief that I wouldn't have to tote them down the stairs myself, I couldn't say. "And you're still here why?"

Nomes overheard me. It was, after all, a really small apartment. "I invited everyone to join us for dinner," she called from the other side of the partition. Like less than ten feet away. "Is that okay, boss?"

I threw in the towel. "Whatever," I said.

"Great," she perked. "I already called ahead for reservations. The Dearborn location, right?"

If it hadn't been before, it was now.

I suggested the rest of them head for the restaurant while I fed

Beelz and Nomes put the replacement comestibles away. Within two minutes, the apartment had grown back to normal size. Beelz had his nose in a bowl of barbecue chicken bits from the deli section.

I waited until Nomes had stashed the Mountain Dew in the fridge to make my move. When she shut the door, I was right behind her. She turned to face me in surprise. Hands flat against the freezer door on either side of her head, I leaned into her.

"Nomes," I said softly. "This was supposed to be a date. Just you and me." The fact that I'd only decided to term it so since the others had left surprised even me.

"But, bo—"

Before she could call me *boss* again, I corrected her. "Bram," I murmured and kissed her.

***

Yeah, I know what you're thinking. *What the shit, Farrell!* Same phrase ran through my mind and I shut it the hell up.

She was kissing me back and, well, the world could just fuck off as far as I was concerned. Then sanity returned. Not to me, but to Nomes.

"Boss." The word feathered across my lips.

"Nomes," I answered, doing a bit more sampling.

"This isn't us."

"Feels a lot like us," I countered.

"You're just riding the wave," she counter countered.

"Wave?"

"Adrenaline."

Yep, definitely. The adrenaline tank was registering at FULL.

"I'm not the girl you dressed up to distract those boys with last night."

"Sugar, you aren't dressed like that now," I reminded her.

"But you're still picturing me dressed that way."

Didn't have to. My imagination had made enough hops on this checkerboard since then that you could "king" me.

Her hands rested on my chest, but she wasn't pushing me away. "We need to return to the way we treated each other before."

"We can do that and then add to it." Like an entire wing.

"Do you really think that's wise?"

It sounded damn brilliant to me.

She frowned. "Did giving you a key make you think…"

"The key had nothing to do with this."

And there went the teeth, worrying that corner of her lip again. "But maybe it does."

"On a subatomic level?"

"On a professional level, boss."

I sighed in resignation. "Bram. Will you ever be able call me by my name? You did in October."

"*Boss* is safer," she said. "Particularly now."

I rested my brow against hers. "You are…"

She waited.

"…infuriatingly right," I agreed reluctantly. "But there's one thing I want you to think about in the coming days."

"What?" she asked.

"This," I said and kissed her again. For quite a long while.

***

"What kept you?" the unwanted dinner guests demanded when we strolled up to the table. Salad and bread sticks were already at hand. Lex and Dawes were drinking wine. Burt had gone for a beer.

I let Naomie slide into the booth next to Burt and settled in next to her. "Dog maintenance," I said. That shut them up.

A member of the wait staff materialized and asked what Naomie and I would like to drink, then asked if everyone was ready to order. The others were. Letting them make their requests, I scanned the menu more for what Beelz would want me to get for his takeout then for a choice of my own. That was always easy. I headed for something with beef. This time out Beef Gorgonzola Alfredo. One for me now, one for the hound to go. Didn't pay any attention to what everyone else ordered. Naomie filled a plate with salad. I made do with a bread stick. I'd lost my head with her already. No need to do so with vegetables. Dawes was man enough to be enthusiastic over the rabbit savories. How very un-wolf like of him.

"Okay, I know why you're here," I said pointing the bread stick at the werewolf, "and I know why Burt is, but you…" I leveled the doughy pointer at Lex. "I've no idea why you are."

She held up a finger—fortunately not the middle one—while she hastily swallowed a clump of lettuce. "Beck Ritter called me. I'd asked her to let me know when her article would appear and send a copy along."

I got a bad feeling.

"It releases in the morning. I thought you needed a heads-up, Bram." While she talked, she rifled through her purse. It was a monster-sized one and even from across the table I could see notebooks and tourist pamphlets took up most of the space. She found her phone and scanned through the messages until she found the one she wanted and then handed the phone to me.

Naomie leaned closer, peering at the tiny screen. We both read in silence. I knew when Nomes hit the final line because she gasped in shock.

I met Lex's eyes across the table. "Has Delia seen this?"

"I thought you should see it first."

"Team Raven sticks together?" I asked.

"Team Raven had damn well better," Lex said. "I sure as hell don't want the franchise shot down before I can profit from it."

I handed the phone back to her and magicked my own to hand. No actual magic was involved because, other than Dawes, the restaurant was filled with generic humans who hadn't a clue. I had Delia on the line before Lex found the number among her saved contacts.

"Damage control, cuz," I told the PR witch. "4th Estate goes live with a story that will make my name an anathema." Didn't want that. I wasn't sure I could spell anathema. "Lex has an advanced copy—Ritter likes her and apparently hates me. Lex is sending you a copy as we speak."

"I'll call you back once I've seen it," Delia promised then disconnected.

Dawes took a sip of wine. I hadn't gotten my bourbon yet or I'd have downed it in one. "Doesn't sound good, Farrell. You going to share with Burt and me, or do we have to wait to see it pop up as a Yahoo news feature?"

I leaned back in my seat, one arm stretched along the outer edge of the table. "It appears I put my foot in it the other day. It was a throwaway line. An exit line. Don't know what I was thinking."

"It was a great line to end a chapter on," Lex said.

It was that, except I didn't write in chapters—or is that dictate in chapters?—I did it by days and I'd doomed myself after one too many breakfasts. "I mentioned that my office blew up last fall."

Dawes cringed.

Beneath the table, Naomie grabbed my hand. "Like in *Raven's Moon*?"

"It made for a great scene, though, didn't it?" She'd probably give me that lecture about using things that really happened being a bad thing to do on the way home, but it was water under the bridge. Well, not *The* Bridge, but *a* bridge. A nonexistent bridge.

"You were lucky to only have a few scratches after that," Burt contributed. "I'd sorta forgotten about it since the car got trashed later that night."

Nomes' grip under the table took on qualities a giant would admire in a girl. My hand felt a bit numb, but I didn't let go. Instead I entwined my fingers with hers. I had recounted the death of the first Mustang in the new book, too. If things continued at this pace, she would soon tumble onto the fact that the story hadn't had a lick of fiction in it. It was a recounting of my first days outside of a book binding.

"Our diligent investigative reporter dug up the news reports and talked to an unidentified source at police headquarters," I said.

"Durkin's gonna shit razor blades over that," Dawes said.

"Oh, it gets worse. I gave her one of the B. Farrell Investigations cards because it had my cell number on it. In fact, it was when she'd asked about the marked-out section that I mentioned the office building's death."

"I drove by the location a week or so ago. They razed the place. Just an empty lot at that end of the shopping center now," Burt contributed.

"At least evidence at the scene proved I didn't do it."

"Just the cause of it, considering it was your office that'd had the bomb tucked inside," Dawes reminded me.

"You're such a cheerful dinner guest."

Lex's hand was pressed to her lips in shock. "Shit," she mumbled. "I told Ritter about the grill blowing up."

I shrugged. "Well, she'd seen the destruction to the house. It was when she showed up to tackle me before Nomes would normally have been on hand to run interference that I sent her away with a misdirection. I told her I'd meet her at Denny's, and then she called you to meet us there as well, Lex."

Naomie frowned. "What sort of misdirection, boss?"

"I told her someone from the city was due to check things out. Sorta implied they might be looking for a gas leak."

"But I'm the one who showed up," Dawes said.

"In all your alien-visitation protection gear," I agreed.

When the others looked to him for an explanation, the werewolf shrugged. "I was working bomb squad that day."

That shut them all up. Briefly.

Burt fortified himself with a long swallow of beer. "Did this reporter learn that, too?"

"Doesn't look like it, but if she does stumble on it, that's just icing on the cake, isn't it? Bram Farrell, soon to be Detroit's least-wanted taxpayer."

"Nah," Dawes drawled. "Those books fill the city coffers through sales tax as well as taxing your ass, Farrell. Not saying they won't lock you up for your own safety, but…"

"You're pickin' up your own tab after that amateur soothsaying," I warned.

"Thought I was doing so anyway."

"Nomes invited all of you. I figured she was buying."

At her gasp, I tossed her a grin. "You are keeper of the company credit card, aren't you?"

She grinned. "Yes, I am,"

"A credit card *and* the key to his house?" Dawes murmured.

"Key to the *office*," Naomie and I said in unison.

"But he's got a key to your place now," Burt pointed out.

"Which I can now return since Beelz and I will be back in our own habitat tonight." I placed said key on the table next to her salad plate. As I had not released her hand—or maybe she hadn't released mine?—it lay there on display. "Thanks for lending your couch to me and the beanbag chair to Beelz. Knowing him, he'll clean your face in payment before we head back to Casa Amberson."

I hoped that put things to rest regarding the holocaust due to hit in the morning, but Lex had been musing on things. Couldn't help wondering whether she was considering how her Young Raven could get into situations where villainous types tried to blow him up.

"All any of that indicates is that you had a real run of bad luck last October," Dawes said.

"Ah, but it gets worse." Not to mention, very creative of Ritter to dream it up. "The article suggests that I had plenty of time to rummage through Calista's old files and find unpublished Raven Tales that I am now claiming I wrote."

"Which is ridiculous," Naomie insisted. "There's the whole new concept of The Raven discovering he's fictional and then getting sucked into an entirely different Detroit than the one he was in before."

"The whole parallel worlds thing," Lex agreed. "Calista had no reason to put a different spin on things, but it makes perfect sense that something had to change in the tales when a different writer took over."

"Thank you," I said. "Case closed."

But Lex wasn't quite done yet. She'd been ruminating on the only thing I hadn't explained.

"If you had an office for B. Farrell Investigations, does that mean you lied to Beck Ritter and actually *are* a private detective, Bram?" she asked.

The answer was, yes, but not under that business name. For twenty books, I'd been the sole investigator for Raven Investigations. But admitting to that would get me locked up in a loony bin. Everyone knew The Raven wasn't a real person. Only Otherworlders knew I was real and every one of them had known the moment I stepped through the portal from that world into this one. Every. Single. One.

"Nope. As I told Ritter that morning, I'm a researcher."

And that's the story I was sticking with. The one that really *was* pure fiction.

***

Delia called while dessert was being ordered and said she'd be contacting the publisher's PR department in the morning to work out whether damage control would be needed. Once they had a game plan, she'd let me know.

Naomie was quiet on the way back to her place. Mentally re-running the pre-dinner table talk I'd prefer her to forget. No chance of that, naturally. I had not held her hand *en route* to the car as we left the restaurant, but I did from the parking lot into her apartment building. Couldn't tell whether she was content or humoring me.

Beelz was happy to see us both, but he believes in slavering over ladies first. I'd left his dinner in the car, but he wouldn't mind that it was a bit cold. Unfortunately, for him, we couldn't take the time to linger with Nomes because of the rendezvous raid with Hammer and his troops. Hopefully, we'd corner Quinton Frost, find he did, indeed, have Eric Winthur held captive and had just been sluggish in getting a ransom note in the mail, and then we'd put him down. Once Eric was safe, I didn't care what Hammer and his boys did to the stalker accountant.

Before Naomie had a chance to take her coat off, I pulled her close.

"You are not going to kiss me again, are you?" She sounded a bit perturbed with me.

"I'd kiss my mother goodnight. I'd kiss my grandmother goodnight. I'd kiss my sister goodnight."

"You have a sister?"

"No. You're missing the point, Nomes."

"The point is, boss, that you shouldn't kiss your secretary."

"Why not? A precedent for such things is already in place. I believe that The Raven kissed his secretary." Which I had back in my old life. True to hard-boiled detective literature form, she'd been a looker, though the clients had been vamps—and I'm not talking vampires.

"He did." Nomes agreed. "But in *Ring Around the Raven,* she got killed."

Oops. "That was fiction, sugar."

"And this is reality. There is a law or something about proper behavior of a personal nature in the workplace."

"Tell Dawes to arrest me. He'd be glad to take my place," I said.

She frowned at me. "No, he wouldn't. He likes Lex."

"He just met Lex tonight."

"The point is—"

"The point is," I interrupted her. "You and I have had a connection since last fall, Nomes."

"Boss." Pure frustration bound up in a single word. But, as noted earlier that evening, she wasn't pushing me away.

"Bram," I corrected and kissed her lightly, then backed away.

"The pooch and I will see you at the usual place at the usual time, Ms. Enright."

The sigh she gave was a deep one. "Are you going to kiss me when I arrive for work?"

I pointed to where Beelz sat at our feet, his neck stretched as he looked up at us. "He does, so why not me?"

"Goodnight, boss," Nomes said.

The hound and I waited until we heard all the locks click into place before heading out.

He decided there was enough room to wolf down the beef and noodles in the car on the shotgun side's floor. I turned the carry-all bag the Garden had supplied into a tablecloth and sat the take-out tray on it. Then we were off for what I hoped would be a rescue operation.

***

To say the neighborhood was unsavory is difficult to qualify. There are degrees of unsavory in all large cities. Always have been, probably always will be. Detroit's downslide was decades in the making, but the city's bankruptcy had been a real blow. The address on the napkin had probably once been a lovely area, but now, it was a land of abandoned and crumbling factory buildings combined with unsanctioned trash-dumping. Homes and businesses were boarded up and had city notices posted on them, no doubt warning that the place was unsafe and, thus, condemned. Definitely forgotten by all but the criminal element (which included both Otherworlders *and* humans) and the braver—or death-seeking—homeless.

A tall wire fence topped with barbed wire curls surrounded the property. There were sturdy but far-from-new padlocks securing the chains wrapped through the gate sections. Since at some point in the past, someone had cut through the fence from top to bottom not fifteen feet away, all it took was maneuvering through the gap to gain entrance. Beelz went through with no problem. I had to hold the prickly bits of cut and rusted fence aside and duck my head to follow him.

I'd brought a flashlight but didn't want to give a police patrol car a reason to bust me. There had been signs on the gate and fence warning that this was private property and that I should keep out. It didn't look like anyone was paying property tax on it, but as a place for nefarious transactions, it definitely had the privacy thing down pat.

The dried and partially snow-covered remains of weeds and wild grasses lined the fence, but not by the opening in it. There, even the snow was well-tramped down. A well-travelled byway, though foot traffic only.

When Beelz halted and growled a warning, I took the Smith & Wesson M&P from my coat pocket. I hadn't put it in the glove compartment where Naomie might stumble across it, but beneath the driver's seat in the car, wrapped in a dark towel that had been acquired during my stop at Dollar General. I'd had an M&P back in fictionland, but it hadn't followed me across from the page. But then, neither had any magic at first. The hocus had pocused my way slowly, but I still wasn't up to the par I'd been on the page. And I'd missed the backup of non-magic firepower. One of the first things I'd done when Calie had vanished and I was still on this side had been to start paperwork for a license to carry. Fortunately, I hadn't left the Smith & Wesson in the Mustang the night before but tucked in my back waistband under my sweater.

"Raven?" I heard a gruff whisper ask.

"Hammer?"

"Yeah," he said and eased into sight, his eyes on the Smith & Wesson in my hand. "I thought you only used magic in confrontations."

"You still haven't read the books," I countered. "You do any reconnaissance?"

"Had the boys ghosting about. No sign of anyone, but that don't mean nothin' with Frost a blood-sucker now. There's locks on the doors, but only one of them is new."

"Haven't picked it yet?"

"This is your party. We're just here to deliver comeuppance."

I gestured with the pistol, not trusting him a minute. "Lead on then."

He melted back into the night as did Beelz and I. Rather than attempt to take point as he had back in October when we'd had a visit with Palermo, the hound was right at my feet.

Hammer's buddies drifted in around us. Whether as an escort or to ensure I didn't try to make a dash for safety was a toss-up. They all stopped six feet out from the door with the new lock. I wondered whether any of the other doors had been locked from the outside and, if so, why no one had considered them as safer entry points. I'd never know. They'd obviously decided this was the way to get in.

"Go on," Hammer urged. "Open it."

I turned my flashlight on, aiming it at the lock. "It's already open."

Hammer glared at his men. "Who picked the damn thing?"

They looked at each other, then looked at him and shrugged.

"You sure it was locked?" I asked.

One of them bobbled his head. "Yeah. I even tugged on it."

"Then the obvious answer is that we are not alone, gents. Watch your six."

While they all craned their necks, peering into the night—like it was possible to see anything—I lived dangerously. I took the lock in hand, removed it from the latch and dropped it into my coat pocket. At least whoever had unlocked the door to lure us in wouldn't be able to lock us in. Still wondering whether I was making a grave error, I flicked the flashlight off again and opened the door.

Nothing exploded. Honest to Odin, I had half expected it to, although I'd no idea how an assassin would have known where I was headed. Of course, there were plenty of other things that weren't assassins who might want to take me out. Ditto with Hammer and his crew. My money was on Quentin Frost booby-trapping the place, though, as a vampire now, he might not have felt it worth going to the trouble to do so.

The vamp snacks let me be the first to cross the threshold. Even Beelz held back until I'd crossed it safely. When he trotted in, the others followed on his tail. This, of course, meant we were all clumped together barely six feet inside the building.

"Split up?" I suggested.

Hammer grunted and waved his men off. They scattered, moving slowly, keeping an eye out for trouble. Then one of them fell over. He didn't make a sound, just… well, laid down on the job. Face first. He didn't move.

I know all this because the lights came on. Not overhead lights, but a bar of security ones placed so their beams arched toward the roof. I wasted no more than two seconds on the downed man and shielded up.

Within the security glow sat an old-fashioned canvas screen, the kind people with movie cameras had set up in their homes in the past when reel-to-reel was high-tech. And then the movie began.

The picture flickered a bit. Probably the old equipment debating whether to work or not. Then it settled down to display a man seated in a leather armchair. From the description the bartender at The Red Dragon had given, this was Frost. The fury-fueled way Hammer lurched forward drove the last nail in the positive identification coffin. Yep, it was Quinton Frost all right.

He wasn't as slick as old vampires, but he was well-dressed, though still pulling off the office casual thing. He smiled at the camera. And not a nice smile either. More like that of a man who believed he had the upper hand.

"Whoever you are, you certainly took your time finding me. But then, the chase had to be merry to be worthwhile. Too bad Wendy didn't come with you. Oh, there is a chance that she did, but adventures aren't really her thing now, are they? No, the sly seduction, the almost-made promises, the deception… Those are more her line of business. I do hope she didn't dupe you into coming to the rescue. You'll end up like me if she did. Or perhaps you won't. Be leaving here, that is. A message needs to be sent. Not only to dear, lovely, lying Wendy, but to her master. The message is, don't fuck with the humans." He paused, took a sip from a wine glass that obviously wasn't filled with wine. "But then, I'm not human anymore, so I suppose that means I can fuck with as many humans as I damn well please."

Whether they were aware of doing so or not, Hammer and his men moved nearer to the screen. You'd think they would know a vampiric mesmerizing when they met one. Perhaps they hadn't known it would work even when the vamp wasn't physically present. Behind my shield, I sure as hell felt the pull.

Which was when my mind flickered to the memory of Naomie's entrancing eyes—something it had begun doing a lot of on its own. While Frost droned on, I leafed through Nomes' smiles, her frowns, that tantalizing way she chewed on her lip, her laugh, how she felt in my arms. How she'd insisted I needed to stop kissing her and then kissed me back, giving lie to every word she'd uttered. And, bingo, the fairly freshly-turned vampire's attempt to befuddle my mind vanished.

Hammer and his men weren't as lucky. Their stances shouted pacification. Except for the guy stretched out on the floor, they stood waiting to do Frost's bidding.

We all watched the screen as Quinton Frost, former accountant, former lover of Wendy Whilsen, former human, licked the last drop of blood from his glass. He turned back to face the camera. "See you in Hell one of these days."

The film ran out and half a dozen packages dropped from the ceiling on cords. The cords gave a last recoil and…

"What the fu—" Hammer snarled.

Whether he finished the curse or not, I don't know because Beelz went Great Dane and leapt on me, knocking me to the floor. And things really did head straight to Pandæmonium.

***

It isn't easy breathing when the full length of a Great Dane has you pinned to the floor and that floor (even if it is cement) is pulsing from a series of explosive devices that sent a few souls on a short cut to Valhalla. If Hammer's men didn't have their fists wrapped around concealed weapons when they went, then the destination was more likely Helheim. The goddess Hel does not treat arrivals in quite the same way as the All Father does. At least, that's what she told me one boozy night at the Antagonist's Lair in my other life.

"Off," I requested of the hellhound. He looked back at the scene of destruction before agreeing to move. I scrambled to my feet. My shield had gone down when he'd pounced, but that was because it's structured to do so. Since he's a friendly, the moment he hit me, I'd thrown a new one around us both. Whatever parts of the building rained on us had bounced to the side, leaving a cleared space where we'd been beneath the shield.

I picked my way over them to check on Hammer and his men. Only Hammer was still breathing. He'd been standing five feet behind the others, but he was in bad shape. He wasn't going to make it.

He was alert enough to grab my arm. "Call a vamp," he gasped. "I'd rather go via a bite than like this."

Didn't bother to argue with him.

Glanced at Beelz, though. Obviously, Frost had been there, or a minion he'd picked up. Someone had to have opened the lock, silently taken down Hammer's man, flicked on the movie, then dropped the lethal packages. "Recon," I told the hound. "Anything that smells of vamp—be they vampire or have the scent of one on them—take 'em down."

Beelzebub vanished and not as in, moving really fast. The hellhound totally vanished. I'd never seen him do that before, but it was the perfect mode for hunting.

I got on the cell and called The Red Dragon. Asked for Wendy. Said it was an emergency. Told them to tell her it was me calling.

"I need you here," I said when she came to the phone and gave her the address. "As fast as you can move."

"Is it Eric?"

"Hammer. He was helping me. I'll tell you more when you get here, but he doesn't have long. Wants a bite."

"I can't turn him without—"

I cut her off. "Not a turn. A bite."

"Keep him alive," she said and hung up.

Keep him alive. Now that was a tricky thing.

Beelz manifested back to the visible world still Dane-sized.

"Nothin', huh?"

We had the silent communication thing down to a science. His stance said it all. Whoever had orchestrated things, they were no longer on site.

I looked from Beelz to the downed Hammer. "Ideas?"

He had nothin'. Just stared at Hammer.

I stared at Hammer, too. He didn't seem to be bleeding out, but he was splattered in what I could only guess were parts of his team of idiots. One of them, I recalled, knew how to read. He'd had one of the Raven Tale books in his hand the day I'd met all of them. He'd lost that hand and part of his skull thanks to Frost.

"Wendy's on her way. Knows it's an emergency. Still, she's at The Red Dragon. It might take a while."

"She'll fly," Hammer said though I could barely hear the words.

"Has a fast car and drives like a bat out of hell, does she?" I asked attempting to… I don't know, take his mind off the direness of his situation?

"No," she said, walking quickly through the now very-opened

door. It had been blown back and was hanging tipsily on one hinge. "He means I changed into a bat. A very fast bat."

She still looked very bat-ish but that could be because I was used to seeing her gowned in red. Something that might have been folded webbed wings draped from ebony-sheened flesh. Her golden hair was black as well. Only her face looked human, though I doubted it had during her flight.

"Hammer," she said, kneeling at his side. As she stretched a wingtip toward him, it became a pale woman's hand. She slid her fingers through his greasy hair tenderly.

"Tell Mr. Pa—" he gasped.

"Hush." She brushed her lips over his to silence him. "Journey well, trusted servant," she whispered then sank her fangs into his neck.

Hammer gave a sigh of pleasure. She stayed in place, feasting, long after the light of life left his eyes.

When she leaned back on her heels, it was to lick a drop of blood from the corner of her mouth. Her fangs retreated. "I trust you'll remove the evidence?"

I nodded. "Just so you know, I am close to finding Eric. I'd hoped Frost was keeping him here, but it was a trap for whomever came looking for him. The accountant left clues to ensure whoever you sent wouldn't leave."

"Yet you are unharmed, Raven."

"I have uncommonly effective backup."

Her gaze went past me to where Beelz stood in his big box store disguise. "I recall very well," she murmured. "It took a week for me to recover from his mauling."

His red eyes burned with the intensity of an active magma cauldron as they met hers. His muzzle stretched in a canine sneer. His look said, "Don't fuck with what's mine, hag."

"Frost," she said. "Let me know when you find him. I'll suck him dry."

"He found one of your kind to turn him, you know."

"Yes," she said, and that *S* went on forever. "Rather than go through the dragon's staff, or Mr. Palermo's office, call this number when the time comes."

I took the card she gave me. Directed the flashlight on it. There was a number ten digits long. "Cell?"

She stood. "I'd best get back. I'm on break."

I held out my hand to her. "Thanks, Wendy. I didn't like Hammer or his underlings, but they got caught in the crossfire. Appreciate that you helped him leave the way he wanted to."

She ignored my hand and was already losing any guise of being human, her hands becoming wing tips, her complexion darkening. But I could still see when she smiled. "Don't thank me too soon, Raven. I'm sure Mr. Palermo will demand something of both of us in payment for his lost ground troops."

When she stepped through the door, I saw one strong wing stroke and she was gone.

I called Durkin.

February 18th

Midnight came and went on its merry way.

"My missing person's case?" I said to a very grumpy police detective. "Well, the trail led me into a trap. I have five dead humans, all the result of some handy explosives, though one was finished off by a vampire at his request."

"I get the strangest phone calls from you," Durkin rumbled. "Address."

Although he left off the question mark, I delivered it.

"Officers will be there shortly. Expect the wagons. You okay?"

"Yep. For a change."

"Then I'll tell them no sirens." He hung up.

Although I know it was bad form to fuck with a crime scene, I went through Hammer's pockets and removed anything that would tie back to Palermo, then psyched myself up to do the same with what was left of the goons. Fortunately, only Hammer had something on him that led to the vampire mafia don—his cell phone. I confiscated it, then looked for the remains of the movie projector and ensured that the entire reel of tape was not going to give Frost's new vampiric life away. There was nothing left for tech types to harvest after my fire ball had incinerated it. My work there done, I walked back to the break in the fence to wait for the local police. Beelz returned to his dachshund form and sat complacently at my feet.

A patrol car was the first to pull up, but another was nearly on its bumper. The light display flashing from the roofs was blinding. I held my hand up to shelter my eyes from the glare as the cops got out.

"Are you Mr. Farrell?" the first one up asked.

I nodded, then gestured back toward the now dark and silent—and even more decrepit—building. "It's not a pretty sight," I said. "Mind if I stay out here rather than accompany you to the scene?"

The cop gestured to the men from the second car to slip through the fence and take a look, then took out his notebook. "You called a detective from the 4th Precinct rather than 9-1-1," he said. "Why was that?"

"He's a poker buddy. I thought calling him would save time and get the required team out immediately."

"Do you live in this area, Mr. Farrell?"

I admitted that I did not but had been out for dinner, decided to take a different route home, and gotten lost. "When the dog indicated he needed a stop, I pulled over. We were about to get back on the road when I saw lights go on in the building back there and then heard an explosion. I ran to see if anyone had been injured. Had taken my flashlight with me to keep an eye on my hound. He sorta blends into the scenery at night."

The officer glanced down at Beelz. The mutt had wedged himself between my feet, put his muzzle on my foot and closed his eyes, to all intents and purposes bored and taking a quick nap. It had the added benefit of keeping his demon-tell eyes from getting attention. "He does at that," the cop agreed. "Did you go inside the building, sir?"

"Yes, I did. The flashlight showed a man down. I went in to see if he was alive. He wasn't. Then I saw the others further in. I moved around to see if any were breathing. Most I didn't have to check. Then I called Chad Durkin and hightailed it back out here to the road. He'd have my head if I did anything more than check on the downed men."

"Did you touch anything, sir?"

It was the dead of night in February in Detroit. I had gloves on. There would be no fingerprints. I still had the padlock in my left coat pocket. Sorta hoped Durkin would be willing to run fingerprints on it. I wanted them to prove Quinton Frost had been the mastermind behind the dramatic set up that had wiped Hammer and his guys out. Being a vampire now, Frost might not have worn gloves. Having been human, he might have fingerprints on file. If he showed up, I had the Smith & Wesson in my right-hand pocket. No silver bullets, but then, they work best—though not always effectively—on werewolves, not vampires, and Dawes hadn't given me any reason to have a beef with him.

"Just touched the couple men who were… er… whole enough to possibly still be alive," I said. Which was the first truthful thing I'd said. "Took a glove off to check for a pulse, that's all."

He asked for my driver's license, made note of my name, address, and who knew what else. Asked for a phone number where I could be reached if they had further questions. As the crime scene and medic teams arrived, he told me I could leave.

It was just past one. I headed for The Red Dragon, a stiff drink, and to give Wendy a more detailed report on the search for her great-grandson.

***

The Amberson mansion sat in the middle of a wide plain of carefully tended grass, which was currently hidden beneath a coating of untouched snow. If it hadn't been dark, the house might have looked brooding. It was a monster of a place. Even before the modern kitchen wing had been destroyed, it hadn't been the sort of joint I would have chosen for myself. It was Calie's taste. You'd think that a guy she made up might have similar tastes, but I'd found soon after crossing that, while she'd dreamed me into existence, the only thing we had in common was that we were both magic-users. Not that I'd minded inheriting the hefty bank accounts, the royalty rights to *The Raven Tales* books, or Beelz, but the rest I'd known had to move on. There were better uses for her fortune than three classic antique, and, thus, never used, cars, and a house where the only rooms lived in regularly were the media room, the bathroom with the Clydesdale-sized shower, the study, and the foyer where Naomie's desk sat. Well, and now and then, part of the kitchen. The part with the coffee maker. Beelz occasionally roamed the estate's grounds, but even he wasn't much interested in venturing out often at this season.

I'd been far more comfortable at Naomie's apartment. Yeah, it was a bit small, but it felt more like a home than the mansion ever did. Could be that was because, back home in that other world as the Raven, I had made do with much smaller and less grand digs.

Could be because at Nomes' I felt welcomed, not… well, I didn't know what. Put up with? Tolerated? I was still new to being human. Which the Otherworlders in my circle of acquaintances assured me I wasn't quite yet. A trace human, but *real* person status was still on the list of things to discuss with old St. Nick.

Naomie had left her mark on the mansion before leaving the evening before. The soft glow of lamps left lit spilled from the tall, currently naked study and media room windows. I'd need to figure out how to cover them. Why make it easy for an assassin to take a bead on me? It was either that or give up watching movies for the night. With my usual computer resting in the trunk of Nomes' car and the spare blown up along with the Mustang, I'd be reduced to watching on the itty-bitty cell phone screen. Or stuck reading a book. Which meant…

Yeah, sheets were going to get tacked up with duct tape. There should be some of the latter in my desk drawer and a closet full of the former, all freshly laundered and longing to be used somewhere. As long as no one peppered me with shotgun pellets while I hung them up, the night would once more belong to Hollywood on the big screen with an Evan Williams close at hand.

The mansion was warm, the furnace winning the battle against the cold nicely. I took the steps to the upper floor two at a time, Beelz following at a slower dachshundric pace, with my mind slotting in items on ye olde mental To Do list. Come dawn it would be back to the hunt for Eric Winthur and his captor, Quentin Frost. *And* a return to ferreting out Solomon Prisk, the ghoul Durkin believed was linked to a growing list of missing persons cases—human persons. I'd have to figure out who the hell put a hit out on me and how to avoid the Heart Burn curse if it was headed my way. I'd also have to live through whatever hell Beck Ritter's journalistic battering had produced and endure the agony of my first-ever tax-paying adventure with the IRS.

Plus, I had to sort out this growing desire to have my life revolve around Naomie Enright rather than anything to do with the fellow I'd been. You know, The Raven. The guy I still was when the occasion required someone to punish and kill a rogue Otherworlder.

Right now, the shower was calling me. I needed to wash away the taint of Hammer's death site.

As there were no further death threats posted on my door, I tossed my coat onto the never-used bed, turned the shower on to make the place steamy, then plucked a fresh set of the usual clothes from the closet.

"What's your viewing choice for the evening?" I asked the hound as hot water rained down on the two of us. "Restart the *Star Wars* saga from Episode IV, go for classic comedy with the original *Ghostbusters*, or kick ass with Jackie Chan?"

He chose *The Avengers* movies. Yeah, they weren't even on the list, but I *had* asked him what he wanted to watch.

It was as I finished dressing and was shoving the Smith & Wesson in place in my waistband (with one or more assassins out there, why take chances?) that the hellhound's snout came up sharply. He turned toward the open door, his growl revving.

There was an ominous *whoosh* and deadly shadows began dancing in fiendish delight on the corridor's walls.

I grabbed my coat. Checked that the cell phone was still in the pocket. The car keys. Yanked open the drawer where extra cash was stashed and shoved it into my pocket. During the thirty seconds I spent preparing to abandon ship, Beelz had done a reconnaissance. He barked a report. Not getting the entire gist of it, I followed him into the hall.

Flames were licking up the walls. In lieu of drapes and the usual area rug in the foyer, someone had tossed Naomie's collection of paperback vampire romances and upholstery cushions from the media room furniture before the door, turning them into an exit-blocking inferno. In both my office and the media room, the wall-to-wall carpeting was ablaze. Fire was making its way up the runner on the stairs. Smoke was gathering, roweling on the ceiling of the grand two-story entryway and on this level.

The scent in the air was heavily tinged with gasoline, a smell I knew well from the twin Mustang killings. Can't blow up a car without that petroleum afterglow.

One of those damn assassins was ruining my evening again. Who the fuck wanted me dead?

Mentally, I reviewed possible escape routes. The back stairs—the old servant staircase—led down to the kitchen wing. The currently sealed-off kitchen wing. There were no handy trellises attached to the outer walls, no sturdy vines staking a claim on the masonry, no convenient lower level roofed areas to clamber out onto. In any case, there was no way a dachshund could do a climb.

But then, Beelz was no ordinary doxy. He was a being birthed in the fires of Hell.

"Can you get yourself out?" I asked.

He gave me a brief nod and went Great Dane.

"Follow me," I said and retreated into the bedroom. Closed the door. Rammed the bedspread against the gap at the bottom of it. A temporary measure. There was already smoke in the room. It took exception to my pushing the window wide open. Or perhaps it was the icy gust of wind that rushed in that it disliked.

Yeah, there was a chance that whoever—or whatever—had started the fire was out there waiting for me, but I didn't fancy being roasted. Better the unknown.

I stood back. "Out you go," I told Beelz. He took an awesome leap and sailed into the night. I slung my legs over the window ledge, pushed off in a flying leap of my own, but fully encased in a bubble shield. I hadn't used one since I'd needed to survive the dangers of The Brothers Woods back in fictionland, but since there was never a friendly dragon or a Pegasus around when you needed one, it was all I had.

The bubble hit the ground, bounced, and rolled. Inside it, I smashed against the sides, went head-over-heels as it continued its way deep into the south lawn. The experience had me swearing by every gods-only condominium complex on ancient record. Bruised but breathing, I lay prone in the snow, the gun digging into my back. If the arsonist was out there watching, maybe he'd think I was dead. Beelz ran up to check on me. He was back in wiener form. I let the shield drop, then erected a new one around us both.

"I'm okay," I told the pooch, barely moving my lips. "Just playing dead. Go into mourning, would you?"

To him that meant stretching his neck, muzzle to the night sky, and crooning a sorrowful cry. Then he lay down, his head resting on my chest.

"Think they bought it?" I asked. He snorted, which I took for, *doubt it.*

Time inched by. Not daring to move or open my eyes in the event the hunter had night-vision binoculars, I waited. The hardest part of playing dead outside in February was not sending breath smoke signals into the night. If I matched a few small vapors with Beelz's, the ruse might work.

At least the burning mansion contributed a bit of heat. It melted the snow. Or maybe that was the heat of the hellhound in his mournful role warming the area.

I wondered how long it would be before anyone noticed that the place was on fire. The house sat half a mile back from the road and the woodlands that edged the estate were thick. But they weren't heavily coniferous. With the brush playing dead and the trees long stripped of leaves, the flames should be visible.

If anyone was up and about in the middle of the night in this neighborhood, that is.

Then I heard the comforting sound of a car engine turning over. The crunch as tires backed over frozen snow and ice. As it grew fainter and fainter, I finally moved slowly to extract my phone from an inner coat pocket. Rather than Durkin, I called 9-1-1 and reported the fire.

Durkin, I knew, would be hot on the heels of the emergency vehicles. He kept his ears peeled for anything remotely related to me. I might not live within the scope of his precinct duties, but I was always a person of interest to him.

I wish I wasn't so interesting sometimes.

Like now.

***

By the time dawn broke, the fire trucks were station-bound. They'd left Beelz and me stranded until help of a different kind arrived. Not satisfied with doing the house an injustice—like it was its fault I lived there—our mysterious fire bug had smashed in a window and dropped burning rags inside the Charger. The rental agency was going to be really pissed.

While we waited, the dog and I stood far back on the drive and stared at the house.

It looked hungry.

Well, *mean* and hungry, though hungry was bad enough.

Thanks to the fire fighters' diligence, it was iced a frost white and featured long stalactite teeth. Unblinking, empty, shadowed, once-paned eyes stared back at us. Quite a few of them, which added to the evil of the thing.

"You got a place in Hell where we can bunk?" I asked Beelz. At least it would be warmer if he did. I was freezing my… well, I was starting to lose feeling in my fingers and toes. Probably other parts would follow shortly. What I had on was damp from my playing dead in the snow and not contributing in the least to body heat maintenance.

The hound sighed.

"Remember January?" I queried. "Our lives were nice and quiet. Just me talking the book out, Nomes' fingers dancing over the keyboard as she listened to the playback. All the naps you cared to take. The movies we enjoyed?" I echoed his sigh. "Think things will ever be that tame again?"

Before Durkin had left the scene, he asked if we needed a ride someplace. I said someone would be along. It might be Burt, though I hadn't called him. It might be the insurance witch. I had called her but at the office where I could leave voicemail. "Had a further bit of bad luck at Calie's," my message said. "You might want to come have a look at it." Let her be surprised. Not happy-surprised. No, this was more of a challenge sort of surprise. Finding any company that wanted to offer me coverage on anything was going to take a miracle. She was probably running shy on those.

The construction crew arrived, took one look at the house and decided to take a sick day. The contractor certainly looked ill. He said he'd call and cancel the specially ordered windows. Seemed a good idea to me. I asked if he had a card. I'd sorta lost the previous one in the evening's apocalypse. There was a good chance I'd have work for him in the future. It wasn't going to be on this site, though. Once all officials gave the go-ahead, I was calling in the bulldozers to wipe out whatever remained. Maybe there were copper pipes I could hock to the salvage folks.

As the work crews headed back down the drive, I glanced at my watch. It had survived my leap from Hell, which was more than I could say for my shoulder, which hurt like I'd spent the evening with it in a torture device. I was alive, though. Sometimes being alive was not a comfortable situation, just better than the alternative.

A few minutes to nine Beelz alerted me to the sound of a familiar car engine. The horrendous lime-green Chevy came to a halt next to us. Nomes' eyes were wide and her mouth gaped as she took in the glory of the ice-toothed ruin of Casa Amberson. Then she was out of the car and…

Well, somehow, being homeless and lacking wheels once more, didn't bother me in the least.

***

Nomes had already stopped for donuts so we returned to her place. It was where the coffee pot was. I carried the computers back inside. While I thawed out in the shower, she toted the only clothes I possessed down to the building's laundry room and ran them through the dryer. Revitalized, or at least warm again, I prepared to face the day.

I waited until well-fortified with Pershing rolls covered in maple icing and nuts—nuts on pastries being tolerated, though the line was still drawn at nuts as hats on high priced bon-bons—then called the car rental agency with the bad news. I'd barely hung up when the insurance witch called. "Holy shit, Bram!" she said. Yeah, she'd been out to see the house. "It may take a while to get checks cut on these claims."

"Totally expected," I assured her. "Do your best. I'd say if you need anything from me, call, but words are about all I've got to my name at the moment." I suppose there was that extremely healthy bank account, too. I'd be siphoning it down by leaps and bounds very shortly.

Delia called next. She hadn't heard about the house. Her topic was how we were going to react to Beck Ritter's article. I recommended ignoring it. Delia said the publishing house had decided to capitalize on it. Although they'd only had the manuscript for a couple weeks, they were going to make publishing history by pushing the release date on *Raven's Moon* up to make a different kind of splash. The online bookstores were going to have pre-order buttons in place later in the day across the board. They wanted me to do an interview with a reporter from a rival news agency and—

I stopped Delia there by telling her about the fire.

"Too bad Ritter's article came out this morning, Bram. We could have blamed it on her, said some psycho fan of Calie's had torched the place."

"For all I know, they did. A sore loser who wasn't happy about me getting the contract for the next book. But I doubt it. Do what you do best, cuz." Which was working PR magic. "Whatever New York wants, I'll do it. Just coordinate things with Naomie."

Hearing her name, Nomes pushed back her chair in the reconfigured Raven Central office in her kitchen. She'd been checking e-mails while I fielded calls. I filled her in on Delia's news, then requested that she abandon the office and join me on the sofa. "There's something you need to know," I said.

She curled up a cushion away from me. She was attempting to follow through on rules of office etiquette, although she had totally forgotten them out at the house. Since she'd thrown herself in my arms and made breathing next to impossible for several minutes, I had nothing to complain about regarding her enthusiastic relief that I was still alive. Well, Beelz, too. He'd gotten his full quotient of attention and, in return, had licked her tears away.

"That doesn't sound good, boss,"

I reached over and took both her hands in mine. "Remember Valentine's Day?" I asked, then told her about Ernie's visit. Not that he was a cupid or that he'd shot an arrow at me, but that he'd been a hit man. A short one, but still… I segued into how the authorities had found evidence that the grill explosion hadn't been an accident. I moved on to the Mustang's demise the night we'd hit the sports bar to talk to Eric Winthur's friends.

"And now the house *and* the rental car makes it pretty clear that you shouldn't be kept in the dark, Nomes. Someone's put out a contract on me. It's dangerous to be in my vicinity. If you'd like to take a vacation to sunny Arizona and hang out with Lex when she heads back to Tucson later today, this would be an excellent time to do so."

She was quiet, but the grip she had on my hands was back to being a crushing one. "I'm staying here, boss."

"Nomes, it's dangerous."

"So is crossing the street at rush hour. I'm staying."

"You should think about it. Reconsider,"

"Staying," she repeated.

"Okay, then here's what I want you to do," I said.

Nomes probably thought it sounded like I'd put her under house arrest. To keep her safe, I left Beelz with her and told her not to leave the building. But as I then gave her something slightly illegal to occupy the day she didn't sulk.

In a nutshell, I set figurative hounds on Beck Ritter's trail. Two could play the investigative game. One didn't have to be a reporter to do so either.

***

I borrowed the lime-green sardine car and went shopping. Sadly, Target hadn't recovered from my last restocking venture. I hit JCPenney, Sears, and Macy's. Between the three, I finally had a wardrobe once more. A slightly more diversified one, but I needed something office casual before I could make a raid on Quinten Frost's office at One Detroit Center. Needed a better car, too. But I knew someone with a better car. Someone I was going to do a big favor for. All she had to do was dig up some information for me.

I called Helena, the CPA witch. "You interested in not working for someone else but for yourself?" I asked.

"Why?" She was suspicious. Heck, I would be, too, if I called myself with a teaser like that.

"Take your lunch at one," I said. "I'll be at your door. We'll be taking your car."

"What's this all about, Bram?"

"I'll explain it to you on the way," I promised and rang off.

My next stop was to the print shop where I'd gotten the B. Farrell Investigations business cards last fall. They ran a new batch of cards for me while I waited. These said Nevar Financial Services. Nevar… Raven backward. I called Frost's office and asked if he was in. They said he was unavailable. I would have been surprised if he *had* been available. It was a cold day with the sun a brilliant distant bit of warmth in the sky. I'd had to buy a pair of Ray-Ban Aviators at Macy's to mute the glare. But if the sun was shining, it was vampire snooze time.

"When will he be available today?" I asked.

"Mr. Frost is in Europe currently, sir. Perhaps another of our CPAs can help you?"

I pretended I'd aced an acting class. "Out of the country? At tax time? No wonder Frost wants to sell the company," I said, going for management level ticked off. Think I nailed it.

"Sell the company? I doubt that—"

I cut her off. "Put me through to whoever that idiot left in charge," I ordered.

She did so quite swiftly.

The guy stuck in the middle of things hadn't heard Frost intended to sell either. But then, it would have been news to Frost himself.

"I'll be there shortly after one with my head auditor to go over the books," I said, taking no prisoners. "Have them available. Everything Frost handled personally, as well as the company P&L and other pertinent documents. The sooner the transfer of ownership is made, the better Nevar Financial's board of directors will like it. But we aren't going to buy a pig in a poke."

Yeah, I was running out of management bluster. However, the sale was made. Not for Frost's company, though I did intend to take it over, gifting it to Helena, but for the scenario that afternoon.

"Yes, sir," the lackey responded. "I'm afraid I didn't catch your name, sir."

"Farrell," I said, disconnected and called Naomie.

"Heading back to dump purchases," I told her. "Lunch needed?"

She gave me sandwich orders for seven people. Damn, when she went on an information hunt, she did so with gusto. I had told her to call in whatever help she needed so getting dirt on Ritter would be swift. I pulled into a drive-thru and passed the order on. Added something for myself, and Beelz's usual choice as well.

There wasn't much room to walk in the apartment when I got there. Two strangers were seated on the sofa, another was in the beanbag chair, a couple more had their backs propped against walls. A long-legged guy had gotten comfy on Nome's bed, pillows piled behind his back. Beelz was next to him, supervising. The humans all had laptops and were banging away at the keyboards. Earbuds were a common denominator.

"Sending you new dirt," one of them called out without taking their eyes off the screen.

"Great!" Naomie sang out. She was at her official Raven Corp computer. Beneath the table, the printer was spitting out sheets of paper.

I cleared my throat and held up the take-out bags.

She looked up and did a quick scan of my disguise. "Boss?"

Yeah, wasn't looking quite the same as when I'd left. "Yeah," I said. "So not me, right?"

"A lot of that going around," Nomes said. Her look said she liked what she saw.

Without the guidance of helpful sales personnel, neither of us would ever manage to pull off a covert identity. I'd told the guy at Macy's that casual office power player was the look I was going for. He'd cut off sales tickets and sent me out into the world a new man. Well, a different one, at least. In place of the usual dark blue or black jeans were dark charcoal wool slacks. The black T-shirt had become a deep wine dress shirt. The collar points looked lethal enough to deliver paper cuts. A black silk necktie had been contorted into a double Windsor and then pulled loose. A black Harris Tweed jacket with a faint hint here and there of wine topped it, and a black honest-to-Sam Spade trench coat (with removable inner lining) was nearly the crowning touch. That honor was reserved for the Belfry Gangster black fedora with a red feather in the band. I did still have my jet Tony Lamas on. The sales guy thought they said casual office nicely, as did my scruffy oops-forgot-to-shave-again jaw line and fledgling mustache. He was probably on commission, but I still upped that tally with an under the table picture of Mr. Grant in a final handshake. Thinking of making this my trademark move.

One of the girls on the sofa turned, took me in, and murmured, "Whoa."

Nomes zipped to my side. "Boss," she said and did a round of introductions with pointing involved. I only remembered the name of the guy in the bedroom—her brother, Cormack. He tossed aside the laptop, hopped to his feet, and offered his hand. "Mack, not Cormack. Little sister's the only one who calls me that. In retaliation for me calling her Niel."

"My name is Naomie," she growled at him.

"Not what it says on your birth certificate, social security card, driver's license, or bank account, *Niela*," he snarled back.

Yep. Based on the way what few sibling characters I knew back in fictionland acted, they were family. Even had a similar mix of features. Mack had a stock of dark red hair, though, not light-sucking black like mine or Nomes' unlikely locks.

I shook his hand. "Bram," I said. "Your sister has a speech impediment that doesn't allow her to use it."

"Yeah, she's weird that way," he agreed. "Is that lunch I smell?"

"Special delivery." I handed the bag to Naomie to pass things around. "Mine's the one with—"

"Extra bacon," she said. "And Beelz's is three patties, no condiments."

She knew us so well.

Work on their… well, I'll call it what it was… *hacking* stopped while sandwiches disappeared. Nomes showed me what they had so far. I suggested she get the master list of Calista Replacement Search contestants from Delia, or at least tell her what we were looking for.

"I might need both you and Mack later this afternoon for a field trip, but I'll call if it's a go," I added as the last of my sandwich vanished.

"Got it."

We were the only ones in the kitchen. Mack had returned to the bedroom and his search assignment. The others had their ear buds back in, their fingers dancing tarantellas over the keys.

"So. You like the disguise?"

"Depends," Nomes said. "Does this version of you plan on bucking office conduct rules?"

I leaned closer to her. "Cupcake, both versions find you more tempting than those incredible maple-covered rolls this morning."

"Just so I know where that is on a scale of one to ten—is it above or below your Evan Williams?" she asked.

"Let's not totally lose our heads, sugar," I admonished, stole a kiss, then headed out the door again.

***

On the way over to pick Helena up for our accountancy raid, I did a bit of musing on who might have put the hit out on me. Ernie hadn't had details and, though one or more of his fellow assassins had taken a shot at disposing of me, there had been no face-to-face confrontations wherein I could shake answers to questions from any. That left logically-considered guesswork as my fallback option.

I could ask Delia whether she had been the only witch benefiting from Lilin deals with moon goddesses thanks to her association with Calista or if there were others. While Delia had turned against Calie last fall, that didn't mean there weren't other folks appropriating new bodies to wear. I needed to ask if there were coven conventions where networking was done, though my creator was more likely to attend fantasy conventions where fans could fawn on her rather than trawl for contacts with other witches. She might have already collected a pseudo Rolodex of magic-using humans long before I'd entered her literary scene. If so, someone on that list might want me taken out, but it would need to be someone with lots of moolah to toss around. And, actually, considering the way Calista had treated underlings, I couldn't really see anyone wanting to get even for her demise. With the queen bee gone, everyone else moved a step up the hierarchy ladder in the witchy world.

Another possibility was that Palermo wanted me out of town, off the map. As the head of the Detroit blood-suckers' mafia, he had the wherewithal to fund a hit, but why would he bother? If he really wanted me taken out, all he had to do was send a horde of lower echelon vamps to overpower me and siphon off whatever flowed through my veins. If it was indeed more magenta ink than physician-sanctioned blood, they might have upset stomachs after the feast, but they'd recover. I probably wouldn't.

No, hit men or women didn't sound like Palermo's style. Besides, whoever was after me had managed to disassemble the shield I had up at the mansion after the propane explosion and the one over the Mustang the other night. Vampires weren't magic-users, just shapechangers with dietary differences.

While I had killed two demons last fall—well, one had really been Beelz's kill—neither had seemed to have pals inclined to be vengeful. Besides, they couldn't have taken my shield down. *No one* should be able to take it down.

I was no closer to having a feasible hunch when I pulled Nomes' Spark into a visitor's parking slot before the accountancy where the coven number-cruncher worked. As requested, she was already waiting for me, her own car keys in hand.

Helena gave in to what she termed my illogical male need to be the one behind the wheel and let me drive her vehicle. It was a dark slate Buick Enclave. She was the mother of three sports-loving boys and needed the space for their equipment, she said. It handled like a dream, but SUVs were not on my radar. The only way Beelz could get himself inside one would be to morph to Great Dane and neither of us wanted him to do that in public.

"You want me to do what?" she demanded when I explained the scenario.

"We're doing a takeover," I explained. "Fudging it a bit, but still… The owner is one Quinton Frost who has gone insane and turned not only stalker, but vampire. I need to know all properties he might have purchased, leased, or has a bid in to buy. I need the addresses by tonight. The office can't reach him while it's daylight because he's in a box somewhere."

"At one of these locations you want me to find him?" Helena asked.

"Yup. I need to take him down tonight."

"Wouldn't it be better to stake him while he's dormant during the day, like tomorrow?"

"Definitely easier, but my backup on this is the vampire community. He's not been following their Roberts Rules of Order."

"Oh," she murmured in a very small voice. My world was nothin' like hers, even if she was a coven-card-carrying member with Calie's former crew. "I just have one stipulation, Bram."

"Mmm?"

"Introduce me as Lynn. I don't go by Helena outside of the coven."

I grinned over at her. "And is there a last name to go with that? I've found lately that I don't know beans about anyone, much less surnames."

"Did you mean it when you said Frost's firm will be mine when the dust settles?"

"Absolutely."

"Then we'll go with my real name rather than invent something to use," she said. "It's Smith."

***

I did the polite when we hit One Detroit Center and held the door for her. When we zoomed up in the elevator to the floor housing Frost Accountants, I let my lovely fake Nevar auditor go first. She looked very professional and intimidating: blonde hair just so, dark suit beneath a long dark wool coat, three-inch heels giving her added height. Her expression was scary. It said, *I know your books have errors and those errors will be found and punished to the full extent of the law.* I wondered if she'd begun her career as a Fed number-cruncher. I let her enter Frost's office first as well, then stepped ahead of her, newly-printed business card in hand.

"I'm Farrell from Nevar. I believe you're expecting me and my associate Ms. Smith. We'd like to get started immediately," I said.

Word of the pending change of ownership had spread. They were all running scared, wondering if that meant they'd each be looking for a new job shortly. "Yes, of course, Mr. Farrell. This way please. We've set everything up in the conference room."

Helena stepped up to bat. "That won't do at all," she informed them. "I wish to work from Mr. Frost's office. If you would show us where it is?"

"Excellent idea, Ms. Smith. That way nothing inadvertently left behind will be overlooked," I agreed and turned back to the receptionist. "Have it all taken back to Frost's office. Is there a coffee machine at hand?"

Nothing like coffee to make it look like one is settling in for the duration.

Minions hustled around us, eager to please.

"If you don't mind, Mr. Farrell, I'll just check in with the home office to let them know we've arrived," Helena said. She stepped out into the hall, moved to the far end to enjoy the view while she called her own office to bow out of work that afternoon. An emergency had come up, she planned to tell them. Then she'd roll into arranging pick-up of her kids via another of the sport moms. That's what her strategy had been in the elevator, at least. She was back by the time all the data the helpful staff had moved had made it back to where it had started. They really hustled with my eyes on them. The Raven stance I took in a handy doorway was out of their way but ominously present.

"Call when you have an answer," I told her, handed over her car keys, then headed out. Burt was unavailable to pick me up but sent a replacement cab to return me to where I'd left Naomie's Chevy. Next stop was a used car dealership. We needed two cars, but at the rate I was going through new cars, it was time to indulge in a bit of thrift. I found a couple of year-old Chrysler 300C sedans, one dark gray, one silver. The two together cost less than either of the decimated Mustangs had. I left the dealership headed for the bank for a cashier's check to pay for them and called Naomie in route. "Grab Mack. I'll pick the two of you up shortly. We have cars to acquire."

"Cars? In the plural?"

"I go through them quickly," I said then disconnected.

They were ready and waiting. Mack crammed himself into the back while Nomes claimed the front passenger seat. I was about to pull back out on the street when I noticed something different in the front yard of her building. "Was that rental sign out there earlier?"

"What?" Naomie turned to look. "Oh, no. I knew it would be going up. The couple in the two-bedroom at the end of the hall just bought a house. They moved out last week."

"The apartment that backs up to yours?"

"Yeah." She sounded curious over my interest.

"Guess that's why it's been so quiet on your floor," I said, but it was misdirection on my part. "You were wondering about the cars we are about to pick up."

"Only in the fact that there are two of them," she said.

"What models?" Mack asked from the rear seat.

I told him. "They're company cars. Your sister's is the silver one."

That caught her off guard. "One of them is for *me*?"

"*Company* car. You can keep the trusty Spark here or move it on."

"Move it on, sis," Mack urged. "Isn't there a cousin who just turned sixteen and is looking for some wheels?"

"What's wrong with my car that you think you can just buy me another one and I'll be all *oh, boss, I worship at your feet*?" Nomes demanded.

I faked surprise. "You mean, you don't?"

She slugged my shoulder. Unfortunately, it was the one that was still smarting from my tumble in a rolling, invisible ball to escape getting crisped.

"Farrell's just not brave enough to tell you why this thing needs to go," Mack said. "It's lime-green, Niel. *Lime*-green. And neither he nor I fit in it comfortably."

"Maybe I like lime-green,"

"Maybe you'll like silver."

Nomes figuratively dug her feet in. "Maybe I'll like the gray. What if I do?"

I flashed her a grin. "I'll immediately take the silver into a paint shop and turn it black, of course."

Mack chuckled. "You aren't gonna win this one, sis."

Nomes threw in the towel. "Would you like to know what we've found out so far in the way of dirt on Beck Ritter?"

I would indeed. "Shoot."

It seems our Ms. Ritter was in possession of a younger sister who wanted to take her writerly talents in a different direction. Their father was a newspaper editor for a small-town daily gazette upstate. Their mother was a high school English teacher who wrote short stories for various literary magazines on the side. The younger Ms. Ritter liked fantasy and longer stories. She contributed regularly to several fan fiction sites, among them Muggle Net, Doctor Who, Dresden Files, and Raven Tales. She'd been one of the first subscribers to leap onto the Calista Amberson replacement search train. Delia had found her listed as Entry #27. I'd gone under the code number #1942. Lex had been #876, she'd told me, saying it made her feel like part of a launch countdown. The sister's entry hadn't made the Top 100 cut.

"Beck is very close to her sister, or certainly seems to be when you tally up all the BFF the sisters post to their online media accounts," Naomie added. "A lot of them end with *call you later tonight*."

"Now that is freakin' weird," Mack contributed from the rear peanut gallery. "We're one of the closest non-dysfunctional families around and there is no way I need to know what my sibling here did with her day. In fact, I think the last message you sent the clan, Niel, was to announce that working for Bram had convinced you to toss all ideas of writing a vampire romance into an active volcano."

That shook me on a Richter scale level. I glanced over at her. "You're giving up your dream of being a writer?"

Her jet hair moved like a model demonstrating a shampoo's special qualities when she gave a negatory to my demand. "Just vampire romances. I'm thinking more along the lines of crime fighting fairytale characters."

"Grandma will only be relieved temporarily then," Mack said. "She stopped lighting candles at church to save you from yourself, you know."

"She's probably funneled the reclaimed funds into bingo nights," Naomie zinged back.

"Are you thinking Prince Charming, P.I.?" I asked.

"There are other fairytale characters. Besides, I'm just thinking about it. No decisions made."

Made sense to me. "I'd say ask if you need help, but I know next to nothing about writing."

"I keyed *Raven's Moon*, boss. Believe me, you know exactly what you're doing. But back to Beck Ritter."

By all means. I needed to get someone off my list, and, while the investigation Naomie was running would likely get Ritter fired if we leaked information to her rivals, it wouldn't result in me needing to kill anyone. Such was not the case regarding the search for Eric Winthur, the hunt for Solomon Prisk, or the various hit persons and the client behind the scenes with a death wish for me. Whether the Heart Burn curse was tied to the assassins or a separate case, I had no idea.

In the meantime, there were cars to retrieve. Housing to be found.

And a vampiric stalker/kidnapper to put down later that night.

***

My life has no middle ground. It is either total sloth or constantly on the go. When we hit the car dealership, they had paperwork ready, had believed the possible lie my insurance witch told about both cars being fully covered, exchanged one large cashier's check for two sets of keys, and we were off and away. Mack opted to drive the silver car, I was in the dark gray, and Nomes was back in her lime-green vehicle. The siblings headed back to hacking into various systems while I headed for the nearest Fontaine Funeral home.

My last visit to one of their locations had been in search of information about a collection of Otherworlders buried in the pretty decrepit looking St. Romaric's cemetery. Quite a lot of

Otherworlders, in fact. Now, I needed to know how many unclaimed gravesites there might be. Five were probably needed after last night's debacle. While the police would search for next of kin, I doubted there would be anyone claiming Hammer and his boys. I'd gotten them killed. Seeing that they received a decent burial was the least I could do in return. I doubted that, although Palermo would be pretty ticked over having lost a handful of mutant scum, he'd care much about burial services. Nate Townshed had those demon boars and I'd bet Solomon Prisk did, too. There was a good chance Prisk took care of recycling containers the vampires had emptied. While such efficient body-removal clearly had a place in my world, when it came to human corpses, I drew the line.

I might need Nate's services later that evening. In fact, it might be handy to ask if he'd like to do a ride-along. He did, after all, work for Fontaine Funeral homes. I'd need to give him a call where no one could overhear my end of the conversation, though.

The bereavement counselor I spoke to thought I possessed sainted—or close enough—qualities to see to the final services for men I had merely stumbled across and not known personally. I had to stick to the story I'd told the police. Only Durkin knew about my world. In any event, arrangements were made for cremation, and tasteful but modestly-priced urns were chosen. As there were no columbariums at St. Romaric's—it being an historic cemetery, though still open for business—I told them to place all the urns in a casket and do a group burial. Hopefully, the police would be able to discover names for the deceased, but I went with a plate—rather than a monument—that said, "Comrades in Arms" and noted yesterday's date. Said I'd let the police know Fontaines would be handling the burial and then called Durkin on my way back to the car to let him know an anonymous taxpayer was footing the final bill. They didn't come more anonymous than me.

Then I headed back to my temporary home with Nomes once more. But, before I went inside, I dialed the number on the FOR RENT sign. Turned out, the building owner lived on the premises. He was home.

He met me at the door. We went upstairs. While he talked—and I didn't listen—I roamed a place that was much larger than Naomie's hobbit-sized one. It had more than two bedrooms. It had two narrow baths that backed up to each other. Just looking at the economic use of space had me missing the shower that was roomy enough to suds down a racehorse and its companion goat. The empty apartment had a kitchen with counters, something Nomes' place did without. The appliances were dated enough to have reached retirement age. The carpet looked newly cleaned, though it was an atrocious color. The walls and ceilings were freshly painted. The interior doors were flimsy enough for a barely trying Great Dane to smash them to splinters. The main door was slightly better. It matched the one on Naomie's apartment on the durability scale—maybe cracking a 5 out of 10—and had an ugly selection of locks making the attempt to lurch it into a more prized security rating.

"How much?" I asked the landlord.

He named a monthly rental amount plus security deposit.

I stopped my inspection. I'd seen enough but dreamed even better. "Not to rent it," I said. "To buy the building."

***

At nearly sixty days past winter solstice, the sun wouldn't have cleared the skies until nearly eight. Wendy would need to be powered up with a good blood-draining—or its equivalent—to be at full power to take down the new-to-the-blood-sucking-world Quinton Frost. There was plenty of time to kick back a bit and have dinner with Naomie. I was not going to tell her I was about to become her landlord. I'd be calling in the contractor first since I was intending to gut the joint. If I hadn't confused her with another coven member, there was an interior designer on my list of go-to gals. Hopefully an architect, too. The neighborhood was teetering on a decision to go to Hell or enjoy gentrification. Hopefully, I'd tip the scales in a good direction. In any event, I'd also be asking for a zoning change so the ground floor could become Raven Corp offices, and a place from which to kick off the non-profit. There were a lot of meetings in my future.

Just had to survive to attend them.

All was fairly quiet at Nomes'. The hackers had finished their assignment and gone home. I'd keep Naomie out of the way for a while tomorrow by having her visit Helena to have checks cut for her friends' and brother's services. She could deliver them in her choice of vehicles. My first stop of the day would be to deliver everything they had collected on Beck Ritter to Delia. In the PR battles of this world, my pseudo-witch cousin was a five-star general.

And I had hunting to do of a more personal nature. I needed to pin another mercenary killer to the wall and shake free further information about the mysterious person who wanted me to move into St. Romaric's next to Hammer and his boys.

Since I'd given my key back, I needed to knock on the door when I strolled down to Naomie's. Beelz's excited bark inside probably clued her in to the identity of her visitor.

She threw the door open in dramatic fashion, posing in the entryway like a runway model, one hip to the side, arm crooked, hand resting on said hip. She was dolled up in the outfit I'd bought her for distraction duty.

"Mr. Farrell." She murmured the greeting.

"Ms. Enright," I growled, quite ready to pounce.

"I believe you need this back." The key I'd returned to her lay in the palm of her open hand.

"I believe I need this much more," I said, and snagged her close. "Office hours are over. Does that mean the rules don't apply?"

She lowered long, curved lashes. "I haven't decided," my previously-bubbly, rather-clueless-as-to-how-I-thought-about-her Gal Friday said. "I dressed to match your new look. We *are* going out to eat, aren't we? I made reservations. Burt told me the name of your favorite steak house."

"Don't want to be on the menu yourself, cupcake?"

"Early days, boss. After all, this isn't really me." She indicated the beguiling outfit with a game show model's sweep of her arm from shoulder on down. The bared shoulder.

"And my get up is me?"

"It's one of you," she said. "The media you. I think Delia will agree. When Bram Farrell, author, takes the stage, this is what he wears."

"You have been around Delia for far too long," I said. "So what time are the dinner reservations?"

"Eight. Is that all right?"

"It's perfect. Gives me time to thank you properly for the awesome job today, Nomes."

"All in the line of duty, boss."

"As is this then." I kicked the door closed and proceeded to make it impossible for her to continue any conversation.

***

Helena called with the required information about real estate in which Quinton Frost was interested as we were contemplating what to have for dessert. Happily, the addresses were within the area patrolled by the 4th Precinct, Durkin's beat. I called him while Nomes ordered molten lava cake for us both.

I gave him the addresses. "You have any calls about late-night activities at either?"

"Oddly enough, yes. One has been discounted because the elderly woman who lives nearby calls frequently about things that are not taking place in the building."

"Like what?"

"A meth lab that wasn't there. An indoor marijuana farm. A cage-fighting operation. A terrorist bomb production unit. She believed they were selling kits on eBay. They weren't."

"And the latest?"

"A sex cult."

"How about the other address?"

"Comings and goings at all times of day. Probably a drug distributor or gun sales to those who don't want to be bothered with official paperwork and waiting periods," Durkin said. "Not my department, or so I'm told, which means they've probably got undercover guys on the job."

"All times of day, hmm?"

Durkin was quick to pick up nuances. "Sex cult address, it is," he said. "You have an ETA? From the background sounds, I'd say you're living it up in a restaurant."

"How astute of you. You must be a detective," I said.

"A *real* one, anyway," Durkin countered.

"Meeting convenes at eleven then."

Durkin smart assed a "Roger wilco, sky captain."

I snorted and snarled, "I look nothing like Jude Law."

"For which I'm sure he blesses his lucky stars. See you at eleven." Durkin rang off.

I texted Wendy. She might be putting in a few hours at The Red Dragon, singing seductive songs or, then again, she might be taking a personal day, er, night. I gave her the address and the time and added that an Otherworld-savvy human cop would be on hand along with a possible necromancer. I hadn't managed to get a hold of Townshed earlier, so I tried him again. This time, he answered. "You up for a hunt tonight?"

"Otherworlder gone wrong?"

"Are there any others worthy of my consideration?"

He said he'd be there.

That was when dessert arrived.

"I won't be home much tonight, honey," I told Naomie.

"*Honey*?"

"Seemed appropriate."

She rolled her eyes. Ah, the Nomes we all knew and loved wasn't gone, just in hiding.

"I'm taking Beelz with me."

"Is it something dangerous?"

"No telling." Well, at least no telling *her*. I'd kept all mention of what was being hunted from my side of the conversations so Nomes would remain clueless. But would it be dangerous? Hell, yes.

"Then we'd better order Beelzie something to go," Nomes said, all complacent-like.

When the wait person came to ask if we needed anything else, I ordered the mutt a New York steak, rare, hold the vegetables, to go. He was going to need the protein. When it came to taking down vampires, a guy needed muscle.

And a heck of a lot of luck.

***

The property Quinton Frost had acquired rather recently had not rated high on real estate lists. It had once served as a school, probably built in the Twenties or earlier. There were numerous holes in the roof, numerous boarded-over windows and the cement steps that led to the double-doored main entrance were cracked and crumbling at the edges. There were lights on inside and a dozen cars—some really swanky ones—parked on the old playground. I wondered if the owners of those spiffy cars complained about the deteriorated condition of the lot.

"A sex club?" Nate Townshed repeated, apparently the only part of what I'd told him that he found interesting.

"Sworn to by the suspicious elderly lady who lives across the way, so, yeah, it's honest-to-gospel truth," I said.

"It's not a sex club." Wendy had arrived in bat form and had kept most of it intact, black being the color choice for the evening. Her face and hands were human, and she had legs and feet, but there was still wing webbing along her arms. She was a sleek ebony everywhere else. As inhuman as her partial morph was, the vampiress was still exuding sex pheromones into the night. Made me wonder whether the promise of taking down another vampire turned her on. Beelz was probably the only one of us males not aware of it. He'd met her with a threatening, low growl.

"Then what do you think it is, Ms. Whilsen?" Durkin asked.

"It's a performance venue. What style, I don't know. Simply that this type of location and the models and number of vehicles lend credence to that supposition, Mr. Durkin."

The four of us were crouched in the lee of overgrown boxwood. Durkin had night-vision binoculars and wasn't sharing. Wendy had night vision; no technology required. I don't know how Townshed was doing, but I wished we were closer. Or moving in. We'd been on the cusp of doing so when another car had pulled in off the street. A man and a woman had gotten out and hastened to the door. Now, they were arguing with someone at the entrance.

"Looks like they weren't given tonight's password," Townshed said.

Wendy shook her head. "No, they're late. The woman just asked if the whipping had begun. The man is offering to pay extra so that they aren't turned away."

How handy to have a vampire with enhanced senses on hand. Saved on the expense of spy gear for an operation.

"Whipping?" Durkin was probably frowning. It was too dark to see. Not only were we in shadow, we were all dressed in black. Many, many layers of black to stay warm. Except for Wendy, of course.

She shrugged. At least, I'm fairly sure she did.

"Ah, they've paid their way in," Townshed noted.

"Then, by all means, let's join the party." I scuttled out of hiding. "Oh, and mind the dog."

"You mean, don't step on him inadvertently?" Townshed asked.

"I mean, don't get in his way," I said as Beelz went Great Dane.

The dog gave me a canine grin, then loped off to take point.

"A bit more warning on what the hellhound just did might have been nice, Raven," Durkin snarled.

The fact that he'd called me by my moniker rather than Farrell, as he usually did, said it all. The cop knew this wasn't his territory; it was mine.

Beelz ran the grounds in quick order. The size and breed might change, but the midnight-coat-with-caramel-markings did not. When he reported back, I led the team in a quick dash for the door.

Townshed tried the latch. It didn't give. I figured Wendy could use vampiric strength and rip it off its hinges. Instead, Townshed knocked politely. The rest of us pressed back out of sight.

A goon answered. A human one. He had a Glock in hand, though that was about all I could see because he'd only opened the door a crack. "Yer too late. Maybe next time," he told Townshed and began to close the door.

Wendy moved and Townshed bounced off the masonry as she shoved him out of the way. She rammed the portal wide and took the guard down with a chop to the neck—and didn't even breathe hard when finished.

Durkin checked the crumbled man. "You broke his neck."

He sounded surprised. No idea why he would be.

"You would have preferred I bite it instead?" She checked her manicure. "I'm saving my appetite for Frost."

Townshed hunkered down next to the corpse. "I could probably fix him."

Although the light in the entryway was dim, it was sufficient to see Durkin's expression. "Necromancers," I scoffed. "Never see a body they don't want to play with."

Durkin got his dour cop face back in place. "Which way now?"

I turned to Wendy. She had the superpowers.

"This way." She headed deeper into the building.

Frost's mind, sad to say, seemed to work along some of the same routes mine did. He'd turned the gymnasium into his game room. It even had bleacher seating.

The place was cold and dark but for the spotlights on the participants in center court. Eric Winthur hung from chains tightened so that his tall, muscular form was kept upright. The man was in pain, his body torn by a recent whipping, one done through his clothing. The tattered remains of a once-white T-shirt and pale gray sweatpants were stained with blood and clinging to some of the lash marks.

Frost stepped from the shadows in a spotless tuxedo, a cat-o'-nine tails in hand, the knotted dangling cords of rope swinging back and forth. Blood stained the cords.

"Fine specimen, isn't he?" Frost coaxed agreement from his audience.

The stands held perhaps fifteen people, a few more men than women, though there was a contingent of them. Each face was intent on the spectacle at center stage.

Wendy had eyes only for Eric, but when they turned to Frost, I clamped my hand onto her arm. "Not yet. We need to know what sort of security measures he's taken."

She inhaled deeply, testing the scents in the air. "Only two vampires. Frost and another. He also has a lackey nearby, someone like Hammer was. Otherwise, all humans with sick fetishes."

For a vampire to call the crowd sick definitely doomed them all to my occasional drinking buddy Satan's eternal torment. Not that I didn't agree with her.

"We still wait," I said.

In the spotlight, Frost circled Eric. "But this was only the first act, wasn't it, my friends? Watching a man be flogged is just the appetizer."

He reached out, took hold of one of the tattered bits of cloth across Eric's back, and ripped it free. The young man's cry as new pain ripped through him nearly had Wendy breaking, but she held still, quivering with suppressed fury.

Frost continued his soliloquy as he stripped his captive's clothing away until Eric was naked, the cruel lashes standing out in relief against his skin as blood seeped from them. Frost dragged his thumb through one trickle, obviously putting pressure behind the casual swipe, for Eric's body bucked in the chains. Frost licked the blood from his own flesh, savoring the taste.

"Time for Act Two," he announced, gesturing to someone outside the spotlights.

A cage was rolled into view. Inside was a being who was pure, infuriated animal. It wrapped human hands around the bars and shook them in what was apparently an impossible effort to escape. Must have been super-reinforced because the beast in the cage wouldn't have been trapped by anything less.

Frost ambled to the prison and took hold of something on top. He set the cat-o'-nine tails down and wrapped a strip of leather around his hand then a length of heavy, linked chain. As he reclaimed the whip, he nodded to whatever cohort awaited his next command.

The cage opened and a woman launched herself at Frost with the clear intent to kill him. The accountant-turned-vampire swung the whip at her. It was the cue for his minion to ram a cattle prod into her back. The electric shock sent her spasming to the floor.

"That's the other vampire," Wendy whispered. "He's tortured her into insanity."

I'd already recognized that, but Durkin and Townshed might not have because the thing lacked fangs.

The chain Frost had wrapped around his hand was attached to a thick collar around the woman's neck. She was filthy and nude. Feral. And she scented food. Her head turned toward where Eric hung dripping.

"Now," I said to my team, but Wendy took control.

"No. Not yet. He's pulled both her fangs and her teeth. She can't feast as required. But she can lick the victim," she said.

I wasn't surprised that she wasn't identifying Eric as kin. Durkin and Townshed didn't need to know. Clarity was required for that last bit, though. "Lick?"

"Look at him." She tipped her chin to indicate her great-grandson. "He knows it's coming and is both relieved and anxious for her touch."

Winthur did indeed have eyes only for the feral vampire.

"Frost has had him for weeks," Wendy whispered. "Winthur has scars from numerous whippings over that time. And healings. Vampire saliva will clean the wounds and cause them to heal faster."

Frost walked his leashed vampire to his victim. The feral creature inhaled deeply of Winthur's blood scent, then licked a dripping wound on his calf.

I've been in some uncomfortable positions before, even chained to a wall in a castle dungeon back in fictionland, but staying still while Eric Winthur was slowly, and fully, lathed by the female vamp was…

Well, the lady across the street had been right on the nose when she claimed a sex cult met at the old school.

In the bleachers, despite the cold, humans were pulling free of their own clothing and grappling, though few took their eyes off the excruciatingly snail pace at which the vampire savored each dripping wound on the very athletic male body on display. Eric's hormones were as primed as my own. In the crowd, someone shouted an order to the vampiress on what he wanted her to lick next.

Frost laughed and jerked her chain to move her to a better position.

"Wendy?" I might have sounded a bit pleading. "Has he had enough healing?" I sure as hell couldn't stand much more.

"She missed a few strips on his back, but Frost won't let her return to them now. You'll need to take Frost on, Raven. Though he has her under control, she's feral and once she's away from his mastery, she'll be the more dangerous of the two."

I turned to my human and hell-born cohorts. "Durkin, Townshed, you've got the humans. Look out for the guy with the prod. Beelz, you're with me. We leave our victim where he is until the vamps have been taken down. Agreed?"

Both Durkin and Townshed manifested revolvers in their hands. I wrapped my fist around my Smith & Wesson.

"Go," I said, then stood up and shot Frost.

He looked startled, but since I'd aimed at the hand he'd wrapped the vampire's leash in, he dropped it, giving Wendy full access to the creature.

Durkin took a stand before the bleachers and held his badge to face the suddenly-frozen-from-fornicating crowd. My hands were full so I didn't catch what he told them. Something about being under arrest.

Beelz leapt for Frost. The vamp ringmaster slashed the cat-o'-nine tails across the hellhound's muzzle. It just made the mutt mad. Those weren't Great Dane teeth he was packing; they were demon fangs.

Frost wasn't fazed, although I'd guess it was the first time he'd seen, much less taken on, a demon in any shape. He slashed again and again. The flying, knotted cords kept Beelz's teeth from making contact.

I called him back. The hound didn't look happy, but he knew I was the only one capable of driving the stake into Frost.

If I got a chance.

To keep the sadistic kidnapper off his game, I slammed him with hurricane-strength wind. He tumbled like a dying leaf and bounded off the back wall, but he was back on his feet nearly as fast. Rather than lunge at me, he brushed off the tux, checked the cuff links, then corrected the tilt of his bow tie.

"And who might you be? No—let me guess. Scruff covered jaw, untamed black hair, all-black ensemble, and capable of magic. I'd heard rumors that The Raven had come to visit this world but had dismissed them as overactive imaginations. It seems I was wrong."

"You were wrong," I agreed and sent a flaming dart his way. It tore a hole in his jacket sleeve.

As though it was the most common of annoyances, Frost patted the fire out. "Somehow, I'd expected better than that from you, but then, you are just a fictional character."

"But a mean one."

Frost laughed. "Then why that feeble bit of fire? Between the covers of one of those books, I doubt you'd be so ineffectual."

"I have a few questions," I said. "You get to live as long as you answer them."

"Live? But for how long?" He gave me an oily smile. "Only moments, I'd guess. But that depends on whether you're capable of getting the upper hand or not. It's difficult to stake a man who's equally determined not to be staked."

"True, but I plan to give it a concerted try."

"So… Those questions of yours?" Frost prompted.

"Who'd you convince to turn you?"

"Does it really matter? Oh, I see it does to you. The little crumpet behind you. How nice of Wendy to come for a visit. Do you think the way she's tearing apart my toy means she's jealous?"

I didn't take my eyes off him, which I'm sure is what he'd hoped I'd do. "Didn't you know? She's temporarily signed on as one of my Avengers crew. We lack a god of Asgard, a billionaire mechanic, and other handy types, but we do have a hellhound."

"You're as glib as I've heard," he mused. "Next question?"

"Why?"

He gestured to the humans attempting to scramble back into clothing and out of Durkin's clutches, then to the sparks flashing behind the empty cage as Townshed battled the goon with the electrified cattle prod, then to the vampiric catfight between Wendy and the feral. "This? Or him?" he jerked his thumb over his shoulder to where Eric still hung, now unconscious.

"All of it."

"I find I require a larger income than the accounting firm can offer. People with too much money who are looking for the next thrill are quite happy to fulfill that need. However, I was still stumped on how to punish Wendy when I started this venue, though."

"Why did Wendy need punishing?"

He gave me a look packed with condemnation and pity. "She wouldn't give me what I wanted."

"Immortality."

He grinned. "Yes. What fool wouldn't want to live forever?"

"Forever isn't in the vampiric promissory note."

"Near enough. How long has old Palermo been around? Centuries. Word is, he isn't the oldest of our kind either. Some count their lifespan in millennium."

"You didn't know there were induction rules, did you? Wendy couldn't turn you without suffering a penalty."

He shrugged. "Others were more obliging."

"Like your crumpet there," I said, nodding back toward the catfight, though I didn't dare spare a glance to see how Wendy was doing against the now-insane vampire because I wasn't about to take my eyes off Frost.

"Don't know why any of them felt she was worthy of a turn," Frost answered. "She didn't like following rules. Wanted to feast where and when she wished. We are far, far superior to our hosts. Who cares what happens to meals stupid enough to stumble within the snare?"

"She agreed to turn you. Why not just drain you? You were just another weak human."

"I left a letter to Palermo in my safe, of course. If she drained me, he'd find out and punish her."

"Kill her," I corrected.

"Best punishment there is. It's what you intend to do to me, isn't it, Raven?"

"Only after my questions are behind us, Frost."

"Oh, yes. So why did I use the magnificent example of manhood dangling in chains behind me? I'm sure you've followed my trail from The Red Dragon. Winthur was too good to pass up. A man fixated on a search to find his great-grandmother, a hag who should have died years ago. An asinine quest if there ever was one. Who the hell cares about finding family that tossed them away? That's what Wendy did with her daughter. Didn't want Palermo to get wind of the kid. Nor of that daughter's son and grandson today. When he cried in his drink over missing a chance to show Wendy that picture from the Thirties that not only looked just like her, but *was* of her, I would have been a fool not to offer my talents as a genealogist to help him. Not that I am one, but that didn't matter because the kid snapped onto the hook like a hungry bass."

It is so nice when the villain wants to brag.

"Then you called in the fake auto problem and took him away," I said, bringing the story to its close.

Frost smiled evilly. Yes, he'd been born to be a villain. I'd bet he even cooked the books for his clients. Helena would soon jettison those fools right into law enforcement hands. She didn't know Durkin, but I'd bet she had old ties to Treasury officials.

"And now you're going to try to kill me," he said, though he sounded disappointed that I'd even make the attempt.

"No," I corrected. "But *she* will."

He'd been so wrapped up in telling me how clever he was that he hadn't realized the catfight had ended, and Wendy was right behind him. Fangs out, she dragged him back against herself and sunk her fangs in deep.

Once he was drained, she dropped him to the floor, then motioned for me to stake him. Instead, I let a fireball float to rest on his chest. The tuxedo caught nicely, and Quinton Frost was soon just a pile of ashes. I also did one on the feral vamp's remains. Townshed found Frost's coat and dragged it through both piles to scatter them. What a team.

While magic is certainly helpful in destroying an Otherworlder, sometimes the ability to distract one is far deadlier. As such, I got to go home to Naomie with no new blood on my hands. And none on Beelz's muzzle either, though he looked decidedly disappointed.

Wendy took off before Durkin's reinforcements arrived and before Eric could be revived. I wondered whether he would return to his search for her or forget he'd been fixated on helping his grandmother learn something about her mother. Maybe he'd get a visit from that great-grandmother in disguise and be mesmerized into forgetting her and what had happened to him. Would lose his desire to continue the search for the woman in The Babe picture.

Townshed and I released the kid from the chains. Although his training as a mortician did nothing to aid Townshed in medical matters, being a necromancer did. He checked over the man's injuries and said, with a straight face, that they'd been licked clean. There shouldn't be any infection, though Eric would always have the scars from the whip.

A police medical unit took Eric off to the hospital while Durkin's crew ran yellow tape about the area. Townshed and I did a vanishing act, heading to The Red Dragon for a last drink. Looking none the worse for wear—and actually enhanced due to draining two rogue vampires—Wendy was on stage for a final set. She allowed a faint smile to curve her lips when she spotted Nate and I at a back table and sang a sultry rendition of "That Old Black Magic" for us.

February 19

Naomie was asleep on the sofa when I got home. I barely recognized her. She had her hair pulled back in a ponytail and was wearing heavy white stocks, a pair of jeans so well-loved the washer had turned them a naturally-distressed pale blue, and a white sweatshirt with the University of Michigan wolverine mascot on the front. On the not-so-big screen, Hugh Jackman retracted his long metal claws and snarled at the supporting cast. I wondered which had come first, the donning of the sweatshirt or the choosing of the movie.

Beelz headed over to give her the doggy version of Prince Charming's princess special, which, naturally, woke her up.

She blinked at us, all delightfully drowsy, ruffled the hound's fur and croaked, "Boss," at me. "What time is it?"

"Late," I said. After The Red Dragon closed, I introduced Townshed to my favorite Denny's middle-of-the-night breakfast routine. Unfortunately, while the bakers were diligently at work, the bakery hadn't been opened yet for business, so no sugary treats were in the offing.

"Everything work out?"

"Yup. Eric Winthur was found, freed, and should be making up with Jamie the moment she hits the hospital if they kept him. Sooner if they sprung him."

Nomes sighed. "Oh good. I like a happy ending. You ready to claim the sofa?"

"Ready to claim the sofa." Not that I'd sleep, but I had thinking to do. "Off to bed you go. By the way, you ever been to Vegas, sugar?"

The ponytail flipped from side to side as she shook her head. "No. Why?"

"Remember me mentioning that hit man who visited me the morning of Valentine's Day?"

She made a sleepy sound that I took for an affirmative.

"Well, I've got the fee together that he's charging to cancel his particular contract on me and need to deliver it. He lives in Vegas. Figured, if you were up to it, we could do a couple days in Sin City, then cruise down to visit Lex in Tucson for a bit. Sound doable?"

Nomes looked at me. "Boss," she said. "My brain is not awake. Spin that all by me in the morning, huh?"

It wasn't a yes, but it wasn't a no, but, still, I felt a bit let down. But then, I was high on vampire take-down juice even if I hadn't been the one taking the vampires down.

"Deal. You need to be tucked in?"

That earned me a grin. "I think I can handle it."

I didn't bother asking about a goodnight kiss, just swooped in and delivered one that might wake her up a bit.

Sadly, Morpheus won that round. She shuffled off and fell face-first onto the bed.

I closed the door behind her, then dropped full-length onto the sofa. Staring at the ceiling was always a good plan when things needed to be sorted out, and I still had a few problems.

1. Figure out how the heck someone could neutralize my shield and fix the problem.

2. Discover who the heck wanted me dead. The *why* would be nice to know, too.

3. If the Heart Burn curse was headed my way, what could I do to escape it, considering the shield disruption was obviously tied to the hit someone had taken out on me? The Heart Burn was definitely an assassin's kind of tool.

4. Figure out what trails needed to be followed to snag Solomon Prisk for Durkin. I did, after all, owe the cop.

Delia might be able to give me some ideas on the shield problem and I'd be swinging by her office with the dirt Naomie's team had collected on Beck Ritter in the morning, so I shelved that until there was data to examine.

I'd been back-burnering the Solomon Prisk case for a while, using the need to write a book as my excuse, but that didn't hold water right now. It was also not a good idea to go after a ghoul when I was experiencing shield impotency. Not something a guy wants to admit to, but it could be worse. Shield first, Prisk second. No third or fourth. There were those assassins out there to identify and then avoid.

The one thing I could do without further interrogation anywhere was to identify who was hiring these hit types. Ernie said he hadn't met his employer, just had that note and a partial payment on the job. If I snagged another of the assassins, would they have a similar story? Chances were the answer was *yup*. Which meant… well, it meant I'd really ticked someone off in the short time since I'd crossed the border between the fiction world and this one.

I heard Beelz lapping up water on the other side of the partial wall and decided a drink was required. Fortunately, I'd brought my buddy, Evan Williams, home with me.

A few sips into the tumbler and old Evan was nudging my mind, but not in a straight line by any means.

Other than the cases I'd cleared up as All Hallows' Eve had moved into All Souls' Day, the only case I'd dealt with since was the damn apocalyptic horn over the Thanksgiving weekend. That meant the suspects who might have one heck of a grudge against me were a minister's congregation and a Bengali woman's friends—though she hadn't seemed to have any or be likely to make new ones when I'd met her—or Otherworlders who worked the come-hither, get-your-jollies-and-die gig. The club-owning red dragon had been ticked over not getting the horn, but then, so had Samael and Raphael. I'd been to The Red Dragon twice in the past few days, and, when I'd talked to the crimson lizard himself, I hadn't gotten a "not welcome" vibe. Raphael had wanted the horn to return to Gabriel who, unlike his brother archangel, was a nice guy and hadn't wanted it back. Samael… well, he couldn't have cared less. As the Devil, he had more than enough souls to fry without counting little soulless me among the crowd.

Which meant I was back to that coven option. I had sorta helped their leader shuffle off to Main Street Hell. While the coven girls seemed rather devoted to me, one might be hiding a desire to do me in. But, if so, she hid it damn well. Every one of them always dropped whatever they were doing when I needed something done. As many problems as my car and now housing disasters caused the one with the insurance agency, I doubted she wanted to have yet another payment to dole out—one for my life insurance. I hadn't taken out the policy. Delia had.

She had inherited the spot as titular head of the coven and was in PR heaven over all the prospective work due to come her way as The Raven Tales rebooted and the Young Raven Tales poised for launch, so I doubted she wanted me out of the way either.

Which left the possibility of an old witch buddy of Calie's elsewhere who wanted revenge for her death. Possibly another of the Lilin, which would mean a vicious little sprite if Calie was a good model of that particular sisterhood.

That was the most nebulous idea, but it also seemed the most logical one.

Of course, that could have been Evan Williams blowing smoke.

Just as earlier in the day when I'd mused on the same problems, I hadn't narrowed in on anything to follow through with by the time Nomes resurfaced and it was going on nine. Because I am such a creature of habit these days, I'd been out to pick up donuts so that proper office breakfast procedures were met.

When she emerged from the bedroom, she was in partial widow weeds again, though, having done quite a bit of shopping lately, I now recognized that the odd hemlines of her layers were what was on the store racks currently. It was simply that she bought all black items and then layered them on to stay warm. I had first met her as the weather was turning late in October and Detroit winters required she dress as she did. I wondered what lay ahead in the wardrobe department come summer.

"Boss, would you mind giving your opinion on some ideas I was working on last night for that fairytale mysteries series?" She handed me a steaming cup of coffee. The machine *did* live in the bedroom, after all.

"Be glad to," I said. "What's the scenario?"

"I'm undecided whether it should be a brother and sister team or not, but the idea is Hansel and Gretel have a detective agency."

"Is this set in the 19th century when the Grimms collected the folk tales?"

"Was considering it."

"Then they are enquiry agents, not detectives. Particularly if the setting is European. That's what Eugène Vidocq and his men called themselves in France after they were kicked out of the Sûreté in the 1830s, and Charles Field used the term when he opened an office after leaving The Yard in the 1850s."

"They did?" Nome's eyes were wide. "Boy, you really dug up research stuff before starting *Raven's Moon.*"

Except, of course, I hadn't. That was either Calie's research or something related to her past spilling off my tongue. Funny, I could get rid of the witch, but I couldn't get rid of some of her memories. At least, not the ones related in some way to me.

Rather than accept Nome's accolade, I shrugged. "What else have you got?"

"I'm having trouble dreaming up a brand of magic that isn't like what The Raven does or any of the magic used in other fantasy books. But I was considering some sort of protective armor Hansel could use. Have it assemble itself around him a bit like Tony Stark's Iron Man suit does, only differently. It's the differently that I'm stumbling over."

"Early days yet, Nomes. You'll work it out." I started on my second donut.

"Did I tell you last night that Lex called before her plane left to thank you for all the help you gave her, and for lending Burt out? She said he was awesome."

"He is awesome," I agreed. Awesomely expensive considering all the hours he'd spent driving Lex around, but well worth it since it meant I hadn't had to.

"Lex said she'd be sending you an outline of what she plans to do in the first book. It's definitely going to be an origin story. You know, how your namesake came to be called The Raven, how he found or developed the magic he uses, that sort of stuff. She wants to make sure it suits the previous Raven Tales and the new ones."

Considering Calie had never felt an origin story was necessary, I was sorta looking forward to seeing what Lex came up with and if, once she wrote it, anything about me would change. I was still a very word-bound being.

"Speaking of Lex, do you remember me mentioning a possible visit?"

"You mean I didn't dream that?" Nomes demanded. "The idea of you asking me to go to Las Vegas to pay off a hit man was so bizarre, I was sure it wasn't real."

"Real, cupcake," I insisted. "You in or out?"

She chewed her lip. Damn, the woman was determined to drive me insane.

"Gotta think about it, boss. It's not like it's in my job description."

"I didn't write a job description for your job."

"The unwritten job description, then."

Women. They'd be the death of me. Particularly if one had hired those hit men.

I ran a hand through my unruly hair. "Okay. Here's the deal. You decide and then make plane and hotel reservations—either for two or for one. Either way, I need to get the money to Ernie before the end of the month. I'd like it to be *way* before the end of the month, so he doesn't think I'm reneging on the promise."

Naomie nodded acceptance of the assignment.

I finished off my coffee. "Now, have you got that dirt I need to pass on to Delia? I'm out the door again the moment it's in hand."

Sixty seconds later, I was in the Chrysler. Beelz had opted to stay in which was fine with me. He'd have been bored with what was on my plate for the day.

***

Delia was treading water (figuratively) as the publicity department in New York filled her e-mail with details for the *Raven's Moon* launch. The book wouldn't hit the stands for months yet, but that didn't mean beans in the PR world. She fell on the info the hackers had unearthed and was ready to boot me from her office until I said, "I have a problem."

I made it sound like I might have only a few weeks to live. A *few weeks* actually might be stretching it if I didn't cure this assassin thing soon.

Delia dropped back into her chair as I closed her office door. Firmly. Quietly.

"What sort of problem?"

I propped my hip against her extremely cluttered desk. "Someone's dismantling my shields. I didn't think that was possible. It's never happened before, but then, most of my life hasn't been lived in this particular dimension either."

"What do you mean *dismantling them*?"

I told her about the note pinned to my bedroom door at the

mansion after I'd sealed the entire place up after the grill debacle. I hadn't even realized the shield on the mansion had been down when I'd gone inside because I'd been going around the exterior taking the smaller shields off the broken windows and doors before the construction contractor arrived. It hadn't registered until I'd considered things last night. From there, I moved on to the bomb beneath the Mustang and the guy who'd triggered it because, without a shield in place, he'd been able to jimmy the lock.

"It stayed whole when I used one to escape the burning house, but that just means either a different assassin was involved or whoever is making the shields fall needs to be right next to one or just a hell of a lot closer than they were getting that night.

"Now I know that in a book, Calie just used the word *shield* and, *poof!* it was there, but in the real world, how do magic-users learn to create a shield? Also, could Calie, in preparing to bring me across, have done the work on creating a shield I could use once I got here?"

"She might have. Throw one up so I can look at it."

As though it were a cone of silence—one that worked better than any Maxwell Smart ever used—I sealed both of us and the desk under an invisible dome.

"You don't use gestures or words to construct one?"

"Never did in a book so why would I even think it was necessary?"

She reached out to touch the surface. From within the dome, it looked like a prism, darts of many colors glittering, sparking, and zipping about. When I'd put the shields in place around the house, I'd noticed there was no change in the outward-facing visual. Everything looked just as it did normally. The shield was totally transparent.

Delia was tracing different facets of the interior dome. "She did do a regular construction for you. I recognize elements from when she taught me to do mine in preparation for my first transfer into a new vessel."

Sometimes it was difficult to remember that Delia was even older than Wendy and not wearing the same body into which her spirit had been born. But it did make her the most knowledgeable witch I knew. She didn't trace her lineage back to the Biblical Lilith as Calie had done, but she had used Lilin magic.

Delia leaned back in her chair. "If called upon to try, I couldn't have taken any of her shields down because I hadn't been involved in their construction, but I'll bet she could easily have destroyed mine because she knew every element used in building it," she said. "It's possible that someone has made a study of shields and found ways to neutralize them, but it's also possible that a user with an identical mix to yours could take yours down, Bram."

"Would Calie have shared the recipe she used for mine?" I asked.

The PR witch snorted. "Calie?"

"Yeah, what *was* I thinking."

"I've never met any of the sisterhood more arrogant and secretive than Calista Amberson, so, no, she would not have shared the recipe with anyone, Bram."

I dropped the shield and stood up. "Thanks for upping the problem quotient, cuz," I said. "Just so you know, I'm headed to Vegas in a few days. I have a cupid to pay off for not killing me and am thinking of dropping in on Lex while I'm in desert country."

"That's two different states and two different deserts," Delia said.

"Tucson's just a day's drive from Vegas. She's thinking origin story for the first book and wants to see how her ideas jive with what's been and what's to come."

"New York is talking talk show appearance, Bram," Delia warned.

"Not until the second week in March. Hopefully, life will have returned to normal by then." I headed for the door, then paused as I opened it. "We have an architect in the you-know loop?"

"Yes." She told me the witch's name. Of course it didn't stick, but it didn't have to quite yet. "Why do you ask?"

"A project in store for her," I said, then knocked her for another loop. "I've bought Naomie's apartment building. It needs help."

***

Armed with particulars courtesy of Delia, I knew there was one thing I needed to do: get away from everyone I knew so that I could jettison the shield properties and build something totally from scratch. Not an easy project for a guy who'd spent his entire life—fictional though it was for all but going on four months—just thinking something into being.

The new shield had to have nothing in common with the one

before. Whoever was taking mine down knew too much about it. I'd half-suspected this would be my project for the day, which was why I hadn't encouraged Beelz to join me. When I'd decided no one could know what was in the makeup of the new shield that meant no *thing* either. As much as I loved the mutt, he was a thing. A demon. I was just going back to that motto of *take no chances*.

The project got more complicated than even that, though. The Raven was engrained in Detroit. I had to have nothing of Detroit in the new shield. Maybe nothing connected to the US either. Or a city environment. Fortunately, Canada was just a trip across the river into Ontario, the city of Windsor and some lakeside wilderness areas. Unfortunately, among all the fake ID materials Calie had supplied me with last fall, a passport had not been one of them.

Since I lacked that handy psychic paper Doctor Who uses to fake documents, I went for the easiest way to attain one. I parked the car near the border crossing and cruised the streets on foot, picking the pocket of any dude who had a passing resemblance to me in height and coloring. Took me five lifts before I had what I needed. Before I left the area, I stopped in five different shops and handed over one of the wallets each time, claiming I'd found it in a booth, in a corner on the floor, on a window ledge—whatever worked. Let someone else be the Good Samaritan who contacted the guy. Then I climbed back into the Chrysler and traveled over to the land where Mounties used to roam. Oh, there still are Mounties, they just aren't mounted or spruced up in red serge jackets except for parades.

Windsor wasn't going to do for what I needed so I traveled beyond the city, to all intents and purposes looking like I was bound for London, further up the road. However, as I didn't have time to just keep roaming around, and it was past lunch time now, I stopped at a restaurant and found a rack of local attraction pamphlets and gathered up everything dealing with parks. Knew I had the right spot when I hit the one about Rondeau.

Rondeau had been designated a provincial park since the late 19th century. It sat on Lake Erie and featured both miles of sandy beaches and old-growth Carolinian forest. The pamphlet told me the park was world renowned as a bird watcher's destination.

Heck, what better place for a guy who went by a bird name more often than not?

Considering it was February, I was the only person in sight, although the park wasn't closed to visitors during the day. I found a spot where the woods were to my back and the lake spread out before me and took a stance that labeled me a New Ager. Since I didn't want anything to disrupt my connection to the land, snow was melting its way into the tail of my coat. I'd taken my gloves off as well as that nifty ear-warming knit hat. Eyes on the view, I spread my arms and kicked the old shield to the proverbial curb. Once it was gone, I felt empty and vulnerable, but it was a temporary thing. I started gathering the new shield components.

Mother Nature is, at heart, the source of all magic. At least, on planet Earth. Her sisters elsewhere probably have the same connection on other worlds. I listened to the lap of the waves, to the call of the birds. It wasn't the season for insect song, but their presence was beneath me in the soil, as was that of small to larger animals in the forest. Breeze caressed my face. The sun was out again and its touch lent warmth to offset the cold. I let my hands brush across what dried grasses there were and found sand that had blown from the beach to nestle among the roots.

My shield came together. It held nothing of a city, nothing of Calie or of my past as a fictional character. I let the budding pull of Naomie Enright's lovely face and how it felt to kiss her, how I felt when kissing her, contribute to the mix. As if it had been an element missing from my previous shield, I felt a slam as the new one took on the strength of Tungsten steel but with the flexibility I needed.

When it felt right, I sealed the mix and pushed to my feet. I needed to test it.

The lake called, offering assistance, so I strolled down to the edge. I built a raft with shield elements and put a dome over it, all invisible to anyone but me, of course. I anchored it to float in the shallows, then I threw a fireball at it. The shield dissipated it in a scattering of flame across its surface, seeming to consume it. I hit it with a blast of wind. The shield boat barely rocked. In fact, I was more inclined to think it was the lap of the lake against the shore that caused the slight bob. Next came a hurricane-strength throw. Again, it vanished as though eaten by the shield. My ace in the hole came next: hellfire. If a shield could chuckle, that's what this one did. I could almost hear it saying, "That all you got, Raven? Come on, dude. Bring it!"

So I pulled the Smith & Wesson from behind my back. Customs didn't know it had come across with me. I checked the magazine, then wrapped both hands around the grip and mentally built a noise-blanketing shield around the weapon and ran a rifled tube to within an inch of the floating dome. The bullet was going to hit with far more power behind it than a usual shot.

And the shield laughed at the effort.

I let the construct around the gun vanish, then turned to the floating masterpiece. "Come ta Papa, baby," I murmured, and it rushed to do what I asked of it next.

***

I was back in Detroit when my phone sang of a TARDIS landing. Fortunately, I was stopped at a red light and had time to unearth it from beneath layers of coat and sweater—not an easy maneuver with a seatbelt restraining my movement.

"Raven," a man's voice said.

Well, I knew what sort of call this was going to be with a salutation like that. Having just frolicked with my caller the evening before, I recognized his voice.

"Necromancer," I greeted. "You know, you really need a terror-inspiring moniker like mine to get word of mouth going about your services."

"Necromancy doesn't usually merit a listing under *Services*. It's more avocation than profession. Usually just mentioning what I do for a living in either of my capacities suffices, Farrell, so I think I'll stick with what I've got."

No imagination these days. What happened to going by nifty nicknames like… well, I could only think of Vlad the Impaler, and I just couldn't picture the dude being welcomed in *Cheers* fashion by his buddies with an "Impaler!" when he walked into a bar.

Which sounded like a lead into a joke, but… I got nuthin'.

"What can I do you for, Townshed?"

"A slight problem. One of my test subjects is having an uncommon reaction to the procedure," he said.

"Ah, the old hospital cover. Where and when?"

"Now and…"

He gave me an address. I had no idea where it was, however, because when one linked the term *necromancer* to anything, the location was not going to be a good one. Turned out, it was another one of the many abandoned factory buildings. I do get to visit the nicest spots. Nate was waiting outside when I pulled into the dilapidated complex that consisted of several buildings, none in what could be called livable condition. In spring when Mother Nature threw the covers back and returned to work, each might look like the distressed version of the Hanging Gardens of Babylon because of the trunks, branches, and roots of trees that had sprouted from cracks in the concrete of walls, floors, and roof. Climbing plants had taken hold, crawling up walls and entwining around support posts that appeared too tired to support anything. Windows were broken out, most likely by vandals, and spray paint provided the only color—and even that was faded thanks to regular battering by the elements. Cables and wires dripped from upper levels where only partial floors remained. Instead of having a warning about trespassing posted on the rusty metal fence and gate (which had been opened and looked like it should be manned by one of Satan's imps), the notice could have skipped straight to *death trap* and been right on the money.

"I lied," the necromancer confessed as I climbed out of the car. "The number of my projects inside is not a singular number. On some primitive level, they melded into a tribe and are both territorial and hungry. But there will be only one thing in there that is a danger to Detroit and needs to be put down."

"Any hints as to which one it is?"

"Let's put it this way," Townshed said. "I lack what you bring to a confrontation."

"No gift of gab, huh? I didn't take anything down other than Winthur from his chains last night, and there was no magic involved in doing that. I just kept the target talking."

"You brought a hellhound and a vampire to the fight." He looked around. "No hound today?"

"Gave him the day off," I said. He wouldn't ask about Wendy. It was still too light for her to be up and about.

"It's best if this is done before sundown." He leaned into the open trunk of his own vehicle to extract a sleek but nasty-looking Ravin R-15 crossbow. Beneath those modest mortician/necromancer chick-magnet dark suits, the dude had to be pumped to Sampson standards. To crank one of these babies in quick succession—which would be a necessity against angry or hungry things headed *en masse* his way—he'd need the biceps of the gods to get the job done. Maybe he planned to take a page from the movies and get more than one of them lined up in his sights so he could take them all out with a single bolt.

"A one-shot wonder, are you?" I chided. "How fast can you get another bolt loaded?"

"Not fast enough," he said and reached back into the trunk. "Which is why I have this as well."

Now, despite the fact that I didn't use weapons other than my Smith & Wesson, I have a lot of time on my hands because I don't sleep, and other than movie marathons, I fill that time with guy searches on the Net. My web history is varied and… well, *varied.* With hit persons (to be politically correct) lining up for a crack at me, I wanted to know what they could bring to the game. Two words described the possibilities: horrific stuff.

The new weapon was a jaw-dropping example of perfection. With an accompanying impressive price tag. A Gunwerks Verdict. A hunting rifle, but not for really big game like elephant, mutant grizzly, or T-Rex. The stock was adjustable, so it could be conformed to the shooter and was built for very minimum recoil. In the hands of a marksman, it was rated as accurate to a mile away from the target. It wasn't a sniper's gun, but perhaps necromancers built toys over which Victor Frankenstein would chew his knuckles in envy. Maybe Townshed's hobby was elk hunting in far northern areas.

Wishful thinking on my part? Yeah, it was.

"And if they get too close for you to use the bow or the rifle?"

He set the rifle down and pulled the Glock he'd been toting last night from his back waistband.

"And when it's out of ammo?"

The Glock went back into hiding but he had a Bowie knife in a sheath under his left arm.

"Gotta say, Nate, you're the most weaponized necromancer I've ever met."

"It's a dangerous profession."

I nodded toward the building. "You sure anything is in there? It's awfully quiet."

"They're in there."

The sun might still be with us outside the building, but its light was making little headway inside the place. There were more than sufficient shadowed areas to hide a battalion of reanimated corpses.

"Are we Butch and Sundancing it? Rushing in to surprise them and just take everything in sight down?"

"That's the plan,"

I did not like this plan. The option to run as fast as I could in the opposite direction gave much better survival odds.

"I'm right behind you," he said, slinging the rifle over his shoulder and taking the crossbow in hand.

That did not make me feel better at all.

"How about at my side?" I suggested and pulled the Smith & Wesson out. It was shy one round, the one I'd amused my new shield by firing at it, but there had been no reason to bring reloads along. Mostly because I hadn't put them on my shopping list. What I'd had on hand had assisted the fire at the mansion when it reached my desk drawer. "We go in, you go left, I go right. We both shoot at anything that's trying to kill us."

And I did mean *any*thing.

Townshed glanced at the gun in my hand. "Somehow, I expected you to use magic, not mundane weapons, Raven."

"Your playthings are human, even if you yanked them back from the spirit world. If a bullet will neutralize them. Magic is overkill," I said. Rather like the crossbow and rifle he carried.

He noted the look I gave his arsenal. "I don't usually have help at hand."

"I don't usually have backup that's packin'," I said. "In fact… you didn't use that handgun last night when you took down Frost's associate on your own. Didn't use a knife, either."

He'd broken the man's arm, destroyed a knee, then choked him out. I'd checked on the body before leaving, just in case Durkin called with a question. The dude had looked worked over by a berserker Bruce Lee.

Methinks the necromancer was uncommonly prepared for killing, considering his avocation supposedly brought dead things back among the living—or he wasn't a necromancer at all. The weapons were a real tip-off.

The moment I stepped inside the death trap—and I'm not just talking about the chance of masonry falling on me—I knew the hunch was more than my stomach inquiring about the next feeding time.

There wasn't a single recipient of a necromancer's tender mercies in the joint. But it was filled with zombies.

Which might seem to be pretty much the same, but that was like saying lemon chickpea muffins were the same as triple chunk chocolate ones. In other words, the only thing they had in common were a few letters of the alphabet.

I vanished into the shadows to my right and shot anything that came near. When the Smith & Wesson was empty, there were still plenty of zombies to go around.

Townshed was handling his cover well. He took the largest—but also the one with the most advanced case of decomposition—down with the crossbow bolt, then opened up with the Verdict. The shots shredded the shambling dead. That was what they were. So far gone, these were mercy killings.

Not a one qualified as a being dangerous for Detroit to have abroad.

I, however, *did* meet that criteria.

To my mind, Nate Townshed met it even more.

I was ready in the event he turned the beady eye of the hunting rifle on me, but it clicked on empty before the final zombie went down so he took the thing out with the Glock in quick order.

No zombies left was a good thing. Townshed with a handgun in his mitt, was not.

He moved forward. Went down on one knee as he checked one of the victims for… well, not a pulse or a lingering breath. He was faking the caution bit. I could feel that they were all goners.

"You still with me, Farrell?" he called.

"Yup." I hastily shifted where I stood, one with the shadows—which were growing darker as the sun dipped, giving the sky that watercolor landscape feel. To return to my car would put me within firing range in a most visible way.

"How long you been in town?" I asked and shifted deeper into the building.

"Not long," he said. "Hey, where the hell are you?"

"Checking that we got'em all." I darted silently in a different direction.

"I'm sure we did."

He ought to know how many there were. He'd rounded them up. We'd danced this number long enough. It was time to bring the curtain down on his masquerade.

"How much you getting to kill me?"

"Kill you? You're paranoid, Farrell."

That was what happened to a guy when he was a target, and I was ensuring that I was a moving one, circling him. I was off to his left when I hit him with a blast guaranteed to sweep the Glock from his hand.

Unfortunately, the guarantee had expired. It knocked him over, but he was still armed. This time, the Glock swung in the direction from which the wind had hit him.

"Who hired you?" I asked as I stirred up a dust devil laden with bits and pieces from the floor. Among them, I noticed a pair of women's panties. They had *Sunday* stamped across the back. It wasn't Sunday, though I was tempted to turn religious and do some prayer bargaining.

When the trash cyclone spun into him, Nate fired a shot toward the fallen support beam it had whipped from behind. The bullet skidded along the girder, ricocheting into the shadows. I was nowhere near either.

"Does it matter?" he demanded, giving up the pretense that he was something other than an assassin.

"To me. I'm curious."

He spun in the direction from which my voice had come, but I'd moved on. He didn't waste another bullet.

"A woman," he said. "Shapely bleached blonde from Cleveland. She's really got a burn on for you."

I wondered how many other former Amberson replacement candidates had turned rabid when I beat them out, but only briefly. Blacken my eye, start a rumor campaign, hint at misdoings as Ritter had. Those were much more logical responses.

"Blondes are a dime a dozen," I quipped. "Gonna take more than that."

"Live long enough, and you'll get to meet her again. She's in town and has been very helpful."

"Like in taking my shields down?"

He chuckled. "Yeah. Real helpful in doing that."

"Bitch in her late twenties or early thirties? Treats you like a lackey? Snaps orders? Blood as cold as the Arctic during the Ice Age?" I stepped into view; a double-layered shield raised between us. It wasn't a full cover, but I needed to tempt the mastermind into the open. She'd be smug, believing she could erase the shield as she had done so many times in the past few days.

"What name is she answering to these days?" I asked.

I knew who was behind the contract on me now. It had been quite a stroll through things I'd heard and learned to reach the answer. A combination that roped two comic book and movie characters who couldn't be killed—Wolverine and Deadpool—to something Quentin Frost had mentioned about some vampires counting their age by millennia.

I knew someone who was possibly 150,000 plus-or-minus thirty years old and had a dandy method of both dying and not dying.

A magic-user who was overly familiar with my magic capabilities and, thus, the make-up of my shield.

My *former* shield.

She'd had numerous names in the past, but I knew her as Calista Amberson. The woman who had created me from nothing more than "what ifs", paper and ink, and had then yanked me into reality.

Considering I'd stopped her—temporarily rather than permanently, it seemed—from completing the ceremony that would let her continue to exist, she had reason to want revenge.

Townshed laughed. "I told her you'd figure out who she was."

"Bet she didn't believe you. Put the weapons aside nice and careful like."

He spread his arms wide, then slowly placed the Glock on the floor, followed by the wicked knife. He'd left the crossbow just inside the door, and it hadn't been claimed by anyone nor reloaded while I'd been busy. He unslung the rifle, put it down as well, then pushed slowly to his feet. He took a step back, then another, putting distance between himself and the weapons. An action I was supposed to take as gospel, I assumed.

"You don't trust me," he said. A real understatement. "I don't have your magical abilities, Farrell. I'm just human. Take the weapons with you and drive away if you wish. I can be patient. I left you a message once, didn't I?

"The one promising to kill me the next time?"

"Well, this is the next time I'm in a situation where doing so is possible without witnesses."

"You didn't try to barbeque me in the mansion?"

"Not my style. I'm not the only one interested in the money offered, Farrell. But burning down a house? That lacks creativity, finesse."

True. What he was going to try wouldn't be though.

"Then you didn't wire the Ford to blow either?"

"Well, actually, yes, I did. Saw the opportunity and took it but that jackass fouled things up by trying to steal it," he said.

"It still took help to neutralize the shield. Is she here this time, too?"

"No," he said, but he lied. While there hadn't been any beings but the two of us and the now-dead zombie forlorn hope team in the building previously, I sensed her presence in the vicinity, but not near enough to be at hand to back him up quite yet. I had to look vulnerable and clueless to lure her out.

Had to remove him from the equation first, though.

"Back another couple steps, Townshed," I ordered, then moved forward and bent to snag the Glock. Whether he'd used it more than once, I didn't know. In any case I was clueless about how many rounds a Glock held—so it might have been empty or it could still have shots available. Either way, acquiring it seemed the logical choice for a man who thought he had the upper hand—the part I'd chosen to play.

The moment my position made it feasible, he lunged forward and knocked me off my feet. He held me down, gloating, while his right hand was poised above me, glowing.

"You guessed right, Farrell. I'm not a necromancer, I'm an alchemist. One who found an ancient recipe to tinker with."

I glanced at his hand. "You knew the Heart Burn curse killed that ghoul because you used it on him."

"It had to be tested."

I struggled but he pressed me down, his stance leaning more toward wrestling than the martial arts I'd suspected him of having mastered and used the night before.

"Goodbye, Raven. Too bad your time in this world is brief." He didn't sound sorry about it in the least. He slammed the glowing hand down onto the center of my chest.

I fought like a mad man, which just made him laugh—*until* I grabbed his forearm with my left and gave his hand a quick snap with my right, breaking his wrist. He cried out at the pain, but I wasn't finished with him. I twisted his still-glowing hand, wringing another cry from him, then smacked it back into his own chest.

And the light scurried to nest in his heart.

Townshed gasped in horror. "That can't happen. It should have transferred to you."

"Not my problem," I said and, grabbing his other hand, forced it to rub the same spot. Activating the curse.

Townshed screamed. Pawed at his torso as though he could countermand the delivered curse's instructions. It was already lighting up the veins in his neck, his face, his hands, the only areas visible considering he had come warded in wool against the cold.

I stood up, letting him writhe at my feet as the curse finished him off. It did indeed take the five minutes he'd mentioned for the curse to kill him.

Why hadn't it transferred to me as intended?

My new shield saved *me* from it, of course. The last thing I'd asked of it, while on the northern shore of Lake Erie, was to do what Naomie considered doing to protect her Grimm boy enquiry agent. Create a thick, close-fitting armor around my entire body.

It had worked even better than expected.

Since Townshed wasn't out in the wintery elements, but sheltered inside the ramshackle factory building, the curse didn't halt as it had on the test ghoul but went from crisping him to full funeral pyre. My sense that his employer was nearby hadn't vanished. But she wasn't at hand either—probably waiting for him to finish me off before strolling in.

While waiting for her arrival, I hellfired the zombie corpses, cooled the ashes with a coating of ice, then let a controlled cyclone sweep them up, along with Townshed's ashes, and spirit them away. Told the magically created tempest to head for E-15, the active volcano cauldron in Iceland and dump the remains inside. I just hoped the wind knew the mountain by its numeronym because I sure as heck couldn't pronounce, much less spell, the fifteen-letter-long Icelandic name. All of that took fewer minutes than the fake necromancer's burn time had.

I'd had my gloves off to toss the magic around and was pulling them back on before touching Townshed's weapons cache when the sound of bored applause stopped me.

She was standing in the open doorway. In feature and shape and age, she was nothing like Calista Amberson, but the stance, mannerisms, and air of entitlement identified the woman as my creator. Her clothing choices leaned toward Cate Blanchard's Hela wardrobe, except this time around, Calie had stolen a blonde's body and she'd foregone a pronged headdress. Considering her personality rivaled movieland's Hela, she was correctly dressed for villainy.

"I'm impressed, Bram," she said, the voice sounding off simply because it originated in a different voice box. "You've got a new shield. I didn't think I'd given you enough intelligence to sort out how to do that."

"I'm not a character on a page any longer, Calie. You can't manipulate me as you please."

"Bram." My name was a patronizing sigh. "Of course I can. You tried to kill me. I'm going to return the favor. It simply isn't going to be as easy as I'd originally thought."

Although the ball of fire I shot at her formed instantly and had Mach speed behind it, she was no longer in sight by the time it whizzed through the spot where she'd stood. She'd moved fast enough to have learned to apparate at Potter's alma mater. My senses told me she was no longer in the building. Nowhere on the property or the neighborhood either. Still, I waited another ten minutes before loading Townshed's deadly toys back into the trunk of his car and slamming it closed. Then I called Durkin and told him where the car was and what it held. Didn't think he'd want any of it falling into other idle hands.

Calie was back. Actually *back*. I'd never asked Samael if he had her on the barbecue in the Inferno. I'd simply assumed that was where she was. It was where she deserved to be.

She'd slipped his catch, though, and had found a new form—whether a willing one or not, I might never learn. And she wanted revenge for my attempt to destroy her on All Hallows' Eve.

But she wouldn't be content with just getting rid of me. She wanted me to suffer first.

I knew what was needed and only hoped my solution would work as well as the new shield did.

Rissy Ponce's nephew wasn't happy when I asked him to put her on the phone. "Can I tear you away from dinner?"

Whether it was because she is a seer or simply recognized the serious tone of my voice, she agreed to be ready and waiting when I arrived. First, I made another stop. At a church.

St. Gabriel's was locked up tight, it not being an evening when services were held. I pulled into the parking lot and shut the engine down. Used nearly the same wording I had when getting in touch with another archangel in November.

I wouldn't say it was a prayer, but then, prayer can come in all kinds of forms, from the pat canon wording to the freeform. Mine leaned closer to putting a call through a switchboard.

"Calling the Archangel Gabriel about a favor he owes me," I said under my breath. Don't know why, but it simply sounded better to say these things out loud.

"I owe you a favor, Raven? Refresh my mind," a heavenly voice said from the shotgun seat.

He looked much the same as when I'd seen him before. Brown hair, chiseled features, worn jeans, generic T-shirt, and gray hoodie.

"Aren't you cold in that?"

"No need to appear bundled up until I head for the volunteer job at the homeless mission," he countered. "The favor?"

"I did get rid of a certain horn for you," I reminded.

Gabe grinned. "I was under the impression it wasn't done for me, but to protect mankind."

"Same thing."

He chuckled. "What can I do for you?"

I told him.

"Needs to be done on holy ground, but I agree it should work. Where would you like to meet and when?"

"St. Romaric's cemetery. You know it?"

"I'll ask Romaric where it is and for suggestions on the most appropriate place. When you're ready, just call my name." Then he was gone.

I headed to Rissy's. We went shopping at the home of a friend of hers who read crystals and used them in jewelry. I explained what I needed.

The woman smiled softly. "I knew I'd made that piece for a

special reason. This seems to be it. Do you want me to program the stones?"

"We're doing that ourselves," Rissy told her, "but I do thank you for the offer, honey."

Purchase in hand, we got back into the car. I called Ruth Lund and told her the extremely large favor I needed to wring from her. The little troll/dwarf said she never could turn one of her regular flirts down. Told her we were on our way to pick her up. "Bundle up. We'll be out in the elements," I warned. She thanked me for the heads-up.

The moon was high in the sky by the time I pulled the Chrysler to the curb before the gate of St. Romaric's cemetery. It was a spooky-looking place at this time of year, at this time of night, but I doubted anything would bother us. Even Otherworlders didn't care to be out on a freezing February night. I doubted the neighbors across the way had been curious enough to leave their comfy chairs or put down their remotes to check who had parked by the burial ground.

I guided my troops through the gate and called Gabriel. He manifested just off the path.

"This way," he said and led the way. What footprints we left in the snow vanished behind us.

As I'd hoped, there was a group of empty graves forming a square of consecrated ground for our use. I hadn't thought of doing so, but Gabriel had brought chairs for the ladies. He and I hunkered between them in our small circle. Boy, girl, boy, girl.

I took the latest purchase from my jeans pocket.

I held the item upright between the thumb and forefinger of my left hand, arm extended so that it was in the center of our circle. "Silver setting for protection, peace, love, and the female connection to the Moon," I intoned. "Obsidian for protection against physical, emotional or psychic attack. Peridot for protection against those who drain energy. Blue Kyanite to shield against coercive or deceptive manipulation. Selenite to create unease in those who wish to harm the wearer of this talisman."

The air around my hand began to glow with white light.

Rissy cupped her right hand so that the palm faced what I held. I felt a tingle as Gaian magic flowed like a rill of rainwater from her fingers. Twists of pale blue rose, entwining gracefully with the encircling halo of white. “To protect with the force of man and the spirit of the Earth.”

Opposite her, Ruth mirrored Rissy’s stance. The green of a polar aurora tinted the manifestation of Otherworlder magic. It swirled, merged with the aura in root-like tendrils and added the damp, musty scent of the forest to the biting cold night. “To guard with the strength of the non-human and of beings long held to be myth.”

Gabriel placed a hand on either side of the women’s, nearly closing the contact, making their hands form a rose bud, its lips barely parted. His hands glowed with rays of celestial gold. When they embraced the conjoined magic undulating within our circle, it felt like we were brushed with the delicate tips of wings. “The light of Heaven, the strength and protection of the angels who now stand guard, I bequeath.”

I looked to the sky above, to the element known as Luna, the evening light that had bought me into this world. I extended my right hand, capturing a beam with the essence of pure silver. The illumination glowed, seeming to pulse in my palm. In a swift move, I slammed it down over the crown of hands, closing the only remaining gap around the blending of metal and crystals confined in their cupped palms and encircled by magic. “I do so seal these qualities with bindings of imagination, of thoughts and intelligence that tie our four worlds together. Protect the wearer for whom we four create this token, be it danger from the forces of man, the divine, the mythic, or the creative world.”

The conjoined, yet separate, magical elements of the nebula flared as if a miniature nova had burst. Nearly blinded, I watched as the intertwined colors flowed around us, spinning ever faster as they consolidated to an ever-tightening orb that then melted into the ring I held, vanishing from sight. In the chill air, the newly created talisman felt warm, as though beating with a heart of its own yet it appeared to be nothing more than a ring chosen from a booth at a fair now.

From the expressions on the faces of the beings I’d brought together, I knew they’d felt the surge of power, too. The magic of a guy made of nothing but imagination made flesh. A wannabe man who had willed protection for one special human into being with their help.

I re-pocketed the talisman, then shook Gabe’s hand. He kissed both Rissy’s and Ruth’s cheeks as a blessing, then I escorted them back to the car. Gabriel vanished as we pulled away from the curb.

As Ruth’s bar was closest, I dropped her back at The Bridge

first, giving her a kiss of gratitude on the cheek opposite the one the archangel had bussed. Then it was Rissy who was returned to her family. If her nephew was taken aback when his aunt's "young man", as she called me, kissed her cheek, he kept any comment to himself.

We had all been quietly solemn on the drive back, a reflection of the ceremony we'd conducted. One basically winged, only the way our hands were held had been briefly discussed before we'd begun. But then, chances were, it was a one-time situation.

Hopefully, it would do the trick. Calie was back. Measures needed to be taken.

It was a whole new ballgame. I had a new shield, one that had protected me against the Heart Burn curse. I still hadn't gotten around to locating Solomon Prisk for Durkin, but I'd had a hell of a lot of distractions to keep me from that job. Mentally, I penciled the search for Prisk on the calendar for March. Right now, I had a cupid to pay off, and whatever three-ring circuses the publisher was going to put me through prior to the release of the book to deal with. Then another book to write. At least I had a story to tell. This time, I'd change some of the names to keep Naomie happy, but, otherwise, no fiction would be involved in the telling this time either.

Nomes and Beelz were on the sofa together watching Kirk and his crew on the *Enterprise* deal with difficulties involving exoplanet people. She looked up with a smile when I shrugged off my coat, then frowned when she read my expression. She sat up. Beelz looked on, his head tilted questioningly.

I knelt like Prince Charming, one knee down, one knee available to rest an arm on, before her. Took her left hand in mine.

And slid a silver band studded with irregularly-shaped, polished shards of obsidian, peridot, blue kyanite, and selenite onto her middle finger and closed my hand over it.

"Never—and I do mean *never*—take this off, Naomie Enright. It is to keep you from harm. Protect you from those who would try to use you against me."

Her eyes were wide. Perhaps a bit frightened, but with good reason. As far as she was concerned, I had totally weirded out.

"Why?" she whispered.

"Because I lied to you before, Nomes," I said. "Magic is *very* real and it's dangerous. Deadly dangerous."

Author's Note

Just as they promise at the end of a Marvel movie, Bram, Beelz, Naomie, and other cast regulars WILL RETURN.

Apologies to the Detroit, Michigan area for putting it through the magic and paranormal wringer once more. And to the border officials for crassly letting Bram con his way across to Canada and then back.

I'm never sure where one of these stories will take me when I first sit down, but it does help that I really enjoy my time with Bram. Sometimes, I feel that his having no need to sleep is wearing off on me. I've spent far too many nights where it was only when the sun came up that I managed to tear myself away from the story and *try* to sleep. I just wish someone would have donuts at hand for me!

If you missed *Raven's Moon* or the short novellas "Raven's Rest" and "Raven's Reward", hie ye out and snag copies!

And so we draw another Raven Tale to its conclusion. Feel free to visit at www.4TaleTellers.com.

Until next time...
J. B. Dane

Made in the USA
Middletown, DE
19 May 2022